A LONG DAY'S DYING

A LONG DAY'S DYING

KEVIN DOHERTY

SIDGWICK & JACKSON
LONDON

For Roz, with love and thanks.

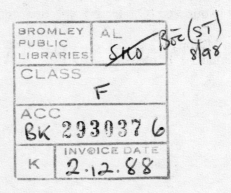
First published in Great Britain in 1988 by Sidgwick & Jackson Limited
Originally published

Copyright © J. K. Doherty 1988

ISBN 0-283-99700 1

Typeset by Rowland Phototypesetting Limited
Bury St Edmunds, Suffolk
Printed by Richard Clay Limited,
Bungay, Suffolk
for Sidgwick & Jackson Limited
1 Tavistock Chambers, Bloomsbury Way
London WC1A 2SG

. . . this day's death denounced, if aught I see,
Will prove no sudden, but a slow-paced evil,
A long day's dying to augment our pain,
And to our seed (O hapless seed!) derived.

John Milton,
Paradise Lost, Book X, lines 962–965.

PART ONE

1

The church was no more than a stone shell, cleared of its pews. At intervals around the walls tidemarks recorded where the Stations of the Cross had hung. Electric cables had erupted from their perished sleeves and dangled uselessly from the vaulted ceiling.

As first light began to seep through the grimy windows of the east chancel, Nikolai Vasiliyevich Serov withdrew deeper into the shadows of the upper gallery. Of the people gathered in the nave below him, only the man called Gramin knew that he was there.

The place was as cold as a tomb. Serov ran his gloved hand over the wall beside him, where an uneven film of ice, an inch thick in places, reflected the glow of his thin cigar. Icicles hung overhead where rain and sleet had penetrated the stripped roof.

A shout, Gramin's hoarse bark and not the first that morning, rang out from the nave.

'Liar! I saw you talking to the Jew in the Lyublino street market. I heard you haggling with him. I saw what you sold him. Why don't you just own up?'

Serov shifted position slightly to bring Gramin into view. With his flat nose and broad body, he looked like the boxer he had been in his army days. The man he was interrogating, if that was what it could be called, was an elderly glass-worker called Yezhov. He knelt on the stone floor at Gramin's feet, his wrists tied behind his back. He was weeping, his shoulders heaving irregularly. Unless he was very stupid indeed, he would know what was coming. Everyone else did.

There were about thirty people watching the two men, ranged in an untidy semi-circle near them. Coarse clothes, gaunt faces, the dregs of the city. Serov knew most of the faces but few of their names. That was Gramin's job, to know names.

'Yezhov! Look at me! What would happen if everyone helped themselves like you did?'

Gramin smashed his fist backhanded across Yezhov's mouth. If he hadn't been holding him upright with his other hand, the blow would have sent him flying. Yezhov groaned. His head slumped forward, blood pouring from his swollen lips.

'Or if you'd been traced back here?'

The fist connected again. A dark stain was spreading down Yezhov's trousers. A puddle of urine began to form around his knees; it mingled with the blood and flowed between the slabs, flooding the cracks in their broken surface.

'You'd have us in Lefortovo, all of us.'

Gramin's arm swept around to encompass the silent audience. The performance was really for their benefit, Yezhov being by now as good as unconscious. Anyway, he wasn't going to be around to profit from their exchange.

'You know what's got to happen now, Yezhov. You know the rules. Like we all do.'

They watched impassively as he forced a bundle of rags into Yezhov's mouth and tied it in position as a gag, then pulled him to his feet and manhandled him past the altar with its shattered slab and up the steps of the pulpit. At the top, he grabbed the noose that swung from a crossbeam and slipped it over Yezhov's scrawny neck.

'Here we go, citizens!'

At the touch of the rope, Yezhov came to and made a feeble attempt to struggle. Gramin rammed a knee into his groin.

'Here's today's lesson.' He draped an arm over the pulpit and parodied the sign of the cross. 'Remember it well, all of you. The same could be coming your way.'

He let go of Yezhov's arms and pushed him hard in the buttocks. What would have been a scream was choked by the gag to a whine, cut short as Yezhov's body fell away from the pulpit and down, and the noose snapped tight about his neck. There was a soft crack as his neck broke. His head was jerked to one side by the sudden pressure of the knot and his body jack-knifed. He swung irregularly to the end of the rope's arc, seemed to hover for an instant, and then began to swing back over the broken altar. Blood welled afresh from his smashed lips.

Serov checked his watch in the cigar's glow. Yezhov was already weakened by the interrogation; he would die quickly. That was no problem; it left longer for his companions to absorb Gramin's lesson.

Outside it was growing lighter. Sunlight reflecting off the snow, undimmed where it found broken windowpanes, slanted across the nave. Tiny strands of hemp, rubbed loose by the friction of the noose, floated through the bars of light. There was silence but for the drip of Yezhov's blood on the altar-slab.

Serov waited while the minutes ticked away.

The sound of the approaching lorry began as a faint buzz in the distance. The revving grew louder and deeper as the vehicle ascended the icy hill to the Church of the Saviour, gears hitching as it wound through the streets of derelict houses. By the time the vehicle arrived

4

outside, the noise was a throbbing growl, felt as much as heard. More revving and the high-pitched note of a warning bleeper indicated that the lorry was reversing towards the church door.

The explosive hiss of its airbrakes was the signal for action.

'All right, let's move!' called Gramin.

At once the people in the nave snapped into action, fanning out across the width of the church. Gramin clattered down the pulpit steps to stand by the arched doors, stopping there to survey the scene.

Serov followed his gaze.

The thirty workers were dispersing themselves into a chain that led across the nave from the main doors and through a smaller door by the north transept. The chain continued down a flight of stone steps to a crypt that ran the width and length of the church. Serov knew that the sides of the crypt were divided into vaults three feet square and six feet deep, each closed by a stone slab with a draw-handle of iron in its centre. He knew this because he had watched Gramin break open the vaults months before, clearing out onto the floor their muddle of brown bones, skulls, rags and dust.

Now it was Gramin who raised the thick iron strip that barred the church doors and dragged them wide open.

The brightness of the snowy morning flooded in, making Serov blink. He made out the silhouette of the lorry-driver, already in position with the first box.

It was by now a well-practised routine. Gramin stepped smartly aside as the driver thrust the box at the first man in the chain. It passed along the line and down into the crypt. Seconds behind it the second box followed.

On the sixth or seventh box, and into the rhythm of his work, the driver allowed himself to glance up and into the church. Yezhov's body had stopped revolving and hung motionless from the crossbeam over the altar.

'Christ save us!' The driver's voice carried clearly in the sub-zero air. His gauntleted hands fell to his sides. Behind him his mate on the lorry's loading ramp hefted another box towards where his outstretched arms should have been, cursing when he found nothing but empty air. He dumped the fifteen kilogramme carton on the tailgate and jumped down to see what had taken the driver's attention.

'He stole some of our stock,' Gramin was explaining. 'Sold it independently.'

The ribbon of workers stood waiting.

'You hanged him for that?' This from the mate; the driver, a wiser man, was saying nothing.

'No choice.' Frozen billows of condensation blew from Gramin's lips. 'Rules, you see. Can't have people going into business for themselves.

Can we, citizens?' He leered at the two men, then laughed softly. 'You wouldn't think of doing such a thing, would you?'

The laugh grew more boisterous and he slapped the driver's shoulder, then walked off along the line. He took hold of Yezhov's foot as he passed and sent the corpse spinning again. He was still laughing as he went down the steps to the crypt.

It took only half an hour to unload the contents of the lorry – East German beef today – into the vaults and slide the closing-slabs back into position to protect them from rodents. At this time of year, in this weather, it would keep almost indefinitely.

Gramin broke open a few of the cartons and distributed packages of the frozen meat to the workforce as payment. They buttoned them under their coats, shivering as the temperature hit them, and hurried off.

Serov came downstairs to watch Gramin clear up. Only one clue remained of their presence: Yezhov's body. Gramin cut it down and lugged it by the heels to the crypt, bumping the head on the steps like a sack of coal. He crammed it into one of the vaults and sealed the closing-slab with some cement that Yezhov himself had mixed earlier. Next he broke the thin skin of ice that was forming on a bucket of water he had left by the stairs. Dabbing a rag into it he rubbed off the steps here and there where the head had grazed and left faint traces of blood. The remainder of the water he sloshed across the puddle of blood and urine on the altar.

As his last job he fetched a shovel from the east corner of the crypt and loaded it with dust. He returned upstairs and scattered it over the most obvious traces of footprints on the church floor. He repeated this several times, going patiently up and down the steep stairs to reload. He threw a whole shovelful on top of the already freezing water on the altar.

All the while Serov stood in the doorway, smoking. He had ungloved his left hand to hold the cigar. His right was deep in the pocket of his black leather greatcoat.

After fetching his last shovelful Gramin set it down by the crypt door, careful not to spill it, and padlocked the door securely. He backed towards Serov, spreading dust behind him as he went.

'That's it, comrade General,' he grunted.

'I've told you not to call me that here.'

'Apologies.'

Serov flipped the cigar butt out through the half-open door. He took a wad of folded banknotes, a mix of roubles and assorted foreign currencies, from his left pocket and handed it over.

'For your additional duties today.'

Gramin grinned broadly and propped the shovel against the wall. He took the wad of notes and turned to leave, his attention focused on the cash.

His forehead hit the oak door with a resounding crack as Serov flung him against it. The impact slammed the door shut. The noises, virtually simultaneous, echoed like a thunderclap in the emptiness of the church. Serov's right hand had emerged from the greatcoat pocket. It held a heavy Makarov 9mm pistol. He twisted Gramin's arm behind his back and pressed the muzzle into the nape of his thick neck; he let Gramin hear the safety catch click off before he spoke. Banknotes scattered to the floor.

'No more Yezhovs.' Serov's voice was quiet, not much above a whisper. 'That's what I pay you for. To make sure no one tries, not just to catch up with them afterwards. Next time I'll do the clearing-up myself. You won't be able to help. You'll be one of the messes I'll be clearing up. Understand?' He pushed the arm a little higher.

'Yes, comrade. Yes, yes.'

'Look in the streets, Gramin. The city's crawling with investigators. People are being rounded up everywhere. These are bad days.' He twisted the arm again. 'Especially after last month.'

Gramin whined softly, like a frightened dog. 'Druzhba Park wasn't my fault.' His cheek was flattened against the door, his eyeballs bulging.

Serov pressed the Makarov a little deeper into the fat of his neck. 'It doesn't matter whose fault it was. We lost people and a good organisation. And I'm stuck with half a million roubles' worth of cocaine I can't market. Think I can afford to have that kind of cash tied up?'

He gave Gramin's arm another twist before releasing him. As he drew his gloves on again the litter of banknotes on the dusty floor caught his eye: dollar bills, deutsch marks, sterling.

'Pick up your money before I change my mind.'

A final glance around the empty church, a careful look outside, and he was gone. Gramin scrambled to gather the money together, locked up and hurried after him.

Five minutes later he was gunning Serov's Chaika into the thin morning traffic on the Mozhayskoye Shosse back to town. Serov sat in the back seat, smoking and staring straight ahead. To any of the ordinary citizens who bothered to look, Serov was just another high-ranking official with his driver. The hill where the Church of the Saviour perched was far behind them.

They spoke only once on the journey, when Gramin asked their destination.

'To Yasyenevo, comrade?'

But Serov shook his head. He had other business to attend to first. Personal business.

7

In the cold light of that same dawn the Kremlin's russet walls stood drained of all colour. Within the walls all was still but for the intermittent patrols of the soldiers of the praetorian guard. Snow gathered on their greatcoat shoulders and fur hats, and was kicked up in flurries by the toes of their high-stepping boots.

In a top-floor room of the Arsenal block that formed the castle's northern corner, two men had sat all night and now saw the dawn arrive.

One was Mikhail Sergeyevich Gorbachev. In his hands lay a bound document marked 'Most Classified'. He had been through it perhaps a dozen times that night. Now he closed it slowly and turned it over in his hands. The red leatherette cover had a rectangular window cut in it, through which was visible the four-line title typed on the first page. It read:

USSR Economic and Industrial Strategy
The Next Five Year Plan and Beyond
Projected Energy Needs and Shortfalls
Preliminary Report of the Oligarchy Committee

The Soviet leader flicked back the cover and glanced down the frontispiece. It bore only two names. One was his own. The other, in a bottom corner, beneath the date, was that of the document's author, the chairman of the Oligarchy Committee and the man who sat watching him from the other side of the desk.

Abel Aganbegyan was the country's most radical economist; since Gorbachev's rise to power he had become its most powerful. He was also a trusted friend.

'You tell me this is the only copy?' Gorbachev asked at last. He lifted his gaze from the document to scrutinise the Georgian's swarthy features.

Aganbegyan's dark-rimmed eyes flickered beneath his bushy eyebrows. He was exhausted; months of intense work and political pressure had taken their toll. The night's vigil had been but the latest in a chain of nights when sleep had had to be pushed aside.

'The only copy apart from my own,' he confirmed quietly.

The room was pooled with soft lamplight, still stronger than the dawn. Behind Aganbegyan, at the far end of the office, were the leather couches where the two men had sat for most of the hours of darkness. On the glass-topped table between the couches was spread an untidy clutter of files, reports and papers. Some of the papers had strayed onto the couches, some had followed Aganbegyan to the desk.

Gorbachev stretched back in his chair, catching sight of his watch as he did so. He sighed and glanced at the lightening windows.

'Dawn. We're a day older, Abel.'

8

His head ached, his eyes were burning with the endless statistics that had swum before them for the last several hours. He removed his glasses and massaged his forehead, his fingers wandering instinctively across the long birthmark. He caught the habitual gesture in mid-act and, as always, swept his hand instead over his thin hair.

'Abel, I thank you and the committee for your hard work. I wish I could also thank you for your conclusions.'

Aganbegyan shrugged. To Gorbachev he looked like a man who was used to delivering bad news, a doctor perhaps. He capped his ballpoint and began gathering up the jumbled papers.

'I saw no point in varnishing the truth, Misha.' There were few others who felt able to use the familiar form of Mikhail Gorbachev's name. 'Too many others have lied to our country for too long.'

'That's why I didn't set them this project.'

The economist nodded. He rose and moved to the glass table and leather couches, where he continued scooping up the clutter of papers and documents.

'The day you asked me to start on this, Misha, we both knew what the outcome would be; we just didn't say it out loud, that's all. I've merely quantified what our instincts were already telling us. So now I've said it aloud for both of us.'

'You knew it would be this bad?'

Aganbegyan took a second or two before he answered. He sat on the arm of one of the couches, a clutch of files in his arms, and stared at the far wall.

'They had thirty years to make it this bad. You can do a lot of damage in that time. I feared the worst.'

The lines in Gorbachev's forehead deepened. 'Abel, our predecessors mismanaged grossly, I grant you. But we can't blame this whole . . .' He tried to avoid the word which came most readily to mind but gave up. 'We can't blame the whole catastrophe on them. World markets –'

'The markets are no excuse.' Aganbegyan's tone was suddenly severe, his tiredness momentarily forgotten. 'Good planning should take account of all eventualities. Besides, the movements you're talking about have only been disadvantageous over the last few months. And they impact on revenue alone; they have nothing to do with capital investment – or the lack of it – which is a large part of the problem.' As he stood up he added quietly, 'Anyway, price movements have nothing to do with the condition of the RBMKs.'

Gorbachev knew that everything he said was true. Brezhnev and his gang of thieves had bled the country white through a combination of economic ignorance and straightforward personal greed. Chernenko and Andropov had been unable to stem the flow, the one too weak, the other too short-lived. Now, with the help of Aganbegyan and a handful of others, Gorbachev had made some kind of start in the rebuilding that was needed so desperately. They had only begun, yet already much had been achieved.

Until this. Which could wipe everything out.

'Abel, this will set the country back by decades.'

'I know.'

Aganbegyan returned to his chair by the desk and they sat in silence for a full minute. Gorbachev's thoughts were on a young law student who had devoured Lenin's theories and writings as eagerly as if the father of the revolution had been speaking to him directly. The student had compared the theories with the reality of his society and had found the latter wanting. It set his path through life. He couldn't change the theories; he didn't want to. It was the reality that had to change.

Now, forty years on, the law student had arrived at the heart of Soviet power; but this morning he was holding a report that told him his life's work might be for nothing. That the great experiment that was world communism might yet turn to dust.

He became aware that Aganbegyan was clearing his throat politely.

'What happens now, Misha? Do you want to share my analysis with the Politburo? It's complex, as you've seen, but I'm sure I can simplify it into something manageable. If that's what you'd like.'

Gorbachev heard the doubt in his voice. Aganbegyan understood a great deal more than economics.

'You know the answer to that.'

The Soviet leader rose and went to the window behind his desk. Snowflakes the size of fifty-kopek pieces drifted past the steamed-up glass. But it wasn't the weather that made him shiver. It was the thought of the men who sat around the Politburo table with him. Yegor Ligachev the arch-conservative, Chebrikov the KGB chief, Georgi Zavarov the militarist: they were the ones who would close in like timberwolves scenting blood as soon as they saw a vulnerability in their leader's position. Nor would they be the only ones. The rank beneath them could prove just as dangerous. Men such as Nikolai Serov, Chebrikov's head of the First Chief Directorate: where would a man like Serov stand? The FCD was the powerful body that operated the KGB's foreign networks; its loyalty and effectiveness would become even more vital with the curtailment of military operations that Gorbachev planned. Could a man like Serov be counted on?

It was the same throughout the country. There were tens of thousands whose loyalty was a matter of guesswork or who would actively obstruct progress because it wasn't in their interests: the bureaucrats and corrupt managers, the time-servers, the black-marketeers.

Gorbachev turned back to the room. The economist had begun to stuff papers and files of graphs back into his two well-worn briefcases.

'Abel, what you've told me must not go beyond this room. Not yet.

Nor must we allow any change to be seen in our conduct. We press on with the business of government – all reform programmes go ahead as planned.'

Aganbegyan nodded. 'I've already dissolved the Oligarchy committee and impounded the working papers. The committee members' loyalty is beyond question. You know that. But as for finding a way out of this –' He finished packing the briefcases and gestured towards the red-bound report. 'We have little time. The situation deteriorates by the day.'

'I'm aware of that. I'll act in the best and fastest way I can.' Now Gorbachev came around the desk and faced him squarely. 'But I have to take care. There are many who would be happy to say that this whole crisis is of my own making in the first place.'

The long session was over. Aganbegyan stifled a yawn as he fetched his crumpled overcoat from a closet concealed in one of the wall's decorated panels. He began laboriously to squeeze his thick body into it.

'A day older,' he muttered. 'I feel a hundred years older.'

Gorbachev smiled wryly as he accompanied him to the door. 'You're indestructible. You'll gallop into the next century like a young colt, never fear.'

But the weary economist paused and looked up at him with eyes that were as dark and cold as the ice on the Moskva.

'Let's hope the next century is worth seeing,' he said softly.

He swung the great door open and two uniformed colonels of the Soviet leader's personal guard clicked to attention. One of them led him off through the palace's echoing halls, his crisp uniform and precise movements contrasting with the economist's slightly shabby figure.

Gorbachev stood on in the doorway, listening as their retreating footsteps faded.

Press on with the business of government, he had told Aganbegyan. Perhaps there were even some things that should be accelerated.

He turned to the other colonel, who snapped to attention again.

'Find me comrade Ligachev,' he told him. 'I want to see him at once.'

Then, before the man could protest at leaving him unguarded, he strode back into his office and closed the door.

'Nikolai? Is that you?'

Galina's voice sounded far away, as if she were still half-dreaming. Serov moved quietly from the bedroom door, leaving it open to spill daylight into the room. He slid the leather greatcoat from his shoulders, draping it over a chair, and crossed to the bed.

'It's me.'

The smile that answered him was sleepy and sensuous, her eyes still closed. The bedclothes rustled and her arm stretched across the pillows towards him. He sat down on the edge of the bed and took the hand, kissing its palm. It smelt fragrant and warm. His body stirred, reminding him of its need.

Now she was pushing herself up on one elbow and shaking her long hair from her face. Her eyes flickered open, blinking against the light, the irises still dilated with sleep. He took in every detail as if seeing her for the first time. Blonde hair, green eyes, milky skin as smooth as glass; like her mother. Devastating.

She watched him watching her, enjoying the effect that she knew she was having, and the sleepy smile broadened into a grin; then her arms closed about him.

'I knew you'd come today. Dear Nikolai. I told myself you would.'

The kiss that followed was open and hungry. He yielded to her willingly enough for a time; when he finally drew away, it was as gently as possible, to let her know his reluctance.

'We're strong willed this morning.' She reached to turn the clock face towards her. The bedsheet fell from her breasts and he felt the sudden pulse of blood behind his temples. She was less than half his age. Every inch of her youthful body inflamed him. There was no part of it he didn't know. Why should there be? He had watched it grow from childhood.

'Eight fifteen,' she mumbled. 'I am impressed.' She peered more closely at him, noting the dark suit, white shirt. 'You're dressed for headquarters.' She fingered the knot of his tie. 'Impeccable. Always impeccable, Nikolai.' Her expression changed to disappointment. 'Can't you stay?'

'Not for long.'

'Why not?' She was pouting, turning it into a game now: little hurt girl.

He pinched her nose gently, as if she were a naughty child. 'Things to do. I've already done a morning's business while you've been fast asleep.'

'Ha!' She eased back against the pillows. 'Not official business, that's for sure. You don't chase about at this hour on official duties. You have minions for that.'

He half-smiled and got to his feet, watching her hand as she ran a fingernail lazily along the seam of his trousers.

'Stay with me tonight, Nikolai. Please? Don't run off to that mysterious apartment of yours.'

She had ended the game now; this time her request was sincere.

'If I can, I'll come back here. I promise.'

He crossed to the wardrobe and unbuckled the shoulder holster. The wardrobe door swung open and he stood looking at his reflection for a moment. She was right about his clothes. He took care. Apart from the heavy Makarov in his hand, he could have passed for a prosperous Western businessman.

Her voice broke into his thoughts.

'I thought I'd go out today or tomorrow. If the snow stops for a while.' Her tone had grown heavy with sleep again.

'Oh? Where? You must have emptied the shops by now.'

The reply was drowsy, barely audible. 'Vagankovskoye.'

He froze, the holster and harness halfway to the hook at the back of the wardrobe, but didn't turn around.

'It's hardly the best weather for standing about in a cemetery, Galya,' was all he said.

He waited but there was no further response. He finished undressing in silence, folding or hanging every garment carefully.

By the time he returned to the bed and slipped in beside her, her eyes were closed again and her breathing was deep and regular, like a sleeping child's.

Vagankovskoye. Well, let her go, if that was what she wanted. Perhaps, after all, there was no harm.

Listening to her breathing, he began to wonder if his visit this morning was to be in vain. Then she moved against him; warm arms encircled him again.

'Dear Nikolai.'

As he embraced her, his gaze fell on the black leather greatcoat, folded across the chair where he had left it. A crooked streak of dirt snaked up the length of one sleeve. For a moment he was irritated, puzzling over what it was and where it had come from. Then he shifted position slightly and saw that it was only dust. Probably from Gramin's shovel. Grave dust.

It would brush off. He put it from his mind and bent his head to kiss the girl's warm body.

2

Georgi Fedorovich Zavarov, Marshal of the Soviet Union and Supreme Commander of All Armed Forces, swathed himself in a dressing-gown and padded out of the bathroom, still towelling his cropped grey hair. Big and powerful, the advancing years had failed to diminish him.

'Think what a good brandy's like after sixty-odd years!' he liked to say. 'That's me! Full-bodied, peak condition, just the thing for a winter's night!'

Or a winter's morning, he thought as he noticed the snow piled on the window-ledge. He sniffed appreciatively as an enticing aroma reached his nostrils. Thick, sweet coffee: the next thing he needed to wash away the cobwebs of last night's drinking.

He turned towards his dressing-room where Ratushny, his valet, would be waiting to help him dress. Instead, he found the majordomo standing by the bedroom window, gazing into the street below.

'Stop gawping, man!'

The little man in the white uniform, a soft creature all roundness and wobbling chins, jumped in surprise. 'Sorry, comrade Marshal.'

'What's going on anyway?'

'I was just wondering who was about so early, sir.'

Zavarov parted the lace curtains to see for himself. Ten floors below, in the centre of Kutuzovskiy Prospekt's fourteen lanes, a limousine sat in the privilege lane, flanked by militia cars and waiting to cut across to their block. Its direction suggested it had come from the Kremlin. The vehicle was a Zil, the model reserved for the Politburo.

'I was just thinking, Marshal, it looks like someone's been up to the Kremlin very early.'

Zavarov scowled in reply. Since most of the leadership had their Moscow apartments along this stretch of road, many of them in the same block as himself, the hunch made sense.

'Never you mind.' He threw his dressing-gown off for Ratushny to catch. 'You just see if you can get me a cup of that coffee I can smell. I taste like a horse's arse.' He headed for the clothes-stand in the dressing-room where his garments were waiting.

But as soon as Ratushny had gone he returned to the window to resume watching the street while he struggled into his uniform trousers.

The limousine had completed its manoeuvre and was crunching through the snow towards the archway that led to the block's inner courtyard. It drew up at the kerb and the driver leapt out. By the time he'd circled around, his passenger had already flung the door open for himself and was stepping out, his feet gliding over the snow by the sill to stand safely on the swept pavement. He wore an overcoat and scarf but no hat, revealing a perfect head of pure white hair.

'Ligachev,' the Marshal breathed softly. 'What have you been up to at this hour?'

He watched as the Politburo's number two spoke briefly to the driver and walked towards the building's entrance, disappearing from his line of vision. A bodyguard had also climbed out from the car but made no move to follow him; the pavement was thick with plain-clothes Ninth Directorate men with radios at their ears and right hands that never strayed far from the fronts of their jackets. When the guard and driver climbed back into the warmth of the limousine and the red and blue lights on the roofs of the militia cars stopped flashing, Zavarov knew that Ligachev had entered the apartment block.

Three minutes later the Marshal was dressed but for his jacket and cap when the doorbell rang. He pushed past Ratushny, making him spill the coffee over his white uniform, to answer it himself.

'Good morning, Georgi Fedorovich.'

Ligachev was round-faced with shining cheeks, like a schoolboy on a winter morning.

'I'm an early bird today.'

He glanced past the Marshal at Ratushny's stained uniform and the dripping tray.

'I haven't caught you at a bad time?'

Zavarov stood aside and waved him in. The majordomo, flushed with embarrassment, took the visitor's outer coat and scarf, then scuttled off down the corridor, mumbling that more coffee would be on its way.

The two men went through to the apartment's luxurious drawing-room and settled in the easy chairs by the log fire, unlit but laid ready for the sake of appearances.

At first Ligachev talked about the weather, about his temporary driver, about anything, it seemed to Zavarov, except whatever might have brought him.

'How is Olga?' was his final question.

'Fine. Not here at the moment. She's spending the week at the dacha. Working on one of her books.'

'Ah yes.' Ligachev glanced at the bookshelf where several of Madame Zavarova's mathematics textbooks were on display. From there his gaze shifted to the Steinway grand piano and the cluster of silver-framed photographs arranged on its lid. One particular picture, faded with age, dominated the group. Zavarov thought his eyes lingered for a moment on it. Then the rosy-cheeked politician turned back to him.

'Mikhail Sergeyevich sends you his warmest regards.'

Zavarov grunted. 'Nice to hear I'm in his thoughts. I reciprocate.' He smiled coldly. 'Did he mention the matter of my establishment?'

'No.' Ligachev pursed his lips. 'That's not what I'm here to talk about.'

Before Zavarov could say anything, Ratushny appeared with a fresh tray of coffee. He had changed his uniform. The Marshal took the coffee and waved him away. He set the tray down on a side-table and began pouring two cups.

'My establishment, Yegor,' he pursued as the door closed behind the majordomo, 'is something you may not want to talk about, but I do. You know the score as well as me. When Chernenko made me Chief of Staff and brought me onto the Politburo as an alternate member, he promised that I could expect full voting establishment in a year or so. Nothing could have been clearer.'

Ligachev looked increasingly uncomfortable but said nothing.

'Gorbachev hasn't the slightest intention of confirming my establishment. Has he?'

Still no response. The Marshal clattered Ligachev's cup down on the table by his elbow. A little pool of coffee slopped into the saucer. Ligachev stared at it and then up at Zavarov. He sighed.

'Mikhail Sergeyevich holds you in the highest regard. It's just that now isn't the best time.'

'Don't patronise me. If Chernenko had lived another year or two, Gorbachev would never have got the leadership. We both know that.' Now Zavarov's voice dropped to a low growl. 'You might have got it yourself.'

Ligachev coloured. 'Ancient history.'

'Why have you stopped thinking for yourself, Yegor? Why do you let Mikhail Sergeyevich do it all for you?'

'Careful, Georgi. Your sharp tongue presumes on my friendship too much.'

'Friendship? You used to be a friend. I'm not so sure any more.' Zavarov returned to his armchair, ran a large hand over his grizzled hair and lit an unfiltered English cigarette. 'We made you Gorbachev's second-in-command as a safety harness, to rein him in. But it isn't working. You've become his creature instead – his little dancing bear. He plays the music, you jig to it.' The Marshal began clapping his heavy hands together, lilting a fairground tune at the same time. The cigarette dangled from his lips, puffs of smoke punctuating the new words he set to the old tune. 'See how Yegor twists and turns! La-la-la! La-la-la! Jump, Yegor! Higher, Yegor! La-la-la-la-la!'

It was a humiliating performance, one that belonged in a drunken NCO's mess, but Ligachev suffered it in silence, merely averting his gaze from Zavarov's and waiting patiently for him to finish.

'It's a question of economics,' he managed finally.

Zavarov snorted with derision. 'It's not a pay rise I'm looking for.'

'What country can keep funding military expansion if there's not enough money to pay for it?'

'Would you rather we let the Western imperialists clean up everywhere?'

'Of course not. But perhaps it's time we learnt to use other methods than brute force of arms. We must become stronger economically. That's where today's battlefield is.' For the first time a defiance had appeared in Ligachev's eyes. 'To take that battlefield we need to make a few changes.'

The Marshal expelled cigarette smoke through flat lips and eyed him with suspicion. 'Changes? What did you have in mind? You and your Mikhail Sergeyevich?'

'The country doesn't have a bottomless purse. We need to spend our money where it makes us strong for tomorrow – rebuilding our industries. It means there'll be less for military investment.'

Zavarov could hear Ratushny rattling dishes in the kitchen. Suddenly he felt cold; he shivered, wishing the man had lit the fire.

Ligachev was in control now. His voice purred on. 'Georgi, I'm just telling you the facts.'

'As you see them? Or as comrade Gorbachev sees them?'

'If military issues are going to take a back seat, we need to get that message across to the country. Not just in speeches. In action. That's why this would be the worst possible time to confirm your establishment. Then there's the Americans and the question of arms cuts.'

Zavarov spat out some shreds of tobacco and wiped his lips. 'Make them a few promises and let them go to hell.'

'No. Mikhail Sergeyevich wants *real* reductions. Not just nuclear either.'

Zavarov's head had begun to pound. 'Men and hardware,' he muttered. The pressure from the new leader had been building all year. 'That's what he's after.'

Ligachev nodded. 'We start with a substantial nuclear agreement with the Americans. Then we move on to conventional forces. Troops and equipment renewal costs – those are the biggest financial problem.'

Now the politician reached into an inside pocket and withdrew a white envelope.

'Which brings me to this.'

He handed it across to Zavarov. The Marshal's name was typed across it, along with the injunction *Confidential*. In the bottom left-hand corner was the single red star with the hammer and sickle picked out in gold within it that was the crest of the office of the General Secretary.

'You're to leave for Afghanistan at once. Your visit will be described as an appraisal of the operational readiness of our units.'

Zavarov rammed the cigarette between his lips and tore the envelope open.

'I've got a score of commanders there to tell me all about operational readiness. As Mikhail Sergeyevich well knows. What the hell is he up to?'

Ligachev drew a deep breath. 'It's all in there. You're to brief the command to begin planning for a phased troop withdrawal. It's only a plan at this stage, of course –'

'No!'

Zavarov scanned the one-page letter. It was as Ligachev said. On a separate sheet Gorbachev had listed specific points on which he sought the Marshal's views after his first-hand appraisal: how many regiments could be withdrawn, over what period, from which regions, at what risk.

'As I said, it's partly an economic issue,' Ligachev was saying. 'But it ties in to our negotiations with the Americans as well. Afghanistan is one of the side issues that always get added to arms control agendas – human rights, Jews, the so-called political dissidents. You know how the White House likes to play holier-than-thou. With Afghanistan, it suits us to show willing this time.'

Zavarov let the letter fall to the table; as he looked up at Ligachev, he made no attempt to hide his scorn.

'Do you really go along with all this, Yegor?'

For the second time that morning, Ligachev avoided his gaze. 'Mikhail Sergeyevich will win the Western public opinion battle with moves like this. That puts tremendous pressure on Western political leaders.'

The cigarette, now a butt, suddenly tasted foul; Zavarov flung it into the fireplace, where it sparked against the dry wood. When he looked up, he found that Ligachev had risen to his feet.

'I can let myself out,' the politician said.

Zavarov stared grimly up at him. 'On that, at least, we agree.'

A few minutes later, his distasteful duty discharged, Ligachev lay back against the headrest of the Zil and gazed out of its smoked glass window with half-closed eyes. But he wasn't seeing the streets of Moscow or hearing its noises.

'Why must I take the letter, Mikhail Sergeyevich? Why not call him in and tell him to his face? Or send an officer of your personal staff.'

'It would be better if you went, Yegor Kuzmich. You're old friends.'

'He'll only cross-examine me about his establishment.'

'Exactly. It's time he knew my thinking. Naturally, you have my authority to answer him in full. That's why I want you to go. It'll be a hard blow for him; a friend can explain it more sympathetically.'

'With respect, General Secretary, I doubt that.'

'Are you unwilling to do this simple commission for me, comrade?'

'Of course not.'

Ligachev closed his eyes fully, the better to study the guilt in his soul. Zavarov was merely the latest in his list of betrayals. That was how he thought of them these days. Why pretend? The process had been going on for months. Ever since he had begun to weaken under the relentless force of Mikhail Sergeyevich's arguments about the changes that needed to be made in the country.

He was responsible for Personnel Affairs in the party. In the old days that had brought him great power. No one got elected – which meant appointed – to a key position anywhere in the hierarchy without his approval. Since high party standing was a ticket to all the best jobs and privileges in the country, he had been able to dispense and with-draw patronage like a Tsar of old, with consequent advantages to himself.

He also had encyclopaedic knowledge of party operations and of everyone who mattered in them. That was what had made him so valuable to Mikhail Sergeyevich. Looking back now, he could see that those who had nominated him as the 'safety harness' had actually played right into the new leader's hands. They had put close to him the man best qualified to guide his hand in the countrywide purge of key party positions that Mikhail Sergeyevich needed to build up his powerbase.

That was how the betrayals had started. Each one drew him deeper into Gorbachev's camp and further away from his old loyalties. For all Zavarov's coarse bluster, he had assessed his old friend's quandary with chilling accuracy.

Except for one thing. Ligachev hadn't stopped thinking for himself. That was what made it all such agony.

As for Zavarov, the rest of his morning slid away in a fug of French brandy. Ratushny came in to clear the coffee-tray, saw the brandy balloon in the Marshal's bearpaw of a fist, and retreated quickly to the kitchen again.

Hair of the dog, Zavarov told himself initially, a pick-me-up after last night's session. Nothing to do with Ligachev or his visit. After two generous glasses, however, the excuse was wearing thin. So the

Marshal abandoned it and fetched the bottle; thereafter it never left his hand all morning.

Noon found him slouched over the Steinway. No longer the proud soldier. Just an old man with too much brandy in his belly. Slumped on a piano for fear of falling over. A piano that Olga no longer played for him. It was over twenty years now since she had touched its keys in his hearing. He knew why.

His thick fingers reached out to trace the curves of the silver picture frame, its reflection gleaming in the dark sheen of the piano lid. The picture showed a soldier of the Red Army with captain's boards on his shoulders. Taller in those days. Slimmer too. No brandy in his belly then. Broad-shouldered. A proud, good-looking wife by his side. One who played the piano for him.

He clenched his eyes tight to shut out the rest of the picture. But it didn't matter: he knew what it contained anyway. For a few minutes he gave in and let the past live again: his foot tapped out tunes that he no longer heard Olga play, the picture in the silver frame moved and he was in it.

The escape was all too brief. When it was over, the picture was only a faded print after all, his hair was grey again and his waist too thick, and the empty brandy bottle and his headache were still there.

The letter too.

He picked it up again. There it was, nicely buried in the middle of the last paragraph:

> *Please make your arrangements to leave at your earliest convenience; your headquarters staff in Moscow will, I am sure, be able to cover adequately in your absence.*

Whatever else it looked like, it was a command: get out of Moscow at once.

Afghanistan. He knew the distances, the journey times. Within twenty-four hours he would be scrambling over the dunghills of Nangarhar or Herat.

On the seventh of November.

Where he would not be, maybe never again would be on any seventh of November, was on the reviewing stand by the Lenin Mausoleum, with everybody else who was anyone, watching his own soldiers, tanks, hardware and missiles file past on Red Square. Taking the salute on Revolution Day.

Exactly where he, the Chief of Staff, should be.

But there was worse. Not only would he not be there; he would be seen not to be there.

Was that the kind of message Gorbachev wanted to send to the country and the West?

Wanted to send to him as well?

'Bastard,' he growled fiercely, swallowing the last of the brandy.

'Bastard,' he said again, louder, as he flung the empty glass with all his strength into the fireplace. The empty bottle followed.

'Comrade Marshal?' ventured an anxious Ratushny, rushing in from the kitchen to see what the noise was.

'The bastard!' Zavarov roared before storming off. Behind him the letter fluttered to the floor.

3

Morning came wet and slow to the capital, the grey dawn creeping slowly over the jumbled rooftops. River and sky were the colour of lead. Scraps of wastepaper and takeaway wrappings, rained-on in the night to near disintegration, clung to the roads and pavements. In the slice of west London bounded by Chiswick High Road and the Uxbridge Road, tube trains rumbled over the elevated tracks above the narrow streets; lights still burnt in kitchens and bedrooms. Like the rest of the city, the streets were waking to another day.

In a narrow terraced house in one of these narrow streets, Edmund Knight let go of the bedroom curtain and closed the scene from view. One thought filled his mind, as it had on so many other days of late, and it brought enough bleakness in itself. Twenty years, he was thinking: twenty years was enough to ask of any man. He had served his time and now was tired. If they challenged him, if they said that so far he had only been required to wait, well then, to hell with them. He had given his readiness. For half his life. The waiting was as bad as doing, they knew that. It was time to finish.

Behind him the bedroom door opened and the woman came in. He watched her cross the room.

'Eva.'

Leaning against the window frame, he spoke her name quietly and she smiled fleetingly at him. She was used to his moods, his silences and stray words. He stood there watching as she turned away and switched on the lamp by the bed.

She wasn't his wife, he'd never had one, but she had come as close to him as he would allow any woman, wife or not. She would never know all of him; he would spare her that.

She was tall, almost as tall as himself, and her body, still damp from the shower, glowed in the lamplight when the white dressing-gown slipped to her feet. She began to comb her wet hair, her whole body shifting from side to side as she parted the fair tresses with long, smooth strokes.

Eva. The name was unspoken this time, locked behind his lips.

Eva, whose home this was; who shared her bed with him and sometimes the big old house in Berkshire that he called home. Who shared the same masters as he did.

Or some of them.

Eva, whom he loved. Who might be all he had now.

She felt him still watching her and glanced around.

'There isn't time, Edmund,' she said, smiling. Her voice was quiet, deep and soft. She knew there was always time. Her head flicked up suddenly, tossing her hair over her shoulders like a dancer, and her face half-turned back to him.

'You're a crazy man.'

He thought about the grey city and the drenched streets. Hated this miserable morning and this ache that was inside him, had been inside him for too long. Then he was behind her, taking the comb from her hand and setting it down. Her back arched and her wet hair was pressing against his unshaven cheek.

'I'm crazy,' he agreed.

Not meaning it; not meaning it at all.

There was one thing he had to tell her. The moment he chose was when they were dressed and almost ready to set out. He had made them late; she was in a hurry and assumed he was too. No time for too many questions.

'I'm going to resign,' he said.

She was bending down by the dressing table to put on her lipstick; her gaze swept up to meet his in the mirror, her mouth still set in the round o-shape. After a moment she tilted her head and returned her attention to her lips.

'Good for you.' She said it with perfect nonchalance.

'I'm serious.'

'You're always serious, Edmund. For the last year you've been serious. Ever since we started.' She took a last critical look at her handiwork, dropped the lipstick into her handbag and put on the jacket that she'd laid out on the bed. Then she turned to face him.

'Once a month you tell me one of us has to resign. Or both of us. I don't find this any easier than you – I know the rules just as well as you do. But let's enjoy it while we can, what do you say? If we're found out, we're found out. Don't make an even bigger thing of it. If you want to resign, resign. But not on my account, and not on this relationship's account. Oh!' She had seen the time. 'Get a move on.'

They left the house and set off in his car for Turnham Green station. The rain had slowed the traffic down and the streets around the common were slow going.

'Is it because of Sir Marcus?' she asked him. 'Have you got the blues because of tonight?'

23

The reception to mark the retirement of their outgoing Director General, Sir Marcus Cunningham, was that evening. They would both be there; it would be a strain, the usual pretence, carefully ignoring each other; but they both thought too much of Sir Marcus not to go.

Knight shook his head. 'I'll miss the old boy – my first branch officer, brought me into the service.' He took the car foward to the traffic lights. 'Twenty years is a long time. So yes, I have my loyalty to him. But his going isn't my reason.'

'Gaunt then?' she said gently. Horace Gaunt was to succeed Sir Marcus; and Eva knew Knight's views on him.

'No, not because of Gaunt either. It's simpler than that. It's just all the things I've always told you – I'm tired of my dirty job, period. Makes no difference who's on top.'

It was the end of the conversation. They were out of time. His calculations had been good. It wouldn't be her style to raise the matter again; she would just watch to see if he meant it.

Turnham Green was where he always dropped her. They would make their separate ways into town from there, he by car, she by tube. Arriving separately, keeping up the pretence. But today he u-turned and faced the car the other way.

'What are you doing?' she asked.

'I'm not going in this morning.' He dropped his hands from the steering wheel and shrugged. 'I don't feel like it. So sod it, I'm going home.' His travel-bag lay in the rear seat, his standard kit when he spent the night with her, and he hooked a thumb at it. 'This Director of Counter-Espionage is going home to do his laundry. Want to come with me? Maybe on second thoughts the laundry can wait.'

She was out of the car at once. 'You're crazy, Edmund, barking crazy.'

Then the door slammed and she was half-walking, half-running into the station. Drawing interested glances, he noted; and no wonder.

He watched for a break in the traffic and pulled off. Crazy? No, he wasn't crazy. Just finished.

He put his foot down and headed for Berkshire.

The house was a Victorian pile in an acre of garden that never got as much attention as it deserved. Eva said the place was far too large for him but he knew that she was wrong. He filled all the rooms somehow: books, old sticks of odd furniture that couldn't be called antique, pictures. Distractions, all of them. He needed distractions.

The answerphone in the study contained no messages, the accumulated mail was junk and bills. He tossed the daily newspapers onto the table and changed into fresh clothes. The ten o'clock pips were sounding on the kitchen radio when he called Curzon Street and told

24

them not to expect him until late morning. He offered no reason and hung up before being asked.

Half an hour later he drove into Guildford and parked at the top of the High Street. It was only a short walk from there to the bank by the Guildhall; when he arrived he went straight upstairs to the Securities section.

'My safety deposit box, please.'

'Certainly, sir. What name?'

'Gough.'

The clerk compared his signature with the specimen on his file card, collected the visit fee from him and delivered him to a small room with a table, two chairs and a telephone. Shortly afterwards he returned with the familiar steel box.

'Ring through when you want it put back, Mr Gough.'

Knight turned the snib in the door before unlocking the deposit box. It was one which he'd supplied himself; the bank didn't provide boxes, only the individual vaults. The benefit was that he held its only key.

The contents were precisely as he had left them. Paper foreign currencies were sorted into envelopes according to country of origin; coinage was bagged in plastic sachets. There were several passports and batches of other official-looking documents, also banded together in orderly groups. At the bottom was a single folded sheet of paper with a list of names and numbers. He took this out and picked up the telephone.

'Gough here. An international line, please. Cash charge.'

He spent the next thirty minutes calling several of the numbers on the list, speaking in French and German. He talked through a different story tailored to each and made careful notes as he went along.

It took until the fourth call before he had what he wanted. The Paris-based precious metals trading agency was eminent in its field and very reputable. The secretary of Henri Vialle, the agency's proprietor and managing director, was courteous and helpful.

'He is occupied at present, Monsieur. Perhaps I can be of assistance?'

'My consultancy firm has been retained by the South African Chamber of Mines to arrange an international precious metals symposium; only leading dealers such as Monsieur Vialle will be invited to attend. It will be addressed by futures exchange officials from the London Metal Exchange and the New York Mercantile Exchange. It will be held in Vienna in the spring of next year. I plan to call on leading traders in the next few weeks to seek their guidance on the symposium's theme. This will not require more than an hour of their time. All I need to know today are the occasions over the next few weeks when I might see Monsieur Vialle. He is, of course, a very busy man. No doubt his diary becomes very full. That is why I thought a telephone call would be wise.'

'Monsieur, your symposium sounds invaluable, but I do not think Monsieur Vialle would wish me to commit to such a meeting without knowing more. In writing, naturally.'

'And naturally, Mademoiselle, I plan to write. In the meantime, if it is easier for you, perhaps you could tell me the days when Monsieur Vialle could definitely not see me? That would help me plan my visits to other dealers.'

Protective secretaries were usually more willing to release information that way around. When Knight hung up five minutes later he had a list of Vialle's least cancellable commitments for the next month, including where in his schedule several of them fell on consecutive days.

Now he selected two of the currency envelopes, two of the bags of loose change, and a passport and plastic wallet containing some folded-over papers. He relocked the box and used the telephone to announce that he was through. He settled with the clerk for the calls and left, as quietly and inconspicuously as he had arrived.

On the pavement outside he checked his watch. The visit had taken three-quarters of an hour. The rain was blowing in bad-tempered squalls and the prospect of Curzon Street was as unattractive as ever. Late morning, he'd told them. Well, very late morning. What the hell.

Back to Berkshire. But not to the house.

By noon he was there. He slammed on the brakes for the cattle grid and pulled the car in to the side of the drive just after the entrance pillars. At last the rain was clearing; above him was the sort of featureless sky he'd associated since childhood with rooks and hooded crows; 'riding shotgun' on the humans, as his father had liked to describe them. He wound down the window and listened. A caw echoed from one of the tall birches and made him smile.

He locked the car and set off. This bottom field usually had a few horses in it. The nuns rented ground and stabling to some of the local families who could afford ponies for their daughters but not the land to keep them on. This morning the field was empty, suggesting that riding lessons were in progress somewhere.

He vaulted the wire into the next field, where he was greeted by a dozen cows who came over to investigate; they lost interest when they realised he wasn't old Jod who looked after them.

Then over another stretch of wire and the land dropped away towards the spinney. Up on his right, hidden by the crest of the rising ground, stood the convent and the school. Although they weren't his destination, he glanced their way automatically and saw the small figure that was just then coming over the brow.

He stopped and watched as the shape drew nearer and resolved itself into an elderly, bespectacled nun. She hadn't seen him yet; all her attention was on the open breviary she was holding. Her lips moved as she intoned the prayers. He waited until she was within speaking range.

'Sister.' He said it very quietly so as not to alarm her. 'Marie-Thérèse?'

She brought the breviary down and tilted her head forward to peer at him over the top of her spectacles.

'Good gracious!' she said eventually. 'It's Mr Knight, isn't it? What a nice surprise. Shall we walk together? If you don't mind my snail's pace, that is.'

They moved on towards the spinney side by side. He noticed that her toecaps glittered with droplets of rainwater from the wet grass; his own were the same.

'What brings you today, Mr Knight? Are you visiting us properly at last?'

He shook his head. 'More selfish than that. I felt like a stroll. Am I presumptuous to enter your grounds?'

'Hardly. We don't see enough of you.'

'Time, Sister. Never enough.'

She chuckled. 'At my age, what don't I know about time? We can save it, Mr Knight, but it still runs out on us.'

There was an old birch tree on the edge of the spinney. They stood beneath it, she puffing a little, and gazed across the fields. Here and there a church spire rose above clumps of trees. Grey roof slates marked the older parts of the village, red tiles the newer developments.

'Your money's always welcome, Mr Knight. An orphanage needs plenty. The children can't eat prayer, whatever the good book says. But there's not much company for a child in a five pound note. We could do with your company more.'

A magpie swooped down to earth and tip-toed through the coarse grass. In the village a clock chimed the half hour.

'I'll see what I can do, Sister. No promises.'

'That's the best way.'

After a while she shivered and made to go back up. He walked her as far as the top of the hill and followed the driveway that would lead him back down to the car. At the little chapel the Notice of Services by the door told him that First Mass had been served as Eva and he were breakfasting; Second as he was dropping her at the station. Father Dominic was hearing confessions now, Father Hugh would hear them from three this afternoon. Evensong was at six.

He stepped inside. The fragrance of candlewax and incense filled his nostrils, then the flat musk of holy water as he crossed himself. Bowed backs and headscarves indicated Father Dominic's confessional.

He was turning the clock back too abruptly; a dizziness came over him and he had to reach out to steady himself against one of the pews. Its wood was smooth, almost oily to his touch, exactly as he knew it would be.

He heard the echo of his heels against the floortiles as he walked up the aisle. He genuflected by a pew and knelt in it. At the front of the chapel an old woman rose from the candle she had lit. He looked up as she walked slowly down the aisle and past him. Her gaze was cast down and she was drawing her coat tight in readiness for outside. He heard the rustle of a curtain on a rail and watched as a young woman stepped from the confessional and made her way to the front. She caught him gazing and blushed, making him look away quickly. The others who were waiting decided by nods who was next, and a gnarled man with a walking stick limped behind the curtain.

What did they have to confess? Jealousies? Something that the checkout girl missed?

He didn't bother to genuflect as he left the pew. He didn't notice whether the rooks were still arguing as he hurried down the drive. The cattle grid rattled like a sten-gun as he revved the car hard over it and turned directly for London.

But there were other voices arguing behind those of the rooks and the crows. Voices from another rainstorm, years before. They ran through his mind all through that day, fading in and out like a weak signal on a crystal set. Frightened voices from his childhood. His mother. His father.

'I stood down.' Rain streamed off his father's windcheater onto the tack-room floor. He busied himself with stripping the wet garments off, a way of avoiding his wife's eyes.

'And?' She had stopped rubbing at the saddle when he came in, bringing a blast of rain through the door with him; now she put the cloth down. But she didn't move towards him.

'And nothing. I stood down, the meeting's over, that's all there is to it. It's over.'

'It can't be over. There are the charges still.'

'There'll be no charges. That's the whole point.'

'Why?'

'There'll have to be a by-election. Our friend says he's prepared to stand. D'you like that? – "prepared to". As if he's doing everybody a big favour, as if it isn't just what he's always wanted. I've given it to him on a plate. The selection committee will adopt him, of course. So naturally there'll be no charges.'

'I still don't understand.'

'How would it look in the papers? – me resigning, him pressing fraud charges. What would that say for all of us? D'you think Central Office would like it?'

'No.' Relief appeared in her eyes as she absorbed the logic of this.

'He's in clover. He's wanted me out for years. Been trying to talk the committee into making me stand aside ever since he joined. Now he's got what he wanted, and for what? – a few thousand. Less than it would cost to buy the damn seat if he could still do that. Loose change to him. Everything to us.'

'We'll have to move.'

'What?'

'Everybody knows. How can we look anybody in the eye? We're finished here.'

'We're finished anywhere. What am I supposed to do with the business? This is no time to sell.'

'Please – we have to go. They'll trample us down.'

'Then we'll learn to put up with it. There's no point running.'

So they didn't run. They stayed put in misery instead.

Glitter and gilt, the Dorchester's Penthouse suite. Red-coated waiters with silver trays, pushing through the hubbub. Knight with a headache and starting to drink too much. Staying away from Eva and she from him. A piano in the corner, playing too loud. The glass doors to the fountain terrace closed against the night outside, making the cigarette smoke hang in the air like smog.

Knight helped himself to another drink and continued watching the group of three men in the furthest corner from him. The grey-haired patrician in the middle was Sir Marcus Cunningham. The smooth-faced civil servant to his left was the Cabinet Secretary. The third man – long and funereal, hollow-cheeked: a man who matched his name – was Horace Gaunt.

The Prime Minister hadn't been able to come. Instead, Home Secretary William Clarke had made the appropriate speech, presented some inscribed glassware to Sir Marcus and then had chatted to him for a few minutes afterwards. Now Clarke was leaving, crossing the room in Knight's direction and towards the door, but having to stop every few yards to shake hands and exchange a word or two with people he recognised. He had a worn air about him that Knight hadn't seen before; a greyness in the square face, yellow in the whites of his eyes, the wiry hair a touch thinner than it used to be. The new job was taking its toll. He drew level with Knight and smiled at him. They shook hands.

'You look tired, Bill.'

Clarke laughed. 'You know how to cheer a man up.'

'Should I lie?'

Once, they'd been close friends. Shared a damp flat at university. Shared a girlfriend or two as well. Twenty years ago.

Clarke shrugged at Knight's question. 'I've had easier jobs.' Behind him his two Special Branch men tried to look inconspicuous. 'How's life treating you?'

'I've had more honest jobs.'

Clarke smiled ironically. 'You chose it.'

'And you chose politics.'

They chatted for a few minutes – about Clarke's wife, Marion, and the children, about how Sir Marcus would be missed, about the old days – then Clarke looked at his watch.

'Division bell's due in a few minutes. I'd better be off. We lost touch, Edmund.'

'Everybody does.'

'I'll call you.'

Knight nodded and Clarke hurried off, the detectives in tow.

Knight's glass was empty again. A waiter appeared and he grabbed another off the tray; it wasn't intended for him but the man was too surprised to protest. Across the room Gaunt was watching him. Like an owl waiting to swoop. Knight raised the glass in a silent toast and Gaunt turned his head away.

It was midnight when he left the hotel. Wondering if he was fit to drive. Suspecting he wasn't.

He paused by the reception desk to glance at the early editions of tomorrow's papers. Snags in the arms talks, the oil price continuing to slide. Opec in disarray, the Arab economies under threat.

'There's a first,' he muttered.

Wishing he was staying at Eva's tonight. Too drunk to make it worthwhile. But wanting her to rub the edge off his loneliness. Block out the memories.

Back in the Penthouse suite the evening was winding up. Sir Marcus had gone. Women were leaving the room to fetch coats and wraps, the men were standing together in little knots.

Horace Gaunt was deep in conversation with a curly-haired man in his early thirties: Dick Sumner, who headed Knight's Soviet section. Gaunt seemed very intense, the hand that held his empty glass fingering his tie, his large eyes earnest. Sumner nodded occasionally at what his new Director General was saying but said little himself.

On her way across the room, on her own way out, Eva saw them and watched for a moment: Gaunt enjoying his arrival at the top, Sumner mindful of his own career, respectful. She realised that she was staring and looked away. Too late; Gaunt had seen her. He patted Sumner's arm, sending him on his way, and smiled over at her. It wasn't a goodnight-are-you-off smile; it was a wait-there. Then he was by her side, his solemn eyes scanning her face. She found that she couldn't look into them but it seemed to make no difference to him.

30

'I wanted to talk to you,' he said. 'Couldn't catch you earlier – Sir Marcus and the Home Secretary and whatnot. Were you rushing off?'

Now she was finding out how Sumner had felt, and shook her head. Respectfully.

The Jaguar rolled up quietly beside Knight in Shepherd Street, just as he was about to cut through the Market and back to Curzon Street, to retrieve his car. The Jaguar's rear door swung open; he stood indecisively on the pavement, looking through the archway for a few moments, then walked back and slid in beside Sir Marcus.

'I might not see much of you for a while,' said Sir Marcus as his driver took them down to Piccadilly, where the traffic was heavier. 'It'll be tough, now that Gaunt's at the top.'

Knight wasn't looking at him. 'I'm quitting anyway.'

The older man's grey eyes studied him in silence, his fingers folding and stretching the pair of gloves that lay in his lap. The car turned down towards St James's.

'This is the drink talking,' he said eventually.

Knight shook his head. Sir Marcus watched him for a moment longer, decided that he was serious, then the grey eyes left Knight's face and gazed along Pall Mall. The fingers crushed one of the gloves in his hand.

'You can't,' he said. 'Not now.'

Knight sighed and settled back for a long session.

4

Serov awoke to darkness and the ringing of the telephone. Alone in his own apartment, stiff from the armchair in which he'd dozed off. Dreaming from the book on his lap. Shaken by the dream. He grabbed at the phone to shut it up.

'Yes?' He shook the sleep from his brain and hauled himself upright.

'I need to see you, comrade.' He recognised Gramin's hoarse tones, mangled by the crushed nose. 'I think it's important. As soon as possible.'

His mind came rapidly into focus. The dream was only a dream. Across the city Galina was waiting for him. In the darkness of the room he picked out the time on the glowing digital display of the video recorder and pulled his thoughts together.

'The Armenian's,' he told Gramin. 'In an hour or two.'

The line went dead and he put the instrument down. He went round the room, switching on each and every light and closing the curtains against the night.

A glass of bourbon later he returned to the armchair and picked up the book where it had slid down the side of the cushion.

Nineteen Eighty-Four. Forbidden reading, of course. As were most of the books in the apartment. All of the major English-language writers were represented. Right up to date, not just the approved classics like Dickens or Shakespeare that the libraries carried. Serious authors, pulp fiction, biographies. British, American, history books, even poetry: they were all here, and in the original English, untouched by the Glavlit censors. It was the library of a cultured man.

He took another draught of the bourbon and surveyed the apartment. His kingdom. In this place where he admitted no visitor, not even Galina, where he was surrounded by tokens of his own intellectual breadth and by luxury goods that would have left most of his countrymen pop-eyed, Nikolai Vasiliyevich Serov defined himself.

Eleven thirty. Time to go. He drained the glass and put the book back on the shelf. In its proper place.

Even at this time of night it was impossible to be unaware of the extra activity on the streets. Not even the weather got in its way. There were uniformed and armed militia and plain-clothes men and women at every Metro exit he drove past, stopping people at random and demanding their identity papers. In some cases body searches were being carried out on the spot. He saw a gang of young people being shepherded at gunpoint into a grey investigators' van, whether for more detailed searching or because they had been arrested, he had no way of knowing. He slowed down as if he was just curious to see what was going on, but as far as he could tell none of them looked like any of the cocaine dealers that had escaped the Druzhba Park swoop. Driving over the Krasnokholmskiy Bridge onto the island, he saw a group of tipsy business types, Westerners judging from their appearance and obvious indignation, who were being photographed and quizzed by three well-built men. That worried him: it was a bad sign if even the tourists and businessmen were being hassled.

With all this going on, he wasn't too surprised when he himself was flagged down a mile later. Traffic inspectors were streaming every fourth or fifth car off the road at the intersection with Great Ordynka Street and directing them into a floodlit sidestreet. Here he waited in line, under the guns of a file of young militia regulars, until a shivering detective came to his car. He saw him take in the fact that it was a Chaika. Although the long, black saloon was unmarked, the officer at once adopted a more respectful bearing.

'Good evening, comrade,' he said carefully, as Serov's window hummed open an inch. 'Sorry to inconvenience you. Might I ask to see your papers, please, and know the object of your journey?'

Serov held his KGB card up to the window. It was the yellow one, the general purpose card that stated only his name and rank, discreetly omitting any reference to his directorage or function.

'No, comrade Detective, you may not ask the object of my journey. Tell your friends in the road to pay more heed to which vehicles they're pulling in. I've got better things to do than sit here half the night.'

'My apologies, comrade General. I didn't realise who you were when I enquired, otherwise of course I wouldn't have done so. I'll have you out of here at once. I'm sorry you've been delayed. What with the traffic and the weather all the inspectors can see are headlights; they can't tell what kind of car they're pulling in.'

'What's this in aid of, anyway?'

'To tell you the truth, sir, I'm not sure. It's a Second Directorage operation. I'm CID, from Pyatnikskaya Street. We're just extra arms and legs. We've been given a list of names to look out for and told to get on with it.'

'The usual tightly co-ordinated operation, eh?'

The detective, glad to feel the thaw in his attitude, went off to shunt the cars in front forward so that the long Chaika could move off. As Serov pulled away he glanced in the rear-view mirror and saw him stamping his feet for warmth while he signalled the queue to tighten up.

At the end of the street were three of the grey vans. Serov heard dogs barking in one as he cruised past.

Back on the main road, he turned south and picked up the Varshavs-koye Shosse. As he left the city centre and the carriageway lights became less frequent, the snow eased off but an icy fog began to close in. Settling back at a sensible speed, he switched his wipers back on and thought about what had happened at Ordynka. Being flagged down was no more than a nuisance; he was carrying nothing he shouldn't be and the car was clean. The real issue was the extent of what was going on in the city; and the rest of the country, if everything he heard was to be believed. That and the fact that at Ordynka he had counted no less than four agencies involved: the Second Directorate, the militia, the CID, and even the City Traffic Control Board. Whoever had set the operation up packed plenty of clout. That was disturbing. With practice they could only get better.

He found a further disagreeable omen at the Ecranas electronics warehouse. A fleet of the now all-too-familiar grey vans and half a dozen police Volgas, headlights blazing, were drawn up alongside the loading bays. He let the car's speed fall while he peered through the fog, and made out what he supposed were members of the nightshift, still in their overalls, being frogmarched to the vans.

After seven or eight miles, well up in the hills by now, he swung west onto Balaklavskiy Prospekt and followed it to Vernadskovo. Here the road became the Aminyevskoye Shosse. Cheaply built apartment blocks lined the right-hand side; on the left, beyond where the Ocha-kovka river paralleled the *shosse*, the concrete blocks of the Olympic Village lay hidden in the darkness. By the roadside, also on his left, he discerned the red and yellow petrol pumps and hut of the filling station, barely visible through the fog. Beside it, in a chain-link enclosure, stood rows of used cars for sale, some under canvas covers, all beneath a crust of snow. He braked, turned into the forecourt and drew up behind the enclosure, the cars within it concealing the Chaika from passing traffic on the *shosse*.

One other car, a Zhiguli it looked like, sat at the far end of the wasteland behind the lot. He studied it in the headlamp beams. Snow covered its roof and bootlid but the windscreen was clear. There were no tyretracks across the snow other than those which it had made.

Serov switched off his engine and lights and waited. Few other vehicles went past on the *shosse*; those which did pressed on without slowing or stopping. All was still and quiet in the vicinity of the apartment blocks. Although he was already behind schedule because of the unexpected delay at Ordynka, he made himself sit tight for a few minutes until he had the feel of the place. Then he pulled on the rubber overshoes that he had ready in the passenger footwell. He withdrew the Makarov from its holster and slipped the torch he kept in the glove compartment into his pocket. Choosing a moment when no vehicles were in sight or within earshot on the road, he slipped out of the Chaika, locked his door and made his way carefully onto the snow-covered moorland where it dropped away from the level of the filling station.

Low bushes and clumps of tough grass frozen into sharp sticks lay hidden under the snow, snagging his steps. The snow also made it impossible to be sure of the contours of the ground, so that he almost stumbled several times before he reached the path that led down to the Ochakovka. He was reluctant to use the torch out here because it would only make the surrounding blackness seem more impenetrable. Anyway, the beam might attract the unwelcome attention of a passing motorist. Or turn him into a sitting target if anyone was that way inclined.

The area had been landscaped when the athletes' village was built, so that the river was trapped into a series of small lakes crossed by arched footbridges. Most of the high fence that had been put up to keep the local people and the athletes safely separated still enclosed the walkways. Although man-sized sections had long since been removed by fishermen and children, apparently no civic or local decision had ever been made simply to take the whole lot down.

Serov made his way through one of the gaps and stood motionless again, watching and listening as before. Thirty feet above him and a hundred yards away a bus passed on the *shosse*. He waited for the note of its engine to fade, then tested the river's surface with his foot, cautiously walking out a few yards. As he expected, the river was frozen rock-hard. He returned to the walkway and followed it towards the footbridge, where a small weir controlled the flow down to the next lake. Only when he was at the edge of the chamber beneath the footbridge did he take the torch from his pocket. Down here, its beam would no longer be visible from the *shosse*.

Just before he switched it on to sweep the sides of the chamber he became aware of someone standing directly ahead of him, his presence felt as much as seen. If he looked straight at the figure, he saw nothing; but by looking to the side, he could make out a vague outline through the darkness and fog. He angled the torch at the region of the figure's waist, where a weapon would be if the man was armed, and switched it on.

'Put it out, for God's sake!' a voice pleaded. It was filled with fear. 'Before someone sees!'

There was no gun. Serov swept the beam up so that it caught the man's face.

Little, flabby Ratushny squinted away from the bright light, his chins trembling.

'Hands,' Serov said. Ratushny held them out, palms forward. Serov stepped onto the frozen river, then into the footbridge chamber and down to the weir's lower level, and rammed the Makarov into Ratushny's soft belly. At the same time he flicked the torch beam around the chamber until he was satisfied that it was empty. He switched the torch off. A truck thundered past on the *shosse*.

'Alone?' he asked Ratushny when the silence returned.

'I swear it.'

'The gun stays here till we're finished. Then you walk ahead of me back to the cars.'

'Whatever you say.'

'So, my friend. What have you got for me this time? Omit nothing. You know how much I like details. For good intelligence I've got all the time in the world. Even on a night like this.'

After the sub-zero temperature outside, the Armenian's shebeen was like a steam-room. Gramin was holding court at a corner table right at the back of the bar. He had his arms around two middle-aged hookers. All three were laughing fit to burst. They were audible to Serov right across the packed hall, even over the general mêlée.

When Gramin saw him approach he whispered something to the women. They rose unsteadily to their feet and looked Serov up and down before tripping off giggling into the hurly-burly. One of them screeched as a bald man with a huge cigar in his mouth crept up behind her and squeezed her buttocks.

'This is what you call a low profile?' Serov slid in beside Gramin at the table and pushed some of the glasses and bottles out of his way.

'It was your idea to meet here,' Gramin said slyly. 'I was only trying to blend in.'

'What's the name of that electronics king? The one from Lvov who expanded his operation here when times were good under Brezhnev.'

'You mean Volkonsky?'

'I saw one of his organisations getting gutted tonight. It's like I told you. They're crawling over this city like maggots.'

Gramin looked sobered by the memory of their exchange. 'Volkonsky can afford a knock or two. Let's drink to his poverty. As for the maggots, may they chew on plenty of carcasses so they run out of appetite before they reach us.'

He ignored Serov's sceptical gaze and poured two good measures of vodka from a litre bottle of Stolichnaya, followed by two glasses of beer from the pitcher that a waiter had just delivered.

'The glasses are clean,' he said when he saw the look of distaste on

Serov's face. 'Well, as clean as you're likely to get here. You don't think I'd have you using the whores' glasses? Drink for your health!'

He tossed the vodka back while Serov sipped. Then he set about the beer. A woman, not one of the hookers, passed the table and fluttered her fingers at him. Gramin winked at her over the beerglass.

'Why did you want to see me?' Serov reminded him. 'You told me it was urgent.'

Gramin belched and put the empty glass down. He noticed that Serov hadn't touched his.

'Good beer, this. If the Armenian pisses in it like they say, that's some piss. Don't you want yours? I'll have it if you're just going to let it die in the glass.'

'Be my guest.' Serov put his hand over the top of the glass just as Gramin was reaching across. 'After you answer the question.'

Gramin wiped his mouth and sat back.

'Remember a guy called Lysenko?' he said.

Serov thought for a minute. 'Jewish?'

Gramin nodded. 'He was one of our pushers at Druzhba Park. I was going to dump him because he'd got himself a habit. Not a good idea for a dealer. But then came the raid. In fact, he wasn't there that night because he was stoned –'

'What do I want to know all this for?'

'I'm coming to that. He works for Melodiya, the music and recording administration. Since Druzhba Park, he's got no sources. He's desperate. He's a garbager now – uses anything he can get his hands on. I ran into him this evening. He tried to score from me. "I've got something to sell," he said.'

'Everybody's got something to sell.'

'Lysenko has a girlfriend. She's a dopehead too – used to look to him for her supplies. Now he's afraid she might go to new pastures. She's a statistician. Works at the Plekhanov Institute.'

Serov shook his head. 'And you're trying to set me up for some kind of trade with Lysenko or his little bitch. What does a statistician have that would interest me?'

'With respect, comrade, I don't think you should be so dismissive. Not until you've heard me out.'

Serov thought about the other things he would rather have been doing at that moment. Galina was waiting. But good intelligence was like grains of gold in a river: it only came to the prospector who kept sifting for it.

He sighed and tossed back the vodka.

'Go on then,' he told Gramin. 'But don't take all night over it.'

5

The north-eastern corner of the Vagankovskoye cemetery was where the newest graves were. The snow was like a shroud over the whole place, as if laid communally over the souls there. Her cheeks raw and numb from the biting wind, Galina came at last to the hedged area where her mother lay. The disorderly jumbles of crosses and head-stones, each grave surrounded by iron railings to keep out prowling dogs, reminded her of the perspective drawings she used to try to fathom in fine art classes at high school: no colour, just grey outlines diminishing as they marched into the distance, interspersed with the bare birch trees.

Death was no easier to fathom. She stared blankly at the laconic inscription on her mother's marble slab. Katarina's name and dates, that was all. No loving epitaph, not even her picture encased in glass on the slab, only the bare facts.

She meant no criticism of Nikolai, of course. How could she? After Katarina's death – death? why couldn't she call it what it was? – he'd taken charge of everything on his own. He'd had to; she'd been worse than useless, close to total breakdown herself. Just another burden for him to bear. He never once complained. God knows how much he'd handed over in bribes just to get hold of the burial plot.

She owed him everything; mother and daughter, they both had. Their home, their welfare, all had come from him. He had always been there, as long as she could remember. A lover to Katarina, a father to herself. Provider and protector to both of them.

And in those terrible months after her mother's death – *suicide* – he'd given her back her sanity.

'I don't want to lose you too,' he would say. 'My Katya's gone – not you too. You can't just give in like this. We must go on, Galya. Just you and I now. Don't close me out. I'll take care of you.'

He cocooned her in care and tenderness, and in the end it worked. Gradually she returned to life, like someone who had almost died from exposure. He thawed her, warmed her, held her close to him until she breathed again.

So she had to repay him. She knew his needs, was woman enough by then to sense them. Who better? She repaid him in the only way she could when he'd given her so much love over so long. She loved him back.

'I was right to do it, Mama,' she said to the marble, drawing her shawl closer about her cheeks. 'I was right.'

Half an hour later she was crossing back through the old town, waiting for a bus connection, when she saw the trolleybus. Number 25. For a moment she stared at it, her connection forgotten. She knew the route, remembered it as if her mother were standing beside her. The trolleybus pulled in a few yards away, and before she could question the decision she had hurried over and climbed aboard.

Within minutes she was at the Dimitrova stop on Great Polyanka Street. She crossed to the other side, cut through the familiar tumbledown alley by the telephone kiosks, and a minute later arrived outside the Tretyakov. In the snow it was no longer simply an art gallery; it was a magic castle from a fairy tale. Her imagination transformed the steeply pitched roofs over the entrance doorways, piled high with snow, into muffs on an old lady's hands, she saw warm jewels in the bright colours of the tiled facade.

She held back, suddenly unsure, conscious that today she had no one to share her fancies with. No Mama. No Nikolai. In fact, if he knew she was here, tantalising her emotions in this way, he would be furious. Pausing in the doorway to shake the snow from her shawl and overcoat, she wondered if he was right. On the other hand, didn't she owe it to him to prove that she could handle her memories and feelings? They had to be faced sometime; she had waited long enough. She stamped the melting snow from her boots and went on.

Just as in the old days, she ignored every other painting and made her way directly to the gallery hall where the Plastov hung. It made her smile to remember how she was always teased for the way she would race right past so many fine works, seeing none of them in her hunger for that one painting.

Suddenly, there it was. *Spring*. Shining out to her the moment she stepped into the room. Drawing her again like a vortex.

Now she was standing transfixed before it, her heart thumping harder than ever. Her eyes devoured the painting.

A woman. Young, with red-gold hair right down to her waist. Behind her a log cabin, its door open. Beyond the cabin and its fence, fields. There was snow on them but it was beginning to thaw, the dark earth showing through in streaks. The woman was crouching to fix a shawl over a little girl's head and shoulders: her daughter. Snowflakes were in the air, fighting the thaw.

But spring would win. There were clues. A bucket near the mother was filled with clear water, not ice. And fresh straw, not snow, carpeted the ground on which she knelt.

Then, the artist's most breathtaking, most memorable inspiration: the young mother was naked. She'd even kicked her shoes aside. She was naked while the snowflakes brushed her skin; naked in defiance of them. Their day was past. Her bare flesh believed in the spring.

Galina bowed her head as the tears started.

'Nikolai,' she whispered. 'You were right. It's still too soon. I'm not strong enough yet. Why did I do this?'

She looked to the side but her mother wasn't there. How could she be? But she wasn't in Vagankovskoye either. No, not under the cold marble with no love in it. Not under the snow that wouldn't melt. She was here, waiting for her here all the time. In the picture, where the snow was melting. Where spring was coming. Waiting for her with soft, white arms. Waiting to enfold her in warm love. See, she was smiling as she unpinned the shawl. She wasn't fixing it on, she was *un*pinning it. Asking where her little girl had been, what had taken her so long.

'Mama!'

The cry reverberated through the long gallery.

'Mama!'

Faces turned to her, voices called out. What were they calling? It didn't matter. Heavy footsteps approached, running. They didn't matter either.

She had found her mama, that was all that mattered.

The man in the crumpled parka puffed slightly as his pudgy body waddled uphill along Gorky Street. His name was Vladimir Chernavin, he held the position of Senior Special Inspector in the Department for Struggle Against Embezzlement of Socialist Property and Speculation, a division of the KGB's Second Directorate, and his mission this morning was the elimination of a piece of the fraud that infected his city. Today his chosen role was that of a man squeezing in a little shopping during office hours, and to this end he carried a cheap nylon shopping bag with a few purchases already in it. These would be charged to the Department but they would end up in his larder. No one was perfect.

He crossed to the north side of the boulevard by the Central Telegraph Office, taking advantage of where the engineers' vans had flattened the hillocks of snow at the edge of the kerb. It didn't escape his notice how some of the engineers were loafing inside the vehicles, with the motors running and the heaters roaring full blast, but he kept his views to himself and continued on his way.

As he passed Soviet Square he scanned the pavement on the other side, to check the whereabouts of the four officers that shadowed him as he had ordered. The two men and two women were armed, an unavoidable precaution these days.

He paused in a side alley to draw breath, leaning against a syrup drinks kiosk and shaking his head at the old woman inside. Next door was Yeliseyev's, the biggest and best food store in town. It was officially known as Food Shop Number One but people tended to stick with the old pre-revolution name.

He had reached his destination. He meandered along the shop-front, pretending to eye the displays of biscuits and canned goods. He watched in the plate-glass windows as one by one his back-up team crossed the traffic coming off Pushkin Square. When they were within a few yards he piloted his bulk through the ornate glass doors.

He went straight to the meat counter, where eight or nine people were jostling together. Some of them had already chosen what they wanted and had been to pay at the cash desk. They had returned to hand over their tickets and collect their goods. But others, like him, were there to see what was to be had.

Chernavin pushed his way to the front and peered along the glass counters.

'No beef?'

'No beef.' The shop assistant looked bored. Her cheeks creased as she chewed something.

In his inside pocket lay the Supply Ministry dispatch note, signed by store director Gulyaev, that confirmed delivery of forty tonnes of beef only the previous week. He knew from the subsequent surveillance reports that it couldn't all be sold already – not over the counter, at any rate.

The assistant swiped at a persistent fly and yawned. 'Hurry up if you want something else instead.'

'Don't rush me. I'm looking.'

'I've got some nice neck of lamb.' She pointed to a tray. When Chernavin shook his head she leant across and dropped her voice to a whisper. 'I could let you have some special chops.' She winked, still chewing. 'Really special. Don't let on.' She produced a greasepaper package and lifted a corner of the wrapping. 'Unofficial.'

'And two or three times the official price.'

She shoved the package back out of sight. 'If you're not interested, there's plenty that are.'

An old woman behind Chernavin clucked impatiently. He slapped the counter, making everyone jump.

'Everywhere it's the same!' He turned to the people behind him. The old woman backed away, clutching her shopping bag before her.

'No beef, never any fresh fruit, now they're cutting down on vodka as well. The only shoes I can get cripple me. All day I queue, all day my wife queues. What do we get? Sore feet and a bit of scrawny lamb. Or we end up paying through the nose for under-the-counter junk I wouldn't give to my dog. I've had enough.' He swung back to the assistant. 'Where's the store director? I want to complain.'

'Comrade, comrade,' the old woman croaked toothlessly. 'I know how you feel. We all do. But I'm getting a bit tired standing here. And you're creating an awful fuss. What's the use? You'll just get into trouble. Take some sausages or something. Some nice salami.'

To the assistant's dismay, however, a hatchet-faced supervisor was elbowing her way through the interested crowd that had started to gather. Some distance behind her a lanky man with a disdainful expression was also approaching.

'What's all this about?' demanded the supervisor. She faced Chernavin. 'Director Gulyaev heard you all the way across the store. You can't carry on like this when people are doing their best. You're lucky I don't call the militia.'

The throng parted to let Gulyaev through. The pudgy man's back-up team closed in.

'What's going on here?' Gulyaev poked Chernavin in the chest with his finger. 'Are you the person who's making a nuisance of himself? All this shouting and hoo-ha. This is a respectable store and I won't allow it.'

'I wanted some beef, that's all.'

'We're out of it. Surely you've been told that.'

The assistant nodded vigorously, chewing again.

'Then kindly make an alternative choice or leave.'

Chernavin nodded to the back-up team. The supervisor noticed and turned just in time to see the two male agents grab Gulyaev. His look of superiority changed to alarm. One of the female agents, a redhead, moved quietly alongside the counter assistant, while the other took the supervisor's arm. Suddenly, what the crowd had been looking forward to as merely the ticking-off of an overheated customer promised to be a good deal more.

Knowing that he was the centre of attention, Chernavin sauntered up to Gulyaev and took his time dipping into the crumpled parka to withdraw his wallet. Necks craned. He flicked the wallet open, revealing his identity card, and spoke in ringing tones so that everyone could hear.

'I, Vladimir Chernavin, Senior Special Inspector in the Department for Struggle Against Embezzlement of Socialist Property and Speculation, arrest you, Eduard Borisovich Gulyaev, director of Gastronom Number One. You are charged with perpetrating, in association with others as yet unnamed, gross economic crimes against the peoples and state of the Union of Soviet Socialist Republics. The maximum penalty for your offences is death and the confiscation of all personally-owned property, whether or not acquired as a result of your illegal activities. You will be detained in custody until the time of your trial. With immediate effect, you forfeit all rights as a Soviet citizen, except the right to legal representation.'

Gulyaev looked near death already. His lips twitched but he said nothing.

'Have you anything you wish to say at this point?'

Gulyaev shook his head. Chernavin flipped the wallet shut and returned it to his pocket. The crowd was very still and watchful.

The redhead guided the shop assistant down from behind the counter to the custody of the other female agent. Taking the girl's place, she planted her fists on the counter and thrust her bosom forward.

'Your attention please, comrades!' she sang out. 'General Secretary Gorbachev and the Politburo of the Central Committee of the Communist Party of the Union of Soviet Socialist Republics have determined to eliminate the vile corruption that petty officials have rolled their stinking bodies in for too long, thereby denying the Soviet peoples the fruits of their own labour.' By now most of the floor was paying attention. 'A foul conspiracy has been uncovered in this store. You see before you some of those involved. Despise them, for in their activities they have despised you. Tell your family, your friends, anyone you meet, what you have seen today. Tell them our leaders are stamping on corruption as you would a cockroach. Most of all, tell anyone you know who may themselves be involved in anti-social or fraudulent activities. Tell them their days are numbered.'

She rattled on for another minute or two, during which time Chernavin led the others off upstairs with their captives.

He took Gulyaev's office on the second floor as his interrogation room. He wanted to get started right away, on the spot, while the rest of the team searched through files and papers for further evidence.

'You'll be for the chop, you know,' he told Gulyaev cheerfully, drawing a paperknife across his throat. He ensconced himself comfortably in the winged recliner behind Gulyaev's desk. Opposite him the director was sitting stiffly upright on a steel and canvas chair.

'I might persuade them to go a bit easy if you cooperate. I already know the basic mechanics of what was going on. You had a smart operation, if you don't mind me saying so. I admire your commercial skills. Really.'

Gulyaev sneered and looked away.

'It was two-tier,' Chernavin went on. 'You diverted portions of legitimate deliveries and sold them to your contact for up to three roubles a kilo – a rouble better than the official price. That kept your books straight and you pocketed the difference – apart from what you handed out in bribes to your staff. Some of them were holding stock back on their own initiative anyway and offering it to customers at over the odds. I was offered some myself this morning. You turned a blind

43

eye to that because it reduced the bribes you had to pay. This place was a goldmine.' He broke off. 'How am I doing so far?'

Gulyaev scowled but said nothing. Chernavin shrugged and ploughed on.

'We know where the stuff went from here.' He glanced at his notes. 'A disused church in Balashikha, east of town. We'll pin down its exact location when we round up the District Food Trade Administration drivers who made the deliveries for you. We have their names.' He leant confidentially across the desk. 'Look, comrade Director, this isn't a personal thing. I'm all for a little private enterprise. Who isn't? Forget my captain's speech downstairs. She's a bit keen. The man I'm really after is your contact. Just a name, that's all I need. Or what he looks like. Or where you used to meet. What's his official job? A smart operator like you would deal only with the top man. Well?'

Gulyaev's lips remained sealed.

Chernavin made an exasperated noise. 'Why protect him? He was fleecing you. Three roubles he was giving you, but he'd be selling to the *kolkhoz* markets for five, maybe six! That's fair? You run the risk and he takes the lion's share. What way is that to do business? What's this crook ever done for you? Apart from get you into this mess.'

At last Gulyaev broke his silence. 'What'll he do for my family if I turn him in?'

Chernavin looked shocked. 'He'll be under lock and key, my friend. What could he do?'

'Plenty, if you didn't get to him fast enough.'

'We got to you, didn't we?'

'When he hears I'm under arrest he'll assume the worst. You should guard my wife and children right now.'

Chernavin frowned. 'We can't give protection to the families of felons. Once you've been convicted they won't even be guaranteed a roof over their heads. If you were helping us it'd be different. I could arrange protection now and some measure of special treatment for them when you've . . . departed.'

Gulyaev looked at the floor. When he answered, it was as if he were thinking aloud.

'Inspector, even if I thought for one minute I could trust you, and told you what you want to know, even if you did talk them into going easy on me – then what? Instead of a bullet in my neck I might get off with thirty years breaking rocks. Is that what you're offering me? Meanwhile, I've put my family on the line.' He looked up and smiled sadly. 'It's not much of a trade. Is it, comrade Inspector?'

Chernavin saw that he was wasting his time. He'd tried; what more could anyone do? He shrugged and dropped the paperknife with a clatter on the polished desk top.

'It's your funeral.'

He came around the desk and clipped a set of handcuffs on Gulyaev. Then he pushed him across the room and into the outer office. The redhead was waiting by the door with a stack of papers. Chernavin waved her inside and glared at the other officers as they sat Gulyaev down.

'Remain vigilant,' he told them. 'I need to review progress with the captain.'

Back in Gulyaev's office he closed and quietly locked the door. The redhead dumped the papers on the desk.

'Make any headway?' she asked.

'Not yet, my lovely Nina.' His eyes fastened on her tightening blouse as she slipped her jacket off and reached up to hang it on the hook behind the door. 'Give him an hour with the gorillas in Lefortovo, however, and we won't be able to shut him up.' He took her hand and returned to the winged chair. She leant against the desk.

'I'm proud of us,' he said. 'It's been a good day's work.'

'I've enjoyed it too.' She leafed through a file.

'As much as you enjoyed last night?'

She giggled.

'By way of modest celebration,' he continued, 'I've decided to send out for some lunch for us all. I'll order up something by phone from the Aragvi. I've also got to send for a secure van for our catch and it'll pass right by the Aragvi. So I thought I'd tell it to stop off and collect the food for us. What do you think?'

'An excellent idea, Vladimir. It'd save any of us having to leave the detainees.'

'Exactly what I thought. Now – do I get a little reward for this well-planned operation?'

Among the pine trees out at Yasyenevo, south of the city, squatted the wedge of concrete and glass that was the FCD's headquarters. In Serov's office on the top floor all was quiet. He'd spent the morning tearing through a mound of paperwork.

The phone rang. He snatched at the receiver.

'I told you – no calls.'

Sergei, his secretary, was contrite but hurried to explain. 'It's a Superintendent Glassov of the People's Militia.'

'Never heard of him. What's it about?'

'He'll only talk to you, sir.'

Maybe it was something to do with being stopped at Ordynka.

'Get the tape machines switched off and put him through.'

A click or two, a delay while Sergei passed his order on to the technical people, then the policeman's careful voice came on the line.

'Am I speaking to General Nikolai Serov?'

'You are. What can I do for you?'

'Sorry to trouble you, comrade General. It's on a rather personal matter. May I speak freely, or would you rather call me back?'

Well, the tape recorders had never been much of a secret.

'You can speak freely, comrade Superintendent.'

'It concerns a young woman we're holding in custody, sir. She was arrested earlier this morning for defacing one of the paintings in the Tretyakov State Gallery. The fact is, we've not been getting a great deal of sense out of her. But she's given us your name.'

Serov closed his eyes and listened for another minute, speaking only in reply to the policeman's occasional questions.

'I'll be there as soon as I can, Superintendent,' he said at last. 'I'll leave rightaway. Thank you for calling me.'

He broke the connection and called Sergei.

'I'm leaving at once. Find Gramin and tell him to have the car outside. I won't be back today.' An afterthought struck him. 'Cancel my appointments for tomorrow.'

He took a few moments to bundle the paperwork into a drawer, then gathered up his coat and jacket. Just as he reached the door the phone rang again. He swore under his breath at Sergei, then retracted when the bell repeated and he realised it was his direct line. It bypassed the switchboard, Sergei and the banks of tape machines, and was as close as anyone could come in the building to a secure line. Few enough people had its number, and they knew to use it sparingly and with discretion. The calls it brought were never lengthy.

He had to answer it. He went back to the desk and threw his overcoat down. A third ring.

'Yes.'

'My friend who's been ill.' The voice was Gramin's. 'The one in need of medication. He's ready to see you personally, for further advice.'

'I want you outside with the car at once. We'll agree something on the way into town.'

He smashed the phone down, grabbed his coat again and was gone.

The heavy van waited outside the Aragvi restaurant until the food was ready, to the consternation of the maître d' and his diners. At last a trolley appeared and was pushed to its rear doors. Rich Georgian dishes, on lidded platters sealed with foil to keep them hot, began to be loaded under the weary gaze of the driver and the three sergeants who accompanied him.

Three hundred yards away, store director Gulyaev had climbed through the open window of his outer office and was hoisting himself precariously to his feet. His face, though drained of colour, had

46

regained its expression of superior disdain. He sneered down at Vladimir Chernavin's officers as they crammed arms and shoulders into the window and tried to snatch at his trouserlegs. Then he turned away, glanced down briefly at the pavement below as if to take his bearings and, closing his eyes, bent slowly over at the waist until he felt his balance go. Only then did he allow himself to push against the windowsill with his toes, launching himself out from the building by three or four feet. He fell gracefully and in silence, head first, like a diver but with his hands locked behind his back and his legs straight. It was only two floors but the precision of his technique was enough to make sure that no cell in Lefortovo would ever hear him disclose the identity of his black market contact.

When the van driver arrived in Gorky Street from the side road running up from Soviet Square, he swore at the shambles that blocked his way. Pedestrians milled around everywhere, there were militia cars at crazy angles across the road, and an ambulance was trying to park on the pavement. The van driver pounded his horn, an illegal act for civilian drivers, and yelled out of the window. It did no good and only got him a foul look from a militiaman trying to persuade the crowd to disperse.

'As if I hadn't enough to worry about,' the van driver moaned to the sergeants. 'Some bastard uses me to run his errands. Now I'll be blamed for letting his food get cold.'

6

The Middle East

As dawn broke over Saudi Arabia's vast southern desert, the Rub' al-Khali, a DC10 took off from a private airfield west of Sharrah. On the aircraft's tailfin, in white on green, were depicted a date palm and crossed sabres, marking the aircraft as belonging to the royal house of Saud.

Three hours later it landed at Cairo and taxied to a quiet spot on the eastern fringe of the airport. Flanked by two large hangars, a commercial charter plane was waiting, its engines already turning. Four Bedouin Arab men dressed in traditional white robes and woollen cloaks disembarked from the DC10 and crossed the tarmac to board the charter. They were the only passengers. Within a few minutes their modest baggage had been boarded and they were gone. No waybills or traffic dockets recorded their passage.

The crew of the DC10 waited until it was safely tucked out of sight in one of the hangars, then made their way to the Meridien Le Caire in the Garden City, where they had reservations for the night.

By the time they'd unpacked, the charter was entering Libyan air space. Three Soviet-built MiGs swooped down to investigate it. They caused the charter pilot no alarm; he'd made the trip several times before. He transmitted his call-sign and the MiG squadron leader tallied it with his briefing notes and waved acknowledgement. The MiGs became the charter's escort. An hour later the four aircraft passed over the Wheelus air and army base east of Tripoli. In a further three minutes the charter was over Tripoli International Airport. It received immediate clearance to land and touched down in the military section of the airport; the MiGs had vanished.

The Saudis hurried down the aircraft's steps and were met by a Libyan officer who led them to two armoured personnel carriers waiting close by.

Within a quarter of an hour the visitors were being driven at speed through the cream-coloured gates of the Bab Al-Aziziya barracks in the centre of Tripoli.

Inside, the complex was a bustle of activity. Jeeps and battered cars bumped along the potholed roads, driven by men and women in various degrees of battledress or as often as not jeans and sweatshirts. More were scattered on foot about the camp, some guarding the various buildings, some on leisure time. Even off-duty, most of them still carried their weapons, Kalashnikov rifles or Uzi submachine guns. They mingled with unarmed civilians who went mostly to and from the main administration block. A steady din of traffic and chatter filled the place.

Among all the stir few people paid much heed to the two personnel carriers.

One man, however, observed their arrival closely, taking care that his interest wasn't noted. He was curly-haired and swarthy but could have been of South European or Mediterranean extraction rather than North African. He was hunched over the engine of an old Fiat car parked outside one of the accommodation blocks, tinkering at it with a spanner and screwdriver. At his feet tools and engine parts were spread out on a groundsheet. The engine chugged unevenly, sometimes dying when he opened the throttle.

From behind the bonnet he watched as the armoured vehicles swung right at the orange-domed auditorium and drew up outside the main administration building.

Next to this block was a half-acre patch of open ground that had once been an ornamental lawn; continuous foot-traffic had worn it almost bare. It was dominated by a straggling Bedouin tent mounted on rough poles. There were six or eight of these poles, enough in that culture to denote a man of importance. Items of hunting paraphernalia hung from the poles and a hooded peregrine falcon perched on a stump driven into the earth.

The tent had always struck the watcher as ludicrous. It was meant as an assertion of the loyalties of its owner, Muammar Al-Gadaffi, the desert Arab who begrudged every moment he spent in urban Tripoli. Yet the military hardware that protected it, including the sophisticated communications gear housed in the administration block, belonged firmly in the twentieth century. All had been bought with the profits of oil sales to the same Western nations that Gadaffi never tired of denouncing.

The man by the Fiat sneered; he found the hypocrisy typical of Libya and its leader. As he watched, Gadaffi himself stepped from the tent's shady interior to receive his visitors. Today, instead of his usual khaki fatigues, he wore traditional clothing like theirs, in their honour.

The Arab who was evidently the leader of the visiting delegation stepped forward. He was taller than the others, including his host, and had a full goatee of the sort favoured by high-caste Saudis. It accentuated his wide mouth and hooked nose. Gadaffi and he embraced, exchanging elaborate greetings.

Eventually the guests were ushered into the men's section of the tent, on the right. There would be the hospitality ritual of spiced coffee, saffron and corn biscuits before business could begin. The watcher caught a glimpse of the tent's brightly-patterned interior before the outer flap fell closed.

He straightened up and wiped sweat from his forehead, shaking his head in exasperation at the engine. With a resigned air he crouched down and slid his body under the engine-block until only his feet were left in view. The engine cut out completely.

The leader of the Saudi delegation was one Saleem Ibn Abdul Aziz Al-Saud, a prince of the royal blood and half brother of King Fahd. This much the watcher already knew. As for Ibn's business with Gadaffi – that was what his masters paid him to find out.

Fastened magnetically to the underside of the blue Fiat's floorpan were a radio receiver the size of a lady's wristwatch and a miniature cassette-recorder connected to it by a thread of cable. The recorder was no bigger than a credit card and not much thicker. The watcher took a tiny earpiece from his shirt pocket and plugged it into the receiver. Everything was coming through loud and clear.

He stayed under the Fiat until he heard the coffee and sweetmeats being cleared away. Then he switched the tape recorder on, using the tip of a screwdriver to activate the tiny key. He put the earphone away, slid out from under the car, started the engine and resumed his labours.

The worst of the day's heat was over when he took the blue Fiat past Supermarket 102 in the downtown area. He turned into the sidestreet at the end of the block, narrowly avoiding a truck that was weaving down the wrong side of the road, and parked in the first space he could find. He strolled back the way he had come until he reached the glass facade of the supermarket. Here he moved to the edge of the kerb and waited to cross the road.

A tubular steel handrail ran parallel to the road about three feet in from the edge of the pavement. Its end was sheared off where a careering car had mounted the kerb some time in the past. As he waited, the man leant back against the handrail and lit a cigarette. It was the last in the packet. He scrunched up the paper sleeve and slid it neatly into the open end of the steel rail. A break appeared in the stream of cars and he loped to the other side of the wide carriageway, turning in the direction of the souk, whose babble he could hear even over the traffic noise.

A minute later a youngish woman hurried across the road in the opposite direction. She was dressed in European clothing: brown cotton jacket, tan blouse and skirt. The cut of the skirt was modest, falling well below the knee, and the blouse was fastened right to the neck. A patterned headsquare covered her brown hair. She wore no makeup. A handbag on a long strap hung over her right shoulder and was held securely under her arm by her elbow.

As she rushed onto the kerb her foot keeled to the side and she stumbled slightly. Luckily the handrail was just within reach; she grabbed at it with her left hand to steady herself.

When she moved off, the balled-up cigarette packet was concealed in the palm of her hand. The stumble had caused her handbag to slide down her arm, so she hooked her thumb into the strap and hoisted it back on her shoulder, reaching across to clasp the handbag with her other hand. The crumpled cigarette packet fell safely inside before the bag was snapped shut.

Half an hour later the Fiat rattled over a red dirt track traversing one of the sprawling estates of jerry-built blocks of flats that littered the south of the city. The driver peered around at the ten or twelve identical four-storey units as if trying to distinguish one from another.

Long strings of kerbstones were concreted into position on the dirt in sweeping lines that led up to and around the flats, promising roads and pavements sometime in the future. On one of them sat a paunchy man in a windcheater jacket and green woollen hat pulled down over his ears. He seemed to be in charge of two small girls who were playing near him, arranging empty tin-cans for a game of some kind. He nodded half-heartedly when they addressed him from time to time. As the Fiat approached, he gave it hardly a glance, yawned and went back to watching the girls.

The driver slowed down and asked something of him, so he stirred himself to go over to the car, bending down by the window while the question was repeated. He rested his left hand on the driver's door where the window-glass had been wound down, his fingers on the inside. When the driver restated his question he nodded and began pointing out directions with his other hand.

The driver heard him through, listening attentively, then thanked him and moved off in the direction indicated.

The man in the woollen hat pocketed the slip of paper that had been pressed into the fingers of his left hand and rejoined his daughters.

The European woman took a circuitous route back to Baghdad Street, switching from taxi to walking, back to taxi, and then repeating the process twice. She spent over an hour on what should have been a journey of only a few minutes. By the time she reached her destination the shops and offices were closed for the day.

51

She hurried along an alleyway that led off the main street and doubled back so that she was walking parallel to it. On her right a galvanised steel fence blanked off a building site, quiet at this hour, while a stone wall about seven feet high ran along on her left, broken by a series of doorways. These led into the rear yards of the commercial premises that fronted the street. Bins and black plastic bags stuffed to overflowing with rubbish stood beside most of the doors, awaiting refuse collections that were never made on schedule. She picked her way carefully around the worst of the debris, keeping a keen eye out for the wild dogs that were reputed to prowl the area from sundown. Her hands were thrust deep into her jacket pockets, her arms pressing her sides in an instinctive gesture of self-protection. As before, the bag was tucked under her right arm.

After about thirty yards she knocked lightly on one of the doors. It was opened at once, as if the person behind it had been awaiting her arrival.

She went straight to a staff bathroom on the first floor, skirting the public area to the front of the building, with its travel posters and brochures.

She locked the door, closed the lid of the toilet bowl for a seat and slung the bag onto the top of the toilet cistern.

She worked with speed and dexterity. In the cigarette packet she found the four micro-cassettes that the watcher had put there. She bunched them together two-by-two in a tissue and swaddled the lot in cotton wool. From her handbag she took a condom, which she broke out of its foil wrapper and unrolled. The bundle of cotton wool fitted into its tip, leaving plenty of length for her to tie into a knot. Before drawing it tight she passed into it a length of fine cotton cord, then knotted condom and cord firmly to each other. She threaded the cord through a wide-eyed leatherwork needle which she forced through the centre of a new tampon, pulling on the cord until the knotted condom was securely attached. She used manicure scissors to snip off the surplus length of condom and the original drawstring of the tampon. Along with the shredded remains of the cigarette packet, these were flushed down the toilet bowl.

Fifteen minutes later she returned to the rear alleyway. Her face was now attractively made up. The drab clothes had been replaced by a crisp, blue-grey uniform, white blouse and red silk scarf loosely knotted under her collar. Instead of the headsquare she wore a chic Trilby-shaped cap. Jacket and cap were adorned by the winged hammer and sickle of Aeroflot.

She glanced at her watch: 1820 hours. Still two hours before SU-420 took off for Moscow via Odessa, but she would need every minute for travelling time to the airport and pre-flight procedures. She put an inch to her step, remembering to watch out for the dogs.

The record of Prince Ibn's meeting with Gadaffi was on its way to Moscow.

The dusk was thickening as the man in the green woollen hat let himself onto the flat roof through the services hatch. The streetlamps on his estate, although installed and fully wired, hadn't yet been linked up to the Tripoli grid, so the security floodlights on the roof were dead. Nonetheless he moved cautiously, crouching as low as he could, aware that his silhouette against the vermilion skyline would be visible to anyone looking out of a top-floor window of one of the adjoining blocks. This was earlier than he preferred to operate but the note had specified all urgency and he dared not delay any longer. At least the job wouldn't take long.

The water storage tank was about fifteen yards from the hatch. When he reached it he was able to straighten up. He eased the lid up just as much as was needed and propped it open with a slat of wood which he kept to hand by the tank.

A nylon fishing-line was tethered to one of the feet of the tank, running up its side to disappear over the edge and into the water. It was virtually invisible against the tank's rubberised exterior. He reeled the line in slowly. Its weighty catch was a heavy-duty plastic box, water-proof to a depth of two hundred feet.

It contained a metal toolbox. He hefted it out and weighted the empty plastic container with two bricks before returning it to the tank.

Half an hour later he pulled his Peugeot off the road at an isolated layby on Kilometre 7 and opened the toolbox out on the passenger seat. It was the type with stepped drawers that spread apart when opened by downward pressure on the carrying-handle. The upper drawers had the usual assortment of well-used tools. But the lower portion was incongruously laid out as a small numeric keypad.

It was the work of a couple of minutes to tap out the list of digits on the slip of paper. He pressed another key once and waited fifteen seconds. A faint whirr indicated that the mini-computer was doing its work. A green light came on to signal that all was ready.

He consulted the slip of paper again and tapped some more keys until he was satisfied with the wavelength reading indicated on the digital LED display panel above the keypad, then extended a telescopic aerial from a corner of the unit. The highway was empty of traffic. He stepped quickly out of the car, placed the transmitter on the roof and pressed another key. The transmission lasted less than half a second, then he and the unit were safely back in the car.

When the toolbox was snapped shut, the unit was automatically switched off and its memory erased. He burnt the slip of paper in the ashtray, crushed the ashes in his hand and cast them out of the window, and set off for home.

All Moscow had to do was slow the transmission down to its original speed, decode it, and the people who ran the watcher would learn that a consignment was on its way.

7

Police Station Number 24, just off October Square, was the nearest to the Tretyakov, and it was here that Galina had been taken.

Serov found Superintendent Glassov an amiable man, more so than the distraught gallery administrator. When this tearful individual finally left them in peace, Serov also discovered that Glassov knew the value of money. The policeman's roundabout approach had a certain polish.

'Seems a shame to lock up such a lovely young woman, comrade General. You and me, sir, we're practical men. What's so special about one old picture? It's not as if she took a knife to it, after all. A few fingernail scratches, that's all.'

'The administrator said she tore the paint to the bare canvas in places.'

'These art people get a little hysterical. It'll fix. We're always hearing how damaged paintings get repaired so you'd never know anything had happening. Amazing.'

Serov passed the superintendent a cigar and glanced at the forms spread out on the table by his elbow.

'I suppose those are the records of the young lady's arrest.'

Glassov nodded lugubriously as he lit up. 'Mind you, records do get lost.' He blew out a smoke-ring and looked appreciatively at the cigar. 'Sometimes finding records here is as hard as finding a decent mechanic to fix your car.'

'You've got car problems?'

'I'm afraid so, comrade General. Top brass like you don't have to worry about that sort of thing. You'll have an official car, no doubt. Don't look so apologetic, sir. You've got more important things to do than hunt for mechanics and car parts. Our citizens don't want you worrying about that kind of thing. Or about whether you can afford a new engine.'

'That sounds expensive.'

Glassov became even gloomier. 'I tracked down a fellow last week who says he can do it. But eight hundred roubles is a lot of money for a fellow like me. Four months' salary.'

Serov produced his wallet and counted eight hundred-rouble notes onto the table. Glassov scooped them into his fist without a murmur and shredded the booking forms.

'The duty medical officer sedated the young lady a short time ago.' He knocked out the tip of the cigar on the table leg, blew on the stub to check that it was dead, and slipped it into a breast pocket. 'Allow me to take you to her.'

Ten minutes later Serov was back in the street, supporting Galina on one arm as he tramped through the freezing slush to the car. He dismissed Gramin and drove her straight to her apartment. She was blue with cold from the cells and her hands and feet were like ice. He set her in the warmest corner of the living-room, turned the heating up full and prepared hot soup, which she supped listlessly. She remained as distant and utterly silent as she had been during the drive.

He knew the symptoms well enough. They weren't just the result of whatever sedatives she'd been given. This was how she'd been in the months following Katarina's death. In some ways she could appear perfectly normal. She would dress herself, eat normally, even continue with her sculpting and painting. The impenetrable silence would be the only clue to her imbalance. Then, without warning, she would collapse in silent tears and lie or sit motionless for hours, completely withdrawn from the world. All he could hope was that this time the relapse wouldn't last too long.

He spent what was left of the afternoon trying to coax an account from her of what had happened; the police report had concentrated on her onslaught on the painting. Something, he knew, had to have provoked it. Had she made the visit to the cemetery that she had been talking about?

It was no use. Try as he might, he couldn't get a word out of her. In the evening he put her to bed and searched the kitchen until he found a bottle of bourbon. The hot liquid was welcome, but it did nothing tonight to burn the tension out of him. He found his mind returning to the changes that were sweeping through Moscow. Dangerous days, he'd told Gramin. Days that could bring not only the annihilation of his comfortable world, but his own death; in the dog-pack the most vicious fate was when the pack turned on one of its own.

He poured another bourbon and looked in on Galina. At least she was sleeping soundly. He returned to the living-room and put on the television to catch Vremya, the evening news.

At first the headlines were just the usual pap. Another speech by Gorbachev about reform; another re-run of the Red Square parades, with no reference made to Zavarov's absence; latest output figures for machine building; more nuclear tests by the US. He let it all wash over him as he sipped the bourbon and took another cigar.

Then the female newscaster spoke a name that registered at once in his mind and he became very still.

'. . . Food Shop Number One, formerly known as Yeliseyev's. The spectacular raid is being acclaimed as a major coup in the mounting campaign to defeat corruption. We have an interview with the officer who led the raid, comrade Vladimir Chernavin. Comrade Chernavin is a Senior Special Inspector in the Department for Struggle Against Embezzlement of Socialist Property and Speculation. This is the KGB division which is spearheading the anti-corruption drive . . .'

Nikolai Vasiliyevich Serov watched and listened with close attention as the pudgy KGB officer detailed the day's events.

The pack was yelping.

The phone rang just as the news was ending. There was no extension in the living-room, only the bedroom and kitchen. He dived into the kitchen to answer it before its ringing could wake Galina. Gramin was on the line. Serov listened in silence to what he had to say.

'You're sure Gulyaev's dead?' he replied at last. 'This man Chernavin said nothing about that.'

'Of course not. He wants to make us sweat. That's the Second Directorate's way. Gulyaev's dead all right. They needed a shovel to get him into the body bag. He didn't just jump – he dived. He wanted there to be no mistake. It must've been a star performance. I'm sorry I missed it.'

'Maybe he was helped on his way.'

'Because they'd finished with him? No. It was his own idea. There are neater ways of getting rid of a person. Anyway, they'd want to keep him alive for a fancy trial.'

Just then Galina moaned. Serov moved to the edge of the kitchen where he could see her through the open bedroom door.

'Gulyaev told them nothing, comrade,' Gramin went on. 'I saw Chernavin's face when he came down to the street to look him over. What's more, I'd say Gulyaev wanted us to know he'd kept his mouth shut.'

'What were you doing there anyway?'

'The loading manager in the Food Trade Administration depot at Mytishchi called me. He'd been phoning the store to set up some delivery dates. I got down there to have a nose around – you know, see who was being taken away. I arrived just after Gulyaev did his stuff.'

'Did anyone see you?'

'Who'd recognise me there? Only the drivers know me and none of them was there today.'

'How many of them were involved at the Church of the Saviour?'

'Four.'

'Where are they now?'

'They took off.'

'They can't hide forever. They need identity cards, their work records have to be kept up to date. They don't have the kind of money it takes to buy new identities.'

He knew how much that was. So would Gramin; no doubt that was why he was remaining silent.

'Sooner or later they'll have to surface, whether they want to or not. Gramin?'

'Yes, comrade?'

'Do you know where they are?'

'I don't.'

'Find out.' Serov spoke slowly and deliberately. 'Find out tonight. And your friend in the depot at Mytishchi. Visit him. Those would be wise things to do. Yes?'

Gramin knew when not to argue. 'I'll do as you say. There's one more thing, comrade.'

'We've been on this line long enough.'

'I spoke to Lysenko. We agreed a venue.'

He began to go through the details; Serov crossed to the breakfast bar and jotted them down on a shopping pad. Afterwards he looked them over sceptically.

'That's the best you could come up with?'

'There'll be plenty of people for cover, comrade. And this is a very natural place for Lysenko.'

'For Lysenko, maybe. What about me?'

'I thought –'

'Never mind.' As he glanced again at Galina's bedroom, an idea occurred to him. 'Maybe it has its advantages. I'll be there. Everything else is as I told you.'

He put the receiver down before Gramin could reply, tore off the sheet of paper and slipped down from the stool.

The open-plan kitchen gave onto a wide-windowed studio that made up most of Galina's apartment. The studio was perfect for her work, bright and airy. As Serov left the kitchen, he detoured to the two sculpting pedestals that were positioned at one end of the room. The work on them, in clay at this stage, was hers. She was good. The finished piece was a female head and shoulders. It was Katarina. The likeness was perfect, unsettlingly so. All the more remarkable for having been done from memory. On the other pedestal, under a damp cloth because it wasn't yet complete, was his own image. When both were finished Galina would make moulds and cast them in bronze.

He knew better than to remove the cloth from his own bust; she had forbidden him sight of it until it was done. His fingers brushed the cloth but left it alone. He continued to the living-room, topped up his bourbon and flopped down on the couch.

A noise startled him a moment later and he looked up. Galina was standing in the doorway of the bedroom. He rose at once and went to her.

'Galya?'

She was tousled and still half-asleep. The green eyes flickered open and tried to focus on him.

'Here I am,' he whispered. He thought he caught the hint of a smile, and smiled back. 'You knew I wasn't far away, didn't you? Did you hear me talking? Is that what woke you? Come and sit down. I'll get you a drink.'

He took her arm and guided her to the couch, carefully putting his own glass in her hand. When her fingers were locked around it he sat beside her and raised the glass to her lips. Its touch made her start slightly, but she took a sip.

'Good.' He forced cheer into his voice, as if he were cajoling a child. 'Now, I've got something to tell you.'

He went over to the audio cabinet and riffled through her record collection. It was extensive; he kept her supplied with all the latest Western releases as well as the output of the Soviet underground bands. The albums he was looking for were grouped together near the end of the row; he took them over to the couch with him.

'I've got a special treat for you, Galya,' he told her. 'I think you'll find it exciting.'

Over breakfast the next morning he watched her closely and spent an hour chatting to her afterwards. She seemed less distant than before. When he suggested that he ought to go to headquarters for an hour or two she showed no alarm. He waited another while, reassuring himself that she would be all right on her own, then set off.

'Tonight,' he reminded her as he took his leave. 'Something for you to look forward to.'

Again the half-smile in response.

The roads were clearer now, especially in the centre of town, the snowploughs having been busy. As if in confirmation, Moscow Radio was broadcasting a report about the billions of roubles spent each winter on snow clearance. It followed this with a lecture on the need for each citizen to be less wasteful with hot water and heating.

He made first for the foreign currency shop on Kutuzovskiy, one of the chain meant for tourists and therefore more likely to have reliable stocks of goods. It was ten o'clock by the time he got there, and the shop was just opening. He parked the Chaika half on the wide pavement just before the underpass at the Dorogomilovskaya intersection, an act that only official vehicles could get away with, and went into the store. Less than five minutes later he returned; his purchases were two pairs of binoculars, which he dropped on the rear seat and drove off.

59

Next he stopped off at the Rossiya Hotel to pick up the West European newspapers that the manager set aside for him each day. He preferred his own scanning of the foreign press to the clippings service at headquarters. That way he got the information he wanted, rather than whatever someone else thought he should have: always assuming the papers had been let through.

A quick glance at the headlines told him that Opec's problems with over-supply and tumbling prices were still the main item; with the consequent beneficial effect on the Western economies.

Out around Tsaritsynskiye Ponds on the southern outskirts, heading for the ring motorway, the roads grew a little more treacherous but became better again in the vicinity of the First Chief Directorate complex; the KGB had the knack of getting itself looked after.

'It's been very quiet, sir,' Sergei assured him as he took his greatcoat. 'You've missed nothing of any significance. Not here anyway.' He followed Serov into his office. 'But did you hear about the raid on Yeliseyev's? And the store director? Mind you, comrade General, you won't find a word about his death in the papers. People are saying the investigators worked him over too hard and killed him by mistake. So they had to fling him out of the window to cover their tracks.'

He grunted a response, took the coffee that Sergei poured, and resumed the attack on yesterday's paperwork, recalling a time when his job hadn't consisted of pushing paper around.

Then a name on a document caught his eye. He stared at it for a moment, taking in the significance of the paper on which it appeared, before picking up the phone.

'Sergei. Come in here, please.'

The document was a top copy plus several flimsies, each a different colour to indicate its destination: a requisition docket. It authorised an amount of expenditure to be debited against headquarters overheads. The sum was insignificant; that wasn't what had caught his eye.

'What's this?' He held it out to Sergei as he entered.

'It's to cover the cost of a funeral wreath, General. We always arrange wreaths for the Directorate's pensioners. In accordance with a scale of allowable values that reflects their rank on retirement, of course.'

'I know that. When did this man die?'

Sergei looked uncomfortable. 'He's not actually dead yet. But I'm assured it's only a matter of days. He's in our private wing in the First Municipal Hospital.' His cheeks coloured as his embarrassment mounted. 'I have an . . . arrangement with the doctors there.'

'An arrangement?'

'Purchase requisitions take a long time to go through the system, comrade General. I've known cases where the funeral was over before the wreath arrived. It makes the Directorate look like it hasn't bothered to pay its respects. So the doctors give me a little advance warning sometimes.' He broke off. 'Did – I mean, do – you know this man, sir?' He peered at the docket. 'Genrikh Kunaev, Major, retired. Is that why you're asking about him?'

Serov nodded. 'I knew him a long time ago.'

'I see, sir. I'm sorry. I didn't mean to give you such an unpleasant shock.'

'It's of no consequence. We weren't friends. Far from it. As I say, it was a very long time ago. That'll be all.'

He let the docket fall back into the tray and folded his hands, watching Sergei retreat.

'Sergei, the *rezidentura* travel rosters – are they up to date?'

The man looked pained at the implication that he might have been anything other than efficient. 'Certainly, comrade General.'

'Bring me the Third Department's, please.'

A minute later Sergei put several large sheets before him. Each was headed by the name of a capital city: Canberra, Copenhagen, Helsinki, London, Oslo, Stockholm. They were the location of Soviet embassies in the countries covered by the Third Department.

Serov turned to the London sheet. The entry he anticipated was near the bottom of the page, along with pertinent information.

Name:	*Kunaev, Viktor Genrikovich.*
Function:	*Senior Cipher Clerk.*
Cover Assignment:	*Commercial Attaché's Staff.*
Travel Details:	*Compassionate Leave of Absence due to Father's Illness. Two Weeks Requested (To Be Spent in Moscow).*

Serov leant back in his chair. So the old fool was still alive, if only just. And his brat was coming home.

He picked up the phone again.

'Sergei. Find Gramin and send him to me. I have a task for him.'

8

The Small Sports Arena in the Lenin Stadium complex could take an audience of about 14,000. Tonight it looked like it would be packed to capacity.

Taking Gramin's advice, Serov and Galina travelled out there by taxi. Parking in the roads near the complex was forbidden, while space inside the park was to be reserved for official use, which would include Soviet, British and American television recording facilities. All vehicles without permits, even a car like Serov's, would be impounded.

The rock concert was scheduled to start at eight but by seven, when the taxi dropped them at the end of Komsomolskiy Prospekt, the fans were already pouring out of Leninskiye Gory metro station to cram the paths through the snow-covered parkland. In the distance another flood of people wound its way from Sportivnaya station.

As they were swept along in the mass of teenage bodies, Serov noticed that Galina was staring all about her. At first he thought she was fearful of the crowd, then he realised: in the sheltered life he provided for her, she had simply never seen people like this before.

A girl with pink hair passed them, arm in arm with a boy whose own hair stood upright, Mohican style.

'I told you you'd see surprising sights, didn't I?' Serov whispered. 'Are you wondering where they've all sprung from? Why you don't see kids like these on the streets?'

She turned to him, wide-eyed with amazement.

'Most of them don't exist, that's why,' he said. 'They're a living conjuring trick. See the green hair? You can buy the dye in the markets – it washes out in the morning, when it's time for work or college.'

Another couple, both wearing outlandish makeup, drew near for a moment.

'Same with the makeup and the hairstyles. That's why so few of the boys have long hair or semi-shaved heads – too permanent. When you see a boy with ear-studs, you can bet they'll be out tomorrow. There's a core of genuine punks, of course, but the majority of these kids are just make-believe.'

He glanced sideways at Galina; she was absorbed, her own wretchedness forgotten for the moment.

At intervals along the route, the militia were standing in twos and threes, many of them as young as the fans. They seemed bemused by the curiosities that traipsed past them but at this stage of the evening showed no inclination to pester anyone. They would form themselves into snatch squads later, searching for dope or drunkenness when the crowd's energy had been sapped by the concert and the risk of general resistance would be lower.

The entrance hall of the Arena was decked out like an old Russian folk-fair. Jugglers, clowns and acrobats from the Moscow State Circus performed here and there across the floor. Clearly, the authorities were out to win friends. The decision wouldn't have been taken lightly to let a Western rock band play before an audience of ordinary Muscovites. In the past, tickets for such an event would have been restricted to the children of the *nomenklatura*, the privileged class. Tonight, it seemed, democratisation and liberalism were in fashion.

As for the English band that the people were flocking to see, Serov knew something of them. In their own country they were considered left-wing, a definition that depended on where the definer was standing, of course. No doubt the songs the band would perform tonight had been carefully vetted by Gosconcert for political acceptability by Kremlin standards.

It had crossed his mind that he might be a little conspicuous in a sea of people Galina's age; it was what had concerned him about the rendezvous. In fact, he saw that the crowd was peppered with men and women his age or older. These he paid close attention to, sorting out the cautious parents or straightforward music enthusiasts from the undercover security personnel. Some would be acting on behalf of Gosconcert, Melodiya or the sports administration. The ones he was most interested in were CID and KGB personnel. Above all, the drugs squad.

At seven forty, bells started ringing. It was time to take their seats.

For the first thirty minutes they suffered a very average band from Leningrad. Their only credentials seemed to be observance of the party line on everything. The audience was apathetic apart from a few stage-managed cheers here and there from supporters or youth Komsomol activists.

Then the lights went out and an immediate hush fell on the auditorium. All eyes were on the dim stage, where shadowy figures moved into position.

Suddenly everything exploded into life. The first guitar chords rang out with startling clarity. Spotlights flooded the stage with coloured light. A driving beat began. The guitarists and the singer strutted forward to the edge of the stage, tantalising the crowd. The songs rolled out and the audience screamed, cheered and clapped. This time it was no set-piece reaction.

Serov watched Galina from the corner of his eye. Her whole being seemed focused on the music. She began to unfasten the clip of the binoculars case that he'd hung about her neck as they left the apartment. He reached over and stopped her; his own binoculars were already out and he passed them across.

The band was as good as any he'd seen in Paris or Hamburg in the Sixties. Their themes were predictable enough: unemployment, peace, racial harmony, the social injustice of capitalism, but more imaginatively handled than the Leningraders had managed. They created an atmosphere in the Arena like a family party. The only uncertain moments were when some of the fans got up and started dancing. The security people insisted that they sit down again. The band didn't agree.

'Dance with us, Moscow!' one of them called in English. The interpreter remained silent for a moment. When his translation finally came over the PA, it was 'Please stay in your seats.'

All around Serov people hooted in derision. 'You think no one but you speaks English?' someone yelled.

When the performance was at its peak Serov took Galina's arm and led her out of the aisle of seats.

'I have someone to meet,' he explained. He took her back out to the entrance hall and into the service area behind the catering stalls. Cold air fanned their faces and they arrived at an open door. He stepped outside and halted to light a cigar, at the same time taking a good look around.

This side of the building was lined with trucks and vans, as Gramin had said it would be. The snow had been scooped to the edge of the parking lot and piled into ramparts four or five feet high. He led Galina slowly along between the building and the backs of the vehicles, taking her arm when she hung back and drawing her firmly along with him.

First they passed the vans of the catering operations, none of them occupied. As they passed through the shadows behind them he slipped the Makarov from its holster and into the side pocket of his greatcoat. Next came the television pantechnicons, surrounded by trails of cable, their generators humming. Light blazed and died in doorways as technicians came and went. Some stood in the night air chatting and nursing hot drinks. As well as Russian voices he picked out English and American accents. There was a luxury coach that presumably belonged to the band. In the driver's cabin a man sat reading the *Nedelya* supplement from that evening's *Izvestiya*. Two or three bored looking girls were dotted about the passenger seats, reading English magazines or smoking.

Right at the end of the parking lot was the Melodiya trailer. Lysenko

64

was waiting between it and the snow rampart, a short, prematurely bald man in jeans and thin leather blouson. His shoulders were hunched, his hands deep in his jeans pockets and he was shuffling from foot to foot, either from nervousness or cold.

'What kept you?' he said as Serov approached. His complexion was unhealthy and oily. He noticed Galina and looked her up and down. 'Gramin said there'd be just you. He said nothing about pussy.'

'Gramin was wrong. Watch your mouth.'

'No offence, brother. What have you got for me?'

'You wanted the deal.' Serov dropped the half-smoked cigar and kicked it into the snow. 'You're the one in need. Let's see what you're offering.'

Lysenko danced some more while he thought this over, his sharp-toed boots compacting the snow into shiny ice. Then he shrugged and reached inside the blouson. At the same time Serov slipped his hand into his side pocket where the Makarov was waiting.

'No surprises,' he told Lysenko. He glanced down at his pocket to make sure the junkie understood.

'All right, all right,' Lysenko said quickly, producing an A4 size document folded in half along its length. It was about twenty pages thick.

Serov took it in his free hand and angled it to catch the beam from a distant arc light. He scanned the first page in silence, looked at Lysenko, then withdrew his right hand to leaf through the next few pages.

'Don't take all night!' Lysenko hissed. His eyes darted anxiously from side to side. They were red and heavily shadowed.

Serov refolded the document and tucked it inside his greatcoat with measured slowness.

'I like to check that merchandise is as advertised.'

'Fine, fine.' Despite the cold, Lysenko was sweating. 'I don't like to rush you, brother, but there's the small matter of what you've brought for me.'

Serov stepped over to where Galina was leaning against the trailer, staring back the way they'd come. He kissed her lightly on the cheek.

'Nearly finished, my love,' he whispered, and took the binoculars case from her. As he did so, she turned to look full into his eyes. For a moment he thought she was about to speak. But she looked away again.

He handed the case to Lysenko, who tore its lid open greedily.

'I see I'm not the only one who likes to check,' Serov observed.

Lysenko pulled the binoculars out and peered into the case. He stuck a grubby hand inside and scratched at the lining. He looked angrily at Serov and was about to say something. Serov reached across and angled the binoculars towards the arc light while Lysenko held on to them. The junkie peered into their eyepiece and his tense expression

65

relaxed. He unscrewed one of the lens retaining rings, dipped a fingertip inside and licked it.

'Pleasure doing business with you, brother! Don't let pussy catch cold.' He clambered up the short stepladder that led to the door set in the trailer's side, wrenched it open and disappeared inside.

Serov turned to Galina. 'Let's get back.'

The rest of the evening seemed to leave her unmoved. Afterwards she shook her head at his suggestion of a late snack at the Sofiya. In the taxi home she either stared out of the window or sat back with her eyes closed. When they got to her apartment, at about midnight, she went straight to bed.

Serov made no attempt to force his company on her. He settled himself on the couch with a glass of bourbon and a cigar. A minute or two later he saw the chink of light under the bedroom door go out.

Behind him on the back of the couch was his greatcoat. He now fished the document from its pocket and spread it on his lap. Here in proper lighting he saw that it was a photostat copy. Some of the pages were off-centre as if someone had been in a hurry when making it. On the first page were typed four lines:

USSR Economic and Industrial Strategy
The Next Five Year Plan and Beyond
Projected Energy Needs and Shortfalls
Preliminary Report of the Oligarchy Committee

Further down were two names: the author's and that of the man for whom alone the document had been intended.

M. S. Gorbachev.

With a morbid fascination, Serov realised that his hands were trembling.

He scanned the document in less than ten minutes, not taking in the detail but enough to get its main thrust. Afterwards he set it down and leant back in the couch, staring at the ceiling.

After a time he realised that he hadn't touched his bourbon; now he knocked half of it back in one gulp. On an impulse, he crossed the studio to the hallway and locked the apartment's outer door, then did the same with the inner door.

Returning to the couch, he began to re-read more carefully. This time he took over an hour and a half, pondering the occasional chart or table that interleaved the text. There were many references to other reports or statistical digests that he didn't have, but for the most part their drift could be deduced easily enough.

When he was done he refilled his glass and went through to the kitchen. Here the window blinds were still open. He didn't switch the light on, so that he could gaze out at the clear, crisp night.

Condensation rimmed the window, setting a white frame to the darkness. In its centre blazed the great red star that crowned the Kremlin's tallest tower, the Trinity.

He watched that star for a long time. Then he decided to call Gramin.

Lysenko was juiced to his red eyeballs. He flopped against the wall of the concert building and let his soul float up to the stars.

His body, however, remained earthbound, and that was all Gramin cared about. In one movement he released the Melodiya trailer's brake and kicked the chock away. The trailer began to roll down the incline towards Lysenko, the massive weight of the recording equipment aboard making it gather speed rapidly. Its protruding towbar was on an exact level with Lysenko's groin.

Lysenko glanced up just before the impact. There wasn't time to move out of the way. Not even time to scream. No one but the stars to hear him anyway.

It was over in an instant. Steam rose in clouds from the snow where his blood drenched it.

9

The old man called Genrikh Kunaev was so frail that he hardly rumpled the hospital bed. He'd been asleep for two or three minutes now, the second time he'd dozed off in the hour that his son Viktor had sat with him.

A nurse approached, pushing a trolley laden with medical equipment. She smiled at Viktor and unhooked the clipboard at the foot of the bed.

'You shouldn't stay much longer,' she advised. 'The major's very weak.' She took the old man's wrist and checked his pulse, then made a note on the clipboard.

'I'll go in a few minutes,' Viktor told her. He moved his corduroy jacket from the bed onto the back of his chair, as a sort of promise to her. 'I don't just want to slip away while he's asleep.'

Suddenly Kunaev's eyes twitched open. He blinked several times and frowned, as if struggling to remember where he was and what was going on. His gaze settled on Viktor and he grunted softly.

'Help me up, son,' he said.

His left sleeve had been rolled back to make room for a catheter that had been inserted into a vein in his arm. A tube brought a clear solution to it from a plastic bag attached to the bedstead. Beneath his pyjama jacket electrodes were taped to his chest; their leads ran over his shoulder to an enamelled box and monitor screen on a shelf halfway up the wall. A green dot raced across the screen, tracing a graph over and over again.

Viktor glanced enquiringly at the nurse. She nodded and helped him raise his father into a sitting position without disturbing the tube or leads. When this was done she plumped up the pillows behind his back.

'Not too long, remember,' she whispered to Viktor. She went back to the trolley and pushed it off to another part of the ward.

Kunaev's arm protruded like a white stick from his sleeve as he reached out for the pebble glasses on his bedside table. Slowly he put them on, one wire leg at a time, and studied his son's thin face.

'You remember what we agreed?' he asked eventually.

'Papa?'

'You know, Viktor. Don't pretend. When your mother died.'

Viktor took his hand. It was liver-spotted and bony, not the strong hand he remembered enveloping his own.

'Don't be silly, Papa. This isn't the time to talk about that.'

'This is precisely the time,' insisted Kunaev. 'Will you go through with it?'

Viktor took a long time before he nodded. He couldn't meet his father's gaze.

'And Anna?' Kunaev pursued. 'She's still for it? You talked it over again with her?'

Another slow nod.

'Do it for her and little Andrei, Viktor. Above all, for Andrei. You owe it to him.'

'Yes, Papa. I know. Let's not talk about it any more.'

'The thing you need. Do you know where in my apartment it is?' The old man's voice dropped to a whisper, all the more emphatic for doing so. 'Can you remember which one it is?'

'I remember, Papa. You showed me and I remember.'

'Get it before the housing people seal the place. Once they do that it could be months before they release anything. You know what they're like. You mustn't wait, son. God knows, they might not.'

'I'll go there tomorrow morning.'

Viktor felt tears gathering beneath his eyelids. It was one thing to talk and plan, quite another to face up to the moment when it came. Now they seemed to be urging it nearer.

He realised that his father was still watching him, and turned away.

'You were always like your mother, Viktor. Sentimental. She could never throw things out, no matter how broken and useless they were. She wanted to hang onto them forever. Just because they'd been good once.'

'I remember.'

'You can't hang onto the past, Viktor. If something's no good anymore, throw it out and make do with the memory.' His voice became a whisper again. 'That goes for countries too.'

'Enough, Papa,' Viktor said gently. 'You should rest now. And I should go, to let you.'

'Rest?' The old man smacked the bed weakly. 'Time enough to rest when I'm dead. Don't rush me into it.'

Nevertheless he settled back against the pillows and let his eyes close behind the thick lenses. Viktor thought he was dropping off again, but after a moment he smiled.

'Speaking of memories, son, did I ever tell you about the day Khrushchev visited us at Izmaylovo? It was just before the bastards hounded him out of power that autumn. He was a real man of the people, our Nikita. Did I tell you how he and I walked like brothers in the gardens and yarned about our childhoods?' He opened his eyes and peeled the spectacles off.

Viktor smiled. He'd heard the story a thousand times. He looked up and down the ward but the nurse was nowhere to be seen.

'I'd love to hear it, Papa. But only if you get some sleep afterwards.'

Kunaev settled back, satisfied. 'It was my last year in charge of the academy. Your mother and you spent the summer out at Serebryanyy Bor. I think you came to visit me sometime early in the summer. Yes, now I think of it, you definitely did.' He stopped and his expression seemed to cloud; the smile faded. 'It was the year they landed me with that young whipper-snapper as my captain adjutant. That's how I remember you visiting me – you met him. You might not remember, I suppose. You were only twelve or so. Now, what was his name? Unpleasant piece of work.'

Viktor lowered his gaze. He remembered the meeting. Not with any clarity; what lingered was his impression of his father's unease and the sense of menace that the stranger emanated. But he knew the stranger's name all right.

'Serov,' he told his father quietly. 'The captain's name was Nikolai Serov.'

It was only three thirty when he walked out of the gates of the First Muncipal but already the sky was darkening. There was the promise of more snow in the air, which tasted fresh and good after the ward. He felt guilty to be so glad to be breathing it while his father lay dying.

Tannoy strains of martial music reached him, rising and falling in volume as the wind shifted. Gorky Park lay just behind the hospital grounds, more or less merging with them; some skaters were testing the ice.

'Life goes on, Papa.'

A yellow Volga taxi drew up by the main entrance. As its passengers got out Viktor hurried across and took it over from them, in case it might be the only free one he'd find.

'The university,' he told the driver. 'Moscow State.'

He wiped a space in the steamed-up window while the car swung around, then huddled in the underheated interior to peer out as they waited to turn southwest onto Lenin Prospekt.

'You a student?' the driver asked. 'A teacher maybe?'

Viktor saw that he was watching him in the rear-view mirror. 'I used to study at Moscow State,' he replied.

'You're the wrong colour for the other one.' The car lurched suddenly into the traffic and Viktor was thrown back in his seat.

They passed the Academy of Sciences on their right. Across the way was the Don Monastery, in whose gardens he used to stroll with Anna, and beyond it, all but hidden from view, Patrice Lumumba University.

Third World students came to the Patrice Lumumba, officially to study, unofficially to be trained by the KGB for other purposes in their homelands. It was their brown and black faces, so conspicuous in Moscow, that had prompted the driver's comment.

'You an out-of-towner?' the man was asking now. 'Please excuse my curiosity, comrade. It's the only thing that keeps me in this job. I like to meet people. You know?'

'I'm a Muscovite.'

'It's the way you're staring at everything, you see.'

'I've been away for a time.'

'In the sticks?'

'No.' Viktor paused. 'In another country. With my job.'

The driver whistled softly. 'You must have a big job, my friend.'

'I wouldn't say that.'

'Another country. Far?'

'England. London.'

The driver peered harder into the mirror. 'Should I know you? Are you government or some big shot?'

Viktor shook his head, smiling. 'I'm nobody special.'

The driver shrugged philosophically. 'I suppose if you were a big shot you wouldn't be riding in my cab.'

They slowed down to join the traffic tailing back from the pedestrian crossing lights on Gagarin Square. The area all around the square and the Metro station was busy with people.

'Look at them,' the driver grumbled. 'Going home already. Nobody works a full day any more.'

On either side of the avenue reared two semi-circular apartment blocks, each wider than the Moskva and crowned by massive, spire-topped towers. They bounded the square like monstrous walls.

'Remember the day Gagarin came to Moscow?' Viktor said suddenly. 'After that first space flight?'

'Who doesn't? This was where they gave him his hero's welcome. Did you go along?'

'My father brought me. He knew some people who lived up there –' He pointed at the block on the right. 'They let us watch from their window.'

The driver was grinning. 'I got drunk, so drunk. Jesus – we all got drunk.'

Viktor laughed. 'I was too young. But yes, it was a big day.' It was one of the best days he could remember; one of those rare days when his father was all his.

'That's a memory I can hold onto, Papa,' he said quietly.

'What's that, comrade?'

'Nothing. Thinking aloud.'

71

'Try getting drunk these days,' the driver mused. 'You could die of thirst in this city.'

'What do you mean?'

The driver chuckled. 'You're right – you have been gone a while. They're cutting vodka supplies. Like in the joke.'

'What joke?'

'I thought everybody knew this one!' The driver slapped his thigh. 'Ivan Ivanovich joins the queue outside a liquor shop. After three hours there's still sixty people in front of him. Ivan can't stand it any more. Pulls a big knife from his belt. "I'll fix Gorbachev!" he says and off he goes. But he's back half an hour later and rejoins the queue, right at the end! So now there's ninety people in front of him. His friend up ahead spots him. "Ivan! You fixed Gorbachev?" Ivan shakes his head. "No," he says. "The queue at the Kremlin was even longer."' The driver whooped with laughter. 'It's good?'

'It's good,' Viktor said, grinning. 'But don't you think you're taking a chance?'

'What do you mean?'

'Telling a joke like that to a complete stranger. How do you know I'm not a Chekist?'

'KGB?' The driver glanced in his mirror again, studied the thin face and tired eyes, and grew serious. 'Not you, comrade. You're like the rest of us. Enough trouble of your own. You're not out to make any for anybody else.'

Viktor said no more.

After Gagarin the road forked in three. They filtered off to the right and picked up the Vorobyovskoye Shosse, curving past the Palace of Pioneers, all fountains and flags, and following the long loop of the Moskva where it cut through the lower reaches of Leninskiye Gory, the Lenin Hills. They began to climb with the contours of the land and Viktor watched the city spread out below him, a panorama of lights.

'Where do you want?' the driver asked. 'Which part?'

The skyscraper block of the university was looming up on their left, crowning the hill. The driver slowed down as he approached the junction with Prospekt Vernadskovo, in case Viktor wanted him to take it and go on up.

'Straight on is fine,' Viktor instructed. 'Drop me at the next junction. I'm not going anywhere in particular. Just a walk.'

'In this weather? You know, comrade, I was right. You must have a lot on your mind if you need a walk that bad. Or a guilty conscience.'

'Maybe,' Viktor mumbled.

The morgue was full of echoes. Vladimir Chernavin was wishing he hadn't worn his shoes with the little steel studs that saved wear on the

72

leather. Clackety-clack, clackety-clack they went as he puffed along beside the morgue superintendent.

'Here we are!' the superintendent said. He stopped abruptly beside a pair of black rubber doors with A23 stencilled on them. Chernavin skidded slightly on the marble floor. The superintendent was peering through the perspex window in one of the doors.

'It's as I told you,' he said, 'Your colleagues are here already.'

'No colleagues of mine,' Chernavin's eyes narrowed as he saw the two CID men. The superintendent pushed the door open and led him in.

'Afternoon, comrades!' the superintendent called. 'One more for the fun and games!'

He grabbed the naked corpse laid out on the bench between the policemen and shook him vigorously.

'Wake up, old son! You're missing the fun! And it's all in your honour!'

'All right, all right,' snapped the senior-looking of the CID officers. 'Why don't you leave us to it? We'll let you know if we need any help.'

The man went off smirking.

'Are you Chernavin?' asked the officer who had already spoken.

'Senior Special Inspector Chernavin. By the way, I wish you people wouldn't queer things for the rest of us.'

The CID man flipped his notebook shut. 'What are you on about?'

'One bottle of vodka used to be enough to get in here without a proper letter of authority from the prosecutor's office. Today it cost me two – because that's what you'd already handed over. Thanks a lot.'

The CID men didn't respond. Instead the younger one lifted the corpse's arm and rolled him onto his side, then began looking closely at his back and neck.

'My name's Mukhin, by the way,' said the senior man. 'He's Stepun. We don't worry too much about rank but for those interested in such matters I'm a major, he's a captain. You're the chap who cleaned up Yeliseyev's, I hear.'

Chernavin stood a little taller. 'You heard right.'

'Nice piece of work. Pity you lost Gulyaev. I understand he was the only one who could've led you to Mr Big.'

Chernavin shrugged but didn't feel like saying anything.

Mukhin poked the corpse's belly. 'Pity about this one as well.' He opened his notebook again. 'Aleksandr Petrovich Burinski. Late of Mytishchi region, where he was a respected member of the community and was employed as Manager Responsible for Deliveries Planning in the District Food Trade Administration depot. Survived and mourned by widow, Helga, and one daughter.' He glanced up at Chernavin. 'I suppose he would have been your next port of call, comrade Inspector.

Like I said – pity. Now, what did they tell you about how he came to be in our tender care?'

'Only that he was found floating in the Moskva last night. Face down by the Proletarskiy Prospekt bridge at the Southern River Terminal.'

Mukhin nodded and went back to the notebook. 'Distance between bridge and water – seventy-two feet. Enough to make sure that he broke through the ice when he hit. When fished out, he'd been dead between eighteen and twenty-four hours. Pathologist says he drowned. Probably unconscious when he went into the water. So full of vodka he could have pickled just as easily. How about that – pickled *and* frozen. Still, rotten luck, comrade – a fellow has a few drinks and stumbles into the Moskva, with no one around to pull him out. You'd be surprised how often it happens in this city. Especially these days.'

'Accident, my arse,' Chernavin grumbled quietly.

'I note your scepticism, Inspector. You would perhaps suggest that the nasty bruise on the back of his head – show the inspector, Stepun – may have precipitated his tumble, rather than being a result of, say, connecting with the ice as he hit.'

'Something like that.' Chernavin bent down to look at the swelling.

'Well, you're free to believe what you please. Play the detective by all means. Good luck to you. Maybe you've got a point: we have a suspicious death on our hands. Persuade my forensic people to come up with some evidence.' He leant across the corpse to put his face close to Chernavin's. 'But I don't know where it's going to take you in the end, comrade Inspector. Which is why I'm not too keen to put my department's time into it.' He snapped the notebook shut. 'So if you'll excuse us, we've got other cases to deal with.'

'Plenty others,' chipped in Stepun. Disregarding Chernavin, he pushed bloated, dead Burinksi onto his back again and went to the sink, where he began scrubbing his hands.

'Like the poor sods whose car blew up this morning,' he called over his shoulder to Mukhin.

'That's right, Captain. Now there's a sorry case.'

Chernavin tugged at the corpse to get it onto its side again. He began probing the bruise at the base of Burinski's scalp, parting the hair to see better.

'Blown to pieces, four healthy men,' Mukhin was saying. 'At least, it looks like four, as far as we can make out from the bits. Several funny aspects to the case, Captain, when you think about it. According to the car's details, as I recall, the driver was a long way from home. With no good reason that we can make out. Wasn't there some odd coincidence or other you were drawing my attention to?'

'Yes, sir. The car driver's place of employment.'

Chernavin looked up sharply.

'Ah yes,' Mukhin drawled. 'Wasn't it the FTA depot at Mytishchi – same as poor old Burinski here.'

'What's that?' scowled Chernavin. 'What did you say?' Burinski flopped onto his back again.

Mukhin looked at Chernavin as if he'd just discovered he was still there.

'By the way, comrade Inspector – you know what you were saying about those two bottles of vodka?'

Chernavin nodded. 'What about them?' Then he shook his head. 'Who gives a shit?'

'You seemed to, earlier. It wasn't true, you know, what you were saying. We only gave one bottle. You've been conned, comrade.'

Stepun shook his head, tut-tutting. He and Mukhin were through the door before Chernavin could stop them.

'Wait a minute!' he shouted. His voice echoed through the hall and made him jump. In his exasperation he meant to slap the bench but his hand connected with Burinski. It had the sound of dead meat. Chernavin looked down at the man in horror.

'Jesus and Mary! Sorry, comrade!'

Then he ran clackety-clack after the two CID men.

The phone started ringing just as Serov was turning the key in the door of his apartment. He got in as quickly as he could, dumped the grip-bag he was carrying and hurried to take the call.

Marshal Georgi Zavarov's voice, distorted by distance and a poor radio connection, was barely recognisable.

'Where in hell have you been? I tried to reach you all last night and this morning. Listen – I've been hearing stories.'

'What stories?'

'I can't say on this line. Don't you realise where I'm calling from?'

'I read the papers.'

'That's more than I can do right now. But word travels. These stories – do I believe them or not?'

'Things here are becoming difficult.'

'How difficult?'

Serov took his time and settled himself on the arm of a chair. He lit a cigar before answering, knowing the delay was making Zavarov sweat.

'The problems have been contained.' He exhaled a long breath of smoke. 'You're safe, for the present – that's what you really want to know, isn't it? So am I. But it's only a matter of time, in my opinion.'

'A matter of time! Then we've got to do something!'

Serov smiled. His gaze fell on the bookcase. Behind it was the wall-safe where he had deposited the Aganbegyan report.

'Maybe there's a way out,' he said. 'Maybe. I have an idea but it's still rough. It needs something to clinch it. I'm prepared to talk it through with you. But as I said, there's only so much time – who knows how much?'

'Next week. I'll be back in Moscow next week. I don't know what day.'

'I'll call you. We won't meet in Moscow anyway. I'll be going to Molodechno. We'll meet there.'

'You want me to go all the way down to Molodechno! That won't be easy for me.'

'Tough, Marshal. Tough.'

Serov hung up, went through to the bedroom, and began packing fresh clothes to take back to Galina's.

Viktor Kunaev stood by the white church with its holy pictures painted on the walls and watched the taxi drive away. He was completely alone. On his right was the broad quadrangle where, in spring and summer, newly-weds came to drink cheap champagne and have their photographs taken with the city as backdrop. He and Anna had done that. He kicked a layer of snow aside; underneath was a litter of champagne corks, empty cigarette packets and film cartons. He smiled wryly; in some regards at least, times hadn't changed.

Beyond the quadrangle towered the artificial ski-slope, silhouetted like a huge children's playslide against the skyline. Viktor's gaze followed it down to its base, where the snow-covered park sloped away to a swathe of darkness that was the river. On the far bank was the oval sweep of the Lenin Stadium. A few beams had been switched on among its batteries of floodlights, enough to show it off. Beyond the stadium the land, locked in the Moskva's ox-bow, flattened out to stretch into the distance and towards the Kremlin.

He took the narrow path downhill and through the trees, drawing his collar high against a sharp wind that was shaking snow from the branches and onto his forehead and lips. Underfoot the drifts grew deep as he descended, deeper than his overshoes. Snow trickled inside them and began to melt, making his socks and trouser-bottoms wet.

He crunched on until he was beyond the cadmium glow of the streetlamps. In the darkness the city's distant lights seemed brighter. From this distance, the traffic noise was no more than a whisper. Far away to his right a Metro train on the Kirovsko-Frunzenskaya line emerged briefly from its tunnel and hurried through the darkness, the light from its windows warm and inviting, then vanished underground again.

'If something's no good anymore, throw it out and make do with the memory.'

The words rang in his head like a bell tolling his fate. The city lights grew blurred as he started to sob.

10

'Good morning, Nikolai.'

It took a moment before the voice speaking softly in his ear registered.

'Galya?'

He opened his eyes to find her leaning over him. She was in her dressing-gown but had climbed back into bed. She kissed him lightly on the lips.

'Coffee,' she said. 'Sit up.'

He took the mug she was reaching to him from the tray on the bedside table and studied her for a moment before speaking.

'Welcome back.'

A tight smile in response.

He sipped the coffee, still watching her. 'How much do you remember?'

She sat back against the pillows, drew her knees up and wrapped her arms about them. 'A few things since I've been home.'

'How much about the day it happened?'

She paused before answering, as if going over it again distressed her. 'The early part of the morning. Going to the cemetery. Then the gallery. Looking at the painting. That's all, until being back here with you.'

'The cemetery,' he echoed softly. 'Galya.' He shook his head but otherwise let it pass. 'You don't remember what happened in the gallery or at the police station?'

She bent her head and a swathe of golden hair hid her eyes and face. 'I know what I thought happened in the gallery. But that's not the same thing as what actually happened, is it? As for the police station – what police station? If that's where you say I was, then that's where I was.' She lifted her head sharply and he saw that high spots of colour had come to her cheeks. She didn't look at him, waiting a moment before she went on. Then: 'There are other things. Other things I've been remembering instead.'

'What kind of things?'

'Things from long ago, maybe. That's how they seem. Confused things. My mother, a man – my father or you, I don't know. The images – you and him – fuse somehow.'

'Galya,' he said gently. 'Your father was never with you. You know that. You never knew him. He died before you were born.'

She nodded and the hair fell forward again. 'In some stupid demonstration. That's what you and Mama always told me.'

'Don't try to make up a past that never existed, Galya. Even if you wish it had. We've been over this. Do you remember anything else?'

As he spoke she had lifted her head and was looking at him. His stomach tightened for a moment: it was the way Gramin looked at him sometimes; or frightened creatures like Ratushny.

But it lasted only an instant before she bent her head, bringing her hair tumbling over her eyes again and uncovering the curve of her neck. The submissiveness of that aroused him and he reached for her. She didn't resist.

'I need to visit my father's apartment – Major Genrikh Kunaev. He's in hospital at present.'

The concierge, a crone in a black dress, eyed Viktor up and down, like a fat crow sizing up her prey.

'Kunaev,' she muttered. 'Kunaev.' She began to turn the pages of a large green register. When she looked up a slyness had appeared in her eyes.

'Heart attack last week,' she said. 'I remember now. Just as he was sitting down to breakfast. Dreadful.'

She stopped at a page headed *Away – Temporary* and ran an arthritic finger down the handwritten list of names.

'Apartment 12G,' she said. 'So you're the major's son?'

Viktor nodded.

'Do you have anything from him that confirms you're to be given admittance in his absence?'

Viktor set his briefcase on the counter, took out the letter his father had written, and handed it over.

'I'll need to keep this,' she said. 'For the records. Very fussy, the District Housing people. It all goes in here.' She tapped the pages of the register. 'And I need to know why you're visiting the apartment.'

'To fetch some items of clothing for my father.'

She wrote it down with painful care. 'Clothing,' she repeated. 'Is the major coming home?'

'Pyjamas.'

She finished writing and looked up at him. 'Never seen you here before, comrade. Shame when folk don't visit their family. My daughter comes over twice a week, regular as clockwork.'

Viktor shut the case and looked pointedly at his watch.

'You'll find the apartment in good order, comrade Kunaev. I tidied it myself. Do you have a key or should I go with you and let you in?' She pulled open a drawer with several bunches of pass-keys in it.

'I've got my father's key.'

She closed the drawer again and nodded towards the lifts. 'Left-hand lift. The other one isn't working.'

He felt her eyes on him all the time he stood waiting for the lift to arrive. When he stepped inside and turned round to slide its black iron gates shut she was still watching. She flashed him an ingratiating smile and mouthed '12G'.

He watched the floor indicators mindlessly most of the way up. He felt perfectly relaxed. When he got bored with the indicators he let his mind dwell on any small thing that entered it. There was comfort in inconsequential things. When the lift reached its destination he opened the gates and stepped outside, following the wall sign that told him apartments G to L were to the right. At the door of the apartment he struggled for a moment with the stiff lock, then he was inside.

Until the concierge's comment he had expected to find the place in disorder. But it was as neat and clean as anyone could wish. He pictured her poking around as she had tidied; it was an uncomfortable thought.

The bookcase was in the bedroom and he recognised it at once. Old-fashioned and low, a glass-fronted cabinet with lockable sliding doors. Just as in his childhood, its top served as a trinket shelf for cufflinks, tieclips, military decorations in flat cases, loose change, bookmatches. He detected the concierge's touch: everything was in orderly groupings that wouldn't be his father's doing.

Viktor opened the briefcase on the bed. With the letter gone it contained only a few transparent plastic bags and a small key, which his gloved fingers fumbled to pick up. He used it to unlock the bookcase.

The books were devoted exclusively to one topic, Russian Philosophy. Many were German, English and French language editions. He scanned across the titles on their spines, his eye lingering only on those which were in English. In the bottom right-hand corner of the bookcase he came to the title he sought. The sight of it made him feel slightly queasy. It was the first time all morning that he'd allowed himself an uncontrolled response.

History of Russian Philosophy

He said the author's name aloud: 'Lossky.' The sound of his own voice was somehow calming.

He finished scanning the rest of the titles to make sure that there was

79

no possibility of error, then slowly drew the book out and slid it into one of the plastic bags. Apart from the faded and slightly discoloured condition of its blue dustcover, it was in mint condition.

He had wrapped several more bags around it and was putting it carefully into the briefcase when he remembered what he'd told the concierge about the pyjamas. Unfamiliar with where his father stored his clothes, he spent a couple of minutes hunting through the bedroom. He tried the dresser drawers, the wardrobe, even under the pillows, but without success. Finally he thought to try the airing cupboard in the bathroom. Sure enough, folded away among towels, bedlinen and underwear, were several sets of pyjamas. He took two out, added a towel for good measure, then returned to the bedroom and packed them into the briefcase on top of the book.

As he was closing the case he heard the scrape of a key in the apartment door and the sound of someone struggling with the stiff lock. He grabbed the case and hurried out into the hallway just as the door swung open.

'Who the hell are you?'

A man stepped in through the open doorway, registering no surprise whatever at Viktor's presence. Viktor was aware of a flat nose over a broad grin.

'You'll be the major's son,' the stranger said amiably. 'Concierge said I'd find you here. I'm Krivchenko. Councillor, District Housing Administration.'

He held a clipboard in one hand and a bunch of the concierge's keys in the other. Now he put the keys in his pocket and produced an identity card of some kind. The hallway was windowless, lit only by whatever light filtered in past him from the landing outside. Viktor squinted at the card but it was gone before he saw anything.

'Councillor Krivchenko, what are you doing here?'

'My job, comrade, that's all. We must all do our jobs.' Krivchenko winked. 'I'm here to check the condition of the place – decorative order, fixtures and fittings, see that everything's in good shape and working properly.'

'Why?'

'Such a lot of questions, comrade! This housing unit's been ear-marked for –' He thumbed through some of the forms on the clipboard. ' – for a young couple who've been posted to our wonderful capital city from Kalinin. They're currently sharing with another family out in Reutov.'

'My father lives here! What are you people playing at?'

The man was still smiling, shaking his head now. 'Don't take it to heart, comrade. Nobody means any harm. An old person goes to hospital, it's only natural that his accommodation unit goes on our list as a possible vacancy. We're building new units as fast as we can but the shortage is still shocking.' He peered over Viktor's shoulder. 'Mind if I come on in now?'

Viktor sighed and stood to one side. 'Can I stop you?'

Krivchenko chuckled as he squeezed past. 'Quite frankly, comrade, no.'

'Comrade Kunaev?'

Black skirts flapping, the crone hurried across the lobby as Viktor pushed open the main door to the street.

'I'm sorry about Krivchenko. You know what pigs these people are – never happy till they make you miserable.'

'It doesn't matter.' He pushed the door again but she rattled on about how hard she'd worked to clean up the apartment. Only when he pressed some money into her hand did she finally shut up. While she was busy examining the cash he strode quickly through the door into the street.

'Bless you, comrade!' she called after him. 'When will your father be well enough to come home?'

Viktor stopped on the steps. 'That's hard to say.'

'I'll keep the apartment nice and clean for him.'

Viktor thought of the housing officer's words. In his briefcase he felt the reassuring weight of the Lossky book.

'Do what the hell you like,' he muttered under his breath. Then he pulled his scarf over his mouth and nose to shut out the sleet, and strode away.

As soon as Gramin heard the lift doors creak shut behind Viktor he threw the clipboard down and hurried out of the apartment. It was a cheap place and none of its windows overlooked the street. He found a stairwell window that did and stationed himself there.

It was a few minutes before Viktor appeared. Gramin waited to see which direction he took. North. Satisfied that Viktor was heading back to the hotel, he returned to the apartment. He nosed around for a while but Serov had set him a tough assignment: he had no idea whatsoever what he was looking for; just some clue to what had brought Viktor along in the first place.

Maybe the story about the pyjamas was true. That little briefcase: there would have been room in it for pyjamas. Little else. Viktor hadn't taken long in the apartment. The place didn't look disturbed in any way.

Gramin checked the time. He had two options. He could set off at once to the hotel to make sure that was where Viktor had ended up. But if he hadn't, what could he do about it? Other than the hospital, there was no way of knowing where else he might have headed.

Alternatively, he could see what booze the old man kept, and insulate himself before re-entering the Siberian gale.

That struck him as the best idea he'd had all morning.

Back at the hotel, Viktor went straight to his room. The time was eleven fifty; in London Anna and Andrei wouldn't yet have set off for the boy's nursery. If he was quick he could catch them.

Getting hold of an international operator lost him some valuable minutes, but at least the line was crystal-clear.

'Anna? It's me.'

'Viktor! It's so good to hear you. How is Genrikh?'

He stalled just long enough to warn her that the news wasn't good. 'The doctors say we can't hope for more than a day or two.'

'Oh, I'm so sad I'm not there.'

'He understands why you couldn't come. He spends a lot of time sleeping anyway. When he's awake he lives mostly in the past. His mind wanders a bit – he forgets things.'

'Such as?'

He sat down on the bed before answering, and caught a glimpse of his reflection in the dressing-table mirror opposite. He realised how tired and drawn he looked.

'Yesterday he'd forgotten who Serov is. He remembers him at the academy all those years ago but he has no idea who he is now – that he runs the Directorate. My Directorate.'

They were both silent for a moment; in the background he could hear Andrei babbling away cheerfully.

'Viktor?' Anna sounded tentative. 'When will you . . .' The sentence trailed away.

He looked back at the dressing-table, where he'd left the book, still in its plastic bags. 'I've got it already. It's safe. It's here with me right now.'

Another pause, awkward this time.

'Would you like to talk to Andrei?' she said at last.

'That would be nice. I miss both of you.'

'Same here.'

11

The memo in Horace Gaunt's hands recorded the details of what passed for a discussion with his Prime Minister. The subject on this occasion had been Opec, specifically the fact that it had decided to hold its next session of price and output negotiations in London. As with all such meetings, the shadow of international terrorism was ever-present; security for the conference had to be beyond reproach.

Gaunt looked around the table in Committee Room 2. Two of his senior directors were present. Joss Franklyn, barely visible through his clouds of pipe smoke, ran operational surveillance, meaning the teams of watchers and listeners and the delicate area of phone taps and mail intercepts. Martin Kellaway, sitting to his left, was in charge of the penetration and monitoring of suspect political organisations, whether left wing, right wing, anti-nuclear, racist, or more exotic imports from Iran and Africa. Opec meant the Middle East, and that meant any number of crackpot factions with axes to grind.

Beyond Franklyn and Kellaway sat the most junior person in the room: Dick Sumner, the curly-haired man whom Eva had observed with Gaunt on the evening of Sir Marcus Cunningham's retirement. It had fallen to him to deputise for his director, Edmund Knight.

'Opec have been rather shrewd in electing to stage their conference here,' Gaunt told them. 'The member countries, as you will be aware, are at an impasse in regard to their individual output quotas. All tiresomely familiar, but this time the situation is made worse by the growing amounts of non-Opec oil swilling about. As a result, the oil price has nosedived.'

'No one to blame but themselves,' Kellaway put in. 'It was them who tripled prices in the Seventies and made it worth our while looking for our own oil.'

'If they could limit non-Opec output that would drive the price up. They see Britain as a ringleader among the non-Opec producers, so they've tried making all sorts of approaches to us, official and unofficial. We have refused their blandishments and prices have stayed down. Where better, therefore, for this conference than on our own doorstep?

They know very well we won't tell them to go elsewhere. We will simply put up with the embarrassment.'

'Like good Brits,' muttered Joss Franklyn. He took the briar pipe from his mouth and glared into its bowl as though it were the cause of his dejection.

'What's the timing of this thing, Horace?'

'Last week in January. Two months from now. Here's our brief, gentlemen.' Gaunt looked down at the memo, where one paragraph had been bordered in green ink. 'In the PM's own words: "You will make all necessary arrangements in regard to counter-intelligence, counter-espionage and counter-sabotage, liaising with the other security, police and overseas intelligence services as you or they see fit."'

'That seems to cover everything.'

Gaunt's gaze roamed to Sumner, who clearly had a question on his mind.

'I was just wondering if Special Branch have been put in the picture.'

Gaunt nodded. 'They were present at the briefing in Number Ten last night. They are charged with the personal security of the delegates, making sure the venue is clean – the usual thing. Anything else, gentlemen?' They shook their heads. 'Then here is how I would like to proceed this morning.' His gaze settled on Kellaway. 'We need an assessment of the potential interest of the conference to the politicals. Especially the Middle East, of whatever faction. Which of them might try to disrupt things, or worse.' Then to Franklyn. 'Joss, I anticipate that your branch's contribution will be supportive rather than initiatory, so we shall pick up on you as we go along.' He turned to Sumner. 'The Soviet position: what might they or their surrogates get up to? Martin, let's begin with you. The politicals are my most pressing concern.'

But before Kellaway could say anything. Gaunt had turned again to Sumner. 'Where is Edmund anyway?'

'He's on a few days' leave,' Sumner muttered awkwardly. 'Some surplus time he'd built up. I believe he's gone to look up a few old friends.'

'Carry on, Martin,' Gaunt said to Kellaway; but the large eyes remained thoughtful and fixed on Sumner.

Paris

Knight took a lunchtime flight and arrived in Charles de Gaulle at two thirty local time. By three twenty he was checking into the Mercure at Saint-Witz, midway between the airport and Paris. His reservation was in the name of Gough.

'Has a package arrived for me?' he asked the clerk.

The youth flicked through a stack of mail beneath the counter and came up with a thick manila envelope. Knight took it and went to his room.

Straightaway he telephoned the courteous secretary at the precious metals trading firm in the centre of Paris.

'You may remember me, Mademoiselle. James Gough. I am at present in Paris, to see other clients, and find that I have some free time. When we last spoke you did not think it would be possible for Monsieur Vialle to see me this week. Do you think that is still the case?'

'My regrets, Monsieur. As I believe I told you, we have important guests who will be in the office with Monsieur Vialle all week.'

He thanked her and rang off. The real Vialle wouldn't get in his way; his schedule was unchanged. God bless organised men.

Knight spent a careful minute or two studying the manila envelope. He'd posted it himself in England a few days earler. Sellotape bound its four edges and it was here that he concentrated his attention. Only when he was satisfied that it hadn't been tampered with, did he slit it open with his room key. A burgundy-coloured French passport slid out, the one he had selected from the security deposit box in Guildford. It carried his photograph but the name of Monsieur Henri Vialle.

The rest of the day and evening was his own. He locked his room and returned to reception, where he ordered a taxi to take him into Paris. While he waited for it to arrive, he picked through the postcards on display at the desk and chose several.

In the city centre he passed time exploring the shops and boutiques around the Champs Elysées before crossing the river to Saint Germain. He bought postage stamps and some Christmas gifts for Eva, then crossed north again at the Louvre and strolled slowly up to Montmartre. He stopped frequently along the way, just to gaze at the buildings, floodlit in the failing light, or the passers-by.

He ate in a small café in the Place du Tertre and wrote and stamped his postcards between courses: one for Eva, the others for his secretary and section heads, all to their home addresses. His friends in Paris, he reported, had welcomed him warmly; the city was beautiful, even at this time of year; tonight they had dined at La Coupole; they saw some famous faces and had fun trying to put names to them. He left the cards unsigned, because that was the rule, just as he made no mention of any names or matters connected with their work, however harmless they might seem.

Later he wandered back towards the Place de Clichy and dropped Eva's card into the first postbox he saw. In the old-fashioned quarter beyond the square the traffic melted into the distance and the streets became narrower. He climbed the cobblestoned hill to the Rue Saint Vincent and dropped some more cards into another postbox. Halfway up the hill, just where the Rue des Saules branched off, he came to the tiny cottage, looking like a weatherbeaten peasant farmhouse, that was the Lapin Agile. He found himself a corner table where he passed an hour or so listening to the songs and poetry. He spoke to no one except a waiter and the cloakroom attendant.

Walking back to the city centre he posted the last cards before taking a taxi back out to Saint-Witz. The hotel was even quieter than when he had checked in; the lounge area was deserted. He asked the night clerk to book him a wake-up call at seven, then went straight to his room and to bed. As he'd hoped, the walking had exhausted him and he fell asleep almost at once.

In the morning he was back at Charles de Gaulle by nine thirty.

London

The silver Metro came onto the Great West Road from Chiswick Lane and crossed through the traffic lights to pick up the dual carriageway that eventually became the M4. In the opposite direction, the morning traffic was still tailed back beyond the Heston services area but the westbound road was clear. Gradually, as the Metro pressed on, the landscape began to open up. High-density housing gave way to ugly blocks of offices, redbrick yielding to grey concrete, and finally to occasional stretches of low industrial building glimpsed beyond the shrub-covered banks of the motorway. The sickly odour of jet exhaust fumes signalled Heathrow and shortly thereafter the Metro left the motorway and turned south.

Eva knew the route well; she had travelled it often enough either with Knight or on her own. It was the route to his house. She glanced at the clock in the Metro's dashboard and calculated that she would be there in about another half hour. With the road's familiarity her speed had crept up. She eased her foot off the pedal a fraction; there was no hurry.

12

Moscow

On Volgogradskiy Prospekt the bus lurched to a halt and Galina realised with a start that she had arrived at her stop. She jumped up and pushed through the people filling the gangway, reaching the folding doors just before they hissed shut.

On the pavement she stopped to take her bearings and fished the torn corner of newspaper from the pocket of her anorak to check the address again. Griboyedov Street. Maps of the city were like gold dust but she had a feeling Griboyedov was just along to the right. She drew up her fur-lined hood and turned into the wind.

She proved to be right about the direction but not the distance. She was frozen to the marrow by the time she got there and found that she'd stayed on the bus for two stops too many. Most convenient of all, of course, would have been the Metro; Tekstilshchiki station was just a few blocks away. But that was a form of transport she would never use . . .

The offices of the *Karacharovo Gazette* were in a squat yellow building whose paint was peeling like diseased skin. Inside she smelt mould, stale tobacco smoke and printer's ink. In glass cases on the walls of the entrance hall someone had tried to brighten the place up by mounting local news photographs: gypsy fairs, markets, folk dances, children receiving swimming prizes, factory openings. The attempt had failed. The brown woodwork and walls drained the life from every shot.

She noticed a small inquiries cubicle on her left and tapped on its sliding glass window. The old man inside glanced up reluctantly from his dog-eared magazine and slid the glass panel open.

'Please, is it possible for me to examine back copies of the paper?'

He shrugged indifferently, holding on to the edge of the panel as if he couldn't wait to get it shut again. She could see that he'd made the cubicle his very own: a hook for his overcoat, a shelf for his tobacco tin and ashtray, a portable radio, a small electric fire for his feet.

'Depends how far back you want to go. We lost a lot in the floodwater thaw of sixty-seven.'

'I only want last year.'

'That's easy enough. You want the reading room. Back of this floor, turn right. There's a woman there to help you.'

'Thank you.'

The glass panel hurtled shut before she'd even turned away.

In his office at Yasyenevo, Serov swivelled his chair, hoisted his feet onto the desk and tallied the score so far.

He began at the top. Mikhail Gorbachev. A man who nursed a mighty ambition: to transform his whole society. But every grand ambition came with its flaw, the seed that could waste its bearer. In Gorbachev's case the Oligarchy committee had identified the flaw. It fell to Serov to use it.

Next, Zavarov. A cornered man. Watching his power being stripped away; worried also that his own grubby deals might come to light in Gorbachev's clean-up. If ever a man was ready to play a part, that man was Zavarov. Again it fell to Serov to define the part.

Ligachev the politician. Could an old ideological leopard change his spots as Ligachev seemed to have done? Or did he just need the right temptation and he too would play a bidden part?

And now this, the Code Red field communication that lay on Serov's desk. It recounted how, in the scorching heat of a Libyan noontime, Colonel Gadaffi had received a delegation of top Saudis in his Tripoli headquarters. Their meeting had been observed and listened to by an agent of GRU military intelligence among the Soviet 'military advisers' that Gadaffi was glad to have at his back. In line with good practice, the GRU report had been monitored by the KGB's Third Directorate, sister to Serov's own. Now here it was before him, telling its story of subversion within the Saudi hierarchy, a hierarchy as closed to outside eyes as the Kremlin's. Subversion in which the Libyan leader meant to have a controlling hand.

Subversion that could well complete the tally of items needed here in Moscow by Nikolai Serov.

Mikhail Tikhrus took another bite of his black bread and cheese and set it aside. He wiped his fingers on his handkerchief before tearing off the three perforated sheets of telex data which had just finished scrolling up on the printer by his desk.

He wore the white shirt and epaulettes of Aeroflot's senior clerical staff. On his long, open-plan office floor of the airline's central Moscow headquarters he was one of only four officers who enjoyed the luxuries of a rubber plant for decoration, two orange screens five feet high for privacy, and one orange plastic chair for visitors.

The telex contained the passenger list of AF720 which was taking off for Moscow from Charles de Gaulle. Already on his desk were similar sheets relating to some dozen other flights from all around the globe. He glanced at the bank of clocks mounted on the wall behind him. Each had a small plate beneath it bearing the name of the capital city to which it related. In Paris it was ten thirty-five; AF720 was smack on schedule.

He scanned down the names on the telex message and had another mouthful of black bread before pushing a button on the base of his telephone. His elderly secretary appeared around the edge of one of the orange screens.

'Something here for our people,' he told her absent-mindedly, still reading.

She approached his desk and reached her hand out for the sheets. But a name on the Paris manifest had taken his attention and he made no move yet to pass the sheets over to her.

'Just a moment,' he mumbled eventually.

She waited while he unlocked a drawer of his desk. It contained a single folder, which he opened without lifting out. There was just one sheet of paper inside. At the top was a telephone number and underneath it a list of names. Tikhrus took a pencil and copied out the name he'd spotted that was common to both this list and flight AF720. When this was done he handed the telex over.

'You may send it now.'

After the secretary had gone he picked up his phone and dialled the telephone number.

'Gramin – this is Tikhrus, Aeroflot. One of the names on your list is on his way to Moscow. He's on AF720, from Charles de Gaulle, Paris. Time of departure 1035 local time, 1235 Moscow time. Took off on schedule. ETA Sheremetyevo 1615 our time. The name is Vialle.' He spelt it out. 'Henri Vialle. Travelling on a French passport.'

He listened for a moment to what Gramin had to say in reply, nodding occasionally and making some notes. When Gramin had finished he said 'Yes,' but the line was already dead. He returned to the telex machine, his bread and cheese forgotten.

The *Karacharovo Gazette* was published only twice a week, so it wasn't that difficult to find the right issue. What she was looking for was compressed into a single column near the top of page 5.

METRO DEATH

Peak hour services were disrupted for an hour on the Zhdanovskaya-Krasnopresnenskaya line last Thursday evening.

The cause was a woman falling onto the track in Ryazanskiy Prospekt station as an eastbound train was coming in. She was killed instantly.

'It was dreadful,' Marina Buczkova told your *Gazette* reporter. 'I heard people screaming and looked round, and there she was. I'll never forget what I saw. It'll be with me till my dying day. If that poor woman committed suicide, which you have to admit is a possibility, what a dreadful way to do it.'

It would be ghoulish for your reporter to repeat the harrowing description which Marina gave of the scene. Marina is a cleaner at the Higher Party School in Miusskaya Square, where she has worked for seven years.

'We must keep this incident in perspective,' Metro Director Boris Krassin said. 'It was a human tragedy, of course. But from the point of view of passenger services, we responded well. Services between Planyornaya and Taganskaya were still able to operate normally. It was only the section out to Zhdanovskaya which had to shut down. I admit that travellers on that line were inconvenienced, but I would point out that their services were back to normal within an hour. I think our workers can take pride in that.'

A date for an inquest has not yet been set. In the meantime, it has been requested that the dead woman's identity should not be disclosed, out of respect for her family. Your *Gazette* naturally respects this request.

Galina stared at the item for so long that the kind-looking woman who ran the back issues department came over to ask if she'd found what she was looking for. There was a worried note to her voice. Galina nodded dumbly and forced a smile of thanks.

There'd never been any inquest. Nikolai knew how to make it worth people's while to overlook niceties like that.

Of course, in a way the newspaper story told her nothing. She hadn't expected it to. It read like the suicide she'd been told about. But that wasn't the point. The point was simply being able to sit here and read it. No screams. No re-run of the Tretyakov. That was what was important. This time, she really was getting stronger.

She closed the paper and took it back to the kindly woman.

'Thank you very much for your help,' she told her, very calmly, and gave her a stronger smile than last time. She was going to practise being strong from now on.

But as she made her way back along the gloomy corridor and past the old man in the enquiries cubicle, one word kept turning over and over in her mind: *suicide*. Like a record jammed on her hi-fi, over and over.

'Is that really what it was, Mama?' she asked the white sky outside. The wind snatched the words from her lips and she hardly heard them herself; only the jammed record.

Serov realised that Sergei was standing at the door; he had no idea how long he'd been there.

'Did you say something?'

'I asked if you'd like me to bring you lunch, comrade General. I'm going to the canteen now. If you don't need me for anything, that is.'

Serov shook his head. 'No food. Tidy this place up a bit before you go.'

He stubbed another cigar out in the already heaped ashtray and rose to get out of Sergei's way. Somehow the act of moving crystallised the decision he'd already been thinking about.

'Sergei, I have to go out of town for a time. I'll leave early this afternoon.'

If Sergei was surprised he didn't show it. 'Very well, sir.'

'Bring me the Eighth Department files. All of them. Between now and when I leave, I'm not to be disturbed. I want Gramin outside with the car at two forty-five.'

A minute later the files arrived. The Eighth Department covered the Middle East, Turkey, Afghanistan, Iran and Greece. The files couldn't be taken out of the building; he had to work through them there and then, making notes or committing to memory whatever might prove relevant to the task he had set his mind for the rest of the week.

Ignoring the growling in his stomach, he lit another cigar and set to work.

13

'I'll drive. Move over.'

Gramin did as he was told. Serov rammed the accelerator to the floor and the heavy car shot away from the kerb, slewing slightly on the icy road. Once beyond the double mesh gates of the FCD headquarters complex, Serov picked up the ring road, the mounds of snow by its verge now beginning to stain black with exhaust fumes, and headed for the city.

'Tell me about young Kunaev.'

Gramin stretched his legs to get his feet under the heater. 'He goes to the hospital twice a day. He's been to the funeral parlour in the Golitsyn annex. He's taken a couple of walks in the hills. He's been to the old man's apartment. Otherwise, he hardly leaves the hotel. He eats in his room.'

'He's met or talked to no one?'

'Only hotel or hospital staff. He phoned his wife once.' Gramin thought for a moment more. 'And he had to talk to the concierge at his father's apartment block.'

'Why did he go there?'

'To fetch clothes for the old man.'

Serov was silent while he concentrated on overtaking a truck on the straight between the two railway bridges near the Danilov. Information. Watch, listen, assess. If relevant, use. But sometimes information simply had no relevance. Maybe the Kunaevs were in that category. Significant once, the old man at any rate; but perhaps no longer.

'I have other news, comrade,' Gramin added. 'I had a call this morning from my Second Directorate contact within Aeroflot. He keeps the Directorate's foreign visitor files up-to-date. He does a few favours for me as well.'

'So?'

'The man called Vialle is on his way to Moscow again.'

'Boyar?' Serov said softly. The name came unbidden, before he could stop it.

'What was that, comrade?'

'Nothing.'

Gramin glanced down at a small notepad that he'd taken from his pocket. 'He's on flight AF720, departed Paris at 1235 Moscow time, arriving 1615 Sheremetyevo.'

Serov kept his eyes on the road, his mind racing. This was something he didn't need. Not at this time. If it was Boyar.

'Which Vialle?' he asked evenly.

'No way of telling till I see him. My man in the Second drew the line at giving me anything from his entry papers about how long he plans to be here or where he's staying. Sorry, comrade. I suppose the real Vialle's too important because of his platinum and gold deals. He gets to come and go pretty much as he pleases.'

Serov swung the Chaika towards the island and the Krasnokholmskiy Bridge. He would have liked to watch the Kunaevs for a little longer, especially if the old man only had a few days left. But it was a question of priorities. He had only one realistic choice.

'Forget Kunaev,' he ordered. 'Get out to Sheremetyevo for Vialle's arrival. If it's the Englishman, don't let him out of your sight. You know what to do.'

Gramin nodded, recalling previous instructions when the Englishman had visited. 'I watch and report. I don't let him see me. I don't interfere in anything he does.'

'Or talk to anyone he talks to.'

'No, comrade.'

Serov checked the cars behind and pulled over to the side of the road. 'I'll be in Molodechno. Contact me only if there's an emergency. Otherwise leave me in peace.' He leant across and unlocked Gramin's door. 'Now get out.'

Gramin looked startled. He stared both ways along the bridge.

'But comrade – my car. It's south at Yasyenevo. I've got to get north to Sheremetyevo. Vialle lands in an hour.'

'Then you'd better get a move on.'

Serov drove straight to his own apartment. There he went from room to room as a cat would pace out its territory. It was his habit after any absence. He didn't check anything in detail so much as sense the atmosphere.

All was in order.

His packing was quickly done. Suits, formal shirts and ties for the meeting and afterwards. These he packed with care, putting them neatly into a separate suit carrier. Then he filled his grip-bag with a more or less random selection of informal clothes.

Next he went to one of the built-in bookcases and swung back the hinged section that concealed the wall-safe. He unlocked it and took out the Aganbegyan report, tossed it on top of the packed clothes and zipped the bag shut.

That left only the call to Zavarov, back by now from Afghanistan. He tried the Marshal's dacha first, reasoning that he would be resting there after the homeward trip. The assumption proved correct.

The Marshal was wary when he heard Serov's voice; he became apoplectic when he heard the proposition that Serov had for him.

'You're crazy,' he shouted down the line, 'He won't come! How the hell can I make him?'

'That's your problem.'

Serov hung up and was back in his car five minutes later. He'd left it on the road to save the time it took to get in and out of the garage under the building. But it was past school hours and a little gang of children had gathered about the car. Big cars always had that effect; adults could be just as bad, if the car was rare enough. If it wasn't an official one the windscreen wipers and a wheel or two could sometimes be gone.

Galina was in the studio, painting, when he arrived. The picture was a new one that he hadn't seen before, a city skyline with heavy clouds and small, tired people. It seemed as bleak as her mood: further evidence, perhaps, that she still hadn't shaken off the after-effects of the Tretyakov incident.

'I wasn't expecting you,' was all she said when he walked in.

'I have to go out of town for a few days. Maybe a week. I came to let you know.'

He draped his greatcoat over an empty easel and moved beside her, peering over her shoulder at the painting. Her hair was drawn back in a ponytail, exposing her neck and ears. He bent to kiss her warm throat. She didn't draw away but equally she made no response to his touch. When he stopped kissing her the brush resumed jabbing at the canvas in short, harsh strokes.

'When do you leave?'

'I'll go from here. I've already been to my own place to collect what I need.' He straightened up and looked again at the canvas. 'What a strange painting.'

'It's just a city.'

'Not a happy one.'

'Cities can't be happy or sad. Only the people.' She put the brush down and wiped her fingers on a rag.

He took her gently by the shoulders and turned her to face him. 'Galya, about what happened at the concert –'

'I told you – I don't remember much.'

Her voice was flat, her eyes expressionless, as if she were somewhere beyond his reach. Today he badly needed to find her.

'I won't see you for a while.'

'We've been apart before.'

But she turned and crossed the floor into the bedroom. He followed, his fingers brushing the cloth over his bust as he passed it. She undressed without a word while he stood watching. Then she slipped his jacket from his shoulders and hung it in the wardrobe. She left its door open and he watched in the mirror as she stripped him garment by garment.

An hour later he was on the road again, thinking that the sensible thing to do was to turn west at once. He didn't. He headed east, picking up the one-way that took him along Petrovskiy, then up past Kazan Station and the Yaroslavl, still the last view of Moscow for those who were off to the Siberian gulags.

When he reached the familiar tumbledown streets his car was the only thing moving in them. Until he got near the top of the hill. Then he saw the sidelights of the first militia car, drawn up by the kerb. The occupants stayed sensibly warm inside as he cruised past. He knew they'd be radioing his approach to their colleagues further up, so there was no point in turning back; his registration would have been noted anyway.

Sure enough, around the next corner a swinging lantern indicated the two policemen who were awaiting his arrival, standing beside their car in the cold air. Behind them the derelict street ran straight up to the Church of the Saviour. Another fall of snow was getting under way. Through it and the darkness his headlights picked out the long, dark bulk of the articulated truck that was parked by the church door. Its tailgate had been thrown open, forming a sloping ramp to the ground. Men were carrying boxes over it into the deep trailer. A group of three other men, all bundled in heavy parkas, stood near the truck. Their backs were to him. One of them, a short, pudgy man, turned for a moment as Serov's headlight beams swept over them. Serov recognised him as the man called Chernavin, the one who'd been interviewed on Vremya. The one who'd come so close to getting what he needed from Gulyaev.

When Serov opened his window to talk to the policemen, he could hear the rumble of a pneumatic drill from deep inside the church. Chernavin was about to have Yezhov's body to add to his perplexing investigations.

Serov identified himself and the officers rebuttoned the flaps of their revolver holsters.

'I heard the activity from down the hill and wondered what was going on.'

'I could ask one of the inspectors to come across, comrade General.'

He shook his head. 'Don't worry. I just wanted to be sure it wasn't anything untoward.'

He reversed the car and made his way back down. None of the three men in parkas bothered to turn around again.

He cleared the city as fast as he could and settled back for the long cross-country haul to Byelorussia. It might take until after breakfast the next day before he arrived, depending on the condition of the roads.

He didn't mind. There was plenty to think about.

The last indignity for the old man was not even being able to go to the toilet properly. He had to do it under the sheets into a cardboard bottle.

He struggled onto his side and grappled to get the hated contraption into position. It needed huge effort and left him panting with exhaustion. But the alternative was to send for a nurse: even more humiliating.

He lay still and let his bladder begin to empty. But he noticed something strange. Instead of the usual sense of relief as the pressure eased, exactly the opposite was happening. It was as if a massive force were swelling inside him, making his ribcage ache to let it burst out.

Vaguely he realised that it was the same as something that had happened before but he couldn't be quite sure when or what it had been. Everything was muddled, and the pain made it impossible to think.

Aah! It was tearing his chest apart now. Why wouldn't it stop? It was like a slow explosion, billowing up within him.

Then he recognised it. A curtain moved aside in his mind, that pain had drawn closed, and he knew when he'd felt this before and what it was.

The cardboard bottle tumbled to the floor and rolled over, discharging its contents over the shiny lineoleum.

Genrikh Kunaev was dead.

Galina lay for a long time in the darkness. From the bowels of the apartment block she could hear the communal lift rising and falling, its motor humming, its doors thudding. The working day was ending and the building's other residents were returning home.

After a time the lift stopped. Cooking smells wafted into her bedroom. Then they too faded.

The wardrobe door was still open. Finally she rose and switched on the dressing-table lamp. The mirror reflected the light against the far wall. Its pattern swept across the wall as she opened the door wider and reached into the wardrobe.

She'd hung his jacket beside a heavy cotton smock of hers. It hadn't been difficult to transfer his keys into the smock as she hung the jacket up. Now she reached into the smock's pocket and took them out. There were four of them on a leather fob. She turned them over in her fingers. One was for a standard cylinder lock. Another looked like a mortice key. The third and fourth she wasn't sure about. She'd find out when she got there. All she needed was the courage to go. A week, he'd said. That was how long she had . . .

As she returned the keys to the smock her eye fell on the wardrobe mirror. He had left the light burning in the kitchen. It fanned across the studio floor, catching the bust of Katarina.

She went through to the studio. Next to her mother's bust was Nikolai's, still hidden by the damp cloth. Now she tugged tentatively at its bottom corner and it slid slowly down, clinging to the contours of the damp clay. First the hair appeared, then one blank eye, then all of the face.

Yes, Nikolai, you asked me if I remember other things, and I do. Like the binoculars you let me carry the night of the concert. Let me carry? Made me carry.

You did that when I trusted you. You used me. You were counting on my trust. It made the whole thing possible. I was perfect – not looking guilty, not drawing attention to myself. Especially the state I was in. I suppose that made me all the better.

All the better too if I'd been caught. No arguments – how could I argue when I wouldn't even have understood? I was perfect.

'Look what I bought for us today, Galya. Just what we need for tonight. I got a set for each of us.'

And if I had been caught – what then, Nikolai? Would you have let me take the blame?

You were planning it right from the moment you bought the binoculars. Planning it when you brought them home.

'A pair for you and a pair for me. So we can get a better view.'

Was that the real reason why we went to the concert, Nikolai? Not for my sake, but because it suited your purposes?

So calculating, Nikolai. All that planning, counting on my trust, using me.

What else have you been planning, Nikolai? Planning for years, perhaps. Because I remember many other things now. Such as when Mama was still alive. How you used to look at me, even then. And I understand the look now, because it's the way you look at me now. How guilty that look made me! – because I thought it was my fault. I thought it was my body betraying me, changing, not a child's any more. Making you something other than the father you'd been to me – making you less . . . safe.

Was that why Mama died, Nikolai? Had to die?

My dear, kind Nikolai. Mama's kind Nikolai.

Galina picked up a heavy cleaver and brought it down with all her might on the skull. It split the clay asunder and tore through the fine chickenwire former underneath.

One blow.

It *was* the Englishman. Gramin decided on a four-man net to cover his movements. A tried and tested number. Less and the subject was likely to start noticing familiar faces; more were tricky to co-ordinate.

He appointed himself anchor. The others were street informers and KGB casuals who couldn't care less about the dividing line between official and unofficial jobs, provided they were looked after. These days booze and Western videos, the raunchier the better, were the preferred currencies.

Already the Englishman had dragged them across half of Moscow: dosshouses, drying-out parlours, wastelands of apartment blocks which even Gramin would have thought twice about walking through on his own, whorehouses, infirmaries. Whatever he was looking for, he hadn't found it yet; but not for want of trying.

Finally, at just gone midnight, he returned to his hotel. He was putting himself up in style, in the Nevskiy.

'Our bird's home,' one of the casuals reported over the radio-telephone. 'He won't be out again tonight.'

A block south, Gramin turned his car engine off and looked around the street in which he found himself. He was just on the edge of the pedestrianised Arbat area.

'He's burned up some shoe leather, that's for sure.' Gramin rubbed his flattened nose, thinking. He lifted the radio-telephone again. 'All of you – you can knock off now. But stay close to a phone in case I need you fast.'

A few minutes later he arrived on foot at the Mariya restaurant. It was tucked away up one of the cobbled backstreets, where not even the tourists could find it.

It was all locked up; the card on the door said it closed at eleven-thirty. But Gramin knew the Mariya better than that and a dim light still glowed at the back. He hammered on the door with his gloved fist until it was opened. A big Turkish-looking type with a full beard glowered down at him.

'What do you want? We're shut.' The Georgian accent gave him away as an immigrant. Some of them would sell their mothers to get a Moscow resident's permit.

Gramin pushed his yellow KGB card under his nose and the man shut up. He took a step back and opened the door just enough for Gramin to get through.

'Be nice,' Gramin said. 'Or I might ask to see your residency permit – and the rest of your stinking family.'

The Turk led him past one or two groups of huddled diners and drinkers. No one looked up as they passed. The business done in the Mariya didn't invite friendliness or curiosity. They came to a dark corner and the Turk took the chairs down from a small table. Gramin sat down.

'Vodka and two glasses. A menu. I want my food fast.'

Half an hour later he'd consumed some cheap red caviar on warm rolls and was hunched over a plate of salted herring when the Turk reappeared, followed by a short-necked man in the brown and gold uniform of the Nevskiy.

'He says you're expecting him,' the Turk growled at Gramin.

'It's true.' Gramin nodded towards the other chair and the man sat down. The Turk lumbered off.

'Take a drink.' Without lifting his eyes from his food, Gramin pushed a glass towards his visitor with the back of his hand. The man filled it himself from the bottle.

'Your friend the Frenchman,' he said.

Gramin grunted and munched on. He'd seen no reason to enlighten anyone on the subject's true nationality.

'He seems to have packed it in for the night.'

'Bed?'

'Yes.'

'Alone?'

'Him and a bottle.' The man's eyes brightened. 'He tips well. Slipped me five roubles to get the vodka up to him.'

'Seen his registration card? How long is he here for?'

'Four days.'

'Get back now. I'll be here for an hour or two. We'll pick him up again in the morning.'

The man seemed reluctant to go. His thick neck bulged over his collar as he gazed down at his drink.

'What's your problem now?' Gramin asked finally.

'You said you'd pay tonight. Upfront, you said.'

'Ahh!' Gramin put his fork down and reached into his back pocket. He counted through a wad of notes and threw some onto the table. The man quickly scooped them up.

'It's short,' he announced. 'By five roubles.'

Gramin belched. 'That's all right, then.'

'What do you mean?'

'That's the five Frenchie already gave you. Now piss off.'

The bottle was half gone but the ache was just the same. Knight stretched out on the bed, setting the bottle on the side table, and swallowed another glassful. His throat was now numb when at first the liquid had stung him like salt in an open wound.

Such fallible creatures, men and women. Strings of neurons that could so easily make the wrong connections. Wrong connections that led to errors.

He had erred. All those years ago.

But didn't everyone? Didn't everyone make errors? Wasn't that how we were supposed to learn?

Yes, but some errors weren't like that, weren't the kind that could be over and done with. Sometimes when an error was made, sometimes it just stayed made.

He closed his eyes and lay back against the pillows.

Yes, some errors stayed made.

Made flesh.

Now lost.

14

Byelorussia

The farm lay hidden among the hills and pine forests west of Minsk. Molodechno was the nearest town, a haphazard muddle of old timbered houses and more modern concrete buildings. Halfway between the town and the farm was a small airfield, hardly used since the war but still capable of being pressed into service. A hundred and fifty miles to the west lay the Polish border.

On the farm's highest ground, deep within its boundaries, stood a stonebuilt house. It had once belonged to a cousin of the old Tsar, used by him as a dacha.

It was nine in the morning when Serov arrived. He was met at the door by Sinsky, a slow-moving beast of a man who stood a full head taller than him.

'Get me some breakfast,' Serov told him. It was now over twenty-four hours since he'd eaten. 'I'll have it upstairs. Then prepare the ash room.'

He went straight to his suite on the third floor. By the time he'd washed and shaved, Sinsky had delivered the food. He ate ravenously before flopping on top of the bed and falling asleep at once.

In the late morning he awoke, washed again to clear his head, and went downstairs. The ash room was at the rear of the house, and was so-called because of its whitewood panelling. It was spacious and bright, and overlooked the snowy fields and forests to the east. A roaring fire, Sinsky's handiwork, was blazing in its huge stone fireplace.

Here Serov stayed, night and day, for the rest of the week. The only person he spoke to was Sinsky, when he sent him to the kitchens for food or ordered him to build up the fire. He slipped into a time zone of his own, eating and snatching sleep when his body could no longer go without. He went back to his suite only to wash or change his clothing. He smoked heavily but touched no alcohol.

There wasn't just one idea; there were half a dozen, each capable of four or five different applications. On the long drive to Molodechno he'd seen the permutations spin out. He could set in motion any option but their final outcomes were dependent on the responses of the people involved. These were what he had to second-guess.

He began simply enough: by writing down everything that had been in the Code Red field report from Tripoli and adding other material from his reading of the Western press and his trawl of the Eighth Department files. Then he reviewed the Oligarchy document again, noting every implication of it that had occurred to him since it had come into his possession. The links between these and the Tripoli information were crucial and he spent many hours on them.

Laying out the likely British and American responses was the most difficult part of the process. Nor were they all he had to predict; he needed also to anticipate how Gorbachev would see them. Where options were balanced he either had to have a plan for each of them or find a way of nudging the decision towards the one he preferred.

When he needed to escape from the room he walked through the forest of pines and aspens, where the silence was broken only by the slither of snow from branches. If he happened upon any of the estate's workers they would move rapidly away or continue quietly with their work until he'd gone past. They might nod a cautious greeting but they never spoke. They feared the man from Moscow.

After four days and most of three nights he became sure that something was starting to emerge, like a statue from a slab of rough stone. For twenty-four hours he closed in on it. On the last evening he pushed the room's furniture against the walls and began sifting through the sheets of notes, spreading some across the floor and rewriting others. Hour by hour he chipped at the idea, clarifying it until it was right. He fell asleep sometime before dawn for a couple of hours, sprawled across the papers, and was woken when Sinsky, without waiting to be ordered this time, brought him breakfast. He ate mechanically and resumed working. By late morning he was sufficiently satisfied to begin disposing of his superfluous working sheets, crumpling them one by one into balls that he consigned to the flames of the fire.

He spent the afternoon looking again for gaps in his planning and ways around them. By four thirty he was as ready as any man could be. He collected his papers together, ordered Sinsky to set the room to rights, and went off at last to his suite to sleep, bath and dress.

He had to be fresh for the most important meeting of his life.

He had given a series of orders to Sinsky. While Serov slept, he rode down to the airfield on a snowplough, bringing with him on its running-boards three other burly farm workers. They stopped short just before the locked gates of the steel fence surrounding the field. After waiting for the others to jump down, Sinsky lowered the plough's scoop and accelerated the plough at the gates, crashing through and leaving them swinging from their mountings. The others finished the job by detaching the mangled gates with powerful cutters and tossing them well out of the way.

In the airfield Sinsky cut a few trial furrows through the waist-high snow until he had located the concrete of the east-west lane. He guided the plough up and down this strip, clearing the snow to either side. Afterwards he drove along at walking pace while the others unloaded some large lanterns from the snowplough's trailer and set them at intervals on each side of the runway. At the runway's end he cleared a wide apron area on the hard earth beside the concrete.

At eight that evening Sinsky emerged from the farm again. This time he was behind the wheel of a silver Mercedes 500 SEL and wore respectable dark clothes. Not far behind him a four-wheel-drive Niva followed, with the three other men aboard. They were also respectably dressed. Short-barrelled machine guns lay in their laps.

At the airfield the two vehicles followed the clearway that the plough had cut earlier. Fresh snow had dusted it over since then but it remained perfectly passable.

The Mercedes pulled to a halt on the cleared apron at the runway's edge, engine and heater still running. The Niva paused for its passengers to step out, then followed as they walked the runway, switching on the flashing lanterns. Then they rode back to wait beside the Mercedes.

In Moscow, Galina was also waiting. She had waited all week for her courage to muster, now it was there and she was waiting for the chance to put it to use.

She stood in a small park opposite Serov's apartment block. It was the closest she had ever come to his place. Near her was a blue and white hut selling ice-cream. She hated the stuff but others consumed it by the bucketful, whatever the season or the temperature. Tonight there was a steady stream of customers from the blocks on the street. They'd take the ice-cream back to their apartments, invariably over-heated because fuel was almost free, and gobble it down while watching television.

The problem that vexed her was how to get into Serov's building. Keys alone weren't enough. There was a doorguard in the lobby and he was stopping everyone that he didn't recognise.

Then the big car drew up and the four whores got out. Top class whores, to have business in that building, but whores all the same.

They were about to enter when one of them spotted the ice-cream hut. The four of them came giggling across the road and bought a huge tub.

Galina stepped from the shadows and sashayed back over the road behind them. Only when they were past the guard and safely in the lift did the girls become aware that she had attached herself to them. They realised what she was up to but didn't seem to mind.

'Busking a little, honey?' was all one of them said.

At the apartment Galina found that she'd been right about the first two keys; they were doorkeys. No one disturbed her as she opened the door and quickly stepped inside. She closed it at once and waited a few seconds before flicking on the lightswitch.

The alarm bell right above her head screamed into life.

For a moment she was paralysed. She thought it was something to do with the lightswitch, so she flicked it off again. The noise continued. Then she realised: it was an alarm with a time delay, sufficient to allow the resident to get to it and switch it off. That would explain one of the other two keys, but to use it she had to find the control box. The racket was deafening. Any second now the doorguard or a neighbour would arrive to investigate. The people who lived here were wealthy enough to care a great deal about security; no one would ignore a noise like that.

She turned the light on again and looked around, wishing she had some idea what she was looking for. She was on the point of giving up and fleeing when she saw the cupboard at the end of the hallway. She raced to it and tore the door open. A green metal box was mounted on the wall. Wires ran from it like tentacles; a stainless steel key-rose glinted up at her in the hallway light.

Her fingers fumbled with the keys. She found the one that fitted and the clanging stopped as suddenly as it had begun. She heaved a deep sigh and listened, still down on her knees by the cupboard.

Minutes passed, in which there was no sound but the thudding of her own heart.

When she did rise to her feet, however, her search didn't get under way at once. For as she moved from room to room, she was stunned by what she found. Only in dreams or foreign films had she seen anywhere like this.

The apartment was large, but so was her own by Moscow standards. It was the contents and style of this place that stunned her. She saw richly patterned Uzbek rugs, Scandinavian hardwood furniture, English soft furnishings. The rooms were full of paintings and fine ornaments. There seemed to be an expensive Japanese television set in every room, and audio equipment that she'd never even heard of. Books everywhere. It was like walking into the pages of one of the Western magazines he brought her.

Most of all, there was him: a pack of cigars on a table, clothes in the wardrobe, his foreign brands of soaps, cologne and shaving tackle in the bathroom.

When she had gawped enough she retraced her steps and began again to walk slowly through each room. This time she had only one object in mind: the safe to which she was convinced the fourth key belonged. She lifted the corners of pictures, she peered behind cabinets and curtains. Eventually, she began tugging at the shelves of the bookcases.

It was her sharp eyesight, not any movement of the perfectly carpentered shelves, that told her when she'd found what she was looking for. Hairline joins in two of the uprights were the giveaway, not matched in the other sections. She ran her fingertips over, under and round the shelves until she found the stud that released the section and swung it out.

So absorbed had she been in her earlier exploration of the apartment that her nervousness had gradually melted away. Now, with the safe before her, it returned in force. She fought it down, telling herself that she was strong, and tried the fourth key.

It fitted.

Yegor Ligachev peered unhappily at the darkness outside the small window by his elbow. He was a politician, not an Arctic explorer.

'Where in God's name is this place, Georgi?'

Darkness was all he'd seen for the whole flight; darkness and the howling blizzard through which they were now flying. The plane had been losing height for two or three minutes and it surprised him that still there was no sign of civilisation to be seen. Not a light, nothing. The warning symbols over his seat were flashing as well, confirming that a landing was imminent. Yet he could see nothing worth coming down for.

He groaned inwardly. He was a fool to have given in to Zavarov. They were both too old for stupid games.

'Where are we?' he asked again.

Across the aisle of the Marshal's well-appointed aircraft, Zavarov snapped the ashtray lid shut on his cigarette. He avoided Ligachev's gaze and blew a last lungful of smoke up towards the air vent.

'We're there, Yegor,' he said laconically. 'That's where we are. Fasten your seat belt.'

Ligachev shook his head wearily. 'I must be insane.'

'What's insane about giving me just twenty-four hours of your time?' Zavarov brushed ash off his sleeve. 'I went all the way to Afghanistan to oblige you.'

Ligachev glared back at him as he did up the seat belt. 'Whatever you're up to, and whatever you're trying to get me into, it can't be right if it needs all this secrecy. I've come with you this far for old time's sake, Georgi, but there's a limit.'

Before he could say more his breath was suddenly knocked from him. The aircraft had set down on a runway with a bone-jarring lurch. What runway?

'Sorry, Yegor,' he heard Zavarov call, the words almost drowned by the screech of rubber on concrete that seemed to be coming from right beneath their seats. 'I meant to warn you. It's a short airstrip – my pilot has to come down hard.'

As if to bear this out, there was a mighty roar as the pilot hit reverse thrust. Ligachev felt himself being thrown forward against the seat belt. Their speed began to fall sharply and he steadied himself back up again, staring again through the window. At least now he could see flashing lights that edged the runway; but beyond them there was still nothing but blackness. It was the same when he looked through the windows on the other side of the plane. No tower, no other aircraft, no buildings, no groundstaff. Nothing.

'A short airstrip, Georgi?' he repeated. 'It's not even a damned airfield.'

'It was once. Relax.'

He wasn't surprised when no one was waiting to meet them off the aircraft. The icy gale lashed hail against his face and snatched the very breath from his lips. Too old, he thought again; old and cold. He felt Zavarov grab his elbow and hurry him away from the plane. He squinted up through the hail and now saw that they were rushing towards two sets of headlights fifty or sixty yards away. But it wasn't the weather for questions or arguments. He went where the Marshal steered him.

A moment later he found himself seated inside a wide, well-heated car that smelt wonderfully of leather and newness. Zavarov slid in beside him, shut the door with a quiet clunk and said something softly to the driver.

As they glided away from the runaway between walls of snow, Ligachev lifted his chin from his scarf and gratefully gulped in the warm air that filled the car. Gradually he felt his circulation return; and with it his curiosity.

'Who is this friend of yours?' he asked, not for the first time.

'I told you. Someone like me who worries about what's happening to his country.' Zavarov turned his head to look at him. 'Someone like you used to be, Yegor. A patriot.'

'You never stop, do you?'

'I can't afford to.'

'Your friend better be worth all this trouble.'

Zavarov patted his arm. 'He is. He certainly is.'

They wound uphill through a dense forest, its trees picked out like spectres in the headlights. Shadows doubled and merged in the beams of the other vehicle that had followed them from the airfield.

After some minutes he became aware of passing through a guard-post, suggesting that they were entering an enclosed estate of some sort. He caught a glimpse of raised barriers and the silhouettes of armed men. Whoever this friend of Zavarov's was, he had himself well set up. At least as well as any of them on the Politburo.

. They continued climbing and then the ground began to level. He became conscious of a strange jumble of yelping and baying noises, high-pitched and eerie. He realised that it had been building for some time but now it seemed to be right beside them. He peered out through the window again. Zavarov showed no interest, watching him instead.

On each side of the car were long wooden sheds, wholly encased in wire mesh and open to the frost and weather. They were raised off the ground on stilts three or four feet high. Boxes or containers sat beneath them. It was from the sheds that the noises were coming. As the headlamp beams swept over one of the units he caught a glimpse of the animals inside. Now he recognised the noises. Even in the luxurious car their sharp smell reached him, drawn in by the powerful heater.

'Foxes,' he said to Zavarov. 'This is a fox farm?'

'Enterprise Number 573, Minsk District.'

'Minsk? We're in Byelorussia?'

The Marshal was smiling at him. 'The pelts belong to the Minsk and District Trade Administration. They're not as sought after as, say, sable, but they enjoy a solid enough market. Most are worn by our own people but many are auctioned in Leningrad and from there go all over the world. People pay good money for them. The money belongs to the state. This little farm, Yegor, is part of one of our nation's greatest sources of foreign exchange.'

'Stop sounding like a textbook, Georgi.'

'You don't like my little economics lecture? Mikhail Sergeyevich would. He's very big on economics. You told me so yourself.'

'What's your point?'

'The money from the pelts belongs to the state. But a fox does a lot of pissing before it becomes just a pelt.'

'What?'

'It pisses. The state doesn't care. Perfume makers do. So we add a few preservatives and sell it to some of the biggest perfume houses in Warsaw, Prague, Budapest. We ship it through Riga to London and Stockholm. When the pack ice closes in we entrain it to Hamburg instead. Foreign exchange, Yegor. Which the state doesn't want.'

'My God!' hissed Ligachev, hardly able to believe his ears. 'You have a nerve to bring me here! Right into one of your crooked schemes.'

Zavarov laughed. 'You've arrived, Yegor.'

Letters in the safe. Not many, only seven or eight. Each still in its original envelope, then all of them had been slipped together inside a larger envelope.

On the floor she'd arranged everything in exactly the order she'd found them in the safe, so that she'd know how to put them back again. A death certificate. Some bits and pieces of her mother's jewellery. Her identification papers.

The surprising thing was that, unlike the apartment, the safe contained nothing of him. Apart from these things of Katarina's, it was a business-only affair; mostly cash and some small jeweller's sacks of diamonds. Perhaps the diamonds were real, perhaps not; he had uses for both.

Now she took the letters a little distance away, as if she knew that they merited a separateness from the wares of his trade, and sat down on the carpet to examine them.

All were addressed to her mother. All were dated before her own birth. Her fingers trembled as she took one at random and opened it.

It was full of love. She bit on her lip as she read it. There was loneliness too. And at the end, a signature. The ink was browning and fading with age, but it was still legible.

It wasn't the kind of name she expected. Not Russian.

Ligachev had failed to notice their approach to the large house. They climbed out, Zavarov still chuckling, and followed the hulking driver to a room at the back of the ground floor. Ligachev made straight for the roaring fire at the far end, set in a wide fireplace such as he associated with old mansions. He unbuttoned his coat and stood warming his tired bones, silently cursing Zavarov. Then he heard a door open and close behind him.

When he turned he saw a tall, well-dressed man waiting at the other end of the room. He was smoking a thin cheroot. Zavarov muttered some greeting but the man's eyes remained on him, Ligachev. As he approached, his features seemed familiar.

'Who are you?' Ligachev demanded brusquely. He found the man's steady gaze and confident manner uncomfortable. The stranger smiled and continued looking him straight in the eye.

'Who the blazes are you?' Ligachev said again.

The newcomer stretched out a hand.

'Serov, Nikolai Vasiliyevich Serov. But let's not stand on ceremony, comrade. Let's be plain. I'm the man who can make you the next General Secretary of the Soviet Union.'

PART TWO

15

Home Secretary William Clarke slammed the door after him as he strode out of the Cabinet Room in Number Ten. It was one of a set of double doors and its twin shuddered with the impact. The Private Secretary, whose office was across the hall, looked up at the noise and stared at him in surprise.

Clarke could feel his cheeks burning with anger. Behind him in the Cabinet Room, as well as the PM, he had left the Foreign Secretary, the Cabinet Secretary and that man Gaunt: Sir Horace now, since the publication of the New Year Honours List. Conscious of the Secretary's gaze, Clarke bent his head in a poor attempt at camouflage and made a show of looking at his watch.

It was exactly two minutes past three. Twenty-four hours from now he might no longer be Home Secretary. In fact, almost certainly not; this Prime Minister never backed down.

He hurried across the hall, grateful to be out of the Secretary's gaze, and tried to recover his composure as he descended the stairs.

He could still hardly believe what he had just been told. It wasn't so much that they had made the decision without involving him, though that was bad enough; after all, he was supposed to be responsible for Gaunt's filthy operation. No no, far more awful was the nature of the decision itself, the action, as Gaunt kept calling it. God, how could they even contemplate such a thing!

In the downstairs hallway his two detectives were waiting for him. The Private Secretary had presumably alerted them that he was on his way. They fell silently in step and accompanied him outside.

George, his driver, was already holding the door of the black Jaguar open for him.

'Copperfields, Home Secretary?' he asked, referring to Clarke's home in Buckinghamshire. At this time on a Friday it was their usual destination.

'No. Queen Anne's Gate.'

Clarke got in. One of the detectives, a man called Fielding, climbed into the front seat; the other went to the black Rover that had drawn up behind them.

The short drive passed in silence, neither George nor Fielding trying to engage him in smalltalk; his mood, he supposed, was obvious to them.

Ten minutes later he was in his office, with his secretary sitting before him. She also had sensed his mood. She waited patiently, knees demurely pressed together and pencil poised above the shorthand pad on her lap, while he gazed unseeing through the window. Eventually he swung around to face her.

'This letter is highly confidential.'

The secretary lifted her eyebrows imperceptibly; she regarded everything in her work as falling into that category.

'It's Saturday tomorrow,' he said. 'You'll hardly want to type this then, but that's when it's being written. Date it accordingly. To the Prime Minister.'

Her pencil jotted the date at the top of her pad, scratched some more, then was still.

'"In the absence of any satisfactory response to my request of yesterday . . . I am obliged, with immediate effect and the deepest regret . . . to resign my appointment as Secretary of State for the Home Office." Not too fast for you, I trust?'

The secretary shook her head. Her pencil scratched busily on, as unperturbed as if he were dictating the weather forecast.

Bloody civil servants, Clarke mused, and gathered his thoughts for the rest of the letter.

'Now for the reasons why.'

He left the office as soon as the letter was ready and settled himself moodily in the back seat of the car. As usual, Fielding the detective was in the front, beside George. The early edition of the evening paper had a story about bomb threats against the Opec conference; it would have nothing that Clarke didn't know already but he scanned it anyway as they picked their way through the traffic.

Hyde Park Corner was well and truly snarled up. George made the Jaguar weave through every gap as if it were a Mini. But instead of heading up Park Lane they swung off towards Knightsbridge.

'It's because of Lancaster Gate, Home Secretary,' George explained. 'The Opec jamboree. Starts Tuesday, doesn't it? There's been all those bomb hoaxes so they've closed off a bit of Bayswater Road and some of the streets behind the hotel. It's a mess and no mistake. Best to avoid the whole area.'

'I see.'

'A-rabs,' George muttered. 'Don't know why we let them come here, sir. Them and their conference. Clogging up our traffic.'

Fielding looked out of the window and tried to suppress a smile, and Clarke returned to the newspaper. They cut through Shepherd's Bush and picked up their route from there. By then Clarke had switched off his reading light and was just staring out at the people and the traffic, lost in his thoughts.

Again no one disturbed him.

Two hours later he had eaten and showered. He sat naked at his dressing-table, letting the warmth of the bedroom dry his skin where the towel had missed. The papers on which he was working came from a red box with a gold leaf crest that lay open by his elbow. There was another one on the nearer of the room's two twin beds, locked shut. The leather that covered both boxes was scuffed with age and use.

Outside, a rising breeze foretold rain. It rustled the leafless branches of the clematis that covered the south-facing wall of the house. Twigs scratched at the bedroom window like fingernails. The small sound, muted as it was by the curtain, was enough to distract Clarke's attention. He shifted in the chair, irritated at his own edginess.

Finally he went to the window and drew the curtain aside. In the dark glass there was only his own naked reflection. He pulled on a dressing-gown, then, leaving the curtain open, he crossed the room and switched out the lights. The moon was high in the sky, full and rich, though soon to be obscured by the scudding clouds. The wind stirred the clematis again and he glanced down at the source of the sound. His focus shifted to the flagstoned terrace where a uniformed policeman stood gazing up at him. Clarke lifted a hand to signal that everything was all right; the officer saluted and turned away. Clarke watched until he disappeared across the dark lawn, his uniform merging with the night. There were men in the woodland too.

Well, he told himself, tomorrow night they'd be gone. All apart from two, who'd stay with him for the rest of his life; that was how it had to be in these terrorist-ridden days.

A sudden, more forceful gust of wind rattled the clematis against the window again, harder this time. Large drops of rain splattered the glass. He blinked, sighed and went back to his seat and the red box.

'Last one,' he said. He squared his shoulders and added, 'Probably ever.'

He read on for about ten minutes, jotting an occasional comment, then peered at his watch where he'd dropped it on the nearer bed. He strapped it onto his wrist and stared blankly at the work that still waited, then at the envelope containing his resignation, propped against the dressing-table mirror. He would deliver it personally to Chequers tomorrow, where the PM was spending the weekend with King Fahd and some of the Opec delegates. Unless he heard from the PM first. No chance.

With that he made up his mind.

There were two telephones by his bed. He rose from the dressing-table and picked up the ivory coloured one. To his surprise he found that the number he wanted was still in his memory. He tapped it out and waited. It was answered after just a couple of rings.

'This is Edmund Knight.'

'Edmund. Bill Clarke here –'

But Knight's voice carried on. 'I'm sorry I'm not here at the moment.'

'Damn.' Clarke slumped down on the bed and waited for the voice to finish.

'Please leave your message and I'll return your call as soon as I can. Thank you.'

Clarke waited for the end of the warning tone.

'Edmund, it's Bill Clarke. I need to talk to you. Sooner the better, really. In confidence. I'm at home this weekend. Could you call me the first chance you get?'

He rang off and sat staring at the receiver for a minute or two, wondering if he was doing the right thing. He became irritated again. Inaction was worse than even dubious action.

He picked up the phone again and tapped in another number. This time it rang for quite a time before being picked up.

'Mr Brook?' said Clarke.

'Speaking.'

'This is Mr Williams. I'd like to call by this evening. I realise it's very short notice.'

There was a silence while the receiver was muffled, a lengthy pause, then the voice returned.

'Nine o'clock, Mr Williams.'

It was a statement, not a suggestion; take it or leave it. Clarke replaced the handset and got back to the box, determined to get it out of the way.

Some minutes later Marion came into the bedroom. Seeing the red boxes, she offered no greeting to disturb him. As she was slipping out again he looked up.

'Did I mention I have to go out this evening?'

'No.'

He saw the slight tightening of expression that was the only sign of her anger and disappointment. Over the years she'd learnt to control the signs. She had to.

'I have to see someone,' he went on. 'Just came up this afternoon. Meant to mention it earlier. Might be back a bit late.' He initialled a paper and began to read rapidly through the next one. Pen in mid-air, he glanced up and flashed her a quick smile. 'Don't wait up.'

Then his head was down again and poring over the page. Marion shut the door softly as she left.

He read through another paper or two before picking up the pale blue

114

telephone. This time he only had to tap out three digits. It was answered at once.

'Home Secretary?'

'George, we'll be going out about eight thirty. I forgot to warn you earlier.'

'All right, sir.'

'We'll be back about one.'

'Very good.'

'Who's on duty tonight?' Now that he was at home only one of the detectives would be taking what they called the graveyard shift.

'Fielding, sir.'

'Let him know I won't be requiring him. Your company will be sufficient.'

'Home Secretary –'

'Thank you, George. Front door, eight thirty.'

At eight fifteen he finished the box and dressed. As he descended the wide staircase he saw Fielding waiting by the door. He moved across the hall to speak, but Clarke stole the initiative from him.

'Sergeant, just the man I want to see. There are two boxes in my bedroom. I've finished with both of them. Please fetch them in the course of the evening and see they're safely looked after.'

'Certainly, sir. Home Secretary –'

But Clarke was already under George's umbrella and climbing into the back of the Jaguar. George closed the door after him and walked around to the front of the car. Clarke saw the resigned face he made at Fielding as he folded the umbrella and opened his door. The detective turned away and walked back into the house.

The car picked up speed when they reached the minor public road that bordered Copperfield's forty acres. They came downhill into Chalfont, almost empty of people and cars, and headed north-west. George knew the best cross-country roads to avoid the Friday evening traffic.

The rain was pelting down now.

The turning into the lane was very tight and the lane itself narrow. George practically had to stop the Jaguar dead to negotiate it. His headlights picked out the two signboards for a moment. The larger one said 'Thomson's Nurseries, Suppliers To The Trade'. The smaller board on the other side said 'Brook Cottage'.

He took it very slowly along the lane; here and there untrimmed hedges scraped the side of the wide car. The rain had stopped but overhanging branches of the trees that fringed the lane dripped water onto the windscreen.

After about a hundred yards the cottage came in sight. Two lights were burning: one downstairs, bright and yellow through the open curtains, and one upstairs, reddish-orange and shaded behind drawn blinds.

George nosed the car into the short spur that led off the lane to the cottage. Clarke got out without a word and went through the gate in the fence to the cottage door.

George reversed into a three-point turn to face the car down the lane again. As he was swinging around he saw the porch light come on and the door open. The man he'd seen on Clarke's previous visits appeared for a moment, then Clarke and he went inside.

George waited until he was parked before flicking the telephone in the car's central console onto standby and punching in the number of the security unit at Copperfields. Its ringing tone was relayed through the car's hi-fi speakers. When it was answered he picked up the handset and the voice of detective Fielding, the man who should have been there with them, came through on the receiver.

'We're here,' George told him.

'Where?'

'Where the hell do you think? The man's a pain.'

'You don't have to tell me, George.'

'You'll have to report it this time. If you don't and somebody finds out, we'll both be for the high jump.'

'I know, I know.'

George put the handset down. 'I bloody well hope so,' he muttered, and switched on Radio 4.

16

Three hours earlier, Viktor Kunaev's four-year-old son, Andrei, was playing in the hallway when Viktor got home to the cramped flat in Porchester Gardens. The boy cried out in delight and ran to embrace his father. Viktor scooped him up and made his way carefully through the strewn toys to the kitchen.

Anna was scrubbing vegetables in the sink. As soon as she saw Viktor's face she dried her hands on the dishtowel and took Andrei from him.

'You finish playing, my love,' she said gently to the boy. Her eyes never left Viktor's face. 'I'll read you a nice story after I've talked to Papa. Then it's bedtime.'

She sent Andrei back to the hallway and set the door ajar before turning to Viktor.

'What's happened? I thought your shift didn't finish until midnight.'

Viktor took off his duffel coat and let Anna drape it over her arm.

'Aren't you well, Viktor?'

His face expressionless, he crossed to the other side of the kitchen. As he passed the washing machine he reached down and swung its door shut. Then he drew a stool out from the breakfast corner and sat down to wait for her.

Anna knew now what it was about. She started the machine, empty though it was, and sat down beside him. They waited in silence while the drum filled with water. Only when it started churning noisily back and forth did he look up.

'It's tonight,' he whispered. 'I have to do it tonight. I know we wanted more time, Anna, but we can't have it. I do it tonight and we go in the morning.'

She sat forward, leaning her arms on his folded coat.

'What's happened?' Her voice was calm.

'Major General Valyukev. You know he's been with us from Yasyenevo this week?'

Anna nodded. The FCD's top brass were forever making inspection visits on field staff in the embassies. Viktor said they liked the travel perks.

'The pressure is on for my recall,' he went on. 'Now that my father's dead and neither of us has family in the USSR they've lost their hold on us. They don't like that.'

'It's just as Genrikh warned us, God rest his soul. But why such a rush now – tonight? Do they want us to catch the first flight tomorrow?'

'No, no. We've got a month as far as Yasyenevo is concerned. The urgency is because of something I overheard this afternoon.'

'An important thing, obviously.'

He nodded. 'Information that I don't entirely understand, but it should go across with us. I still want to take the other material as well. That's why I have to go back to the embassy. I said I was feeling ill, so that I could come here to give you some warning and get myself ready.'

Now she straightened up and patted the palm of her hand on his coat. 'So. God's will.'

She fell quiet again, trying to adjust to their new situation. Her eyes roved around the little kitchen, part of their home for the last eighteen months and now never to be seen after this night.

Viktor understood her feelings; it was the same turmoil that he'd been through in Moscow, while his father lay dying: the difference between planning and doing. They both knew they were leaving more than this flat behind: for all Moscow's shortcomings, there had been good things about their lives there as well. Friends, special places, the emotional currents of a society that didn't put material values first: Anna and he were leaving all of that behind.

He reached across the table and took her hand.

'I know it's such short notice, my love. But it's what we planned. The timing is all that's being forced on us. The decision itself was always our own.'

His words seemed to strengthen her and she tightened her grip on his hand. 'Then maybe we shouldn't even wait for morning. Why not go tonight, after you get back here? Especially if what you heard is so urgent.'

'Too dangerous. You know they watch this place. Most of the apartments in the building are the Directorate's, so we're easy to keep an eye on. Better to leave it till morning and it'll look as if we're just going shopping.'

She pursed her lips as she thought this over. Andrei came in with a problem about one of his toy cars; the battery had fallen loose.

'The money,' Viktor said, putting the child on his lap and taking the car. 'Where is it?'

'Where you put it.' She smiled. 'As you said, at least KGB apartments don't get burgled.'

She took a plant down from a small shelf and handed it to him. Some five- and ten-pound notes lay curled between the plastic pot and its glazed container. The amount was less than a hundred pounds at the last count, but it was more than enough for food and tickets to where he had in mind. He was glad that they'd had the foresight to set it aside. The banks were closed.

'And the things I need tonight?'

Anna went to a drawer and took out a pair of kitchen scissors, a roll of Elastoplast and a large handkerchief. She rolled the scissors and Elastoplast up in the hankie and put them in his duffel pocket.

'Now you're all organised. When will you go back?'

He gave the car back to Andrei and kissed him on the forehead. 'I'll leave it for an hour or two. If I'm ill I can't recover too soon. You're trembling, Anna.'

'It's just because there's so much to do.'

He set Andrei down and the child began playing at his feet.

'We've rehearsed it, Anna. You helped me and I know just what I have to do. There's nothing to worry about. On the contrary –' He stood up and put his arms about her. ' – there's everything to look forward to. For Andrei most of all.' He lowered his voice to a whisper. 'He has nothing to forget, my love, nothing to leave behind. Freedom to think and speak as he wants, Anna, to grow into a free man – that's what lies ahead for Andrei.'

'I know, I do know. I'm just a little tense. Until it's all over.'

'And it will be – within just a few days. You'll see.'

He hugged her close, hoping that what he said was true. Andrei looked up and, laughing, pushed his way between their legs. Viktor picked him up and included him in the embrace.

'Just a few days, Anna.'

He hugged his little family all the closer in case she might read the doubt in his eyes.

The Soviet embassy sat halfway along Kensington Palace Gardens, only a few minutes' walk from the flat. It was a road that, even in daylight, was made dark in all seasons by the large trees and the oppressive bulk of the block-like buildings that lined it.

The rear section of the embassy, the part that had the forest of strange aerials on the roof, housed the secure and electronically screened warren of rooms where the KGB personnel, the *rezidenti*, conducted their business.

Viktor was cleared by the watch officer through to the *rezidentura* section. Here he mounted a short staircase, not as imposing as the main staircase at the front of the building, but with a set of maroon velvet curtains that covered its side wall as if to make up for what it lacked in design grace.

He pressed the concealed button underneath the banister rail and went up to the first half-landing. He drew back the curtain to reveal a steel door, and waited in sight of the viewing glass set two-thirds of the way up it. After a moment the door swung open and an armed guard beckoned him into a room about the size of a small bathroom. Although they were on first name terms, the guard still made him produce his *rezident* pass and fed it through the scanner built into the metal desk.

Viktor looked around the room at the security systems that he was about to violate. In a top corner a camera shielded by bullet-proof glass clicked a photograph every fifteen seconds for as long as anyone was in the room with the guard. Behind the desk six television monitor screens covered the area of the embassy from which he had come, as well as the corridors and certain offices of the *rezidentura* annex that he would shortly enter. Happily, because of the confidentiality of the cipher section, his own office couldn't be monitored.

The guard turned to a door on the opposite side of the room. It was also steel and had two combination locks and a card-key system. He set one of the combination locks, inserted Viktor's pass into a slot in the door, and set the other lock. With some effort he pulled the door open for him to pass through.

It closed with a sigh of expelled air and Viktor set off down the familiar corridor. For the last time. More steel doors led off to various offices on either side. Two doors of white-painted wood led to the incinerator rooms where he and the other clerks disposed of the routine material that was generated daily. Nearby, another door led to a much larger and more powerful incinerator. Only the chief of the *rezidentura* could enter this room. Its incinerator was designed to his own specifications for the destruction of whole files, cipher books, agent dossiers and other bulky material.

Behind one of the steel doors on the left was the cipher room and next to it the historical files vault. Opposite was a conference room.

Near the end of the corridor was Viktor's own tiny office. Once inside, he locked its door behind him before sliding open a drawer of his desk and unlocking the safe.

There were sixteen files that he planned to go through. He removed them from the safe and stacked them on the desk. A number of the documents in the first file had their top right-hand corners folded down. This was a marking process that he had begun from the day he got back after his father's funeral. Every day he had set aside a few minutes to identify the material that he was planning to extract.

Now he ripped each of these documents out, not wanting to waste time undoing the fastening to get at each one, and began making a pile of them in the open drawer. When he finished he swept up the little shreds of paper that had fallen out and dropped them into the bin.

He went through each of the other fifteen files in the same methodical way.

The stack of papers with which he ended up was about four inches high. Viktor ran his thumb along its edge. It was about as much as he'd calculated.

Now came what he knew was the most dangerous part. If anyone came to his door it would be difficult to clear away quickly the signs of what he was up to. And he knew from the rehearsals with Anna that it would take another fifteen minutes or so.

He pulled his duffel coat off and threw it over the chair, and got out the Elastoplast, scissors and handkerchief. He cut the Elastoplast into about thirty strips four inches long, which he tacked by their corners along the edge of the desk.

Then he stood up, undid his belt and dropped his trousers, the loosest-fitting pair he owned. Sitting down again he raised his feet, ludicrously tethered by the trousers about his ankles, onto the desk, took a wad of documents, rolled it around his calf and fastened it tightly to itself with strips of Elastoplast. He used the handkerchief to wipe his calf dry of the perspiration that was starting to cover it and the rest of his body in a slippery film, and taped the top of the wad in position against his leg.

Finally, he rolled his sock up over the papers and repeated the process with the other leg, then taped another wad to the inside of each thigh and pulled the trousers up, zipping his fly but leaving the top clasp and the belt undone.

Next he pulled up his jumper and shirt and lined his belly and sides in the same way, slipping each handful of documents an inch or two inside his underpants for additional support and taping them in position as before.

When he'd finished the whole job he tucked his shirt back in, fastened the trouser clasp and drew the belt as tight as he could bear. There seemed no possibility of the papers slipping.

He tidied up as quickly as possible and relocked the desk and safe. The roll of Elastoplast was finished but he returned its cardboard former and the scissors to his duffel pocket. Then he put the coat on and forced himself to stand absolutely still, watching as the second hand of his watch made two complete revolutions. While he waited, he breathed deeply and evenly to calm himself.

Taking a final look around the room, he ran his hands quickly over his clothes to smooth them and check for bulges, and stepped outside. The clock in the corridor said that he'd been in the office thirty-five minutes.

The process of leaving the *rezidentura* annex was the reverse of entering.

'You weren't long,' the guard grunted at him.

'I don't feel well.'

The man seemed to be taking far longer with his pass than before, but Viktor knew that was only an illusion induced by his nervousness. He tried not to look at the camera in the corner, then wondered why it mattered; by the time the photographs were seen by anyone he would be beyond their reach.

He hoped.

The guard contented himself with only a cursory glance inside his briefcase and wished him goodnight.

He was as lucky in the front lobby, where the watch officer was too absorbed with the paperback he was trying to read under his desk to do more than wave a hand lazily at him as he passed. Similarly, the guard who stood by the front door hardly looked at him.

Outside, he drew up his duffel hood against the heavy drizzle that was setting in. The wrought-iron gate at the foot of the short drive swung open to let him through, remote-controlled by the guard at the front door.

There were still risks to calculate. The embassy stood on what the British called Crown land. If he had been found out already and someone followed him, would they wait until he got to a public road before trying to grab him? On the other hand, what difference could that make? A kidnap was a kidnap, wherever it happened.

Twenty yards along from the embassy was a wooden and glass sentinel hut used by the British policemen who guarded the road. One of them was sheltering in it from the rain. Surely no one would try anything within sight of him or the others at the end of the road?

The policemen were armed. They claimed not to be; the British disliked policemen with guns. But one summer day when they were in their shirtsleeves, Viktor had seen a revolver in an officer's trouser pocket. Would they be prepared to use their guns in defence of a Soviet citizen? He doubted it.

The policeman nodded a courteous greeting as he passed, but Viktor was walking with the concentration of a man crossing a minefield, his mind on every step and slight shift of papers about his body, real or imagined.

It was a blessed relief when he got onto the main road, good just to be away from the claustrophobia and stillness of the embassy's road and among the reassuring bustle of traffic and people.

He turned right and began walking along Bayswater Road. The traffic on the east-bound carriageway was still jammed solid because of the re-routing and detour signs around Lancaster Gate. The faces of the drivers looked short-tempered and irritable. The rain, turning into a downpour now, would add to their problems.

One part of Viktor wanted to follow the quiet streets home. He felt like a walking parcel, one that might fall apart at any moment. But a stronger instinct told him to stay where there were crowds. He'd taken enough chances for one night.

So he picked his way between the jammed cars to the other side of the road and stuck resolutely to the broad, busy pavement. As he passed the underground entrance and turned into Queensway, he noticed the headline on the news-stand. It was the same story that William Clarke had read earlier: More Opec Bomb Threats.

When he finally got home he was so relieved that he hardly felt a thing as Anna tore the strips of tape away. The papers closest to his skin were soft with sweat. She hung them over radiators and pegged them out on clotheshorses. He saw the funny side but she couldn't.

Then they switched on the washing machine and talked about what they had to do in the morning.

17

Buckinghamshire

Midnight. Moonlight broke through the clouds above Brook Cottage and gleamed on the old vixen's coarse coat as she moved from the hedgerow into the field. She picked her way between the rows of young conifers and pot-growing shrubs where the fieldmice scurried. They made easy pickings for her. She snapped one up and continued her progress along the rows.

When she reached the greenhouses at the end she followed her customary line around them, veering south towards the lane. She paused by the verge, her nostrils twitching at the alien stench of engine oil and metal that suddenly reached them. She padded softly along to investigate, keeping to the cover of the hedge.

The car was stationary, its width blocking the lane. Its fat tyres flattened the grass. A man sat inside it in darkness.

The vixen kept very still, her belly to the wet earth, her senses sharp and calculating. They gradually told her that the man in the car was asleep, that there had been no movement from him or the car for a long time, and that all was quiet at the cottage. But she waited to be sure. That was why she was an old vixen.

When she was certain, she left cover and continued down the lane. She didn't meander aimlessly as a dog might but loped confidently straight ahead.

She had vanished under the holly hedge on the other side and was halfway across the next field by the time the white Sherpa van approached, its wheels slicing through the puddles.

The driver slowed to not much more than walking pace and glanced in his rearview mirror. Instinctively his passenger shifted position slightly to watch the road behind them in the wing mirror. The driver satisfied himself that no cars were approaching from either direction and switched his headlights off. He wanted to allow time for his eyes to adjust to the moonlight before he turned into the lane. His instructions warned him that it was narrow and he didn't want any noisy mishaps.

At that moment the moon slipped behind a bank of cloud and they overshot the lane anyway. The passenger saw it go past and clicked his fingers, pointing back. The driver braked. As the Sherpa stopped, the passenger produced two pairs of clear surgical gloves. Both men put them on.

They reversed back along the road, very slowly so that the engine noise was kept to a minimum, turned into the lane and drove up it at tickover speed. When William Clarke's black Jaguar came into view the driver turned his engine off and let the Sherpa roll to a halt fifteen or twenty yards from it. He left the vehicle in gear to avoid the ratching of the handbrake.

The clouds parted and a shaft of moonlight fell on them as they stepped out into the lane. The driver was thickset and bald; his passenger was taller and thin-faced. Both wore black trousers, black sweaters and dark jackets.

They didn't close the Sherpa's doors but just eased them back until they felt the locks touch the striker bars. Then, like the old vixen, they stood motionless and silent for a full two minutes, waiting while their senses absorbed all the information that the damp night air brought them. They heard an owl's distant hoot, small rustles in the under-growth. But no clicks of a cooling engine from the Jaguar nor anything else to alarm them.

The bald man reached inside his jacket and withdrew a silenced automatic pistol. His companion already had his gun out. They walked carefully to the Jaguar, never taking their eyes off it.

The bald man took up position by the driver's door and waited until his companion was beside the other. Pointing his pistol at the driver's head, he took a pen torch from his pocket and shone it for a second on the inside of the car door, just long enough to verify that the lock button was raised. He nodded to his companion, who put his hand ready on the door handle.

George started awake, still muddled with sleep, as his door was wrenched open and a hand clamped his mouth. He winced as his knee collided with the steering wheel. By the time he reached for the gun beneath his jacket the holster was empty. Instead he became aware that something cold was pressing against his forehead. The muzzle of a gun. He looked up. Silhouetted against the night sky was the man whose hand was over his mouth. The dim glow of the car's interior courtesy lamp reflected off his bald head. He was watching George with great seriousness.

A movement to the left caught George's attention and, unable to move his head under the bald man's grip, he swivelled his eyes to their limit. A man with skeletal features was leaning across from the passenger seat, levelling two pistols at him. One of them, he saw, was his own. He smelt a faint whiff of latex and realised that it was coming from the gloved hand over his mouth.

'Out. Not a sound, friend.'

George felt sick; he did as he was told. There was no sound but the wind in the trees as they shepherded him across the lane to the cottage.

'Open the gate.'

In the cottage only the downstairs light was now burning.

'Over there.' The bald man pushed him towards the light and followed him along the path. He peered into the window for a few seconds before pushing George up to it and putting his lips to his ear.

'Knock when I tell you. Then signal towards the door – let him know you want to be let in.' The pistol jabbed into George's ribs, angling up towards his heart. 'Don't be a hero.'

Out of the corner of his eye George noticed that the other man had taken up position beside the front door.

He looked in through the window. In the scullery sat the man who had opened the door to Clarke. He was watching television, his back to the window. The volume was very low and no sound reached George.

'Now, friend. Knock!'

In the distance George heard a vixen howl for her mate, a high, short scream that split the night and made him jump. At any other time he would have heard it as a sound of loneliness. Tonight it was the sound of freedom.

He shivered in the damp air and rapped on the pane.

No one saw the dusty Volvo station-wagon, its lights doused, that had drawn up at the foot of the lane. Nor the two women who stepped out of it. One of them crouched on the car's bonnet, raising herself above hedge level, and trained a pair of night-vision binoculars on the cottage. She was as soberly dressed as the bald man and his companion. She was fine-featured and pretty, and her jet-black hair had been cropped so that it was virtually a crew-cut. Her movements suggested an athlete's physical strength and control.

When the door of Brook Cottage opened and the man inside was overpowered, she whispered something to her companion and passed her the binoculars. Crouching low, she hurried along the lane, drawing a camera from inside her corduroy blouson. In the pale moonlight the Sherpa and the Jaguar were clearly visible, though not their registrations. But the woman with the crew-cut knew that the infra-red film would see and record all.

By the time the screaming started she had returned to the Volvo. She and her companion sat listening, their faces void of all expression. When the screaming finally stopped, the Volvo drew quietly away.

18

Moscow

No snow had fallen all day; the blizzards that had lashed the city for a fortnight had eased off at last. The contrast made the weather feel almost mild, although temperatures were still well below zero.

The snowploughs took advantage of the lull, clanking through the city and lining the thoroughfares with walls of snow. Five of them together swept across the vastness of Red Square in a staggered line, engines roaring and lights flashing.

The break in the weather lifted people's spirits. They had been held under virtual siege and now they were able to move freely again. It was the Winter Festival season. The special performances at the Stanislavski and Nemirovich-Danchenko theatres were packed, the queues outside even the bad restaurants seemed endless, crowds thronged to the circus, the cinemas and sports stadia, or just strolled through the streets and snow-covered public gardens.

Sverdlov Square was a particular attraction. Tonight the people who surged out of the Bolshoi felt no urgency to get home. Free troika rides, a tradition at Festival time, departed at intervals from Marx Prospekt; while people waited for the next carriage to arrive there was the huge New Year fir tree for them to admire in the centre of the square, encrusted with its thousands of multi-coloured lights.

Even the policemen seemed less forbidding than usual; they too were glad of the kinder weather. With the populace less cooped up and driven in upon one another, they could expect fewer broken heads and skewered corpses. The reduced availability of alcohol helped as well, of course.

Nikolai Serov saw this lifting of winter's oppression, understood it all, understood the vein of relief that pulsed through his city. But it was as if he was looking at it through eyes of glass: analytical, capable of understanding, but finally, indifferent. He had his own long course to run yet. He had mapped it well, he had no doubts of that, but there were many others besides him who had to be steered through it.

Others such as Zavarov, whom he was to meet tonight.

It was not a time for talk. It was a time to listen, to hear where there was doubt and eliminate it, to keep men and events pressing in the right direction.

He found the Marshal already at the agreed meeting place under the Karl Marx statue. His great red face was bordered by a fur hat and ear muffs, and a bulky overcoat made his shoulders and chest look even larger than usual. He swigged from a silver hip-flask and offered it to Serov as he saw him approach.

'No thank you, Marshal.'

He wondered how much the man had already had to drink, and waited patiently while the old fool made a show of looking him up and down.

'A man should never refuse a mouthful of good Armenian brandy,' Zavarov said. 'At least, you shouldn't. You're a walking bag of nerves. I've never seen you looking as tense as these last few weeks.'

Serov watched a policeman over by the subway; he was chatting up a girl but his hand stayed resting on the holster in his belt.

'I've got a lot on my mind. Who hasn't? Drinking is no answer. And you smell like a distillery.'

Zavarov grinned. 'Ah well. I'm sticking with the only answer I know.' He took another mouthful, swishing it through his teeth before swallowing it; then he capped the flask, patted it fondly and slipped it into his pocket.

They moved off together from the statue, instinctively avoiding the brightness of the New Year tree and heading for the more shadowed edge of the square. A group of attractive women, expensively dressed but not hookers, passed them in the opposite direction. Zavarov's gaze followed them.

'Tell me, General,' he said, his eyes still on the women, 'What do you do for sex?'

'What a man usually does. What business is it of yours?'

'I didn't mean to be impertinent.' Zavarov held his hands up apologetically. 'I just meant I'd never seen you with a woman. Nor has anyone that I know of. You must have a little something tucked away somewhere.'

'Been asking around, have you?'

'Of course not. It was just a joke, that's all.'

Serov took his arm, like a man about to swap a pleasantry; but his hand squeezed the soft muscle through the heavy coat like a vice, and his voice was flat.

'Save your jokes, Marshal. Keep them to yourself till this is all over. Then you can crack them all the way to hell, for all I care. Don't ask about my private affairs again – or make comments about them – or even think about them. You understand?'

Zavarov nodded dumbly. Serov released his arm and began walking again. The Marshal stood for a moment rubbing his bruised muscle, then caught him up and they walked on together in silence. They met one of the policemen but the light was behind them and he didn't even bother trying to look into their faces.

At the corner of the square Serov stopped to light a cigar and drew deeply on it before speaking.

'Update me.'

He turned around and leant against a bench by one of the snow-covered flower beds that enclosed the square, turning so that he could see anyone that might approach them along the path in either direction. At present there was no one within sight or earshot.

Zavarov propped his forearms on the barrier and stared across to the other side of the square.

'Everything's going along just the way it should be. Naturally, Mikhail Sergeyevich has his moments of doubt. That's only to be expected – he thinks it's a high-risk plan. But he seems to suspect nothing.'

'Seems to?'

'He definitely suspects nothing.'

Serov watched him closely; without shifting his gaze he asked, 'Ligachev – how's he doing?'

Zavarov smacked his gloved hands together in a gesture of satisfaction. 'Absolutely no problem. I'm delighted. I look upon him as my special responsibility. Why not? I helped bring him back to the fold. All that nonsense about reconstruction and new directions – pah! I told you how well he performed the day we sold Mikhail Sergeyevich on the plan, didn't I? He continues to play his part well. The thought of all that power keeps him going, I suppose. Your boss, Chebrikov, he's good too. At the start I had my doubts about him – but now he's all right.'

'As I said he would be.'

The ear muffs wobbled as Zavarov nodded his great head. 'You were right, General, you were right.'

'Chebrikov's with us for the same reason as you. Because even if this fails he'll be no worse off than if he'd never tried.'

Zavarov looked uneasy at this assessment of his motives but put up no argument. 'Well, I'm glad we've got him. Mikhail Sergeyevich places great value on his advice.'

Serov had been keeping an eye on another of the policemen and now the man was slowly coming their way. It was time to begin walking along the path again. Time also to get to the main point.

'Now tell me about the money,' he said softly.

Zavarov lit a cigarette. 'Today Ligachev approved the portion of the funds that's to be drawn off from Central Committee reserves. Chebrikov and I have already authorised the amounts that will come from our budgets.'

'You're being discreet?'

'Believe me, we couldn't be more careful if we were embezzling the money for ourselves. The chance of anyone detecting what's going on must be one in a million. The funds should start moving next week.'

'You're cutting it fine. It should all have been set up already. The London operation gets under way next week. After that, things will happen fast.'

Zavarov looked pained. 'We're not magicians. There was no way we could organise matters more quickly. Don't forget how much cash is involved here. We can't just deliver it in a few suitcases, you know.'

Serov grunted, giving no clue if he accepted what the Marshal said.

'Listen,' Zavarov went on, a note of complaint entering his voice. 'Isn't it time you told me how things are going at your end? Remember what Ligachev said at Molodechno – the whole thing blows apart if you can't deliver your part of it.'

Serov shrugged. 'Find something else to worry about. I can handle my end. The people in London know what they're doing.'

Zavarov glanced nervously across at him. 'Are you really prepared to go through with your role?'

Serov laughed. A family group of grandparents, parents and teenage children were standing nearby. Some of them glanced over and smiled, pleased to see someone else enjoying a pleasant evening. He returned their smiles politely.

'Comrade Marshal – would I have started this if I wasn't prepared to go through with it – all of it?'

By now they were back at the Marx statue. Serov stopped by its base and stared at the inscription.

'"Workers of the world, unite!"' he read aloud, 'There you have it, Marshal. That's exactly what we're doing.'

He stood looking up at the statue for a moment, then he turned and gripped Zavarov's shoulder.

'Don't drink too much, comrade Marshal. Difficult days lie ahead. Days to be sober in.'

He strode quickly off before Zavarov could say anything or ask further questions. A short distance away he looked back: just in time to catch the flash of reflected light as the Marshal pressed the silver flask to his lips.

Missing her was what took him to Galina's apartment. Perhaps Zavarov's salacious question had something to do with it as well. But when he got there he just stood in the middle of the studio floor, smoking, and wondered what purpose he had served in coming.

It was as if she was due back any minute. A record on the turntable, magazines on the couch, the bed even turned down, waiting for her warm body. Paintings still stood on their easels, including the city scene with its oppressed people that had puzzled him. On the paint-stained table there was a row of jars filled with cleaning fluid. Her brushes had been left soaking in them; she never left them like that longer than overnight for fear of warping their bristles.

His skin prickled, as if a sixth sense was telling him that he was being watched, and he swung abruptly around: so instantly that his hand hadn't even reached the Makarov under his greatcoat. But of course no one was there.

Only Katarina's bust.

The breath that he'd been holding came out harshly, shaded blue with cigar smoke.

Her empty eyes were in shadow, making it all too easy to believe that they weren't really empty. Maybe Zavarov was right: he was a bag of nerves.

He stepped quickly across the studio floor and moved the pedestal an inch to dispel the unnerving illusion of the watching eyes.

His own bust, or at least its remains, stood on the adjacent pedestal, and he stared at its wreckage for a long time. In Galina's absence he'd finally removed the cloth: whether merely to satisfy his own curiosity or also to spite her in some secret way, he wasn't sure. What he was sure of was that the shock of finding his image demolished like that had chilled him to the marrow. Just remembering that night of discovery made him shudder again. Why had he come here?

He picked the cloth up from the floor where it had lain since that night and threw it over the wrecked bust.

He was on his way out of the apartment when he turned and crossed to the work table. He selected the largest cloth from a pile of cleaning rags in the corner.

He draped the cloth over Katarina's bust and left.

19

Saturday dawned fresh and clean after the rain. It was just first light as James Thomson's Land Rover pulled in at the foot of the lane that led to Brook Cottage. Old James got out and studied the Nurseries sign for a moment. It was definitely more askew than yesterday.

He hoisted himself over the low fence and tugged at one of the uprights. Loose. He tried the other. Just as bad. His face puckered in annoyance; he'd have to make time to fix it later.

He reviewed the rest of his plans for the morning as he swung the Land Rover into the lane. Light jobs were what he stuck to these days. Sorting out trays of bedding plants, grouping and pricing them: that was his agenda today. He glanced at his sandwich box and smiled. He'd start with a nice cup of tea. First things first.

A transistor radio lay on the seat beside him. As he bumped along he started to tune it, glancing down at the dial. He finished and looked up again just in time to see the big black car. He cursed and hit the brakes. The Land Rover lurched to a standstill.

James folded his arms across the steering wheel and tilted his cap to the back of his head to contemplate the problem. There was no way he could get past the Jaguar. Both its front doors were wide open but even if he got out and closed them the car was still too wide. He'd take half the hedge with him if he tried to squeeze past. And he didn't want to be blamed for scraping that expensive bodywork.

He pumped his horn lightly a couple of times and stretched up in his seat to watch Brook Cottage. No one appeared. Over the chatter of the radio he heard a dog barking somewhere across the fields but otherwise there was no sound, no movement. He waited a minute more and pumped his horn again, slightly more insistent notes this time. Still nothing.

'Come on,' he muttered. 'You can't be that far away. Not the way you've left your motor open to the world.'

Exasperated, he climbed down from the Land Rover for the second time. He shook his head sadly. Big cars had become a common enough sight in the lane since the young couple had come to live in the cottage last year. Not that James minded. Their visitors usually parked with more consideration, that was all he cared about.

'Common courtesy,' he said.

He hoped this morning wasn't the thin end of a wedge. Come to think of it, their friends usually came visiting in the afternoon or evening. James looked up at the lightening sky.

'Funny time of day to call.'

As he walked past the Jaguar on his way to the cottage a faint beeping sound caught his attention. It was coming from the car. He peered into the interior and spotted the telephone.

'Flash,' he said.

He straightened up and looked at the cottage. Now that he had a clear view, he could see that its front door was lying as wide open as the Jaguar's. Taken together, it all suggested that someone was just dropping in, not intending to stay long. Which made it all the more daft that they'd wandered off someplace where they couldn't hear his horn.

'Hallo!' he called out. He waited but got no response. He repeated it, louder, cupping his hands around his mouth. Still no answer.

Without really meaning it, he muttered something about moving the damned car himself and glanced inside it again just as he was about to walk on. That was when he noticed the keys still in the ignition. He laughed at the thought of really sliding in behind that wheel and having a go.

'Oh yes,' he chuckled.

Then something jarred. It took a moment to figure out just what it was.

The dew. An even film of dewfall was spread across the roof, bonnet, windscreen and boot. Some had also gathered on the interior lining of the open door nearest him.

It wasn't rain. There hadn't been any since last evening. Besides, rain didn't settle like that. Especially if a car was driving through it.

If it was dew, he thought uneasily, then the Jaguar had been there all night. With its doors lying open. Why would someone leave a car that way?

Something was wrong. What about the cottage door? Had it been open all night as well?

The car phone beeped again, startling James. He began backing away, as if he feared the phone. His hand bumped against the gate and he turned to stare at the cottage.

'Hallo,' he called again. 'Anybody home?'

Reluctantly he pushed through the gate and went up to the front door. He had to hold it from swinging away from him as he banged with the knocker. No answer. He banged a few more times.

He went in. The downstairs was just a scullery and a sitting-room. Both rooms were empty, although the television was on in the scullery.

The Open University motif filled the screen. The announcer's voice was saying something about tropical rain forests. The volume was low, barely audible.

'Hallo?' James called at the foot of the stairs.

He listened and thought he heard a slight scuffling noise. Just for an instant, then it stopped. It came from one of the bedrooms; there were only two. He'd have to go up and see. He climbed the stairs slowly and looked in the open door of the first room.

The bodies seemed to be all over the place. He was too shocked to take in exactly how many there were. There was blood everywhere. The smell now hit him and it was awful, a metallic stench of blood mingled with something rotten.

James threw up before he could stop himself. Then, as he hung his head in the doorway, clinging to the jamb for support and watching the strings of vomit trickling from his mouth, he caught the quick movement in the corner of the room. He tried to focus on it but the retching had filled his eyes with water and the image was blurred.

He wiped his eyes and tried again. This time he made out the unmistakable muzzles and white-tipped brushes of the foxes. With a snarl they dashed right at him. He jumped out of their way and they tore past him and down the stairs.

James cursed after them until his lungs ached. He pushed himself from the doorway and lurched up against the banister rail. Bloody pawprints stained the stairs.

Through the front door and scullery window he saw the foxes race across his land. He watched, gasping for breath, until they vanished. Something else caught his eye, this time in the lane. A black Rover was approaching. He stared at it, wiping his eyes again, while it drew up behind his Land Rover. Two men in dark raincoats got out. They paused for a moment by the abandoned Jaguar, then hurried towards Brook Cottage.

'Up here,' James whispered, and crumpled down by the bedroom door.

Viktor and Anna Kunaev had been up since six, each having slept hardly a wink. Because of Viktor's fear of arousing suspicion they waited until nine o'clock before setting out.

When they stepped into Porchester Gardens everything about them suggested that they were off for a morning in town, perhaps a visit to the sales. Thousands of other young couples were setting out with the same objective that morning. They might have been planning to return some toy of Andrei's that they'd already bought and found faulty, because a large, colourful toy carton was tucked under Viktor's arm.

They stopped off for a couple of minutes at the post office on the corner before strolling south along Queensway. They walked abreast or in single file as the numbers of people allowed, and took it in turn to hold Andrei's hand.

From Bayswater they took the Circle line south. Unlike the other shoppers they didn't change for Oxford Circus or get off to Kensington, but stayed on as far as Embankment, where they hurried through the station and took the Northern line to Waterloo.

When the escalator brought them up to the British Rail concourse they turned left and checked the departures board at that end of the station. Anna took Andrei into the W. H. Smith shop and helped him choose some comics and a picture book. Viktor went to the opposite side of the concourse and bought tickets.

They boarded the train on platform twenty at nine fifty-eight. The tickets were one-way.

Knight got home from Eva's a little after ten. The answerphone had a call from someone selling double glazing and a message from a local bookshop. Knight sorted through his mail and newspapers as he listened.

'Edmund, it's Bill Clarke.'

Knight stared at the answerphone.

'I need to talk to you. Sooner the better, really. In confidence. I'm at home this weekend. Could you call me the first chance you get?'

He put down the papers and played the message again, hearing a tenseness in the voice that he hadn't noticed the first time. Clarke was angry or rattled about something.

There were two numbers for Copperfields. One was Clarke's official line and would most likely be answered by a Special Branch man. The other number was the one he gave to family and friends, and would be picked up by himself or Marion. Knight found the personal number and keyed it in.

'Who is this?' a man's voice asked, one that Knight didn't recognise.

'Hello?' he said tentatively.

'Who did you wish to speak to, sir?'

What was a Special Branch man doing on Bill Clarke's personal number?

'William Clarke. Is he there?'

There was a pause before the voice answered. 'I'm afraid Mr Clarke's not available. Could I ask who's calling him?'

But Clarke had requested confidentiality.

'This is a personal call. When will he be available?'

Another pause, longer this time, as if the man were consulting with someone, or as if that someone were listening in and feeding him his answers.

'That's hard to say, sir.'

'Is Mr Clarke actually at home or not?'

'Not at the moment. If you would tell me who you are, sir?'

'Is Mrs Clarke there?'

'I'm afraid she's not available either.'

It made no sense: Clarke not available and not even at home. He'd said he would be. Something might have come up, but that didn't explain what a Special Branch man was doing on his line. Why wasn't Marion 'available' either?

'Sir? Are you still there? Perhaps you'd like to tell me why you wanted to speak to Mr Clarke?'

If someone was listening in, the chances were that they would also be trying to trace the call.

The Special Branch man was still in mid-sentence when Knight put the receiver down.

20

He heard the car pull into his drive a couple of minutes later. He was crossing the hall and detoured to open the front door; he was expecting no one.

A white Sierra from the local taxi service was ticking over a few yards from the door while a man leant into its window to pay the driver. There was a brightly illustrated cardboard carton, like a box that toys came in, at his feet. Behind him stood a woman looking up at the house, and near her a small boy clutching an armful of comics. The woman saw Knight at the door and immediately lowered her gaze. Her hand sought out the boy's.

The man picked up the carton and turned as the Sierra drew away. He put his arm around the woman and stared at Knight for a moment.

'Mr Edmund Knight?'

'That's right. Good morning.'

Knight stuck his hands into his pockets and waited. His visitors seemed uncertain what to say or do next. There was something waif-like about them, as if they were lost. He studied them more closely: their faces, their clothes. Something troubled him about them but he couldn't yet pin down what it was.

The man passed the toy carton to the woman and stepped closer. He was in his early thirties, the woman a little younger.

'How can I help you?' Knight prompted.

'My name is Viktor Kunaev,' the man said. 'This is my wife, Anna, and our son, Andrei.'

His accent was all the confirmation Knight needed. Their faces were faces that could be seen in any street in Moscow, their clothes were what might be picked off any rail of indifferent garments in a Moscow store. That was what had felt out of place about them.

'How can I help you?' he repeated, more reserved this time.

Kunaev paused for a moment and half-glanced back at his wife. 'I am a Soviet citizen. I work in our embassy in London.'

Knight glanced instinctively down the drive. Kunaev noticed and smiled.

'It's all right, Mr Knight. I was very careful. We have not been followed.'

'Why should you be?'

'For the same reason as my coming here has surprised you. Because of the jobs we both do. In our different ways and at our very different levels, of course.'

'What would they be?'

Kunaev produced a cheap-looking wallet and opened it. A passport and some other items lay inside, not tucked in its pockets but arranged on top as if he'd deliberately prepared them for this moment. He handed them over and glanced back at his wife as Knight began to look through them. As well as a Soviet passport there was a junior-grade Soviet diplomatic pass. Both bore his photograph. The diplomatic pass was in English and identified him as a member of the Commercial Attaché's staff. A third item, in Russian, was a security pass for entering the embassy. Knight noted that it admitted him to the unmarked building in Kensington Palace Gardens as well as the block on Bayswater Road that most members of the public thought of as the embassy.

But it was the fourth item which Knight found of most interest. He recognised it at once as a KGB pass: almost certainly First Chief Directorate. Like the embassy pass, it was in Russian. He turned the card over in his hand; on the reverse it had an electronic strip like a credit card, suggesting that it could be used as a key in one of the building's security systems, probably the FCD annex.

His face still expressionless, Knight returned the documents and put his hands back in his pockets.

'I'm no expert, but the passport and diplomatic pass seem to bear out who you say you are, Mr Kunaev. For what that's worth. But the other items seem to be in Russian; I'm afraid I can't make head nor tail of them. I'm no wiser as to what's brought you here. Or what any of this has to do with me.'

Kunaev sighed. He put the articles away and returned to his wife's side. 'Very well, Mr Knight. I am sorry we troubled you.' He took his wife's and son's hands and began walking back down the drive.

'Mr Kunaev?'

They stopped. Kunaev looked back at Knight. The boy whispered something to his mother. She drew him close as she answered.

Knight moved inside the doorway and extended his hand in invitation. 'Would you and your family like to come inside until we sort out this confusion? It looks like more rain. We'd be better off indoors. And perhaps your little boy is tired or hungry.'

The Chief Constable was on the fourteenth fairway and his ball was in the rough again. Fingering the spare ball in his pocket, he picked his way through the coarse grass and wondered if the other players were far enough away not to spot if he did a switch. He stole a glance over his shoulder to assess his chances.

That was when he saw the maroon car. It was sitting quietly on the road that cut across the fairway, just on the crest of the low hill. It must have only just arrived, for he'd crossed the road himself not two minutes ago and it hadn't been there then. While he was staring at it the headlights flashed once.

'You'll have to excuse me,' he called back to the others. 'Business.'

The Chief of Special Branch was waiting for him in the back seat, with the window open. As the Chief Constable drew near, the two detectives in the front got out and strolled a few yards away.

The Chief Constable slid into the back beside his visitor. 'What brings you all the way out here? Apart from the bracing air.'

The Special Branch man slid a forefinger around inside his tight collar.

'Murder,' he said. 'Multiple murder.'

'Sounds nasty. Still doesn't usually interest you chaps.'

'What if one of the victims was a politician? What would you say then?'

'Depends who he was.'

The Special Branch Chief pushed a button in his armrest and the window began to rise with a soft swish. He waited until it was completely closed.

'The Home Secretary,' he said.

The Chief Constable whistled softly. He sat in silence for a moment, knowing the rest would follow without being asked for.

'In embarrassing circumstances,' the Special Branch man added eventually. 'The kind of thing that'd give the media great joy.'

'I see.'

'May we turn to practicalities?'

'A cover-up?'

Staring ahead, the Special Branch man nodded. 'And it better be good.'

In fact, Andrei needed the toilet. Knight showed Anna where it was, then set out some biscuits in the kitchen. He led Kunaev into the living-room and, without bothering to offer any explanation, drew the curtains at both ends of the room and put the lights on.

He waved Kunaev to an armchair, sat down opposite him, and looked at him expectedly.

'Well now, Mr Kunaev. Perhaps you'd like to explain why you've come here.'

'I know who and what you are, Mr Knight. That and the identification papers I have shown you – all of which you understood perfectly well – should be enough to convince you of my identity. In due course you can verify it further by checking through the diplomatic lists. I have no idea whether your people also have me on record as a *rezident* within the embassy, but again, the passes I have shown you should be adequate proof of that. So – let us not waste further time on pretences.'

Knight heard him through in silence and continued watching him for another minute, then got up and went to the hi-fi unit. He found the microphone and held it up for Kunaev to see.

'You don't mind this, do you?'

Kunaev smiled. 'Not if it means you are taking me seriously.'

Knight snapped a blank cassette in place. 'It means nothing one way or the other.' He positioned the microphone on the low table between them, switched the machine on and set the volume controls while he announced the date, time and location.

Kunaev seemed perfectly at ease, showing no more than polite interest as he observed these preparations. Knight returned to his seat and gestured towards the microphone.

'Over to you, Mr Kunaev. I might just add for the record, before you begin, that you're under no obligation to say anything at all. You can leave my house this moment if you wish, and I won't lift a finger to stop you. You understand that?'

Kunaev nodded. Knight pointed at the microphone. 'I understand,' Kunaev said aloud.

'Please repeat what you said to me when you first arrived – who you are and so on. Explain what identification you've shown me.'

Kunaev did as he was asked, speaking clearly and carefully. Just as he was describing the identity papers, Anna and Andrei came into the room; she glanced at the microphone but said nothing, and led the child to a corner at the other end of the room. She fished a few toys from the cardboard box, sat down with Andrei and began to play quietly with him.

Kunaev finished what he was saying and became silent. Knight was about to prompt him when he realised that his eyes were on his wife. She had looked up from the child's game and was returning her husband's gaze calmly and steadily; it was as if a pact between them were being ratified. After a moment Kunaev turned to look directly at Knight again.

'I seek asylum from your government for myself and my family,' he said.

'Wouldn't it be less dramatic just to ask your own government for permission to emigrate to Britain?'

Kunaev laughed. 'I said no games. FCD personnel do not qualify for exit visas. Somehow I think you know that.'

'If my government were to grant you asylum?'

'I will participate in whatever debriefings you require. We want only fresh identities and the opportunity to make a life for ourselves here.' Kunaev looked again at his wife and child, then added, 'And protection from acts of reprisal.'

Knight nodded thoughtfully. 'You haven't yet mentioned what position you claim to hold in the *rezidentura*.'

'Claim to hold? I am the senior cipher clerk. I report directly to the chief of the *rezidentura*, Colonel Aleksandr Lyulkin. I am responsible for handling both incoming and outgoing signals. All embassy traffic comes via me, whoever it is for. If it is ordinary embassy material or for GRU – military intelligence, but you know that – I just pass it on and they decode it themselves. All we decode is KGB traffic.'

'You've said you're willing to be debriefed. Does that include a detailed account of your work and the other members of the *rezidentura*?'

'Yes.'

'Their identities and ranks?'

'Yes.'

'What about information on your military intelligence people in the GRU section?'

'It is limited. We are brothers in arms but we are competitive brothers. We keep our distance. I do not even see their cipher books. But yes, I will tell your people what little I know.'

Knight sat back in his armchair. 'And your government's illegals network in this country?' He raised his eyes to see Kunaev's reaction.

'Mr Knight, you know the conventions as well as I do. There is no crossover between illegals and *rezidenti*. Nor between their activities.'

Kunaev's expression was open, his eyes untroubled. Either he was a very good actor or he really knew as little as he claimed.

For a moment, however, Knight sensed that he was about to say something more. But his son ran across to him and began chattering.

The moment passed; Kunaev fell silent again. Anna came over and retrieved the boy.

But there was something there, Knight knew. Something more than Kunaev was saying.

And something about the man himself that he couldn't yet put his finger on.

He would eventually, though.

21

In the meantime, the cassette was still running.

'You're offering to betray your country, Mr Kunaev.'

Knight saw Anna look up sharply from the other end of the room. It was the first indication that she understood English.

'You're prepared to become a traitor. How do you feel about that?'

Kunaev returned his stare angrily. 'I do not see it as betrayal.'

'The Soviet authorities will. Why are you prepared to do it? What *is* your motive?'

'That need not concern you, Mr Knight. Nor your government.'

'On the contrary. It's of tremendous interest to us.'

'In case I change my mind, you mean? Or in case I am trying to – what is the expression – set you up?'

Knight looked steadily at him. 'Both have been known. Please answer my question.'

He saw Anna catch her husband's eye; she nodded almost imperceptibly. Kunaev sighed.

'People grow tired of being told what to think and believe. Tired of a system that allows no alternative.'

'You've got a leader now who claims to be a reformer.'

Kunaev laughed. 'Gorbachev? More Leninist than Lenin? We have heard big promises like his before. Remember Khrushchev? If comrade Gorbachev survives, we will see how many of his fine promises he fulfils.'

'You think he might not survive?'

'Some promises are easy – like "You must all work harder", or "We will stop you getting drunk".'

'Why do you think Gorbachev mightn't survive?'

'Mr Knight, stop trying to find out if I know something about that. I do not. All I am saying is that if Gorbachev is pushed aside like Khrushchev – or dies unexpectedly – the men who will take over will be throwbacks. Worse perhaps than those we had before Gorbachev. Do you think that is what Anna and I want for Andrei?'

The boy looked up at the mention of his name.

'There is my motive, Mr Knight,' Kunaev added, nodding in his son's direction.

'What if Gorbachev does survive?'

Kunaev frowned. 'Will he really let Andrei be a free man? Or will it be a freedom that is conditional on saying and thinking the right things? Perhaps a slightly different set of right things from what others before Gorbachev would have prescribed, but prescribed even so.'

The cassette was approaching its end. Knight stopped the machine and flipped it over. When he looked around, Anna was standing behind him.

'Are you satisfied with my husband's motives now, Mr Knight?' She folded her arms and looked at her husband. 'You see, we are not motivated by simple greed. We do not ask to come to your country because we want to own cars or swimming pools. If that was all we wanted there are better places than Britain.'

'The betrayal.' Knight looked away and switched the machine on again. 'How do you justify betraying your own people in what you've both done and said today?'

She laughed in his face. 'Is it betrayal to want to cut down to size a system that pens and herds people like animals? The Soviet peoples have never known freedom, Mr Knight. Never. We went from being oppressed by tsars in palaces to being deceived by tsars in committees. They wore rough coats like the rest of us at first. But they soon got a taste for silks and satins. They moved back into the palaces and dachas and the guarded houses. They put their children in special schools. They ate rich food while the rest of us fought over scraps. Now they have limousines and servants, and everything is just like before. This man you call a reformer – Gorbachev – his wife and daughter dress like fashion models in Paris or New York. Seventy years ago the Soviet peoples thought they had a revolution. What revolution? We still await the revolution, do you not see that? We are still waiting for the real Bolsheviks. Until then, who are we betraying?'

She stopped as suddenly as she had begun, seemingly taken by surprise by her own outburst. Then she wrapped her arms about herself and returned to Andrei. Kunaev was watching her with unconcealed pride.

It was time, Knight decided, to tighten the screw a little more. He turned his attention back to Kunaev.

'Very well, Mr Kunaev. I think you and your wife have made it clear why you want to join our capitalist society. But capitalism is about trade. What have you got to trade?'

'I have already told you.'

'A few titbits about the *rezidentura*? Mr Kunaev, you're proposing defection, not a trip to the seaside. Defection is an emotive word. It gets politicians ruffled. Especially when our two governments are feeling their way towards some kind of working relationship again.'

'You worry that my defection might upset the process of détente?' Kunaev laughed. 'You flatter me. I am not that important.'

'That's just my point. You don't seem to be important at all. But your defection will still cause some political discomfort.'

'What are you trying to tell me? That you refuse my appeal for asylum because I am not an important man?'

'It's not up to me either way. But you may not have much to offer to make the political fuss worthwhile.' He saw Kunaev's face darken. 'Let me explain it like this. We've got satellites that can tell us if an SS-20 shifts the angle it's pointing by half a degree. We can count every soldier you deploy anywhere in the world. Those things are important, but technology means we can find them out for ourselves. What's important nowadays, Mr Kunaev, is the political motive behind things – what's actually in a leader's mind when he deploys his troops. When the warships start moving, is it really only a military exercise or something more? Now in that context, political motive – what can you offer us?'

There was a long silence. Again the exchange of glances between Kunaev and his wife.

'I went through the *rezidentura* files last night,' Kunaev said at last. 'I brought out a lot of material.'

Knight shook his head. 'If what's in the files came in on the airwaves, we probably monitored most of it anyway.'

'There is more. I have certain information.'

'Let's hear it.'

Kunaev made no response. His whole body had tightened up. His eyes slid away from Knight's. Knight recognised the signs. He'd brought Kunaev to the brink. Now he had to leave him no choice but to jump.

'You may as well tell me, Mr Kunaev. It's going to be a bit difficult for you to go back to your friends now. What would you do? Return whatever you stole from the files and say you didn't mean to take it?' He paused before delivering the body blow. 'How would you explain your visit here if your friends found out about it? *When* they find out?'

Kunaev let out a long breath of air as if he'd just pushed to the surface of deep water. Anna was watching him like a hawk.

'You'd do that?' he whispered.

'Just tell me the other information, Mr Kunaev, and we won't have to hypothesise.'

Kunaev bit his lip, then looked up. 'There would be conditions.'

He had just launched himself on the jump.

'Conditions?' Knight repeated comfortably. 'State them.'

Kunaev sat quietly for a moment, as if gathering his thoughts. When he looked up, the tension of his body and face had gone.

'They are not difficult to meet, Mr Knight. First, you must give me your undertaking that my family and I will be put under the immediate protection of the police or secret services.'

'The police don't involve themselves in this sort of thing. But I'll arrange for the protection you require.'

'Can you move us to a safe house during today?'

'Certainly.'

'My last condition is that there must be at least two people present when I tell you my information.'

'Why is that important to you?'

Kunaev shrugged and avoided his gaze, looking instead at Anna. 'I am on trial, Mr Knight. I just want it to be a fair one, with witnesses – that is all.'

'On trial?'

Kunaev smiled humourlessly. 'In our profession, we are always on trial. Never more so than when we change allegiances. Would you not say so?' He waited but Knight said nothing. 'Those are my conditions. Will you meet them, Mr Knight?'

Knight shrugged. 'I anticipate no problems.'

It was time to let Gaunt know about the Kunaevs and have him prepare the politicians.

He wasn't at home; Knight left a message for him to call back.

Dick Sumner was at home. There was surprise in his tone when he recognised Knight's voice.

'Problems, Edmund?'

'Hard to be sure. Go on scramble, please.' As soon as he heard the click on the line he pressed the button on his own phone. 'I need you to get here as soon as possible. You'll be here for the rest of the day, including the evening. Details when you arrive.'

'Understood.'

'Make some calls for me before you leave. First, get hold of Protective Security. We need a couple of men here, plus a woman officer. Armed. At the double but tell them to be discreet. Any fuss around here will stick out like a sore thumb. Tell them to pack a bag – they'll be on duty for the rest of the weekend. And to come in a couple of cars – they'll have three passengers. Next, we need one of the safe houses. In the country would be best but within reasonable reach of London.' He thought of the Kunaev boy. 'Somewhere with space. Maybe a bit of garden that'd suit a young kid. Anywhere come to mind?'

Sumner thought for a minute. 'What about the place at Stratfield Saye? There's play equipment in the garden and a big games room.'

'Anyone there at present?'

'As far as I know, only the staff.'

'Tell them they've got customers from tonight. Two adults and a child, plus the security people. They'll all be staying until further notice.'

By now Sumner was beginning to form some rough idea of what was going on. 'You're having an interesting weekend, Edmund, by the sound of it.'

'You could say that. Last of all, get hold of a staff stenographer and bring him with you.'

'The calls will take ten or fifteen minutes. I'll be with you in an hour or so.'

Knight returned to the living-room, where the Kunaevs were sitting side by side on a settee with the boy between them. Anna was reading him a story; Kunaev was deep in his own thoughts.

'The arrangements are made,' Knight told them. 'We can make a start probably an hour from now.'

It was coming up to lunchtime and it seemed an appropriate time to break. He wondered what food he had in the house. As if reading his mind, Anna looked up from the storybook.

'You live alone, Mr Knight? My husband says you do.'

'Your husband seems to know a lot about me. Including where I live, for a start.'

'No doubt your people in Moscow know the same about his superiors. The reason I ask is – would you like me to prepare us some lunch? It seems unfair to expect you to do it.' He must have looked uncertain, for she laughed gently. 'We have not come here to poison you, you know.'

He smiled apologetically. 'Let me show you where everything is.'

They went through to the kitchen. He suggested a few sandwiches and showed her where to find meats and salad.

'How old is your little boy?' he asked.

'Four. Do you have children, Mr Knight? Perhaps you were married once?'

He looked at her for a moment before answering. 'I've never been married. Families aren't such a good idea in my line of work.'

She flashed him a shy smile. 'I too am learning that.'

The phone rang. Knight went through to the study and it was Gaunt. The hollowness on the line meant he was calling from his car. As with Sumner, Knight asked him to switch to scramble.

'Take a deep breath, Horace. I've got a visitor. A Soviet who wants to defect. Someone from the embassy. I think he's genuine.'

'Good Lord. Diplomatic or *rezident*?'

'*Rezident* apparently, but no one very big. A cipher clerk. He just rolled up to my door this morning. Plus wife and kid.'

'Do we know him?'

'I don't. Dick Sumner might.' He updated Gaunt on the morning's events, concluding by stating his intention to conduct Kunaev's preliminary debrief himself.

'Where will you take him?' Gaunt asked.

'We'll make a start here. Then I'll move him to a safe house from this evening. Probably Stratfield Saye.'

'A cipher clerk. I wonder how much use he'll be.' Gaunt didn't sound enthusiastic. 'I'll be home for the rest of the day, Edmund. I'd like you to keep me informed. I won't raise any balloons with the politicians until we see what your debrief brings.'

Knight hung up but remained in the study, realising that he'd forgotten about Bill Clarke; talking to Gaunt about politicians had reminded him.

This time the number rang for a long time before someone answered. 'Yes?'

It was the same voice as before. Knight hung up.

22

They were finishing lunch when Sumner arrived. The stenographer who came with him was an elderly man whom Knight had met once or twice before.

Knight and Sumner spoke privately in the study. Sumner recognised Kunaev's name from the diplomatic record index; but that was all.

'Looks like you've landed a *rezident* we didn't know about, Edmund.'

'He's no big deal.'

The security people arrived as they were talking. On Knight's instructions, one officer stationed himself in his car outside the front door while the other agreed to take up position in a rear bedroom overlooking the garden. As he was opening the car's boot Knight realised what was about to happen and went to him; sure enough, a rifle lay in the boot.

'Break that down and case it before you lift it out,' he told the man. He nodded his head towards the front door, where the Kunaev boy and his mother were watching the goings-on. 'They'll be in the kitchen later, but for now have a care.'

The debrief took place in the living-room, still with its curtains closed. Knight did the questioning. Sumner listened and watched, jotting his own notes and comments. The stenographer made a verbatim record; later he would present two versions: the verbatim one and another that had been distilled into coherent prose, with all the hesitations and repetitions edited out. The cassette machine would prove a cross-check for his work but it was also there to capture the spoken nuances of tone or emphasis that no written record could provide; later the psychologists from PsyOps would comb through it.

The first ten minutes were devoted to Kunaev's general background, both personal and career. It was no more than a preliminary canter through dates and places so that an early check could be made to verify that he was who he said he was. In his weeks ahead with a specialist interrogator – months if he proved worth the trouble – a more searching investigation would be made. It would cover events great and small in his life, the people whom he'd known, descriptions of locations and people: nothing would be too insignificant.

It was when Knight reached the question of how Kunaev had chosen the method and timing of his defection that they came to the heart of the interview.

'Why did you come to me, Mr Kunaev? It's brought you well beyond the Greater London zone permitted to your rank. If any of your people had spotted you, you'd have been in difficulty to explain what you were up to.'

'You are the head of Counter-Intelligence. I know of you. Also your address. Not those below you.'

'Why not walk into one of our offices any day of the week?'

'The information I have cannot wait until offices are open.'

'Better tell us then.'

'Our *rezidentura* has just had a security audit. Major General Valyukev descended on us from Yasyenevo.'

Knight glanced over at Sumner, sitting slightly behind Kunaev and out of his view. Sumner coloured. His section should have picked up on the arrival of someone as big as Valyukev, whatever cover had been used to get him in and out of the country.

'We came through satisfactorily,' Kunaev continued. 'But yesterday afternoon I overheard Valyukev and the head of our *rezidentura*, Colonel Lyulkin, talking together. I heard Valyukev say something about illegal rules.'

Knight looked sharply at him. 'You said yourself that you people have nothing to do with the illegals. So what did Valyukev mean?'

'What I said was true. I know next to nothing about our illegals network in this or any country. But I know the operational principles. All the *rezidenti* do. That is essential. Illegals spend years to build their cover identities. Everything would be put at risk if there was any contact between them and KGB personnel from the *rezidentura*. The *rezidenti* might be known to your people and under surveillance; they would lead you right to the illegal. So, under no circumstances is there ever such contact.'

Knight nodded. 'And this was what Valyukev was referring to?'

'No, I do not think so. Lyulkin said something such as: "If that is what Moscow wants for this operation, then certainly I have no problem with that." Do you see? It suggests that they were talking about an operation that is out of the ordinary, not just an existing situation involving illegals.'

'Did you hear what this operation might be?'

'No. But I know what it is associated with. The Opec conference begins on Tuesday. They referred to that.'

Knight leant forward. 'Go on.'

'I then heard Lyulkin ask about a mobile unit – I could not hear everything but he asked when it will arrive in London. Valyukev said it was here already, to be here in time for the conference. He called it the oil meeting. He said the unit had to have time to orientate itself well before the meeting begins.' Kunaev paused. 'I think you must know what a mobile unit is?'

'Where your people are concerned, it usually means an assassination squad.'

'I doubt if you would accept that as a description of an SAS unit, which would be your closest equivalent. This particular unit, you see, is a Spetznaz team.'

'Sabotage, kidnapping or assassination then. What size is the unit?'

Kunaev shrugged. 'Neither of them said.'

Knight scrutinised the man's face closely. There was no hint that he was telling anything but the truth, in terms both of all he had said and that which he claimed not to know.

'I have now told you all I heard, Mr Knight – and that the *rezidenti* are to stay well clear.'

In the silence that followed there was only the distant and incongruous sound of Andrei's laughter. Knight sat looking at Kunaev for some time before carrying on.

'Why did Valyukev tell Lyulkin anything? Why not just let this Spetznaz operation go ahead on its independent course with Lyulkin none the wiser? Wouldn't that have been the best and easiest thing to do?'

'Illegal rules include an escape provision. I think the same arrangement must apply in this case.'

'How would that work?'

'Every illegal, if he must abort his assignment, has the right as a last resort to secure help from the Soviet diplomatic mission. There are arrangements regarding codes which only the ambassador and his head of *rezidentura* know. Both of them must be involved, and both of them must be satisfied with the arrangements that are made to give the illegal safe passage.'

Knight nodded. Kunaev had described a standard network cut-out. Only if the ambassador and the head of *rezidentura* had both been compromised would the illegal be at risk.

'The Soviet Union places great importance on looking after its illegals, Mr Knight. It goes to great lengths to protect them or get them back. It is an important factor in maintaining their morale. These people need every such consideration. Theirs is the loneliest job in the world.'

'Spare us, Mr Kunaev.'

'I would assume that the Spetznaz unit has been provided with similar escape facilities, so this is why Lyulkin had to be told. Before you ask, I do not know what the code arrangements are. Valyukev could have told them to our ambassador anytime last week. They met two, three times. He could have told Lyulkin either before or after the conversation that I overheard. I cannot help you on that matter.'

'What else can you help us with?'

Kunaev laughed. 'What else do you hope for?' He became serious again. 'Perhaps you would like to see my files now?'

Knight was still enmeshed in the implications of what he had just learnt. 'What?'

'The files I told you about, Mr Knight – that I took from the *rezidentura*. That you are convinced are probably so worthless. I need to step outside this room for them.'

Knight nodded. 'Go ahead.'

When Kunaev had left he nodded for the stenographer to stop the tape, and turned to Sumner.

'Take over the rest of this session, Dick. I'd better pass this on.'

Kunaev reappeared in the doorway, carrying a stack of papers.

'From the cardboard toy box?' Knight asked him.

Kunaev nodded. 'I could not walk out of our apartment this morning with a fat briefcase. I would not have got twenty paces. I went to much trouble to acquire these, Mr Knight, so I was not going to leave them behind either. Whatever your opinion of their worth.'

At the other end of the phone Knight's words seemed to devastate Gaunt. For a moment he actually wondered if they'd been cut off, then he heard Gaunt's laboured breathing and the creak of a chair.

'Horace?'

'Yes, yes.' Gaunt allowed himself one softly whispered swearword. 'The PM will be apoplectic. Bloody Spetznaz. After the sweeping-up we're meant to have done. God, we could do with knowing more. But if this man Kunaev has cleared out the blasted *rezidentura* files as he says, then I fail to see how we can send him back to find out more.'

'He'd never have gone anyway. He's made his break and devil take the hindmost.'

'We'd have changed his mind for him. We have the wife and child as collateral. You still stick by what you said earlier, Edmund – he's the genuine article, not a Trojan horse?'

'I'm as convinced as I can be.'

'Sumner there with you?'

'Yes.'

'We'd better get moving to find these gorillas. Damn quick too. Boost the conference security.'

'I take it there's no question of calling the whole thing off?'

'None whatever. The PM would never accept the loss of face.'

'Where are the delegates today?'

'Those that spring to mind as targets will be at Chequers this evening for a reception. Lesser dignitaries are being left to their own devices. Edmund, see what else you can get out of this chap. Any morsel would help.' He sighed. 'I'll get onto the PM. We'll put the Met on alert. We'll want them to draft in men from other forces. We need house searches and rounding up everybody who might know or have heard something.'

The line clicked and echoed as he hung up.

Knight punched out Clarke's number again. But again there was only a voice he didn't know, a different one this time. He hung up without saying anything and left the study.

He heard the broadcast as he was crossing the hall to go back to the debrief. In the kitchen Anna was listening to a play on the radio. At first he thought that it was part of the performance: the actors' voices faded and another voice cut in. He stopped at the living-room door with his hand on the handle, and listened.

'We interrupt this broadcast to bring you a special newsflash.'

The announcer's voice had the unmistakable timbre that the BBC reserved for deaths and disasters. Knight pictured listeners the length and breadth of the country looking up from newspapers, standing with half-filled kettles, hushing children.

'The death late last night has just been announced of the Home Secretary, the Right Honourable William Clarke, MP. The announcement was made from Downing Street by the Prime Minister's Press Secretary just a few minutes ago. Mr Clarke is understood to have died in a car accident in which his driver was also killed. No other vehicle was involved. The Prime Minister is reported to be deeply shocked and has paid tribute to Mr Clarke as "a politician of real ability and integrity who will be sadly missed". The Queen has sent a personal message of sympathy to Mr Clarke's family and tributes have come from Opposition leaders and senior politicians of all parties. For further information we now go to . . .'

A giddiness came over Knight. He leant against the living-room door for support and had to push himself upright by means of the door handle. He waited for the moment to pass before he could make his way back into the study, where he flopped down in the high-backed chair and stared blindly out of the window.

Then he rewound the answerphone tape and listened again to Clarke's message. Then again. And again. He played it five or six times before he called Sumner out of the living-room and shared the news with him.

He made no mention of the answerphone message.

23

Moscow

The lane and the street were both called Kropotkin and they crossed at right angles. The little group of French Communist Party officials stood in a tight knot at the intersection, their smiles as bright as the cold afternoon sunshine, and listened with interest to their guide. She said they were in one of the city's most characterful quarters, where the old nobility had built their fine homes in the previous century. Some of the mansions, as they'd seen, had been returned to the people and now housed art galleries, the Academy of Arts, or had been turned into museums to the honour of Tolstoy and Pushkin.

'Let us continue,' she said. 'You will see why Kropotkin called this area our little Faubourg Saint-Germain.'

Laughing at her joke, they climbed aboard their waiting coach and headed for Smolenskiy Boulevard, where they turned north in the direction of Arbat Street.

Serov watched them go. The building whose rear courtyard he strode into a minute later was neither fine nor noble. It stood on the corner of Kropotkin Street and Zubovskiy Boulevard, a grey stone monstrosity whose brass plate by the main entrance on Zubovskiy announced it as the Institute of Industrial Law. That was a lie. It was the Serbskiy Institute of Forensic Psychiatry. Officially it was run by the Ministry of Health. But that was another lie. The Serbskiy belonged to the KGB.

Professor Ogarkin grabbed a paper tissue from the box on his desk and blew his nose loudly.

'The girl shouldn't even be here, comrade General, as you well know,' he mumbled nasally.

Serov turned from the window where he'd been watching an ambulance arrive in the yard three floors below them.

'Don't I look after you well enough?' he said.

'That's not the point.' Ogarkin's fingers scrabbled for another tissue but the box was empty. He picked it up and peered into it, prodding the end of his nose with the used tissue and sniffing disconsolately.

There was a fresh box on the shelf where Serov was leaning. He tossed it onto the desk. Ogarkin tore it open and blew his nose again.

'I'm thinking of the risks you're making us both take. This is Section Four you've got her in, that's the thing. It's meant for politicals only. The young woman, your . . . ward –' He said it with some circumspection. 'She's hardly what you'd call a political, is she? A dissident?'

Serov moved to the desk and leant across it. 'And you, my fine comrade Professor, are hardly what I'd call a doctor. What's more, the Commissariat of Psychiatric Medicine would say the same if they knew about the little games you used to play with the deranged schoolgirls the Ministry of Education sent you.'

Ogarkin coloured. 'That was years ago.' He grabbed yet another tissue and put it to his nose, his eyes watching Serov over it.

Serov straightened up from the desk and went back to the window. 'The past is never that far behind us,' he said quietly.

He watched as two male nurses dragged a man from the ambulance and began frogmarching him toward the building. He was strait-jacketed and screaming hysterically. Eventually one of the nurses slammed an elbow into his face. It was impersonally done, with professional coolness; the man slumped over and stopped screaming.

Serov turned back to Ogarkin.

'Professor, it might say "Ministry of Health" on the nameplate by your front door, but don't forget who your real bosses are. It's the KGB that pays your salary – not to mention providing this elegant building and its distinguished offices.' The dingy walls and worn linoleum hardly fitted his description, but that was neither here nor there.

'Most of all,' he added, bending over Ogarkin again, 'on a more personal level – don't forget who sets up your discreet weekend trips down to Batumi every summer. You like your Black Sea cruises, don't you? With all those nice little stewardesses. You certainly wouldn't want that to stop. Or anyone to learn about it.'

Ogarkin slumped in his threadbare chair, his head down. Serov's coat had fallen open as he leant over the desk and the butt of a revolver had been clearly visible inside it.

Serov studied him in silence for a moment longer before pulling a tissue from the box and shoving it into his face.

'Now wipe up and take me to see her,' he said. 'Let's check how the great professor's most important patient is doing.'

The room was about three metres square. It could have been a prison cell but for the heavily padded walls. There was an iron bunk bolted in one corner, two chairs and a table, also bolted in position, and a barred window. Galina was sitting on the bunk, her legs folded below her. Her green eyes stared fixedly at the far wall.

'She needn't be in there,' Ogarkin whispered. He was holding open a hatch in the door while Serov peered through.

'Every morning after breakfast we take her to the lounge area. Not the one used by the other detainees, of course – we take her to the one that the nurses and orderlies use. We talk to her or leaf through picture books – anything to try and get some response from her. But it's always the same. She stays there for about an hour, then wanders back here and waits for her nurse to open the door. In the afternoon, when it's time for her therapy sessions, she comes with me willingly enough. But frankly, the sessions are getting us nowhere. She hasn't spoken a word since she arrived. And she just wants to come straight back here afterwards.'

Serov straightened up from the door. 'What therapy are you using?'

Ogarkin snuffled into a tissue and put his watery eyes to the hatch. 'On that point, comrade General, it would help me if I knew what had caused this regression. I could design her treatment with greater confidence. As things are at present I'm working in the dark. After her mother's death she was bad enough. But this is far worse.' He looked up into Serov's face. 'If only I knew what brought this about. Something triggered it. Don't you have any idea what it might have been?'

Serov pushed the professor's hand roughly away from the hatch. It clanged shut.

'The trouble with you, Ogarkin,' he said, 'is that you're more used to inducing psychiatric symptoms than curing them. Open this door.'

'It's not locked,' the professor said quietly, and swung the door open. 'It's her who closes it, not us.'

Serov stared through the open doorway but didn't move.

'She likes to paint and draw,' he told Ogarkin. 'You'd know that if you were worth anything as a doctor. Fix her up with some paints and so on – an easel and brushes – sketch pads, pencils – canvas – those kinds of things.'

Ogarkin nodded. 'It's worth a try.' He turned to leave, but Serov's arm suddenly reached out, blocking his path.

'One more thing.'

'What?'

Serov turned to face him. 'If you so much as touch her while she's here,' he whispered, 'I'll rip you wide open.'

He went into the padded room and drew the door softly closed behind him.

On his way to the car afterwards, an old man caught his arm on Ostozhenka Street.

'A few kopeks, comrade. For bread. Only for bread.'

There were laws against begging and the police enforced them rigidly. The penalty was automatic imprisonment, often in a camp. The official logic was straightforward: no one was poor, everyone had work, therefore beggars were parasites and enemies of the people. But there were always some who were desperate enough to take their chances.

'A few kopeks.'

Serov turned and the old man's eyes met his own. They stared at each other for a moment. Then the beggar's fingers slowly released their hold. Whatever he found in Serov's eyes, it was enough to force his own gaze away. He hunched deeper into his filthy coat and shuffled off.

Serov continued on to his car and drove away.

There was an old song and Galina couldn't remember all the words. She hummed it softly over and over. She'd been humming it for weeks now; sometimes it seemed like she'd been humming it all her life. It was there first thing in the morning and she fell asleep at night with it still going round and round inside her head.

There was something about footprints through the snow. She could remember that. And a little boy. He couldn't keep up and he was crying.

> *The footprints are so deep, mama.*
> *The gaps between are long, papa; too long for me.*
> *I fall behind.*
> *I stumble.*
> *Wolves are howling – can you hear them?*

I want to sit here but they come and take me into other rooms. They talk to me but I'm not interested. I come back here because what I want to do is to finish remembering the rest of the song.

And now here you are at last, dear Nikolai, come to visit me. Have you brought the rest of the song?

There's snow on your boots, if that means anything. Snow on your boots but your hands are warm. They touch me. Your breath is on my ear; it carries words but none of them fit the song. All I can do is stay here, watching, listening and waiting until the words come.

Now you're leaving. I disappoint you. But you disappoint me too. You brought no song.

> *There are shadows on the snow, mama.*
> *Two shadows side by side, papa; two shadows waiting.*
> *I fell behind.*
> *I stumbled.*
> *The wolves have stopped their howling.*

Ogarkin slid the hatch open again and looked in. She was still staring blankly at the wall. She seemed to him like a doll that a bored child had abandoned and tossed carelessly into a corner.

He went quietly into the cell and stood before her. Her blonde hair was swept back and slightly tousled. The green eyes were like cool jade. She was the most beautiful creature he'd ever seen. So young and vulnerable.

'Galina?' he whispered. She blinked but made no other response. He reached down and touched her hair. It was soft and cool but when he pressed his fingers into it he felt the warmth of her skull.

He ran his hand down to the nape of her neck and stroked the top of her shoulder inside her blouse, then let his fingers find their way up to her cheek. It was soft and unblemished. He felt the down over her cheekbones and traced her eyebrow with a fingertip. Still she made no move away from him.

He stepped closer, so that her face was only an inch from him and he became dizzy just at the thought of her closeness. When he looked down he saw that some stray strands of her hair were even brushing against his trousers. He heard the uneven rasp of his own breathing and saw his chest heaving under the white coat.

'Galina?' he said again. 'Won't you tell me what's the matter?'

No answer. He took a tissue from his pocket and wiped his damp nose. His hand returned to her head; he touched the lobe of her ear, her neck again, the delicate ridge of her jaw.

Then he remembered Serov's warning.

He drew his hand back sharply from the girl's head, turned on his heel and left the room.

24

London

Before they sent the bald man over, they'd made him polish his English pronunciation and colloquialisms until he sounded like a native. They fixed him up with a four-day crash course and he'd worked with the linguistics advisers from eight in the morning until nine at night. In what was optimistically called his leisure time he'd played video cassettes of English television plays and films; because how the English used their lips and facial expressions was as important as the sounds themselves.

When he took the flat in Cricklewood he was just another working man living wherever the work took him. He had identification and references: driving licence and banker's card, a letter from a firm of builders in Hendon saying that he was a new foreman just joining them, and a letter from the landlord of the last place he'd rented, saying that he was a good payer and a clean tenant.

That Saturday afternoon he strolled up the Broadway to a busy hardware shop and bought a few tools and bits and pieces. When he got back to Mulgrave Road he had a cup of coffee and looked over some maps with the thin-faced man.

Afterwards they spent an hour welding some steel brackets inside the Sherpa's loading bay. They cut an opaque plastic shower curtain to size and rigged it up behind the seats so that the van's contents couldn't be seen through the front windows. They blanked out the rear windows by taping surplus strips of curtain over them.

When they were done, there were still a couple of hours before it would be time to set out; they passed it poring over the maps again.

Oxfordshire

That evening a cold snap set in. The barometer fell below freezing. The flat fields around Kidlington took on a dusting of frost and on the Cherwell the water voles retreated deep within their burrows.

After prayers Ibraham Abukhder set out on his jog, alone as usual.

His fellow-students in the air training school were either gathered around the television in the residential quarters' communal lounge or exploring the nearby pubs.

He followed his regular route south from the school, past the shops and the repair garage. All of them were closed now until Monday; but, as ever, an assortment of vehicles was parked on the garage forecourt or in its side alley, awaiting service or repair. Ibraham automatically checked off the models: a Granada, an old Morris Minor, an Opel, a white Sherpa van.

He cut left down the quiet road that formed the second side of his triangular route and focused his thoughts on his body's performance. His legs felt good and strong, no signs of flagging yet. His breathing was still steady and unforced, his heart wasn't hammering. The old ankle injury twinged a little but that was just a reminder, not a real warning of trouble.

He was within a few paces of the bench before he looked up and saw that someone was sitting there. The unexpected presence made him start; he wasn't expecting a messenger tonight. He slowed to a walk in order to make the figure out.

In the darkness and scarcely helped by the dim street-lamp thirty yards away, he could only make out at first that it was a man. As he drew closer he saw that he was stocky and bald-headed. Ibraham had never seen him before. This man had never been sent before. But by the time he realised this, it was too late.

The bald man was on his feet. He was looking straight ahead, as if something beyond the hedge had caught his eye. Then he turned and looked directly at Ibraham. His right arm lifted in a leisurely, almost slow movement.

Ibraham saw the pistol. He saw the dull orange gleam of the street-lamp on its metal.

He ducked low and made to throw himself into the hedge. But the white Sherpa van had pulled up behind him. He hadn't heard it coming. As he turned for the hedge it shot forward, cutting off his escape. The bald man moved towards him and he heard the van door fly open and feet clattering on the road as someone jumped out.

He braced himself for the bullet that was surely coming and submitted himself to the will of Allah. But the bullet didn't come. Instead the bald man held the revolver to his head while the other, a thin-faced man, jerked up his track suit top. A bony arm encircled his neck, holding him motionless. He felt a sharp jab in the flesh near his spine. A minute passed, then the hold was released, leaving him gasping. The thin man walked to the rear of the van while the bald one kept the gun pressed to Ibraham's skull. He seized his arm and began walking him towards the open rear doors. Ibraham found that his legs had turned to jelly, as if he'd run too far. His vision blurred and he felt dizzy. He recalled the European students' descriptions of the effects of alcohol and wondered if this was what it was like.

By the time they got to the rear doors the bald man's grip on his arm was the only thing that was keeping him on his feet. The hand let go and he folded over on the van's scratched metal floor. His legs and feet were pushed in after him and the bald man climbed in beside him. His wrists and legs were tied quickly to some steel brackets on the floor. The last things he felt and heard were a clang as the doors were fastened shut and a sharp lurch as the van accelerated away.

His fear had gone; he no longer felt any alarm. Just a very deep sense of peace and an irresistible need to sleep.

Forty minutes later the Sherpa approached Aylesbury from the west on the A418 and skirted the town to pick up the A413 to Stoke Mandeville. A mile or so along this road it turned sharp left to cut through a modern housing estate. It crossed a couple of roundabouts and turned left onto a back road that wound through farmland and over the canal before rejoining the A418.

The thin man got to the T-junction with the A418 before he realised that he'd gone too far. He switched on the courtesy lamp and looked more closely at the hand-drawn map on his lap. The bald man slid the curtain behind them open a little and flashed a torch over Ibraham. He was still out cold.

No other traffic had drawn up behind them, so the thin man reversed the Sherpa until he found a place to turn and take the van back the way they'd just come.

They found the lock-up garage on their right, close by a small hamlet of houses before they got back as far as the canal. The wooden owl that was supposed to be their marker was there above the doors but they'd missed it in their concentration on the winding road.

The bald man got out and undid the padlock on the garage. He threw its doors wide and waved the Sherpa back until its rear end was inside by a couple of feet.

The garage contained a Yamaha RD350 motorcycle with a distinctive red and white fairing. Folded on its pillion was a set of black racing leathers; on top of them sat an all-in-one helmet and tinted visor. The helmet was in the same red and white as the machine's fairing. There were a pair of tall black boots and a set of gauntlets on the floor beside the bike. A stout plank was propped against the wall.

The men hooked the plank to the rear of the van for a ramp and manhandled the Yamaha up it into the loading bay. The bald man climbed in to tether it upright to the brackets on the van's side while the thin man loaded the leathers, helmet, boots and plank in after him. Ibraham never stirred.

Two minutes later they were on the road again; even if someone had been watching from the nearby houses, they'd have seen nothing.

An hour after that the Sherpa was in north-west London. It came off the North Circular at Neasden and picked up Walm Lane, following it to its northern end, then past the church and the synagogue where it became Chichele Road. It turned off left just before the Broadway and chugged through the network of little streets where Irish, Eurasians, Jamaicans and original English rubbed along as best they could.

The pubs were closing when the van arrived at the terrace in Mulgrave Road. The thin man got down and walked around to the van's nearside door. He opened it and gave his bald friend a hand with their other friend who seemed to have had more than one drink too many. He was a young man in a tracksuit.

They manoeuvred Ibraham between them and got their arms about him so that they could help him walk to the front door. There was some laughter as they did this, though none of it came from Ibraham. He stumbled a lot and in fact so did they, as if none of them was completely sober. The young man called something out once or twice. But a block away the Galtymore Dancehall was blasting showband music into the night and his words were lost.

It was a common enough sort of scene for that area on a Saturday night; not the sort of thing that would attract anyone's attention.

But the pretty woman with the crew-cut black hair saw it all. Across the way and a few doors down, she sat at an upstairs bay window and noted everything.

She was very still apart from her fingers, which occasionally tapped in time with the showband music. All afternoon and all evening she'd sat there, watching. On a tripod beside her was mounted the camera. Again it was loaded with infra-red film; tonight it was also fitted with a 300mm zoom lens, precisely aligned with a neat hole in the net curtain that screened her from the road, and focused on the Sherpa and the flat.

She had tracked the bald man coming and going during the afternoon, popping in and out of the van with his colleague as they worked in its loading bay, and setting off with him in the early evening. The camera was recording them returning now with the young man in the tracksuit slung between them. Its motor whined almost non-stop as they went up the path, such was the woman's interest.

Behind her the door opened and her friend came in. She tossed the Volvo's keys on the table and went off to make coffee. When the lights went out in the ground floor flat across the way, the black-haired woman undressed and climbed into bed. She was asleep by the time her friend had settled herself in the chair at the window, coffee-mug in hand. The thump of the dancehall music became her lullaby.

25

Knight dragged himself slowly from the deep well of sleep and struggled to bring his mind and senses into focus.

Sunday morning. Six thirty. Still dark. The steady drip of rain outside. Like a conversation; or an interrogation. Question, answer, question, answer.

Yesterday. The Kunaevs.

'Viktor Kunaev,' he muttered, now fully awake as memory returned. 'What the hell am I to do with you?'

Sumner had taken over the debrief as he had requested. In the evening, when all of them had been packed off to Stratfield Saye and Knight was alone again, he had listened to the recording of their exchange.

> KUNAEV: The information about the Spetznaz unit is only one reason why we have come to you at this time. Even without it we would have to make our move now. Yasyenevo have decided to recall me. My father died last month. He was my only family in the USSR and the people in Moscow like to have someone to hold as security.
>
> SUMNER: Tell me your father's name. Tell me a little about him.

A long pause. Finally:

> KUNAEV: His name was Genrikh Genrikhovich Kunaev.
> SUMNER: What did he do, what was his work?

Another pause.

> KUNAEV: He held the rank of major.
> SUMNER: He was a military man?
> KUNAEV: Why do you need to know this?
> SUMNER: It all helps us to verify if you are who you say you are.

It was true, but only partly. Kunaev had blundered into the mention of his father; the reluctance in his subsequent responses made that clear enough. Sumner would have been a poor examiner not to pursue it.

SUMNER:	I said, was he a military man, Mr Kunaev?
KUNAEV:	He was a major in the KGB. He was in retirement at the time of his death.
SUMNER:	I see. What was his area of operation prior to his retirement?

Again silence.

SUMNER:	Please answer the question, Mr Kunaev.
KUNAEV:	He held a post in the First Chief Directorate.
SUMNER:	Can you be more specific?
KUNAEV:	It was merely a minor teaching post.
SUMNER:	Teaching what to whom?
KUNAEV:	He kept the matter of his work very much to himself. I do not understand why you ask this. It is I who wish to defect, not my father. My father is dead. All I want – all I and my family want – is peace in a free country.

'Silly man,' Knight said aloud, and got up.

At the convent, cars already lined both sides of the lane up to the small chapel. The Mass was just starting as he stepped inside. Old Jod, expecting no further customers, had closed the inner and outer doors and gone to his usual place in the rear pew. He glanced around and grinned toothlessly at Knight as he slipped into the pew beside him.

Father Hugh, who glared at his congregations if their responses weren't sufficiently loud or convincing, was extracting some hearty chanting this morning. Jod slid a Mass card along the pew. Knight wouldn't have dared not to take it; he glanced down to find the place and let the ritual sweep him along.

He noticed some of the sisters among the worshippers, kneeling in a group near the front. From behind, one looked much like another and he couldn't tell if Marie-Thérèse was among them or not. The children occupied four or five of the pews next to them.

He didn't take communion and left as soon as the Mass was ended, before Old Jod could catch him.

When he got home he called Stratfield Saye. One of the Protective Security officers came on the line.

'Has Matt Parrish arrived?' Knight asked him. Parrish was a specialist interrogator from PsyOps Branch.

'Yes, sir. He got here shortly after breakfast. Him and Mr Sumner. They're at work now with our houseguest. Did you want to speak to them?'

'Don't disturb them. I'll leave it.'

As he prepared lunch he switched on the television in the kitchen for the news magazine programme. The presenter's voice was speaking over the opening graphics:

'Oil prices continue to hit new lows, last week dropping to half last month's levels. That brings them to a third of what they were in 1980. In real terms, oil is the cheapest it's ever been since the 1970s.

'But yesterday, in a spectacular move timed to coincide with this week's Opec meeting in London, Saudi Arabia declared its decision to double its output. This will drive prices down even further; just how low is anybody's guess. Today we ask –'

Knight looked at the screen and saw that the presenter's next words were also the title of that week's edition, appearing on the screen as he spoke them:

'Opec – what price peace?'

Apart from William Clarke's death, Knight had missed the rest of the previous day's news. Now he paid attention. The screen changed to a long-shot of the presenter in the studio. He looked up from his notes and spoke into the camera as it closed on him.

'Yesterday's surprise move by Saudi Arabia, which was almost certainly engineered by Sheikh Yamani with the blessing of King Fahd, has angered many in the Arab world. Later we discuss its implications. But we start with a look through Opec's troubled history since its emergence in the 1970s as a major force affecting world economies.'

Library footage paraded glimpses from Opec meetings of previous years: leading figures, usually Arabs, stepping from limousines outside the world's premier hotels, being mobbed by press and television crews, giving off-the-cuff interviews or formal media briefings.

Knight watched closely, his lunch forgotten. He saw Yamani in the early days: sleek, black-haired and Westernised, conspicuous in his business suit among the Arab dress of his Opec colleagues: the very picture of the sophisticated, Harvard-trained lawyer.

He was a man who had served three kings in succession. The footage showed him in company first with King Faisal, then with Faisal's successor, Khaled; last of all, the ample frame of King Fahd sometimes accompanied him. Always, somewhere in the background, would be other Saudis: all that Knight retained of them was a general impression of flowing robes, dark skin and trim beards.

There was one exception. He began to observe a man that the camera often captured at the periphery of scenes. Unconsciously he began looking out for him. He was a tall, imperious Arab, about the same age as Yamani, with a hooked nose and full goatee. Always he wore traditional robes and headcloth. He was never to the foreground; but once Knight became aware of him his presence brooded over every

164

scene in which he appeared. Sometimes he was slightly out of focus but Knight still recognised him. He wondered idly what it was about him that had compelled his attention. As the footage progressed, he realised: it was the way in which he seemed always to be watching Yamani or Fahd from his unfathomable eyes.

The final clip was one from the media briefing of the day before, when Yamani had made his startling disclosure of the double-capacity tactic. Again, there at the long table was the tall Arab, just to the left of centre, sitting two or three seats away from Fahd and Yamani. His hands were folded on the table and he had the icy stillness of a wax statue. As ever, the eyes were on his king and the oil minister. Fahd was silent, for he spoke no English and was there only to add his authority to Yamani's announcement; this briefing was directed at a political audience. Yamani was grey-haired now but as urbane and magnetic as ever, the power of his presence a match for any Hollywood star.

Then Knight saw it: the look that the tall Arab flashed both of them. Yamani was talking about his 'freefall price strategy'. Even from the safety of the TV lens Knight was chilled by that look. It was of a kind that he'd seen perhaps only three or four times before in his life. 'If looks could kill,' was what ran through his mind.

Then the camera began to close in on Yamani; as the distance shortened, the name card on the table in front of the tall Arab came into focus for an instant, then was off-screen entirely.

Not before Knight had seen the name stencilled on the card. Saleem Ibn Abdul Aziz Al-Saud.

Then the footage was gone and the studio presenter was back, turning to some expert analyst.

Knight saw no more of the tall Arab.

Apart from the Opec development, the main item in the Sunday papers was Clarke's death. There were photographs of the wreckage of his black Jaguar and a flattened telegraph pole on an isolated country road. The reports said that Clarke's driver had died from a heart attack; it would be for an inquest to decide whether this had been the cause or the result of the crash.

As Knight scanned the reports he realised that he had allowed yesterday's other events to drive Clarke's death to the back of his mind. Now he felt guilt and remorse; he thought about Marion and the children, what emptiness there would be in their household today. He compared his own discomfiture as he had awoken this morning with what Marion must have felt, and didn't feel proud of himself.

He sighed. As Clarke himself had pointed out, they had lost touch. But that didn't excuse Knight from offering what comfort he could to the man's widow. He decided to drive up to Copperfields and visit Marion after lunch.

But a shock awaited him there. Marion Clarke's feelings were not as he had supposed.

'I hope he rots, Edmund. You haven't come here to give me your sympathy, have you?'

He stared at her. She was in black, but that was her only widow-like feature; and the glass of gin in her hand was certainly not her first that afternoon.

'The story about a car crash is balls,' she said. 'He was with one of his floozies. Did you know he was up to his old tricks again?'

Knight hadn't known.

'He started up again about a year ago. Not long after he took office. I could generally tell when he'd been with one of them or when he was going off to meet one. That's where he went last night. I don't know who she was – far less want to.'

'What happened?'

'There was some kind of fracas. The police think it started with the girl getting killed. They say Bill did that.' She gulped at the gin. 'I wouldn't put it past the bastard. The girl's pimp had a gun. You can figure out the rest. The car crash is just a yarn – a cover-up.'

'Where were Bill's detectives?'

'Detective – there was only one.' She laughed up at the ceiling, a short and bitter sound. 'And he was sitting on his arse in the security room here. Take a drink with me, Edmund?'

'I'd best be going. I just wanted to see how you were.'

She walked him to the front door. As he stood on the threshold, he noted how the house and grounds were crawling with plain-clothes and uniformed policemen. He wondered about the official mentality that rushed to slap so many bolts on an empty stable.

He made to kiss her cheek but she turned her face and brushed his lips with her own.

'Don't be such a stranger in future,' she said.

He looked into her eyes for a moment, then turned and walked down the steps to his car.

Bill Clarke had been screwing around but that didn't make him a killer. It was time to think about looking up some old contacts.

He waited until evening, then drove in to London. The pub in Shoe Lane was just as busy as on week nights. Most of the drinkers were journalists or in some way connected with Fleet Street.

He worked his way through to the bar, ordered a pint of best and a large Scotch, paid and told the barman to keep the change.

'Is Riley in?'

The barman hooked his thumb towards the ceiling to indicate the upstairs room.

Riley was in a booth near the fire, his city overcoat on over his suit despite the heat that the logs were throwing out. Knight waited until the youth who was talking to him went away before approaching the table.

'Evening, Doug.'

The journalist looked up from the notes he was scribbling; his big, florid face had the automatic smile that he switched on for everyone who might be bringing him a story.

'Edmund.' The smile vanished. 'Long time no see.'

Knight set the Scotch in front of him. 'I saw your bit today about Bill Clarke.'

Riley's face took on a guarded look. 'Rotten business.'

'Especially when you consider what really happened.'

'Oh yes?'

'You owe me, Doug. I'm collecting. I want to know some things. Like what the police found, who she was.'

Riley looked anguished; the palm of his hand pressed the air above the table in a gesture of silence. 'Christ's sake, Edmund, keep it down. If you knew the knives that are being held at throats over this –'

'I won't rock any of your boats. I just want to know where it happened, how, and the girl's name. Then I'll go away.'

'Why do you want to know?'

'My business.'

'You've got contacts at the Yard. Talk to them.'

'Okay.' Knight stood up. 'Take me off the list next time you want to check a source or a name.'

Riley looked up at him for a time. 'Wait here,' he said, picked up his drink and went downstairs.

When he returned twenty minutes later, he put a slip of paper on the table. 'That's the girl's name and the address of the place. Christine Pangton. Nothing known on her. No suspicious connections or history that we're aware of. There might be if we dug, but we're not likely to. Looks like she was just a working girl. But good background, educated, a cut above the rest. Good quality hooker. Clarke could've run across her in any of a dozen places in town. The man's name that I've given you was her minder. Lived on the premises with her – this place called Brook Cottage. He might also have been her lover.'

'What about how it happened?'

'Murder Squad report suggests that Clarke killed her. *In flagrante.* Strangled her. The minder shot Clarke and his driver, who must have shot back before he died. Bang Bang, all dead. Juicy story, if we could run it.'

'It's sick.'

'It'd sell papers.'

'Why did he strangle her?'

'He didn't mean to, I suppose. Pangton was strapped to the bed, face down. S and M. She was wearing a leather bodice with reins. The reins were tangled around her neck. She had long hair. Maybe Clarke didn't notice the reins were still tight after he let go. Or maybe he got carried away. Hung on too long, got too rough. Who the hell knows how people do these things?'

Knight put the slip of paper in a pocket. 'Thanks, Doug. Sorry I had to get heavy.'

'Sure you are,' Riley replied.

The club was in one of the streets between Kensington Church Street and Holland Park. It was strictly members-only but there were no membership cards. If Greaves didn't know a face, it didn't get in. That was all there was to it.

He took a moment over Knight's face. Then he gave his little, formal smile.

'Mr Knight, isn't it? We haven't seen you for a long time, sir.' He inclined his head slightly and stood aside for Knight to pass.

The building was long and deep. Knight walked along the corridor on the ground floor, past the restaurants with their Roman statuary and where the waitresses wore linen togas, until he came to the rear lobby. As he stood waiting for the lift, he could hear and feel the beat of a disco from the basement.

He rode up to the third floor, past the casinos, gymnasia and massage rooms, walked right to the front of the building again and knocked on the last door he came to. The woman who opened it had a drink in her hand.

'God almighty – Knight! Where have you been hiding?'

'Hello, Thea.'

Thea was handsome rather than beautiful. Her aquiline nose was in keeping with the toga which, like her girls, she wore. She was twice the age of most of them but it didn't show in her figure or her skin.

Knight sat down and took the whisky she offered him.

'Christine Pangton,' he said. 'Was she one of yours?'

Thea slid one hip onto the desk in front of his chair. The toga fell slightly open. She put a cigarette in a long holder and lit it.

'Bill Clarke?' she asked.

He nodded. Lurid news travelled fast.

'Chrissie used to be mine, yes. Nice girl. Only about nineteen or twenty. But she'd been on her own for about six months.'

'Was it here that he first met her?'

Thea nodded. 'About nine or ten months ago. She had a boyfriend of sorts. I hear he was killed too.'

'Was he her pimp?'

'Minder rather than pimp. Chrissie didn't need anyone to hustle for her. Word of mouth was enough. That's why she was able to leave me, when she realised she could go it alone without having to pay my commission. I was sorry she went but I could understand. I'm even sorrier now.'

'What tricks did she do?'

'She could afford to be fussy, so she was. Mostly she kept it clean. Show business type – never worked with children or animals. Also no drugs, no rough stuff.'

'S and M?'

'She might stretch a point for a client she knew well. But she was a sensible girl.'

'She'd have to be tied.'

'There are ways, Knight. Symbolic bonds. Silk cords with slip knots, no chains. No real danger.'

'That's how she'd do it if she had to?'

'Anyone with any sense would.'

'Did you know her boyfriend – the minder?'

'I met him briefly a few times.'

'Violent?'

'Can't tell these days. He was a big lad but he seemed quiet enough.'

Knight put down the half-drunk whisky. Thea slid her hip a little further onto the desk and swung around to stub out the cigarette. The toga parted, revealing the inside of one long thigh. She saw him looking.

'All work and no play, Knight?'

'Another time.'

'Don't forget,' she said automatically. She paused and became thoughtful. 'Why are you asking these questions and not the police?'

'Maybe they will.'

'If they do, what should I tell them?'

'Exactly what you've told me. Goodnight, Thea.'

Each student in the air training school at Kidlington had his own separate study-bedroom. Therefore no one had noticed Ibraham's absence on the Saturday night. The fact that he wasn't at breakfast on Sunday wasn't noticed either. There were many students, of various nationalities; even among his own people Ibraham was a loner. When he failed to show up for flight instruction on Sunday afternoon his instructor asked if anyone knew why but the other students simply shrugged or shook their heads. The instructor was puzzled that Ibraham, a conscientious young man, hadn't bothered to send an explanation via one of them. But it was only a puzzle, not a concern. He marked Ibraham absent and made a mental note to have a tactful word with him next time.

On Sunday evening, by which time Ibraham had missed four of the day's prayer sessions, one of his fellow countrymen decided to inform the Student Welfare Officer. The Officer called the Chief Instructor and together they checked around the other students and members of staff; that was when they established that it was twenty-four hours since anyone had last set eyes on Ibraham. Puzzle turned to worry. He was, after all, Libyan. His government paid well for the training he received at the school, and for the dozens of other young Libyan airmen who attended it each year. In these days of tightening budgets, their business was very welcome.

The school's Principal was phoned at home; he decided that it was time to call the Oxfordshire police. A Panda car prowled Ibraham's jogging route but found nothing.

The Principal phoned Ibraham's embassy, the Libyan People's Bureau, then still in St James's Square, and was given the home number of a junior attaché. He called him and explained the situation. The attaché knew something more than the Principal did: that Ibraham had low-level terrorist connections, that he was an occasional courier. His private and unspoken assumption was that Ibraham had gone on some job and simply been careless about leaving a cover story behind. So he listened politely to the Principal's worries, made reassuring noises, thanked the man for letting him know, expressed the view that it would probably turn out to be nothing more than a case of a young man up to the kind of thing that young men usually got up to, and made a mental note to tell Ibraham's superiors that he was getting careless.

The Oxfordshire police did three things. They quizzed Ibraham's fellow students on his routines and people he associated with or had been seen to meet; not that that got them far. They searched his room and personal effects for clues of any kind. And they logged his disappearance with the central computer at Scotland Yard. Libyans were among the several political or otherwise suspect groups whose movements were monitored in this way. Ultimately the information would reach the files of Martin Kellaway's Political Branch at Curzon Street.

But Ibraham Abukhder would be only one man among dozens that were being sought that weekend. By the time his name and background would be seen to stand out, it would be through events that would themselves make obsolete any further need to search for him.

26

The house at Stratfield Saye was discreet in every way. The country lane in which it stood was just under a mile long and contained about ten other properties. There were a couple of small cottages, a farm, a kennels, and three or four other large houses. These had pleasant names like April Meadow and were the sort of country homes favoured by corporate executives and barristers.

The house in which the Kunaevs were being looked after was bordered by woodland that helped to screen it from the road. There were no observable security measures other than a burglar alarm box on the front wall, which was a standard feature of all the big houses in the road: but there were no guards on the gate, no steel fencing, no dogs in the grounds. Such things would have drawn attention, ruling out the anonymity that was considered essential to good security.

The couple who ran the house and who were thought by the neighbours to be its owners were a military-looking gentleman in his fifties, who was 'something in the Home Office', and his disabled wife. Her disablement was taken as the reason for the resident housestaff and the occasional comings and goings of people assumed to be doctors or physiotherapists.

This was as far as neighbourhood curiosity went. It was the kind of backwater where people valued their privacy and had little time or inclination to know about each other's affairs. There were no coffee mornings, no cocktail parties at Christmas, no summer barbeques; and definitely no questions asked.

'Monday,' Anna said as she knotted her son's shoelaces. 'You're supposed to be on days this week, Viktor. They'll discover you're gone this morning.'

Viktor shook his head. 'They'll have noticed the log book at Porchester Gardens already and seen we didn't come home on Saturday. They'll know already.'

They looked at each other in silence.

'Breakfast is at eight,' he said, not wanting the tension to build up. 'That gives us time for a walk in the garden first.'

Anna zipped Andrei into one of the jump suits that the housekeeper had given her. Changes of clothing had been found for all of them; most of the garments were second-hand but at least they allowed what they'd arrived in to be laundered.

No one interfered with them as they found their way out to the garden, but Viktor saw Anna glance over her shoulder when they got to the swings. A security man was watching them from the kitchen window. He was leaning forward with his elbows on the sill; a cup of coffee was by his elbow and cigarette smoke curled up from an ashtray beside it.

'Did you want to talk?' Anna asked. 'Is that what this is about?'

Viktor nodded and lifted Andrei into the safest-looking swing.

'I knew it.' She looked upset. 'You think they're listening when we're in our room.'

'I don't know. It's possible, even probable. I'd expect them to.'

She pushed her hands down inside the pockets of her anorak. 'When you say things like that, we might as well be back in Porchester Gardens with that washing machine.'

Viktor started pushing Andrei back and forth. The boy giggled with pleasure.

'Look,' Anna said, and nodded at the house. The security man was now strolling up and down the rear patio. He poured the dregs of his coffee onto the lawn and stared down the garden after them. Viktor turned from the swing to watch him; then he watched Anna.

'Forget Porchester Gardens,' she corrected herself. 'It's as if we never left Moscow.'

'No.' Viktor came from the swing and drew one of her hands from the anorak. 'He's on our side. And that's not how I remember Moscow. Protection was one of the things I asked for.' He kissed her fingertips. 'You're upset because it hasn't been as easy as we thought. Yet you can't blame these people for that – they have to be careful.'

'That man Knight – he bullied you.'

Viktor nodded. 'Of course. I might have been a trap.'

'He said your files are worthless. After everything you went through.'

'They probably are. How do I know the British don't already know the information they contain? That doesn't mean Knight has done anything wrong.'

'He practically told you to go back. "We don't want you here." He practically said that.'

'Of course. No one wants a defector. We're a nuisance, we need to be protected, we're expensive. That's all right if it's someone important. But who is Viktor Kunaev?'

'Money. Always money.' She pulled her hand away and thrust it back into the anorak. 'And when you talk about not being important, you sound like him, like Knight.'

Viktor sighed. 'That's because I understand his rules. They'd be mine too if the situation were reversed. This is why I wanted to talk to you. It's a difficult time, Anna. You must keep being strong.'

'How long do I have to be strong for? Months, years?'

'Days, Anna. They're starting to accept we're genuine and not a trap. They believe what I told them about the Spetznaz operation.'

Andrei was slowing down and had started calling for more pushes. Viktor went over to oblige him. As he pushed he looked across at Anna.

'Tonight,' he said, 'I'll tell them about the *avoska*. I'll begin this morning, in fact. That's when I'll tell them my conditions.'

'Conditions. Everything's so cat-and-mouse.'

'That's the world I live in.'

'If Knight doesn't trust you, do you trust him?'

'No.' He stared down the garden, suddenly looking very grave. 'That's also the world I live in. That's why I set conditions. We had to go to Knight because I had no other name. But I don't trust him or any of them – I can't. Not yet anyway.'

He shook the mood aside and lowered himself into the swing beside Andrei's, grinning at him as he flew past. He crooked his fingers and made grabbing motions until the child was almost crying with laughter. Behind him Anna poked with a toe at a fungus clinging to a tree-root.

'This cat-and-mouse world of yours,' she said after a while, 'where no one trusts anyone else. I thought it was like that because Yasyenevo was in charge.'

'Some of it,' he said over his shoulder, still playing with Andrei. 'But some of it is because, well – because that's how my work is.'

She left the tree and came over to stand behind him. At the head of the garden the security man was lighting another cigarette. Anna laid her hands on Viktor's shoulders as she watched him.

'It's a sad world, Viktor Genrikhovich,' she said to the back of his head. 'This world that people like you and that man Knight have made. I'm not sure how much I like it. London or Moscow – what's the difference?'

Viktor turned around in the swing to stare up at her. She looked disheartened. But before he could say anything the figure of the security man caught his eye. He was waving and pointing at his watch.

Anna saw too.

'Breakfast,' she sighed. 'Our new little tsar says so.'

She lifted Andrei down from the swing and set off up the garden, leaving Viktor to follow.

An hour and a half later, Sumner thrashed his old Citroën along the unclassified roads that riddled the Hampshire countryside. He roared through tiny villages that lay like forgotten worlds in the remains of the morning mist. Old women in bread shops and postmen on unsteady bicycles turned their heads to stare after him.

He joined the motorway at Junction 5 and let the needle climb to ninety before he was satisfied. If a patrol car flagged him down, he decided, it would be their hard luck, not his.

He dug the cassette out from his briefcase where it lay on the front passenger seat, put it into the car's player and rewound it. He let it play from the beginning until it was cued to the passage he wanted. His finger was on the eject button when he decided that he wanted to hear the passage again for himself, and he pressed play instead. He heard it through, then re-cued the cassette and took it out. As he stowed it back in the briefcase he shook his head in amazement. This sort of thing was meant to have ended years ago. But it was like indigestion: it kept rumbling on when you thought that there was no more left.

The strange thing was, he should have been shocked and dismayed, or something equally worthy, and nothing else. But in his heart there was a small, secret nub of elation. The sort of feeling you might have on finding evidence that a supposedly extinct species had survived after all; especially if you'd always felt that times had been more exciting when it was around.

No patrol cars appeared and the M3 went past in a blur of preoccupied thought as he considered how to report his news; similarly the outskirts of town and his approach to inner London.

By the time he was seated before Gaunt and Knight in Gaunt's office he had decided that the cassette needed little embellishment by him. He'd brought a portable cassette player along with him. Now he took it out and put it on Gaunt's desk, then set the cassette beside it.

The two men looked at him, waiting for an explanation.

'It's the recording of something new from Kunaev,' he said. 'This morning he announced that he wanted to go into another session. Right there and then. We were surprised. Parrish had been planning to leave it till this afternoon.'

That was enough. He dropped the cassette into the machine, closed the lid and pressed play. Matt Parrish's persuasive tones filled the room.

'. . . ready when you are, Viktor, but I want you to set the pace. You just say whatever it is in any way you can. Now – what did you want to talk about?'

There was a moment of silence. When Kunaev's voice came, it was very soft, abstracted; almost as if he were talking to himself.

'It is a question of who I can trust.'

The cassette rolled on while Parrish let the remark remain unanswered for a time. Sumner glanced at Gaunt and Knight but their eyes were fixed on the cassette player.

'Viktor, we've been all through this yesterday. We're on your side. You made the jump across to us. That took a lot of doing. Do you think we're going to let you down after that? What is it you're frightened of?'

'Not you, I do not think. You are not big enough, high enough. That is why I am telling you. But beyond you? That is a problem.'

'I'm sorry, Viktor, I don't understand.'

'I have proof . . .'

The voice trailed away. Again Parrish waited before pushing him on.

'Proof of what?'

'They destroyed Nikita, the men in the Kremlin. My father loved him. But they called him a peasant and sneered at him. He wanted to give the country back to the people – that was the real reason they hated him. After Brezhnev and the other crooks took control, my father became fearful for the future. Fearful for himself, for my mother, for me. So he arranged some protection – he called it his *avoska*.'

'His what, Viktor?'

'You have never lived in Moscow, Mr Parrish. Or not as a Muscovite. In England you go into your shops and buy what you want. If you have the money. But money alone is not enough in Moscow. The shops are so often empty. Or filled with rubbish. So you carry always a little string bag. Folded in your pocket or the corner of a handbag. In case something good appears in the market one day. The bag is *avoska*. A just-in-case thing.'

'This *avoska* of your father's, Viktor – what is it?'

'That does not matter. Not yet. What it proves is all that matters.'

'All right. What does it prove?'

Another long silence followed, punctuated only by the faint, regular squeak of the cassette's reel mechanism. Sumner didn't dare fast-forward the tape for fear of missing the vital seconds. Knight looked up inquiringly but he avoided looking at him. Gaunt's head was bent; his eyes were closed.

Finally, Parrish's voice resumed, very gently.

'Viktor, will you tell me what the *avoska* proves?'

When Kunaev made his answer, his voice was little more than a whisper.

'It proves that there is a traitor in your organisation, Mr Parrish. A mole, as you would say. No ordinary mole. Not like the others that you people get so excited about. Always you are so busy looking for them that you do not think who or what else might be among you. This man is a sleeper, you see – of a unique kind. He has been climbing the ranks of your organisation for twenty years, waiting for his time. By now he should be at the highest level. The highest level. That is what he was groomed for.'

Sumner reached to the tape machine and pressed stop. Gaunt's face was inscrutable as he looked up at him.

'Who else has heard this?'

'Only Matt Parrish.'

'Stenographer?'

'He wasn't present. The interview was unscheduled.'

Gaunt sat back in his chair and swung away from them. They waited for his judgement. A minute ticked by.

'We have here an allegation,' he said at last, still facing the window. 'A grave allegation, yes, but still only an allegation. It may be true, it may not. Until it is proven – if it can be – it is imperative that as few people as possible learn of it. That becomes our first priority.' He sucked in his narrow cheeks. 'I'll have to tell the PM, of course. And the Cabinet Secretary. Not the Joint Intelligence Committee, however – damn thing leaks like a sieve.' He took a deep breath. 'Our second priority is to see if it is true.'

'And if it is,' Knight asked quietly. 'Then who do you tell?'

Gaunt's morose eyes regarded him evenly. 'In that event, it becomes even more important that as few people as possible learn of it.'

Knight turned to Sumner. 'Has Kunaev said exactly what his proof is – this so-called *avoska*?'

Sumner shook his head. 'As soon as he got that far he clammed up. Said he wanted to think before he told us any more. When we saw he was determined, we called it a day and I came here at once.'

Knight made to rise. 'He's had his thinking time. I'll go back with you now and we'll talk to him some more.'

Sumner shook his head again. 'There's a problem with doing that, Edmund.'

'What?'

'Kunaev refuses to talk to anyone from now on except Matt Parrish and myself.'

He looked at the men's faces; both were still tense but he saw realisation dawning in their eyes; he rewound the cassette for a second or two and pressed play again.

'. . . waiting for his time. By now he should be at the highest level. The highest level. That is what he was groomed for . . .'

It was Knight who put it into blunter words: Knight who, as Director of Counter Espionage, was the most senior man after Gaunt himself.

'He's pointing at you and me, Horace,' he said. 'He says it's you or me.'

Sumner was despatched to make arrangements with Parrish for a further session with Kunaev; but Knight made no move to leave Gaunt's office.

Gaunt looked at him warily. 'Are you about to suggest that we discuss this?'

'Don't you think we should?'

Gaunt straightened some of the things on his desk before looking at him. 'Until we have proof – whether from Kunaev or in some other way – it seems to me that such a discussion is entirely without benefit. Each of us would of course deny the allegation. We might each try to lay it at the other's door. Neither action would be proof of anything. We would be no further forward than we are now. I fail to see the point. We will await Kunaev's proof – if it exists.'

'Don't you think your reticence could be interpreted in another way?'

Gaunt uncrossed his thin legs. 'Don't waste my time, Edmund. Your eagerness could be interpreted in just the same way. You're demonstrating my point perfectly.' He sat forward and spread the palms of his hands on the desk, a signal that he wanted to get on, that their meeting was over. But Knight still remained where he was.

'We have other business, Horace. What I really wanted to talk to you about. Bill Clarke's death.'

'Bill Clarke? What an awful thing. I was with him only that afternoon. We had a meeting with the PM. When I heard the news I just couldn't believe it. Such a terrible waste –'

'It was no accident.'

Gaunt withdrew his hands and sat back again. 'What are you saying?' His face was giving nothing away.

'His death wasn't an accident. Not in the car, anyway. I don't think it was an accident at all. To start with, as you well know, there was no car crash.'

Gaunt blinked slowly. 'I know this, do I?'

'You're wasting my time now. I know about the hooker, about Brook Cottage, about all of it.'

'That's classified information, Edmund. Extremely classified.'

'Classified?' Knight shook his head sceptically. 'Half of London knows what really happened. Or think they do. The sex games that went wrong.'

'Who told you this?'

'That doesn't matter.'

Gaunt drummed his fingertips together softly.

'The facts of the matter are these,' Knight went on. 'Everyone's doing what they were set up for: putting together a cover-up to protect Clarke's name, his family's peace and the government's standing. But the sex was a decoy. Or at least, the way it ended. We've obligingly created a cover-up on top of one that was already there. The media's been taken in just as effectively as the rest of us. They've stopped digging for anything else because they think the sex is all there is. They've been frightened off because of the pressure to keep the lid on what is in fact the wrong cover-up. Someone's murdered a senior member of the government – not to mention three other people – and we're helping them get away with it.'

'Do you have justification for any of this?'

'Some. What started me off was this.' Knight took a folded sheet of paper from his pocket and tossed it across the desk. Gaunt unfolded it and scanned it quickly.

'What is this?'

'Bill Clarke called me on Friday night. That's the message he left on my answerphone. He was badly upset about something.'

'It could mean anything or nothing. You two were old friends. What's odd about him calling you?'

'We hadn't been in touch for months. And you haven't heard how he sounds. Worked-up, rattled.'

'I'd like to hear that recording. Do you have it?'

Knight shook his head. 'It's at home.' He stood to leave. 'Here's why I'm telling you this, Horace. Bill Clarke was a friend once. Now he's dead. No one cares a toss, not even his wife. He was no saint, but he wasn't a killer either. His widow thinks he was, and a lot of other people. That's how he'll be remembered. But it was the other way around – someone murdered him. I don't know if it was connected with why he wanted to see me or not. Either way, someone's been very clever and the Murder Squad and Special Branch haven't got a clue – or maybe don't want one. I think we owe it to Clarke to get to the truth. You'll have to talk to Special Branch, raise merry hell if you have to.' He drew a deep breath. 'If you don't, I bloody will.'

He left the office before Gaunt could reply.

In the corridor he almost bowled Joss Franklyn over.

'Steady, old man,' Franklyn said through his usual cloud of pipe smoke.

'Sorry, Joss. Wasn't looking.'

'In a paddy with Gaunt, more like. What's he been saying to you? Ticking you off about these Spetznaz boys getting in? Mustn't let him get to you.'

'No, nothing like that.'

Franklyn took the pipe from his mouth and peered into Knight's face. 'You need a break, Edmund. What about some opera?'

'What?'

'I've got a couple of tickets for tonight. Wife's poorly, can't come. Why don't you come with me, it'll take you out of yourself. *The Barber of Seville*. Lots of fun.'

Knight laughed, thinking of the Kunaev debrief that was barred to him anyway.

'Taking out of myself,' he said. 'That I could surely do with.'

Franklyn held up the folder in his hand. 'I'm on my way in to see Gaunt myself, let him know what I'm doing with my people in regard to the Spetznaz unit. Only be about ten minutes. I'll pop down and see you after and we can sort out times. Sound all right?'

Knight nodded, grateful for the man's kindness. Franklyn stuck the briar back between his teeth and, pulling a face for Knight's benefit, tapped on Gaunt's door.

Later, with Franklyn gone, Gaunt sat back and thought. He thought very hard indeed. He swivelled his chair in small motions from side to side, his bony elbows resting on its cushioned arms and his legs crossed again. He steepled his fingers and let his thumbs beat a soundless tattoo against one another. These were his only outward movements. His head was down, his great eyes seemed to be fixed on some secret inner scene.

His secretary crept in at some stage and left a file of letters on the corner of his desk. She said nothing to break his concentration, and closed the door on her way out as quietly as if a baby had been asleep in the room.

After fifteen or twenty minutes he sat upright. He laid his arms on the desk top and breathed deeply, like a man waking from a catnap.

He picked up the receiver of the black phone by his elbow and tapped in a number. All the telephone lines in that building and its satellites spread around London were among the most secure in the world. There was no need to bother with the scramble button.

'Gaunt here. I think we have a problem.'

He paused, fastidiously aligning his jotter and pen and listening to the question that was asked.

'Mr Edmund Knight,' he replied.

He listened again.

'There is a complication. I have been giving it some thought. I have concluded on a course of action. I think we must implement it at once. It requires your sanction.'

He listened a third time, then rang off. He stood up, ignoring the file of letters, gathered his camel topcoat from the hatstand, and left the office.

27

Moscow

The money began moving at midday; the money that Serov had fretted over.

Director Smolny of the Foreign Trade Bank was alerted by his deputy that some major transferrals were being effected. He capped his fountain pen, clipped it safely away in an inside pocket of his dark suit, and followed the deputy to the communications room. Their progress was stately: two plump burghers as filled with importance as a good chicken Kiev is full of Ukrainian butter. Heads turned to watch them pass, sensing that something of moment was afoot.

The telex machine was still chattering when they arrived in the marble-floored room. Two whole sheets had been filled and a third was two-thirds done. Smolny clasped his hands behind his back and waited. Halfway down the fourth sheet the machine's print head fell silent; the sheet reeled up to the end and stopped.

A second or two passed, just long enough for the men to assert that theirs was not a hurly-burly world, before the deputy looked questioningly at Smolny. The director nodded once. The deputy went to the machine, carefully detached the sheets, folded them in sequence and handed them to him. Like the good servant delivering a newspaper on its silver tray, it was not for him to glance at the sheets in advance of his master.

Smolny slipped a set of half-moon spectacles onto his nose, lifted his eyebrows to settle the spectacles comfortably in place, and scanned the long list of account numbers and amounts.

'These are substantial receipts,' he remarked after a time. There was approval in his voice. 'Very substantial indeed.'

The deputy adopted a look of mild gratification. His head tilted and a small smile came to his damp lips.

'What accounts would these be?' Smolny wondered.

The deputy cleared his throat softly. In that place it had all the significance of a lengthy speech.

Smolny peered at him over the spectacles. 'Yes?'

'I believe they're some of the secure accounts, comrade Director.'

Smolny stared for a moment, then went back to the telex sheets. KGB account numbers. Registered against a series of dummy organisations and non-existent individuals; a way of moving funds about. Smolny sighed. When the Foreign Trade Bank was used, it generally meant that the funds were to leave the Soviet Union. Sooner or later; he hoped later.

The credits, he noted, came from three sources, all at the State Bank. He didn't need the deputy's assistance to know which they were. Their importance and prestige made their codes familiar to every senior banking officer in the capital. One was the Central Committee account, the second a holding account normally used for military procurement budgets, and the third was one of the KGB's own Treasury accounts.

Satisfied that no more was to be learnt from the telex sheets, he thrust them at the deputy.

'See that these transfers are verified and recorded.' He took off his glasses and waved them at the deputy. 'And don't delegate it – do it yourself.'

With that he swept back to his office, pleased to contemplate what the aggregate of the receipts would do to the day's balances. To say nothing of the week's; the month's if they were left that long; perhaps even the accounting quarter's: he could keep hoping.

An hour later the deputy tapped respectfully on his door and peeped his head round it.

'Comrade Director, further instructions have been received on those secure accounts.'

Smolny looked up as sharply as if his head had been on a spring.

'What?' He stopped jotting digits on the ruled sheets spread over his desk and held his pen in mid-air. His other hand clasped its cap anxiously. 'What instructions?'

The deputy looked mournful. 'We are to wait till five pm today. By then banking hours will have begun in Panama.'

'Panama?'

'We are to transfer everything to a series of accounts in one of the Panamanian banks.'

Smolny's fingers were pressing on the cap of the pen so hard that they were turning white.

'Five pm?' he echoed.

The deputy nodded. 'I'm afraid it means that not a kopek of the receipts can be counted in today's balances.' The slightest hint of that small smile reappeared on his damp lips as he withdrew and closed the door quietly.

Serov was going through Valyukev's inspection report on the London *rezidentura* when the phone rang. Valyukev himself was on the line.

'Everything seems to be in good shape in London,' Serov told him.

Valyukev's response was a dry little cough. 'That's what I want to speak to you about, comrade General.'

'Indeed?'

'Lyulkin just called me. Viktor Kunaev – the cipher clerk that you said had to be recalled now that he has no surviving family here –'

'I remember.'

'Lyulkin told Kunaev on Friday.' Valyukev paused. 'He hasn't been seen since.'

Serov drew a deep breath and let it out slowly. 'Exactly what are you telling me, Major General?'

'Kunaev was last seen by Lyulkin on Friday afternoon.' Valyukev sounded like he was reading directly from notes; which he probably was. 'On Saturday morning the watch detail on duty at his living quarters recorded him setting out with his wife and child. On Sunday morning the watch officer made his routine daily check of the log and noted that they still hadn't been recorded returning home. He phoned their apartment but received no answer. He alerted Lyulkin and was authorised by him to enter the apartment. There was no sign of them although all their belongings were still there.' He was taking shelter in minutiae.

'Has anyone checked hospitals and police stations?' Serov asked wearily; often these people forgot the most obvious things.

'Lyulkin checked those in the vicinity of the Kunaevs' home, without coming up with anything. He didn't want to put out more extensive enquiries for fear of raising British suspicions.'

'We have a problem, comrade.'

'I've left Lyulkin in no doubt about my views on his responsibility in this matter, comrade General.'

'I expect they'll be much the same as mine about yours. Have we started damage assessment?'

'Yes, sir.' Serov heard him breathing heavily. 'There's a number of papers –'

'Get up here. Bring a list of the papers with you. Get a gloss of them from Depository.'

'Yes, comrade General. At once.'

Serov put the phone down and took a cigar from the open packet on the desk. He peeled off the wrapper and dropped it in the bin.

'What a surprising young man you are, Viktor Kunaev,' he said. He put the cigar between his teeth, flicked his lighter and studied its flame. 'Almost as surprising as your father.' He lit the cigar and called Sergei to tell him to show Valyukev in as soon as he arrived.

It took them an hour and a half to go through the checklist of missing papers; Valyukev brought copies of some and the glossary summation of the remainder.

'Things could be worse,' Serov admitted, rising to his feet. 'At least as far as this material is concerned.'

Valyukev relaxed visibly but still looked wary; he knew he wasn't yet out of danger.

'You briefed Lyulkin on the Spetznaz unit?' Serov asked.

Valyukev nodded. 'I didn't refer to it in my report because you said there was to be nothing on the record.'

'You stressed that to Lyulkin?'

'Certainly.'

'And told him to keep it to himself?'

Valyukev looked slightly indignant. 'Of course, comrade General.' He realised the import of Serov's question and added, 'I'm certain he wouldn't have mentioned anything to Kunaev.'

Serov nodded, looking thoughtfully at Valyukev. 'You may go now, Major General.'

He returned to his desk and, still standing, began leafing through a document. Valyukev's gaze slid to the side, as if he were looking for an ambush of some sort. He rose uncertainly and saluted. Serov returned it casually and Valyukev made for the door. But as he opened it Serov spoke.

'Comrade Major General.'

'Sir?'

'Make arrangements for Colonel Lyulkin's recall to Moscow for full interrogation as soon as possible.'

Valyukev breathed a quiet little sigh of relief. 'Yes, comrade General.' He turned back to the door.

'And let me have a set of personnel transfer papers when it's convenient for you to do so. After you've sorted out Lyulkin's recall will do. There's no hurry. Have the papers completed except for the destination. I'll see to that.'

'Transfer papers, sir? For Lyulkin?'

Serov was engrossed in the document he was reading. He flicked a page and didn't bother looking up again.

'No,' he muttered absently. 'For yourself. That'll be all, Major General.'

Kunaev didn't seem to pose any significant risk. He knew nothing of the Spetznaz unit. His defection was no more than irritating as far as his work in the *rezidentura* was concerned. The materials he'd taken with him would provide confirmation of some minor operations in which the *rezidentura* had been engaged. They could be aborted without disastrous consequences. The British, assuming that was who he'd run to, probably suspected their existence anyway. Meanwhile, nothing major had been put in jeopardy. A few transmission codes would become obsolete.

That was it. That was the most damage Viktor Kunaev could bring about.

Serov puffed lazily on his cigar and wondered where would be a good place to send Valyukev.

Vladimir Chernavin, Senior Special Inspector in the Second Chief Directorate's Department for Struggle Against Embezzlement of Socialist Property and Speculation, was a broken man.

Standing inside the front door of his apartment, he opened his dressing-gown and scratched absently at his soft paunch, unable to take in the meaning of the letter that had come for him.

It was signed personally by the Director of the Second Chief Directorate and copied to that individual's immediate superior, the KGB's First Deputy Chairman; which meant that it had been written at the latter's instigation. Which meant that it had probably been the idea of Chairman Viktor Chebrikov himself.

Chernavin read it three times before he even understood it. Even then, he wasn't convinced that he'd got it right and went back to the start again.

'Put the Yeliseyev investigation in abeyance?' he said at last, addressing the letter as if it were its author. 'Food Shop Number One? When we're so close? Even if we did lose Gulyaev. There were killings as well – the body in the church, the one in the river, the bombed car! Now I should shelve the whole thing? You can't mean that! Surely not!'

So he read the letter through for a fifth time; and in the end he was left with no option but to conclude that that was precisely what the Director did mean.

Oh yes, there were a few complimentary words for his handling of the investigation to date, and reassurances that no criticism attached to his or his team's efforts and skills. But the Director's view, after the most careful consideration and consultation with other senior colleagues – 'Aha!' cried Chernavin, 'There! I knew it! Chebrikov!' – was that other cases on the comrade Senior Special Inspector's files seemed more likely to bear fruit at present. And, after all, the resources of the Department were not limitless and had to be focused in a disciplined manner. Besides, the Director suggested consolingly, it might be that some of the other cases on the comrade Senior Special Inspector's files would, in the end, connect back to the Food Shop Number One affair. The Director finished by wishing him luck with these cases and looked forward to seeing his customary outstanding results in due course.

Chernavin crumpled the letter in his hand and returned to the bedroom. Nina's ample frame waited for him in the bed, her red hair spread over his pillow. She sat up as he entered.

'They can't stop writing to you even when you take a day's leave?' she said. 'What an important man you are. Come back here quickly. You're mine today, important man.'

He walked to the bed in a daze; the letter fell from his fingers and she snatched it up.

'Anything interesting?' She started to unfold the letter, spreading it on the coverlet and running her hand over it to smooth the creases.

'I've been muzzled,' he said quietly, still dazed. 'Like an old Borzoi hound that's had his day.'

'Oh dear.' She scanned the note thoughtfully. Then she grinned, patted the bed and tugged at his dressing-gown.

'Come here and I'll make it up to you. Woof woof.'

'Come and see, Galina.'

Ogarkin laid the large package on the chair and began tearing off the paper. He paused as a sneeze overwhelmed him and afterwards crammed the tissue into the pocket of his white coat; it already bulged with a collection of used tissues.

She stayed where she was, motionless on the bed, but her eyes followed his fingers as he pulled the string aside and the contents spilled out.

'Oil paints,' he said, picking out the dark wooden case and presenting it open before her. He was like a little excited magician. The case held two rows of paint tubes, brushes, jars of linseed oil and spirit, a box of charcoal and a palette-knife; there was a palette-board clipped inside the lid. It was the kind of beginner's case that might be given to a child but her heart lifted to see it.

'An easel.' He struggled to unfold it but gave up and leant it against the chair.

'Canvasses.' They were canvas-boards in fact, second-best by a long way, but she was gladdened to see them nonetheless.

'Sketch pad. Pencils. Apron. Everything you need.' He flung the apron over the chair and stood back to survey his booty triumphantly, his gaze flicking back and forth to her face.

She looked at the display in silence for a few moments.

'Cleaning rags,' she said under her breath.

He jumped as if she'd shrieked at him. 'What?' His face was a mixture of incomprehension at her words and delight to hear her say something at last. 'Cleaning rags – what do you mean?' He stopped staring at her for a moment and looked again at the array of items.

'Ah!' he exclaimed. 'Now I see it. I forgot cleaning rags! Idiot! I'll send someone around the wards rightaway. We must be stuffed full of old rags.'

He turned for the door but stopped abruptly as he reached it, and came back to her. He dived a hand into the coat pocket, thankfully not the one the used tissues had gone into, and pulled out a clutch of clean ones. He dropped them on the bed.

'Here! Here! These'll get you started.'

Then he was gone, leaving her staring at the ridiculous handful of tissues. As his footsteps faded she heard him sneeze again. The footsteps stopped and there was a moment of silence; she imagined him reaching for the tissues that were no longer there. Then she heard him swear and snort loudly. The footsteps hurried away.

That night, Serov found Gramin in the Armenian's, at his usual corner table. For once he was alone.

'The night's young, comrade,' Gramin explained, waving a stubby hand at his surroundings to illustrate the point.

Serov looked; by its usual standards, the shebeen was under-populated. A few blowsy prostitutes sat yawning on barstools, spinning out their half-litres of beer until a client or two arrived to offer them something better. A group of elderly men, out-of-towners by the sound of their accents and exaggerated laughter, were drinking too much too quickly in a booth in the corner along from Gramin's. Their eyes wandered often towards the hookers, and they muttered and laughed some more. Some younger types were engaged in grave, whispered conversation on the other side. Serov's guess was that their purpose was business: a deal of some sort was being thrashed out. They'd probably move on when they'd concluded it. Little profit for the Armenian there.

'One day soon this place will be raided,' Serov remarked.

'Raided?' Gramin shook his head. 'Never. The Armenian's too well connected. Safest place in Moscow, this. That's why I like it. Health!'

Serov watched as a tumblerful of vodka vanished.

'Remember young Viktor Kunaev?' he asked when the glass was back on the table.

'Of course. His old papa handed in his card last month. Viktor came over to see him off. I kept an eye on him for a few days for you.'

'He didn't seem to do much with his time.'

'That's right. Hung about the hospital, mostly.'

'There was one afternoon when he went to his father's apartment.'

Gramin nodded. 'And fetched some pyjamas.'

'But you said at the time you couldn't be certain if that was all he collected.'

'I remember. He might've been getting something else. That's what you said when I told you he had a briefcase with him.'

'I want you to tell me everything you saw that day. Was he carrying anything else, for example?'

'Well,' Gramin said slowly, 'I even went so far as to talk my way into the old boy's apartment. I had a good nose around after the son had gone. I was still none the wiser, though.'

'Tell me everything anyway.'

The car park was starting to fill up by the time Serov was leaving. The luxurious Chaika looked almost second-rate among the Saabs, BMWs, Renaults and Volvos that were arriving. You could drive around Moscow for months and see nothing better than a Moskvich, but if you knew where to look it was a different picture. Serov didn't mind; one day his turn would come.

One day soon.

He got on to the forest road out of Scholkovo and headed back to town, still pondering Gramin's account. There were no clues in what he'd been able to remember. If Kunaev had taken anything, it was small enough to fit into a pocket or that briefcase, and sufficiently innocuous to take through security and customs at Sheremetyevo and London without raising any eyebrows. According to FCD Administration, Kunaev had made no special baggage exemption arrangements before leaving, which, as embassy staff and particularly as an embassy *rezident*, he could easily have done.

Serov shifted restlessly in his seat and drummed his fingers on the steering wheel. Maybe he was seeing danger where none existed. Like his scepticism about the Armenian's ability to survive the present purges.

The road widened and its crust of snow thinned as he passed the ring motorway, marking the city limits. A huge illuminated sign swept past overhead; one of the words on it caught his eye.

Izmaylovo.

He smiled. Why not take a look? Idle curiosity, nothing else. The past was never being far behind. In Moscow, sometimes, it was never far away either.

He inched the car right up to the gates of the mansion until its bumper rattled against them, and climbed out. Most of the street lamps had failed but the Chaika's headlights showed him as much as he wanted to see.

It was a sorry sight: sandstone walls that now were stained and discoloured with damp, windows long-since boarded-up, a jungle of Virginia creeper, leafless in this season, that threatened to engulf the entire hulk of the place.

He gripped the bars of the gates and shook them to see if they were locked. Rust flaked off in his hands.

He sighed and turned away. Standing there in the snow, which was deep enough in that forsaken road to have piled itself into man-high drifts against the walls of the old academy, he closed his eyes and remembered.

It was summer again and he was – what? – twenty-four? twenty-three? Sunshine glinted on the arched windows, he felt the warm coarseness of the sandstone under his hand. Overhead, chevrons of geese thirty or forty strong made for the lakes of Izmaylovo Park; the crack of their wings against the hot air seemed the loudest sound that was likely to disturb the stillness of those walled grounds.

Inside, in the coolness of the mansion's great rooms, sat Major Genrikh Kunaev, in an office cluttered with books and mementos: a dry old man in a dusty room.

Old? He seemed old even then, with his shiny, bald skull and those pebble glasses. Peevish and dried up.

Somewhere in another room a voice droned on: a lecture. The clatter of a typewriter escaped through an open window to the gardens. And old Kunaev looked up as Captain Nikolai Serov was shown into the dusty room to meet him for the first time.

'Your academic qualifications are a little thinner than I would have wished, Captain.'

'I'm sorry, comrade Major. Where I grew up there weren't that many schools and colleges left standing after the Germans had been through. And I was too busy worrying where my next meal was coming from to have much time for book-learning.'

'Those days were hard for all of us, Captain. I see you made time to get yourself full party membership, though. That's an unusual accomplishment at your age, even without having to combine it with a military career.'

'I've never thought about whether or not it's unusual. It just seems to me that willingness to serve the party should rank high in the priorities of all young people with energy.'

'Indeed, Captain? Well, I'm sure you're right. You'll pardon my comments regarding your modest educational attainments. I don't mean to give offence.'

'None taken.'

'It's just that the young people who attend this academy are . . . rather special, intellectually. I'd like my Captain-Adjutant to be able to relate directly to them.'

'I understand, comrade Major. I'll make special efforts.'

'You will. Good.'

Serov's eyes snapped open and the wintry night returned.

'Damn you to hell, Kunaev,' he said. 'If you're not there already.'

He shivered as he felt the cold suddenly penetrate, and drew the leather greatcoat closer about him.

Lunacy, he thought; lunacy and pointless, to stand there cursing an old man's ghost. He had much to do tonight. Far wiser to be off and see to the needs of the living. He climbed back into the car and turned the heater to full.

The mansion's boarded-up windows, like blank, empty eyes, stared unwavering into the night as he drove off.

'She was only a child, Georgi.'

Zavarov shook his head. 'She was a grown woman, Olga. Nineteen years old. I was shooting Germans in the Ukraine when I was nineteen.'

He took the silver-framed photograph gently from Olga's hands and stood up to return it to the piano. He still wore his heavy outer coat and overshoes; he hadn't made time to take them off when he'd come in and heard her sobbing.

Sobbing; she seemed to do nothing else these days.

The overshoes dripped melting snow on the carpet as he crossed the room; he pushed them off onto the small rug under the piano stool and went to the liquor cabinet.

'Here,' he said as he brought her over a brandy. 'For once, drink it and don't argue. Medicinal reasons.'

She forced a smile. 'You'd know, wouldn't you?' She swallowed a mouthful and pulled a face as it went down.

'What hurts most of all is not knowing,' she whispered when she'd caught her breath. She clasped her arms about herself and began to rock slowly back and forth. The brandy washed up and down the sides of the glass with her movement. 'Not knowing where she went. Or why, Georgi – why? Not knowing where she is now. Or even if she's still alive. My dear God.'

Zavarov turned back to the cabinet and poured a brandy for himself. As he knocked it back he clamped his eyes tight shut and wished silently for strength. Strength to get through the next few weeks; strength to keep carrying Ligachev, who wasn't nearly as self-assured as he wanted Serov to believe. And strength to cope with Olga and her ceaseless maundering.

'Don't go over it again, my love,' he said, sounding more tender-hearted than he felt. 'Not tonight.'

For want of something to busy himself with, he collected the overshoes and slipped off his coat on the way out of the hall. There was a rustling sound as he reached the half-open door; it seemed to have come from the far end of the corridor. He folded the coat over one arm and went along to investigate.

He rounded the corner at the end and stopped dead. Ratushny's flabby face was peering up at him, looming pale against the darkness.

He couldn't have looked more guilty or scared if he'd still been standing by the drawing-room door.

'You worthless little maggot,' Zavarov hissed.

Ratushny's mouth opened to say something, his chins quivering. But before the words could form, Zavarov dropped the overshoes and cracked the open palm of an enormous hand across his jaw. The majordomo folded silently to his knees, blood spilling over his white uniform as the coffee had done on that fateful morning when Ligachev called. He cupped his hands as if to catch the blood and pressed them to his face.

Zavarov bent over and seized him by the scruff of the neck.

'Get to your rooms,' he rasped in Ratushny's ear, 'before I tear you in half.'

Olga's voice, still tearful but now anxious as well, called from the drawing-room.

'What's that noise, Georgi? Is anything the matter?'

Ratushny scuttled off, dripping blood, and Zavarov flopped against the wall. He forced calmness into his voice.

'It's all right, my love,' he called, 'I'm just being clumsy. I dropped my overshoes, nearly tripped on them. But I'm all right.'

He clamped his eyes shut again and tried to drive away that beautiful young face in the photograph that floated up before them.

28

London

The bald man arrived at the Opera House at seven fifteen and went straight to his seat in the downstairs part of the auditorium. He dropped a coin into the mechanism on the back of the seat in front of him and unclipped the opera glasses. In the last moments before the lights dimmed he amused himself by scanning the auditorium. His survey included the Grand Tier.

He saw Knight and Franklyn arrive just before the overture began. They had prestigious seats at the end of the Tier's front row, where it curved around towards the stage; only the private boxes were closer to the performers. When the bald man saw Knight settled in the seat at the end of the row he put the glasses away and sat back to enjoy the evening's performance.

He smiled as the Count fell in love with Rosina and Figaro schemed with him to win her hand; he laughed at gloomy Don Basilio and Bartolo; his shiny head swayed in time with Rossini's melodies; he called out 'Bravo!' with everyone else in appreciation of the ensemble at the end of Act One.

At the interval he let himself be swept along with the chattering crowds as they flooded out of the auditorium. But instead of going to the bars and buffets as they did, he picked his way through the flow of people towards the toilets. He was still smiling.

He stood in a cubicle with the door locked until he knew that the toilets were empty. His suit jacket was hanging behind the cubicle door. The lightweight nylon jacket that had been folded up in its inside pocket now hung over it, to give the wrinkles a chance to fall out. It was wine-coloured, like the uniform of the Opera House staff. At a distance no one would note the absence of braid or the fact that it was the wrong material.

Four leather slings were strapped about his body, two under each armpit. The suit jacket had concealed them earlier; now he slipped on the nylon jacket and buttoned it up carefully.

He stood there patiently until he heard the distant strains of the aria, *'Il vecchiotto cerca moglie'*. It was his signal that Scene One of Act Two was drawing to a close; it was time for him to go to his position.

He moved from the cubicle to the outer door, opening it half an inch, then an inch, as he watched and listened. The foyer was deserted.

He stepped out and closed the toilet door gently. From the foyer he turned confidently down a corridor that ran along the building's perimeter.

At length he came to some narrow stone steps that led upwards by the outer wall. Instead of the rich carpets and polished wood of the public areas, here there was only cold stone and brick, plastic and lead. Bare pipes criss-crossed the walls; low-wattage bulbs left shadows in corners and turnings.

The stairway wound up behind the Grand Tier and on up again behind the Balcony Tier. The music grew in volume as the stairway rose higher. At this level only the wall separated it from the performance, whereas on its lower level small offices, toilets, boiler rooms and plumbing had intervened.

At the top of the staircase a scuffed wooden door faced the bald man. He was at his destination. He knew exactly where he stood; he had studied the plans. Beneath his feet curved the great dome of the auditorium. Forward of him it swept towards the stage, behind him to the Balcony Tier, and on either side to the wings of the Grand Tier.

A hundred feet below him, Rosina's anguish mounted as Bartolo told of the Count's unfaithfulness and swore his own love for her. The music soared in an orchestral thunderstorm that symbolised the torture in her soul.

The bald man unbuttoned the nylon jacket and drew the components of the Mauser SP66 sniper's rifle from the leather slings. The Mauser was one of the world's most accurate weapons, and the model in the bald man's hands had been customised to break down into the four pieces he now began to fit together: the barrel, the stock, the butt and a Smith & Wesson image-intensifying night-sight. The butt was distinctively formed, shaped like a pistol grip with the shoulder rest extending behind it; the design, even to the adjustable cheek-rest and the thumb-hole behind the pistol grip, gave the user the best possible and steadiest hold on the weapon. The muzzle was already fitted with a silencer and a flash hider, the latter intended to prevent the firer being dazzled by the weapon's flash at night.

When the Mauser was assembled and its bolt primed, the bald man pulled the scuffed door open, snatching his hand back at once to the rifle. The music drowned the click of the doorlock and his foot stopped the door before it smacked against the jamb.

The room was long and narrow. It curved with the dome that formed one of its sides; its far wall sloped away towards the apex. This wall was open to the auditorium below, like a long, thin window; huge lights were ranged along it, flashing lightning to the stage as the storm roared on.

There was only one man in the room. He was bearded, wearing jeans, and sat on a stool before a complex panel of switches and slide controls.

Something made him turn around as the bald man entered, perhaps the change in air temperature caused by the open door. His eyes widened in alarm.

Unhurriedly, even as he was moving into the room, the bald man steadied the Mauser and touched the trigger, firing from waist level and releasing the first of the magazine's three rounds. A torrent of blood spurted from the technician's chest and he toppled backwards with the force of the 7.62mm bullet. A puff of plaster indicated that it had torn right through him and embedded itself in the wall behind.

The bald man was beside the technician as he fell, able to catch an arm and lower him gently to the floor. Sidestepping the pool of blood, he checked that the man was dead, then straightened up and chose a good spot at the thin window.

From the privileged seats of the Grand Tier the spectacle of the storm was exhilarating. In the main room of Bartolo's house Rosina flung herself to the floor, bosom heaving. The music climbed to a crescendo, swelling through the rapt auditorium. The floodlights had dimmed to a flicker, trembling on the verge of darkness. Lightning flashed across the sky beyond Bartolo's windows, throwing into relief Rosina's sobbing form.

High on Bartolo's walls were recessed alcoves in which sat scrolls, books and pottery jars.

The thunder rolled. In a fine piece of dramatic timing, one of the largest pottery jars toppled from its alcove to smash on the floor at the precise moment that the thunder crashed. The thunder rolled again; another jar tumbled, there was another mighty crash.

Joss Franklyn was enthralled; he had an even better view than in Act One, sitting now in the seat that Knight had occupied earlier. He'd forgotten to extinguish his pipe after the interval and had returned to the auditorium with it clamped as usual between his teeth. An usher had spotted him, he'd doubled back to find an ashtray, and when he finally got to the front row the curtain was rising. But Knight had moved up a seat so that he could slip in at the end of the row; and that was where he now sat.

The bullet thudded into his heart just as a third pottery jar shattered on the floor.

Beside him Knight felt him shudder, and thought he was jumping in surprise at the crashing jars, like himself. Only when Franklyn's head and shoulders began to slump forward did he turn towards him.

'Joss?'

He touched Franklyn's arm. There was no response.

'Joss? Jesus.'

Franklyn was falling sideways, away from him, and into the aisle-space.

A heart attack was Knight's first thought, and he knelt down to undo Franklyn's collar and tie. But his hand met a damp wetness.

'What the –'

There was a sickness in the pit of his stomach as he hurriedly tore the man's jacket and shirt open. The music pounded on, drowning the sound of ripping cloth as Franklyn's soaked shirt split. Knight bent his head close to the man's chest. Even in the semi-darkness he could see that it was one large, dark stain. This close, the smell of the blood was overpowering. For a moment Knight stared in disbelief, finally, slowly, beginning to grasp what had happened. Then, whispering Franklyn's name over and over, he tried to be practical. He could make out no details to find where the wound was and had to run his hand across Franklyn's chest, gagging at the feel and tang of the warm blood. At last his fingers slipped into a hole large enough to accommodate three of them; it was jagged and fragments of bone had been pumped out by the blood, catching in Knight's fingers. Swallowing a mouthful of bile that made his eyes stream, Knight grabbed his scarf from the seat and pressed it forcefully in place in what he knew by now was a futile effort to stanch the flow.

An usherette arrived, carrying a shaded torch. Knight glanced up at her, sweat and tears blinding his vision.

'First-aid unit, do you have one?'

The girl nodded. 'St John Ambulance.' She was staring in round-eyed horror.

'Fetch them. Quick as you bloody can, girl!'

As the orchestral storm began to subside, the occupants of the nearby seats became aware of the activity at the end of the row. Heads began to weave and peer. Knight sensed the same kind of mixture of concern and morbid interest that followed road accidents.

'What's happened?' a man behind him whispered.

'Heart attack.' Knight said. He dropped Franklyn's wrist, where he'd been searching for a pulse, and bent closer to lay his finger against the side of his neck. He saw then that Franklyn's eyes were rolled back so that the whites showed, and realised that he was wasting his time. It made no difference: he kept searching for some sign of life anyway. As he did so, he scanned the opposite half of the Grand Tier, looking for the gunman.

No, he concluded, not from over there. Not possible among all those people. His gaze swept up the dome and he saw the long, narrow opening towards its top. For an instant he thought he saw a movement but it could have been his imagination.

He looked down from the opening to the stage. A strange, bluish light now flooded it, unchanging and obviously wrong. It made the faces and costumes of the artists appear ghostly as they carried on with the performance.

The ambulance team arrived and he moved back out of their way. He watched as they set to work; he'd found no pulse but was reluctant to leave Franklyn until he knew their verdict.

They took less than a minute to reach it. They were equipped with torches and he heard one of them swear softly as he moved the scarf and saw the damage underneath. He looked questioningly up at Knight.

'Nothing to be gained by making it public knowledge,' Knight whispered. 'A heart attack's all anyone needs to know.'

The man nodded his understanding. In his shock he was willing enough to submit to Knight's authority. 'Is who did this still here somewhere?'

'It's possible. Keep it to yourself.'

Knight wiped his blood-caked hands on the blanket folded across the stretcher and left them to it. As he strode up the short aisle to the exit doors he met the manager coming the other way. The usherette had probably sent him. Knight grabbed his arm.

'Those stage lights – the ones that are all wrong – are they controlled from up there?' He pointed to the narrow opening at the top of the dome.

The manager nodded, anxious to get past him. 'I'm sorry about the lighting, sir. We have a technical problem. I'm sorry if it's spoilt –'

'I want to get up there. To the lighting place. How do I do that?'

The manager began to protest, so Knight steered him back to the exit door and outside.

'Now you listen. Here's what you do. First – phone the police. Tell them there's been a shooting.'

The man turned pale, his jaw dropped, but Knight carried on.

'Tell no one else or you'll have pandemonium. Ask the police to get some men here at once. The killer's probably left already but just in case he hasn't, some of them better come armed. Bow Street station is right opposite you, so they'll be here in no time.' He took out his Home Office pass and put it in the manager's hand. 'Read this out to them. It'll mean something to them. Explain I told you to do all this. Let the performance continue in the meantime and never mind your lighting problems. We don't want all these people in the way if the killer's still in the building. When the police get here, they'll take over. They'll block the streets outside. If the performance ends before they arrive, make an announcement for the audience to stay in their seats. Got all that?'

The manager nodded uncertainly.

'Now tell me how to get up to that bloody lighting place.'

Two minutes later, as Knight stood breathless in the long, curved room at the top of the dome, he saw the reason for the lights' failure. A young stage manager, who'd also come up to investigate, had arrived before him and saw it too. He was standing with his back to the technician's body; Knight stood beside him, looking down at it.

'See anyone else when you got here?'

'No. Only him.' The man half-turned to the body. 'Isn't there anything we can do?'

Knight shook his head. 'We wait for the police to arrive. That's all.'

Somewhere below them the singing stopped and applause began to ring out. The performance was over.

The bald man skirted Covent Garden, where the shops were closed and the stalls had been cleared from the cobbled courtyards for the night, and turned down Southampton Street and into Maiden Lane. He had thrown his overcoat on over the nylon jacket and was carrying his suit coat folded over an arm. There were plenty of people around, both tourists and Londoners, and he walked at a businesslike pace but not hurriedly, so no one paid him any heed.

No one, that is, except the black-haired woman with the crew-cut. She now wore white cotton trousers, a colourful blouse, brimmed hat and fashionably-cut raincoat. She carried a sightseer's map of London and the camera swung from her wrist by its strap. There were several thousand women like her in London that night.

Without raising the camera to her eyes, she had run off a sequence of shots as the bald man had left the Opera House, the chatter of the autowind drowned by the traffic; now she turned into Maiden Lane just in time to record him climbing into the white Sherpa.

Then she continued on down Southampton Street to where the dusty Volvo station-wagon was waiting for her on a yellow line.

29

Moscow

Serov let himself into his apartment and poured a glass of bourbon to take away the chill that had followed him home from Izmaylovo. As he drank, he fetched the old leather grip-bag, went into the bedroom and flung open the wardrobe doors.

Molodechno was the last occasion for which he'd had to pack. How different from that trip this one would be.

He checked each garment before he folded it away in the bag. If the labels and laundry tags were Soviet or East European, he returned it to the wardrobe and substituted a garment of American or West European manufacture.

His approach to the task was spasmodic, distracted. He retired often to an armchair or the couch in the bedroom, to sit there in thought. Or he paced back and forth through the other rooms. He kept the bourbon topped up and was seldom without a cigar. From time to time he looked up and his gaze seemed to devour his surroundings, as if he were committing them to memory.

When the clothes were sorted, he turned his attention to the safe behind the bookcase. The Aganbegyan report was where he had stored it on his return from Molodechno. He transferred it and the other contents to a lockable, steel-lined briefcase. Among them were the letters and other items which Galina had found.

On one of the side tables he kept a scrapbook. It was filled with snapshots, mostly of Galina and Katarina. The most recent shots were only of Galina. He started to slip some of the prints from their mounting sheets. But the selection was difficult and he found himself stopping often in indecision; in the end he replaced the prints and dropped the whole album into the briefcase.

Then he was done. He lowered himself heavily into the armchair, as if what he'd completed was some onerous physical task, and took a final look around. His eye settled on the section of bookcase that concealed the safe. Automatically, he scanned the book titles on the shelf; there, where he had left it that night, was the Orwell. *Nineteen Eighty-Four*.

But no, he wouldn't be taking it. Or any of the books. Where he was going, he could replace them all. Ten times over if he wanted to.

His last task before retiring for the night was to read through the English Sunday papers. Although he was coming to them a day late, there was one item that he had already noted that morning in the international news summaries that passed across his desk at Yasyenevo, about which he wanted to know more.

It was the account of Home Secretary William Clarke's death.

'Car accident,' he repeated thoughtfully as he moved from paper to paper and studied the accounts and photographs.

Eventually an amused smile came to his lips. He knew all about the car crashes that could befall politicians and other leaders; also aircraft crashes, drug overdoses, dangerous swims, capsized yachts, insane gunmen working alone, and a legion other bizarre ways of removing awkward individuals. Exactly what had Clarke done to merit his fate?

He shrugged. He would find out in due course.

Soon.

In his narrow bed at the Serbskiy Institute, a bed and in a room not much superior to those of his patients, Professor Ogarkin lay awake. He was pondering Galina's progress.

Maybe Serov was going to be proved right, he admitted to himself; maybe the paints would do the trick.

He had watched from a window that day as Galina paced the courtyard below, looking up at the building from all angles. She was carrying the wooden case, a canvas and the easel. One of the nurses was standing in a nearby doorway to keep an eye on her. The nurse was shivering because of the cold but Galina didn't seem to mind it.

At last she had put the easel down, right alongside one of the walls, and spread its feet. She mounted the canvas on it and crouched down to open the paints case on a nearby step.

Ogarkin had smiled and turned to Serov, who was watching with him.

'Maybe we'll have some developments now,' he had said, relieved that even Serov looked pleased for once. 'Call back next week and see.'

'I can't,' Serov had said.

Well, Ogarkin thought to himself as he looked back on the incident, the comrade General was a busy man. He couldn't keep chasing about forever just for the sake of one girl.

The professor blew his nose one last time and tried to get some sleep.

Yegor Ligachev drew a hand down either side of his face, stretching the skin beneath his eyes until it stung, then combed his fingers through his pure white hair.

The Party Congress was drawing near; too near. His office was awash in drafts of speeches, wordy resolutions from well-meaning party bureaucrats, and the endless proposed annexes that every new Five Year Plan generated like spring pollen.

He sighed: a long, hollow sound that seemed to echo back at him from the high corners of the room. There were so many who came to scratch at the doors of power; so many arguments; so many factions to meld. It all pressed down on him.

And Serov's plan was the weightiest pressure of all.

Once, when he was the secretary for Novosibirsk region, he'd made the long flight south to visit the cottonfields of Uzbekistan. There was a storm in the air, a great hot cawl of electrical tension that closed over the plains the day he arrived. It was like being caught inside a net of crackling energy. The tension made him want to scream, just to try and break the spell. Eventually, when he could stand it no longer, that was exactly what he did: he drove alone one afternoon to the heart of a limitless plantation where there was no other human being for miles and screamed at the white sky until his voice broke and he was drenched in perspiration.

These weeks of waiting were like being trapped in that net once more. Coaxing Mikhail Sergeyevich through every step. Fighting his own instinct to yield to the scream again and abandon the whole enterprise. Finally, and worst of all, realising that it was too late to scream. There was no way of going back: the enterprise had taken on a life of its own, as indifferent to those caught up in it it as the Uzbek storm.

Like Faustus, he had signed his compact; and like him, all he could do now was wait.

Georgi Zavarov waited too. Olga was in bed, although it was doubtful whether she was asleep, and Ratushny had coughed and moaned for a while in the far reaches of the rambling apartment and run considerable amounts of cold water. But now the apartment was still. The litre bottle of brandy lay dead at Zavarov's feet. A second one stood open on the mantlepiece by his folded arms. He never bothered with a glass these days.

He lowered his head like a grizzly giving in to sleep and rested his forehead in the crook of his elbow. The heat of the log fire bathed his body and he spread his legs to absorb more of it.

'Only heat you've had down there for a long time,' he muttered. The slur in his voice pleased him. What else was there for him to do these days but drink? Whatever Serov had to say about it.

He knew he couldn't trust Serov. Working with him was like dancing with a cobra: sooner or later the bite would come, however sweet the rhythm.

As ever, Serov was up to something. Zavarov was certain of it:

something beyond even the bounds of this fantastic scheme that he'd drawn them all into. For all the chance any of them had of fathoming it, they might as well try and count the stars.

So he waited. Because Serov's icy analysis had been right: he had no choice. It was that or watch Gorbachev turn his armies into toy soldiers and his missiles into washing machines.

He waited and he drank. He humoured Olga. And he prayed to God for strength.

The money from Moscow, the passage of which through the Soviet Foreign Trade Bank had first pleased and then distressed Director Smolny, had since then passed half the banking day in the Banco Nacional de Panama and half in the Bahamas.

Now, as Tokyo awoke to tomorrow, the telexes in the Saitama Bank began singing like birds of the morning. They told of the yen's overnight performance on Wall Street and Threadneedle Street; they enumerated batches of transactions from every corner of the globe; and they detailed a long list of transfers as the Soviet money now moved on from the Bahamanian corporation accounts that had sheltered it to certain others on Saitama's books.

The transfers were perfectly legitimate: payments by one trading partner to another for goods, commodities or services. All the corporations had histories behind them in the house of Saitama; their business dealings with one another always had proper documentation when it was needed. There was no apparent connection between them, other than a trading one.

The financial cat's cradle that Serov had constructed was underway. Zurich, Bonn, Amsterdam and London were yet to be added. By the time it was complete, its unravelling would be the kind of job that could make rich men of international lawyers and finance specialists, and fools of the clients who hired them to attempt it. The attempt was unlikely to be made.

30

Stratfield Saye was asleep. It wasn't a place for late hours.

Only in the house where the man from the Home Office lived were lights still burning. One was in a small room at the front, where the security man leafed through a paperback and listened to the night-time creaks of the old timbers. The other was in the games room at the rear, where four men had gathered to listen to Viktor Kunaev.

Viktor took in the scene as he entered. The room was becoming familiar territory to him now; as were its people.

Light was provided by two green-shaded bulbs suspended from the ceiling on long flexes. They had once hung over the billiard table but now illuminated two high-backed chairs positioned to face each other in the centre of the floor. One chair was his, the other was for Matt Parrish.

Viktor had never seen the room with the billiard table in its rightful position; since the start of the debriefs it had remained pushed against the wall, where it was tonight.

Here Parrish stood, a patient and wise-looking man, leaning against the table. He was big and raw-boned with a farmer's weatherbeaten face. It was honest and Viktor liked the uneven look of it. He was in the act of taking a cigarette from a white packet as Viktor came into the room; he looked up at him and nodded.

The table also served Parrish as a resting-place for his ashtray, the tape recorder and a clutter of coffee cups and mugs. Ring-shaped stains marched along the edge of the green baize, each session adding to their number. Two folders, which Viktor now recognised as transcripts of their sessions, lay open nearby.

At the edge of the double pool of light sat the tireless stenographer, his muted typing machine on a folding card table. Viktor's gaze finally came to rest on Dick Sumner, sitting opposite the stenographer, his fingers playing nervously with the flights of a metal dart.

The scrape of a match being lit broke the silence; Parrish held it between his cupped hands for a moment and the flare cast a glow across his features.

'Well, Viktor.' He paused to put the flame to his cigarette and inhaled a mouthful of smoke. 'Here we all are again – just as you asked.' He shook out the flame and swept the match in a wide arc before dropping it into the ashtray. The gesture encompassed all of them.

Parrish settled himself more comfortably on the edge of the table. Viktor went to his chair and sat for a moment in silence, thinking over what he planned to say. When he was ready and looked up again, he was aware that all eyes were on him; but none as sharp as Parrish's.

'I believe that when your organisation is training people for intelligence work, Mr Parrish, you describe the Soviet personality as secretive and distrustful.'

Parrish smiled. 'It's a generalisation that some trainers use. Old hands, usually. I think it's a dangerous simplification. Sorry if it offends you.'

Viktor shook his head. 'I have behaved according to type.' Parrish drew deeply on his cigarette but showed no inclination to reply. Viktor continued. 'I have good reasons. In the FCD – in fact, in all parts of the KGB – we work as if we are in a hall of mirrors. Take the Border Guards. They watch our frontiers to make sure no one escapes from Soviet territory. But there are other troops positioned behind them. Their task is to watch the guards. We have guards to guard the guards. That is how we are. We march in a circle – sometimes we get nowhere but we always know where everybody is.'

Parrish shrugged. 'So?'

'Tonight I do not want us to march in circles but I have tried to arrange certain precautions. A hall of mirrors. You and Mr Sumner – you are here to watch one another.' He paused to lend weight to his next words. 'Mr Parrish, do you remember when I said I did not know who I could trust?'

Parrish nodded. The room had become very still.

'That is because the man I have told you about – mole is not a good name for him: he is more important than that – I do not know his identity, you see.' He looked from one to the other and added, 'Life would be so much simpler if I did.'

Parrish was puzzled. 'You said you could prove conclusively who he was.'

'Yes, and that is true. But the possession of proof does not always mean that you know something yourself. You will understand in a minute.'

Parrish's cigarette smoke drifted up through the light. His gaze followed it into the darkness as though he could trace in it the implications of Viktor's circuitous logic. 'Viktor, are you saying you're worried that the person could be in this room right now?'

Viktor shrugged. 'It struck me as a possibility.'

Sumner cleared his throat. 'You said it was someone high up.'

Viktor smiled. 'Which is why I have decided to talk to you after all.

This man was of university age when I was about twelve years old. He was at university here in England. You are roughly the same age as me, Mr Sumner, so it cannot be you.'

Parrish did a quick mental calculation. 'I would've been at university about then.'

'And that is why I spent a long time wondering about you. But – with respect – on balance I do not think you occupy a high enough position. Mr Sumner is right, you see. This man was recruited because he was considered to be one of the brightest people of his generation. Whatever else the KGB may be, it is very efficient in its selection of agents – its long-term judgement is seldom wrong. If you had been its choice, I would expect you to be more senior by now. Sorry, Mr Parrish.'

Parrish laughed softly. 'I'm not sure if you've just paid me a compliment or the opposite. However, I take it your mind's sufficiently at rest now to get on to the matter of the – what was it you called it? – the *avoska*?'

Viktor sighed. 'At rest? As much as it can be. I can lead you to only one man.'

Parrish frowned. 'Are you suggesting there's an entire network, a ring?'

'Yes and no. There are other sleepers, yes. Whoever and wherever they are, however, they do not depend on one another as a conventional ring would. Each one does not even know who the others are.'

'Then that's conventional at least. You mean there's a system of cut-outs between each of them.'

Viktor shook his head. 'A ring needs cut-outs only if the members are inter-dependent for the task they have been set. I said these sleepers are not. Every one of them works on his own. The programme was Khrushchev's personal idea. It ended after he was ousted.'

'One at a time then,' Parrish said. His cigarette had burnt itself down to the filter and was giving off an acrid odour; he crushed it in the ashtray, ignoring the ash that spilt onto the green baize of the table. 'Whoever and wherever the others are, let's stick to the one we're interested in at the moment.'

Viktor nodded. 'Tomorrow we go to London. All three of us.'

'London?'

'You will take me to a post office and I will collect a poste restante package in my name. It should be there by now – I posted it on Saturday as Anna and I left London. I will give the package to Mr Sumner. You will witness me doing this.'

'And then?'

'Mr Sumner will take the package directly to your forensic scientists.'

'Forensic scientists? What is this package?'

'A book. Merely a book. A book about Russian Philosophy. In English. But I would not recommend you or Mr Sumner to read it.'

'I see,' said Parrish, though he didn't.

'You would leave fingerprints. Fingerprints will stay on paper for up to thirty years. Did you know that? This book already has enough fingerprints. Some are my father's, of course, because the book belonged to him.'

Parrish believed he was beginning to understand. 'And the other fingerprints?'

' – Are those of the man you seek. There are not even the fingerprints of a bookshop owner or a browsing customer. My father ordered the book direct from the lists of the English publisher. Perhaps a worker or two in the printing house handled it, but that need not worry us. Fingerprints, Mr Parrish. That is why Mr Sumner will need his forensic scientists.'

There was silence. The stenographer's fingers stopped tapping. Viktor rose and stretched.

'And now, if you will excuse me, I would like to go to bed. Anna has said she will stay awake for me. I do not want to keep her waiting. This time is stressful for her and she needs much sleep.'

Sumner watched Parrish. He nodded. Viktor smiled and waited for one of them to unlock the door.

At Mayfair's Holiday Inn, the young Portuguese doorman called Jesus finally emerged from a door behind the porter's counter and came over to where Eva was waiting for him in the lobby.

'Good evening, miss.' He knew her face from previous visits but not her name.

'Sir Horace Gaunt is expecting me. He said you'd be able to find me a parking place.'

'I see what I can do. Everybody want favour tonight.' It was his way of ensuring that she made it worth his while.

The spot that he found for her was smack in the centre of the small courtyard at the side of the hotel, beside the rows of ten or twelve other cars that were already there. She groaned when she saw how visible she'd be to anyone who chose to glance that way from the front door.

Gaunt took a quarter of an hour to appear, by which time she had a crick in her neck from staring fixedly in her mirror. He folded his long body into the Metro's front seat.

'What's all the panic about?'

'There's no panic, Sir Horace.'

'That wasn't my impression when you phoned me.'

'Sorry. I've simply made my mind up about something.'

'And it couldn't wait until morning.'

'I'm making sure I don't change my mind.' Even as she said the words, she knew they were wrong. Two errors in not many more sentences: apologising to him and admitting the possibility of doubt. She was handling this abysmally; not at all the way she'd planned it. Best to get it over with.

'I want out. Now.'

'Out of what?'

'You know perfectly well.'

Gaunt stared out of the side window at the comings and goings on Berkeley Street. She actually wondered if he was about to accede to her demand. But when he spoke his tone was icy.

'My dear, you got yourself into this when you climbed into bed with Edmund Knight. That being the case, I have no power to get you "out" on the terms which you no doubt mean. At this point you have only one way out and I'm not at all sure what you would do afterwards.'

'What's that mean?'

'It means, after leaving the service I'm not sure how you would survive.' He turned to look at her. 'After all, you have been indiscreet, to say the least. Life could be such a trial if you left under the wrong circumstances.'

'Are you threatening me?'

'By no means. Merely reminding you of your obligations. I see I'm alarming you. I mustn't go on. I will say this much, however: I will overlook this conversation. I advise you to do likewise. I would also remind you that it would be unwise of you ever to mention our . . . arrangement to anyone.'

'You mean to Knight.'

For a moment he had that faraway air again, as if their conversation wasn't really as important to him as he would have her believe.

'Not to Knight, not to anyone,' he said. 'Whatever happens.'

With that, he muttered goodnight and manoeuvred himself out of the car. He was waiting in the hotel doorway when she roared past onto Berkeley Street. She only caught a glimpse of him, didn't want him to see her looking, and just gained an overall impression of his dark figure standing there, hands in pockets, sharp elbows tucked in against his sides.

It was only when she was driving along Knightsbridge, still trembling as her mind went over the abortive encounter in random snatches, that she became convinced that he had been smiling.

In the house at Stratfield Saye, Sumner took Knight's call.

'Joss Franklyn's been shot,' Knight told him. 'He's dead.'

There was a silence, then Sumner whispered, 'How did it happen?'

Knight ignored Sumner's question.

'Where's Kunaev?' he demanded.

'Tucked up in bed, I hope.'

'Tell security to keep on their toes. Joss's death might have nothing to do with Kunaev but who the hell knows.'

'Spetznaz?'

'It's possible. What did Kunaev have to say for himself? Did you get anywhere?'

Still half-stunned by the news about Franklyn, Sumner spilled out an account of the debrief. Afterwards, Knight returned to the police interview room to wait for whoever wanted to talk to him next.

'Fingerprints,' he said quietly to the room's bare walls.

Two hours had passed.

'Why aren't you asleep?' Anna whispered.

Viktor rolled over on his side to face her. It was too dark to see but he could feel her breath on his cheek.

'I could ask the same of you,' he whispered.

'Your tossing and turning would wake the dead.' She snuggled closer and sighed. 'You lecture me to be strong and now look at you. What are you worrying about? Were they difficult with you tonight?'

'No. It went the way I wanted.'

'What is it, then?'

He thought for a moment. 'Tomorrow the shop will be empty.'

'Don't talk in riddles, Viktor. We have no money to go shopping.'

'It's I who am the shopkeeper. What I sell is information. But I've had to do what no wise shopkeeper should – I've given my goods away on credit. I had no choice. That's how it works. Tomorrow I hand over the last thing on my shelves. After that, they're empty. No more *avoska*, even.'

'You have to hope your customers pay up.'

'That's it.'

'I told you – you've made a sad world, you and that so-important Mr Edmund Knight.'

'Not just us, Anna. Not us.'

Her fingers touched his brow, like cool cotton soothing hot skin. He closed his eyes and tried to picture a small boy growing to be a man in a free country; it wasn't as easy as it used to be.

31

Morning. Bleary-eyed and unshaven, his head throbbing from lack of sleep, Knight drove straight from Bow Street to Berkshire. No detour to Eva's. And no question of going in to Curzon Street.

He was at the end of his road when he saw the Range Rover turning into his drive. He stopped the car, shook his head to clear the sleepiness from his brain, and drove back to the village. He tried to think but his mind was in utter chaos.

He passed the dairy and the shops, saw a parking space and thought about pulling in. Indicated, at the last moment changed his mind and carried on. He did the same thing again at the pub by the green: to the irritation of the cars behind him, who'd put up with his first indecision. One of them honked and he turned down the side road skirting the green, to get out of their way.

He was leaving the village now, on the far side from his home. The cottages and shops were behind him and there were only the occasional lanes and hedges of the larger houses on either side. He knew them all. Not who lived in them, often not even what the houses looked like, tucked out of sight as many of them were. But he knew the shape of the road, the pattern of its trees and bends; all was imprinted on his mind like the furniture of a familiar room in darkness.

But it felt as if he were driving through an alien land. The sky seemed cracked in every leafless branch.

The village surgery came in sight. He glanced into the parking area as he passed. The morning surgery was underway; six or seven cars were parked by the fence and people went in and out of the surgery entrance. He stopped at the next side road, turned and drove back, and drew into the surgery parking area. There was a space at the far corner and he pulled into it and switched off his engine.

Time passed. An hour perhaps. No one bothered him and that was all he wanted. Perhaps he dozed off, like a small animal seized by a predator; or perhaps his mind went to the no man's land where sleep and wakefulness shaded into one another.

He started, and looked about him sharply. The flux of people and cars had ceased. Now there was only one other car besides his own. He studied it more closely and made out the Doctor sticker in its front window.

Morning surgery had closed. Soon the doctor would be off on his visiting rounds. Knight started the car again and drove back to his own side of the village, looking hard at every car he met.

There was no movement in the vicinity of his driveway, but when he walked close enough to peer along the hedging that edged it, he saw that the Range Rover was still there. No visitor would wait for that long. No normal visitor.

He hurried back to his car. There was only one place he could think of to go.

The cattle grid made his teeth judder as the car rattled over it. He drove straight up past the chapel and followed the road over the brow of the hill and down to the central block of the convent.

The secretary's office was on the left off the front hall. The door was open, so he walked on in and waited for the matronly woman behind the counter to pause in her typing. After a moment she looked at him to show that she was ready for his enquiry.

'I'm looking for Sister Marie-Thérèse,' he said. 'Do you know where I can find her?'

The woman smiled; her world was pleasant and orderly. 'Let's see if she's in a class.'

She rose and consulted a large chart that covered most of the width of the wall by her desk. It logged all the school forms by class and day of the week. She began running her finger down the Tuesday columns. On the fifth or sixth column she said 'Aha,' and kept her finger in position while she glanced at the wallclock above the chart. Then she turned back to him and told him where to go.

He dawdled at the noticeboards until the bell went, and arrived at classroom C3 just as it was emptying. Twenty or so girls, thirteen-year-olds, filed out and split up to go their different ways. They were well-behaved and those who noticed him nodded a respectful greeting.

Marie-Thérèse was cleaning the blackboard when he went into the room and closed the door. He coughed quietly to catch her attention.

'Good gracious!' she said. 'Mr Knight – you do have a habit of popping up on me in unexpected places.'

She set the duster aside and rubbed chalk off her fingers. The sunlight glinted on her spectacles as she glanced down to flick more dust off her grey gown.

'I didn't mean to startle you, Sister.'

She looked up and smiled at him, waiting politely for whatever he wanted to say next.

He couldn't hold her gaze. 'I've come to ask you for something.'

She began packing her books into the leather satchel on her table.

'Ask away.' She finished packing and eased herself stiffly into a chair behind one of the students' tables, gesturing for him to do the same.

He remained standing. 'I need your help.'

She joined her hands on the table and made a slight movement with them as if she'd gathered as much. 'Good. You've given us plenty, it'll be a chance for us to pay a little back. Would it be spiritual help you're looking for?'

'My priority at the moment is more temporal.'

She smiled and made the little hand-movement again. 'I don't recall Our Lord turning away from those that needed temporal help. Tell me what you need.'

He prowled uneasily towards the window and back again before answering. 'Somewhere to stay.'

'I see.' She pondered for a minute. 'Is there something the matter with your house?'

He smiled and shook his head. 'The house is fine. I just need to . . . get away for a while.'

She leant slightly forward, her head tilted on one side like a little wise bird, and stared hard at him. He felt as if she were opening him up and looking inside.

'Get away?' she repeated. 'There's no retreats on at the minute, I'm afraid.'

'That's not what I had in mind.'

Her lips drew into a thin line. She sat upright again; there was a sadness in her face now. 'Are you asking for sanctuary?' she whispered.

'If that's what I should call it.'

She didn't move or speak for a moment. He heard the sound of hurried footsteps drawing nearer along the corridor outside, then someone strode past the door and the footsteps faded away.

'What kind of trouble are you in?'

'Trouble?'

'It's the only time people come looking for sanctuary.'

He paced again towards the window. 'I won't burden you, Sister. I'm asking enough as it is. If you haven't got somewhere, it doesn't matter. I'll find somewhere else.'

'Where?'

He shrugged. 'I'll find somewhere.'

The wise head tilted again. 'You haven't got anywhere else. You wouldn't be coming to me if there was somewhere else.'

He said nothing.

'All right, Mr Knight. Forgive my probing. It's all very well for God – he knows what terms he's doing business on. But the rest of us have to check things out a little. Now then.' She unclasped her hands and put them in her lap, palms down. 'We have the retreat house. That'd be the best place. As I said, it's not being used at the moment.' She paused before adding softly, 'You'd be out of harm's reach there.'

'Harm's reach?'

She shifted the angle of her head fractionally; the lenses of her spectacles flashed sunlight at him so that he couldn't see her eyes any longer. 'Just an expression, Mr Knight. Now, does the retreat house sound all right to you?'

'It sounds just fine.'

She rose to her feet and became businesslike. 'It's well away from the school and the playing fields, so no one will see you there. No one will bother you.'

All he ever wanted.

'I'll have to speak to the Mother Superior, of course. But I'm sure she'll agree. I'll take you there in the meantime and you can settle in. Are you here by car? It's a long walk. For me anyway. Have you brought luggage?'

'What I'm standing up in.'

'We'll get you a few things, if you're not fussy. Let's be going then. I'll just have time to talk to the Mother Superior before my next class.'

He picked up the weighty satchel and followed her out.

It was as much as the two cars that had driven in from Stratfield Saye could do to keep in view of one another. Sumner couldn't recall seeing the London traffic so bad in years.

'Relax,' Parrish told him as they crawled towards Hyde Park Corner. 'What do you think the Soviets might do – pick him up by helicopter from the middle of this lot? He won't be making a break for it either – we've got his wife and kid, remember.'

In the same way as his own people had his father as a guarantee, thought Sumner. Aloud he said: 'Why should he want to make a break? He came to us of his own free will.'

'They always have second thoughts,' said Parrish.

Sumner forced the Citroën into a gap that made Parrish wince, and craned his neck to look for the Maestro with Viktor and the two security men aboard. He caught a glimpse of it as it slipped between a bus and a brewery truck at the foot of Park Lane.

'Got you,' he breathed, and put his foot down.

Parrish closed his eyes as the tail of the truck passed within inches of his window.

'Nothing on the news this morning about Joss Franklyn,' he said when he'd regained his equilibrium.

'They won't let the media say anything.'

As they came onto the straight the Maestro filtered to the right at the

211

slip road intersection and positioned itself in the middle carriageway, facing Mayfair.

A suspicion crept into Sumner's mind; it grew to a certainty and he smacked the steering wheel.

'The cheeky sod,' he exclaimed. 'Look.'

By now Parrish was watching the car as well. He nodded as he took in its location and understanding dawned.

'Mount Street. Our own backyard.'

Sure enough, when the lights changed, the Maestro swung back down Park Lane and took the first left. Sumner lane-hopped ruthlessly and was at last able to close the gap.

There was no possibility of parking legally in the busy street so the two cars wasted no time trying. Instead they double-parked bumper to bumper right outside the post office and put on their hazard warning lights.

The security men climbed out of the Maestro and hemmed Viktor in. Parrish and Sumner joined them and all five made their way into the post office. Inside, they almost doubled the size of the queue.

'Jump the queue, for God's sake. Over there.' Parrish caught the arm of one of the security officers and indicated the parcel counter across from the door, where a clerk was finishing with someone. 'He'll do – persuade him.'

The clerk looked askance as the two burly men and Viktor approached together. He listened to what one of the security men had to say, looked at Viktor's passport when it was passed under the glass, and went off through a door at the rear of his enclosure. A minute later he reappeared with a package wrapped in brown paper, which he passed through. It was the size of a large hardcover book.

Ignoring the black glances he was getting from the people in the queue, the security man brought it across to Sumner and Parrish; Viktor and the other man followed.

'This is it?' Sumner asked.

Viktor nodded. 'Open it and see. Carefully.'

Sumner took a penknife from his pocket and gingerly slit the wrapping paper along three edges. He peeled it back gently, not wanting to lay a finger on the book, and stared at the faded blue cover.

History of Russian Philosophy by N O Lossky.

'Take Mr Kunaev back to Stratfield Saye, please,' Sumner said to the security men. 'Thank you, Mr Kunaev.'

Viktor shrugged glumly. His shop was empty.

'Sir Horace is waiting for you but Mr Knight hasn't come in yet,' Gaunt's secretary told Parrish and Sumner fifteen minutes later. 'Maybe he's making a late start after last night. You heard about Mr Franklyn, I suppose? Sir Horace sent a memo around this morning.

Poor Mr Franklyn. He shouldn't have been smoking with a heart like that.'

Parrish turned to Sumner. 'Let's go ahead and put Horace in the picture anyway. Edmund can join us when he gets here.'

Sumner looked down at the book with its torn wrappings. Something had happened that he couldn't fully explain. Just twenty-four hours ago it had all seemed so exciting. Now it was as flat as ice. It was the look in Viktor Kunaev's dulled eyes that had done it. Something, Sumner realised, had died. But what? Trust? Perhaps, but not trust in a system. In the end it wasn't a question of systems or ideologies. It was a question of people.

Wasn't that a kind of death: when a man ran out of that kind of trust?

'You go in,' he said quietly to Parrish. 'It doesn't need two of us. I'll take this to forensic.'

32

Surrey

In the countryside thirty miles west of London, the A30 passed through the commuter heartlands of Egham and Virginia Water, then ran through Sunningdale and on to Bagshot. Between these two towns, in the vicinity of the village of Windlesham, it followed a dead straight line for two miles.

It was six thirty in the evening when the bald man came onto this stretch from Bagshot direction, travelling east. It was the peak commuter hour and the westbound carriageway was an endless thread of headlights.

He let the speed of the Yamaha RD350 drop to thirty, holding it steady at that until he reached the Windmill pub, on his left. Here he swung into the car park and brought the bike around in a wide arc to face the road again. He planted his feet on the ground either side of the machine, switched to sidelights and let the engine continue idling quietly.

He wore the black racing leathers, long boots, gauntlets and red and white helmet that had been with the bike when they collected it. The darkened visor was clipped shut, hiding his face completely.

Some modifications had been made to the Yamaha. An aluminium pannier was fastened on either side of the rear pillion and a third box, large and square, was mounted behind it. They were painted red and white to match the helmet and the bike's fairing; the rear box bore the words 'Jet Despatch' and a London telephone number. A radio speaker and handmike were slung beneath the handlebars. A black plastic rocker switch was screwed in place beside them, adjacent to the clutch lever.

He had been waiting about two minutes when the radio crackled and a voice said 'One-Seven', the last two digits of the telephone number. He lifted the handmike and acknowledged the signal by repeating the number into it, his voice muffled by the helmet.

The eastbound traffic was steady, but nowhere near as heavy as that coming from the direction of London, and the Yamaha had the advantage of speed and compactness; it slipped into the eastbound stream without difficulty. The bald man rode east for another half mile, indicated a right turn and pulled into the filling station located at that point on the road. On the forecourt he swung past the pumps to the airline, hefted the bike onto its stand and dismounted. Again he left the engine running.

The airline was close to the road, on the perimeter of the forecourt so that motorists using it wouldn't obstruct the pumps. He crouched down behind the Yamaha and fumbled with a tyre valve, leaving its cap in place but pretending to be connecting the airline. From this position he surveyed his field of action.

On the other side of the road, exactly opposite the garage, a wall seven or eight feet high ran along the edge of the footpath. It was red-brick with a sandstone coping. Halfway along its length it was interrupted by the sweep of a short drive, which led to a set of black and gilt iron gates. Large facing stones had been set into the curves of the wall on each side of the drive; the words carved in them stated the name of the manor house set in woodland behind the wall. By the drive and immediately inside the wall stood a Victorian gatehouse, built in the same brick and sandstone. A television camera in a weatherproof steel housing towered above one of the gates' pillars; it looked down from a height of about ten feet so that its lens could view the whole approach area. Beyond the gates the drive wound out of sight through the woodland and shrubbery.

His gaze shifted back to the road. He had a clear view for almost a mile to the east. In the distance a large coach was approaching, its lighted windows visible above the foreground traffic. He scanned the other vehicles before sweeping his gaze back to the coach. He couldn't yet see what was following behind it. Dropping the airline, he reached inside one of the side-mounted panniers and withdrew a steel box about four inches square He slid down a recessed switch on its side and replaced the box in the pannier.

The coach had come close enough now for him to catch a glint of the white vehicle that was following behind it. He mounted the Yamaha, kicked up the stand and rode at once to the roadside.

The glint of white became the Sherpa van. A moment later he made out the gold Corniche and the dark-coloured Rover that were sandwiched between it and the coach. They were over to the crown of the road and, although the coach was still obscuring his view, he knew that both would be indicating their intended right turn into the walled estate.

The coach thundered past, its slipstream rocking the Yamaha against his leg. The Corniche was gliding to a halt about ten yards away; before it could cross to the black and gilt gates, it would have to wait for the eastbound traffic to ease. The bald man counted four men in the Corniche and another four in the Rover as it drew up behind. The gaze of the Rover's front passenger rested briefly on him, then moved on elsewhere.

He took the steel box out of the pannier and clamped it tightly under his left arm. Reaching back again, he drew out a circular tube about the size of a beercan and with a similar kind of ringpull. He eased the ringpull up without breaking the seal and wedged the tube between his thighs.

The Sherpa had come to a standstill behind the Rover, just at its nearside corner. It looked as if the driver was unsure if he had room to squeeze past on the inside. He was inching the van forward and towards the nearside; the other traffic behind him would remain blocked until he got through.

The bald man moved across the clear carriageway that this provided to the middle of the road, where he stopped and sat facing the Corniche. Over his left shoulder he watched for a break in the eastbound traffic, revving his engine as he waited.

An Audi was approaching; behind it the road was clear. He glanced back at the Sherpa; it had now got past the Rover and was moving westwards again, followed by the traffic that it had held up. The bald man's companion was at the wheel; he drove past without a glance.

The Audi came up on the other side and the bald man released his clutch and moved forward. He did so just at the same moment as the Corniche began to swing across his path. The car's nose dipped sharply as it stopped; the peak-capped driver raised his left hand and impatiently waved the Yamaha on. The bald man acknowledged with a nod and moved forward again. He hugged the crown of the road, so that he was only inches from the gold Corniche.

Drawing level with its rear wing, he braked abruptly and dropped his right hand from the throttle. He ripped the ringpull and leant forward to roll the tube beneath the Rover. Instantly, billows of blue-grey smoke began to flood out from under the car. He took the steel box from beneath his left arm and smacked it against the side of the Corniche, just behind the passenger door and close to the petrol cap. It locked solidly in position, its limpet-magnets clinging to the metal.

He saw the face of the robed Arab who looked out at him from the back seat: the face of Saleem Ibn Abdul Aziz Al-Saud. A hooked nose surmounted a wide mouth and jet-black goatee. The prince's large eyes, their irises black and liquid, regarded him with puzzlement rather than alarm. He began to sit forward, peering towards the rear wing, to try and make out what had caused the clunk. None of the other occupants of the Corniche, also Arabs except for the driver, seemed to have noticed anything.

The bald man's hand returned to the throttle just as the doors of the Rover flew open. All four men leapt out, only to begin spluttering helplessly as the gas filled their lungs. He caught a glimpse of the automatics in their hands, trembling uselessly as he accelerated swiftly past them. The close-fitting helmet protected him from the gas for the short time that he needed.

Four seconds had passed since the moment when the Corniche driver had waved him on.

He gunned the Yamaha east towards Sunningdale, keeping as close to the middle of the road as the oncoming cars allowed. In his rearview mirror he saw the men from the Rover crouching to try and take aim. One of them had stumbled over to the Corniche. Prince Ibn and the others were now climbing out; they also had begun to cough. Cars travelling east were braking and swerving to avoid the activity in their path.

Pistol shots rang out but came nowhere near the bald man. He stretched his left thumb across the Yamaha's handlebar and flicked the rocker switch. A ball of flame consumed the Corniche and spread back immediately to the Rover. An instant later the roar of the explosion reached him and he felt the impact of the shock waves in his back, like a kick.

Even as he triggered the explosion he was braking; he'd only travelled about five hundred yards. He slewed the bike across the path of a Sierra that was already skidding to a halt because of what lay ahead, and turned into the road that had come up on his right. The Sierra's tyres screeched and he heard the crunch of colliding metal. As he entered the side road he stopped and put his foot to the ground; he allowed himself a moment's glance back at his work.

The flames reached to the tops of the trees that lined the road. Oily black smoke curled above them to disappear into the night sky. In the heart of the blaze nothing could be seen of the Corniche, the Rover or any of the bodyguards. Prince Ibn and the other Arabs had vanished.

On the other side of the road another car lay on its side, caught by the blast as it was passing. There was no movement in or near it. Its roof was torn off.

The traffic was now in chaos on either side of the scene; more shunts had occurred, adding to the pandemonium. The bald man heard shouts and screams above the crackle of the flames; there was the noise of running feet as some of the bolder or more foolish drivers left their cars and raced towards the inferno. Others were trying to u-turn out of the crush of vehicles, to get away from the scene as fast as possible.

Men had rushed out from the garage, carrying fire extinguishers, and were trying to douse the flames; it was plain that they were wasting their time. Even through the crash helmet and visor, the bald man smelt the acrid stink of burning rubber and petrol.

No one was stirring from the direction of the walled manor house.

A second blast belched blue and yellow flames from the blaze as the

Rover's petrol tank exploded. The men with the fire extinguishers were flung to the ground. Some of their clothes caught fire as the petrol sprayed them. The press of vehicles trying to leave the scene was increasing. Car horns and racing engines added to the clamour as drivers urged each other out of the way. The rip of tearing metal indicated that some had decided that parting with a bumper was the least of their worries.

The bald man became aware that eyes were watching him. The Sierra driver was moving towards him.

The bald man was in no hurry. His registration would be noted, there would be descriptions of the bike and himself. So he waited until the Sierra driver was within a few feet before dropping the Yamaha into first and roaring off with the throttle wide open. His speed alarmed the people who'd emerged from their homes to see what was going on. Some of them stared as he flew past. More witnesses, he thought; which was fine by him.

Two or three miles away, deep in a quiet copse at a spot called Valley End, the Sherpa waited. When the thin man who had driven it there heard the Yamaha in the distance he threw open the van's rear doors and slid the plank into position.

On the floor, tethered as before, Ibraham was stirring. He tugged against the ropes and tried to turn his head to see what was going on. His eyes were dilated, his expression stupefied.

The thin man climbed up beside him and fetched a flat plastic case from the front seat. He opened it on his lap, withdrew a syringe, and filled it from a glass vial.

Ibraham focused on him for a moment and shook his head, muttering something incoherent. The thin man ignored him and grabbed his left arm. Ibraham's sleeve was already unbuttoned; the thin man pushed it up to his elbow and pressed his thumb into the soft flesh of his inner arm until the vein stood up. Ibraham's small struggles were as weak as a butterfly's.

The syringe pierced the vein and the struggles began to subside, eventually stopping entirely. The thin man watched Ibraham's face as he pumped the heroin home. One tear plopped in the dust by Ibraham's head, then his breathing became regular again.

A minute later the Yamaha pulled into the copse and the thin man rose to his feet. He pushed Ibraham well to the side and jumped out just as the Yamaha ascended the plank and came to rest in the loading bay. The bald man dismounted and began tying the bike in position while his partner stowed the plank and closed the doors.

Then they made themselves comfortable and waited.

Back at Windlesham the fire engines and ambulances were making the best of their gruesome task. The road was awash with oil, petrol and extinguisher foam. Gobbets of charred flesh and limbs littered the scene, twisted metal was scattered everywhere. The medics' priority was the living. Some of the burning men had been wrapped in blankets and were receiving attention by the roadside, but the worst casualties had been loaded into the first ambulances and driven away. There was no help to be given to the occupants of the passing car. The traffic was stacked bumper to bumper for miles in either direction. The police were doing their best to set up detours via the side roads but they could see that it would be many hours before normal flow was restored. They and the other emergency services were having an increasingly hard time getting to and from the scene, and were being forced to use the pavements and the verges.

The television cameras and the press hadn't yet got through, but one amateur photographer had been busy. It was the woman with the crew-cut. She and her companion had driven the Volvo into the filling station after the man on the motorbike and had caught everything on film until the tear-gas forced them to close their windows. Their shots included the motorcyclist and the white Sherpa.

By the time the police started enquiring from car to car for witnesses, the camera was out of sight and the women seemed just as upset as everyone else. They had seen nothing until the explosion itself, and then they'd dived for cover. Or so they said.

When the road was clear, they were just two travellers among many that day who seemed only to be glad to be leaving such a scene of carnage.

It was one thirty in the morning, still and silent on the downs and heathlands, when the Sherpa, having travelled south to pick up the A3, reached the outskirts of the small town of Hindhead. It turned into the gravelled car park north of the town and stopped in its far corner. The deep gorge known as the Devil's Punch Bowl fell away beneath it, hidden in the darkness. An occasional set of headlights traced the route of the road that curved around the rim of the gorge.

There was no sign of life in the beauty spot's car park. It was too cold a night for lovers and the hikers had retired to their hostels long ago.

The thin man got out of the van and set the portable transmitter on a bench at the edge of the parking area. He switched it on and tapped the microphone with his knuckle while the bald man checked the reception on the Yamaha's receiver. Everything was coming through loud and clear.

Leaving his partner in position by the bench, the bald man took the wheel of the Sherpa and drove slowly back onto the A3.

He was no longer wearing the motorcycling gear. The leather suit, boots and gauntlets had been put on Ibraham; the helmet was in the bike's rear-mounted pannier, whose lid had now been removed.

The road was empty and he took it slowly around the mile-long loop. At the tightest stretch of the left-hand curve a crash barrier separated the opposing traffic lanes; an earth bank screened the inner lane from the steep drop beside it.

As the road came out of the curve, the crash barrier ended. On the right was a dirt track leading into the gorse-covered Hindhead commons.

The bald man accelerated across the road, before any traffic should appear and see him, and took the Sherpa well down the track and out of sight. He turned off the engine and lights.

Ibraham was regaining consciousness again. By the time the bald man had manoeuvred the motorcycle down from the van's loading bay, the cold night air had revived him further.

'Ibraham – can you hear me?'

The Libyan nodded uncertainly. He started to shiver. Sweat was breaking out on his forehead.

'More,' he croaked. He looked up pleadingly. 'Please, please. Ohhh –' The sigh was like a death rattle. 'I am so cold.'

He sat up unsteadily and hugged his knees. For a moment he stared at the gauntlets on his hands, uncomprehending, then shivered again and buried his face against his knees. Sobs began to shake his body in long, irregular waves. 'Allah, what have they done to me?'

The bald man fetched the plastic case and recharged the syringe. The sobs continued but there was no resistance as he took Ibraham's arm, pulled back the leather sleeve and inserted the hypodermic into his vein.

'I've got good news, Ibraham,' he said as he pushed the plunger steadily down.

'What?' Ibraham's head was still pressed against his knees but the shaking was beginning to ease.

'We've heard from your people. They've agreed to pay up. We're going to make the exchange now. Come on.'

He helped Ibraham down from the van and onto the bike, and began trundling it back along the dirt track. Ibraham looked down and realised what he was sitting on.

'You've ridden one of these before, haven't you? Airmen are good with all kinds of machines.'

Ibraham nodded, still sniffing and sobbing. 'Where are we going?'

'You're going to ride down the road to meet up with your friends. Not far.'

A dazed smile spread across the young Libyan's face. 'Who is there? Ahmed? Salim?'

'Yes, yes. They're all there, waiting for you.'

By now they'd crossed the A3 and were passing the spot where the earth bank began. No vehicles had passed them. The bald man pushed the Yamaha into a break in the gorse bushes and started the engine. He held the throttle so that Ibraham couldn't rev it accidentally. A car flashed past; the bald man waited until its engine note died away.

'One-Seven,' he said into the handmike.

'One-Seven,' came the immediate reply.

Ibraham stared at the radio unit, noticing it for the first time.

'That was my partner,' the bald man explained. 'He'll let me know when your friends arrive, then I'll show you where to ride to, to meet them.'

They waited for another three or four minutes. A few cars passed in both directions. The bike was positioned so that Ibraham had his back to the road and paid the cars no attention. The bald man stood facing him, making sure that he didn't touch the brakes and bring on the brake light, and keeping him chatting. He checked that Ibraham understood the basics of gear-changes and use of the clutch, but the exercise became more meaningless as the heroin sent him higher. The bald man didn't mind; it wouldn't make much difference in the end.

Then the radio crackled again and the voice said 'One-Seven.'

The bald man didn't acknowledge this time. He planted the crash helmet on Ibrahim's head, not bothering to fasten the chin strap, then pushed the bike as fast as he could and got it positioned on the road and into gear. A clap on the back and Ibraham wobbled off, gathering speed as he entered the long curve.

He was on the wrong side of the road, riding without lights.

It might have been the sight of the approaching headlamps that panicked him, or just the fact that he couldn't ride the Yamaha after all. The bald man thought the latter, since he didn't see the bike's brake light as it keeled over and skidded away from under Ibraham. Bike and rider separated in opposite directions in the path of the lorry that bore down on them.

The lorry's huge tyres shredded on the road in the attempt to avoid the inevitable. With a shriek of tearing metal the bike vanished under one of the wheels. The noise obliterated any sound that the Libyan might have made as the nearside wheel smashed against him. His body was flung spinning into the air. It arced over the earth bank and into the steep gully on the other side.

The bald man was back in the Sherpa and passing on the other side of the crash barrier even before the trembling lorry driver had climbed down from his cab.

The red and white crash helmet spun to the side of the road and bounced against the kerb. It rolled along for a few feet, met a buckled motorcycle wheel, and was finally still.

The night returned to silence.

Moscow

But in Section 4 of the Serbskiy Institute, the silence of the night was shattered. Running footsteps echoed up the long, dark stairwells, accompanied by anxious shouts and laboured breathing. Doors slammed and keys jangled in locks.

The residents of the wing moved restively in their sleep behind their locked doors. Some started wide awake.

The noises were the noises of alarm, of panic: rare emotions in that place. So what if some inmate needed urgent help, or hung himself in his cell, or had his knuckles white around another's throat? These people were politicals, dissidents, they had no rights, they'd ceased to exist. They were human oxen, nothing more.

Ogarkin, in dressing-gown and slippers, was first at the door of the cell, followed closely by the haggard nurse who'd raised the alarm. This patient was different, and the nurse knew it.

The professor threw the door wide and stumbled into the room, where the nurse had left the light burning. What he saw stopped his feet and almost his heart as well.

Galina lay in a tangle of bedclothes drenched in blood. Even the beautiful golden hair was streaked with blood. The grey padded walls too. There was a pool of blood on the floor, where one arm dangled down. Its wrist was torn open. The other arm was thrown back beside her head; its wrist had an open gash as well.

'Oh Jesus! Holy Jesus!'

Ogarkin fell to his knees by the bed. He remembered the down on the girl's soft cheek and touched it gently. The flesh was warm.

Something hard dug into his knee; he shifted position and looked down by the bed. He picked up the palette-knife that lay there and stared at its blade, crimson and sticky.

'Impossible,' he croaked. These things were blunt. He'd even thought to check this one himself in the shop.

He looked again, and wiped the blood on a sheet. He ran a finger along the edge of the blade. It wasn't how it had been in the shop; now it was rough, like sandpaper, and a coarse sharpness had been honed along one side.

Then he remembered her in the courtyard; right alongside the wall; crouching by the step: the sandstone step.

A male nurse pushed in beside him and rapidly began to prepare two tourniquets.

'Professor?'

222

Ogarkin looked around to see who'd spoken. It was one of the doctors. He'd already reached over Ogarkin and torn open Galina's blouse; now he was waiting with his stethoscope. He lifted its end to make his point. Ogarkin realised that he was in the man's way and stood up. He felt a sneeze coming on and realised that he'd come without tissues.

The doctor knelt down in his place. He put the stethoscope against Galina's chest and listened. He was very still and so was Ogarkin, the sneeze conquered.

The doctor moved the stethoscope an inch and listened again. Then he looked up at the professor.

PART THREE

33

Berkshire

The retreat house was as isolated and peaceful as Marie-Thérèse had promised. On his first afternoon Knight climbed the creaking stairs to the dusty attic room and scraped a hole in the grime of the dormer window. Peering through, he found that he could just make out the top of the convent roof beyond the trees to the east. In the fold of hills further on lay the village and somewhere beyond that his abandoned home. In the other direction, though he had no window from which to view them, the downs stretched to the next county. North, he knew, was woodland; to the south were farmland and the motorway.

In the last of the afternoon light he brooded by a half-open window in the library, surrounded by Thomas à Kempis, Father Brown and endless lives of the saints. The sounds of the schoolgirls playing reached him across the frosty fields. Then a bell pealed and the laughter faded.

Sometime in the early evening he was startled by the honk of a car horn outside. He was in the small dormitory that he'd chosen for his bedroom. He crossed to the window in time to see the retreating tail lights of old Jod's Mazda pick-up. By the time he got downstairs its engine note had faded to nothing. He unbolted the kitchen door and took in the carrier bags that had been left on the step. One contained an assortment of rough clothes, the others were full of groceries. As he unpacked the bags he smiled and silently thanked Marie-Thérèse.

The passage of the days that followed was marked by a cycle of sounds that soon became familiar to him: the children's laughter from over the hill and the peal of the school bell, clock-chimes from the village when the wind was right, birdsong in the morning and the scratch of mice in the evening, the thump of hot water in the pipes throughout the house as the boiler followed its twice-daily routine, the tread of his own feet on the floorboards as he wandered from room to room.

He grew used to the crucifixes that guarded every doorway, perfect in the smallest detail as if their realism bore witness to the faith of the artisans who had moulded them. The images pressed themselves into his memory without any effort on his part; when he closed his eyes a random selection of them would appear for his inspection: a fingernail, folds of linen, the curve of a lip within its fringe of beard, a punctured ribcage, thorns, the knuckle of a slim toe.

He grew accustomed also to being watched over, wherever he was, by statues of the Virgin Mary, her hands extended in blessing or supplication, or by portraits of a Jesus whose bleeding heart shone in His chest as if the flesh and bone had been replaced by perspex.

In the dormitory he came upon a Latin missal, its gossamer pages plumped up by brittle crosses of palm-leaf. A variety of childish hands had inscribed them with the dates of Palm Sundays long ago; he grouped the crosses on the bed and found that they spanned four generations. He discovered that some of the books in the library had names written on their fly-leaves in matching handwriting, with dates that overlapped with those on the crosses. Missal and books together, he realised, recorded a part of the house's history before it had passed into the convent's ownership. Over several evenings he enjoyed the therapy of organising this material in an attempt to retrace a past that seemed, in its distance, easier to confront than his own.

As far as wider and more contemporary events were concerned, the house had neither television nor radio, nor newspapers landing on its doormat, nor any other message from the world outside. Marie-Thérèse kept her distance and old Jod never appeared again. Knight might have been living in a sealed time capsule, without even so much as a calendar to count the days; only as he was strapping on his wristwatch on the first Saturday did he notice that January had given way to February.

Only a mile away, the Range Rover drew into his drive again. Four men got out. Three stood by the vehicle while the fourth went to the front doorstep. He carried a flat briefcase which he set down at his feet and opened. It was filled with keys and lockpicks arranged in a purposemade polystyrene bed. When the door swung open some minutes later, the other men joined him and all four entered Knight's house.

In west London, Gaunt arrived at Eva's with two men whom she didn't recognise. She sat with him in the sitting-room, wincing at the sounds of them moving through the rest of her home. They were shifting her furniture about and scuffling through cupboards and drawers. There was no mention of a search warrant and she knew that there was no point in demanding one.

'Don't be alarmed,' Gaunt told her. 'They're only taking a general look. I've told them not to be too enthusiastic. Unlike the people at Edmund's place. Not that I expect to find much either here or there. I think he's been far too clever for that. Don't you? By the way, where do you think he's gone?'

No answer.

'Twice a year,' he mused. 'He always took time off twice a year. June and November-ish. Just a few days. Not his main holidays, just a few spare days. Leftovers. Or as if he was saving them all along. Odd.'

'So what?'

'Odder still, this time. No reason given. He just . . .' His eyebrows rose questioningly. 'Well, he just vanished. Not subtle this time.' He produced a leather notebook from an inside pocket and slid a slim ballpoint from its spine. 'You weren't planning anything special today, were you?' He set the notebook on the arm of the chair. 'So we have plenty of time. I'd like to go back to the beginning. I'm sure you must know the sort of thing I'm looking for. Let's begin with names – names of people or places he ever mentioned to you, whatever the context. There must be scores.'

She shook her head. 'You really didn't know Knight, did you? You really did not.'

On the evening of the second Sunday, Knight took the heavy mackintosh that was hanging on the back of the kitchen door and pulled it on over the old cardigan and shabby corduroys that he was wearing, and strode out across the fields to the chapel. At its porch door he stood listening for a moment. The chant of evensong reached his ears. He closed the door softly and walked down the side of the chapel to wait in the darkness.

When the small congregation emerged a quarter of an hour later, he moved where he could see the nuns as they stood to the side to gather their flock of schoolgirls together. Marie-Thérèse appeared at the edge of the group. The girls and the nuns started walking back to the main block of the convent and Marie-Thérèse fell behind, as he'd hoped she would. He followed quietly along the lane and was soon able to draw alongside her.

'Surprising me again, Mr Knight?'

As the last of the cars reversed down from the chapel, she peered at him in the flicker of headlamps, taking in his heavily stubbled chin and shabby clothes. There'd been an old flat cap in the pocket of the mackintosh and he'd pulled it on.

'You'd pass for a tramp,' she told him. 'One of the poor souls that come up here every day for a bite to eat.'

'I can't pay you yet for the food or the clothes. I'm low on cash. I could give you a cheque, but –'

'Someone might be keeping an eye on your bank account?'

They walked on for another few yards in silence. He looked sideways at her before pursuing the request that had brought him to her.

'I haven't seen or heard the news since I came here. I'd like to do some catching up.'

'You'd be welcome to use the television room in the main block anytime you like.'

He shook his head. 'I'd be just as happy with a newspaper or two. The back issues for the last two weeks would be useful as well.'

'The school takes most of the main dailies. You'll have to take your chances on the back issues.'

'Where do I find them?'

'The sixth form reading room. Go there any evening and you shouldn't be disturbed. The girls go into dinner in a few minutes, then they have study time. You'd have the reading room to yourself from this time.'

They had drawn close to the main convent block. It was well-lit and girls and nuns were scattered about the doorways and corridors. He stopped by a tree, at the edge of the darkness. She understood his reticence and came over to join him.

'I'll tell you how to get there.'

Five minutes later he watched from the darkness as the corridors emptied; through the arched refectory windows he saw the tide of heads bend in prayer, then disappear from his view as the girls seated themselves. A moment later the white caps of the serving staff began bobbing about the hall. Dinner was served. He made his way in the direction that Marie-Thérèse had indicated.

The grim events he found recorded in the headlines of the last week and a half were not what he expected. An assassination, yes; but not of any of the target figures he'd assumed.

SAUDI PRINCE ASSASSINATED

The prince in question, he discovered, was the Saudi with the chilling gaze who had seized his attention two weeks before: Saleem Ibn Abdul Aziz Al-Saud. He had turned out to be a victim and not the potential protagonist that, if anything, Knight would have been inclined to take him for.

His death had occurred on the day that Knight had come to the retreat house: Knight read with sadness of the other casualties that the bomb had claimed. But there was a political cost as well. The Opec conference had been aborted. For Britain that was embarrassing enough in itself; Knight recalled Gaunt's words about the Prime Minister's reluctance to call it off. Worse, however, was the fact that Prince Ibn had been under British protection at the time of his murder; if the Soviets' purpose in killing him on British soil was to drive Britain and Saudi Arabia apart, the strategy seemed to have worked. Within a day of the assassination the headlines showed how the Saudi government was reacting:

SAUDI ARABIA MAY SEVER
DIPLOMATIC RELATIONS
WITH BRITAIN

The development that followed on from this came as no great surprise; in the knife-edge relationships that characterised the Middle East, there was always someone who was ready to exploit every situation:

GADAFFI CLAIMS BRITAIN, USA AND SAUDI
GOVERNMENT BEHIND IBN'S DEATH

At first sight, the accusation had all the hallmarks of the Libyan leader's usually wild pronouncements. But on this occasion he seemed to have some grounds for what he was saying. Ibn, he claimed, had been at loggerheads with Fahd and Yamani over their oil strategy. Knight remembered the prince's brooding presence in the newsreel footage; that he loathed Fahd and Yamani had been clear enough. Now Gadaffi seemed to be supplying the reason. Whether his revelation at this critical time was Soviet-prompted or not, it was certainly making a substantial contribution to the process of alienating Saudi Arabia from its Western allies.

The pattern of the Soviet strategy was making sense. Until, that is, the next development occurred. By then a week had passed since the assassination:

KILLER OF SAUDI PRINCE WAS LIBYAN,
BODY FOUND

The dead Libyan, a young man called Ibraham Abukhder, was said to have known terrorist connections. He had died within hours of Ibn's assassination but nothing had been released while the police and Special Branch checked who he was and the evidence that he was the likely assassin. There were plenty of eye-witness accounts of him bombing Ibn's car, and the press were convinced that his action must have been sanctioned by Gadaffi. But in fact, as Knight read through the press reports, it became apparent that they were initially not based on any official statements. Official silence prevailed for two more days, despite questions in Parliament and the stir that the media was creating.

Finally, however, the Foreign Office had been obliged to end the speculation, confirming everything the press had said.

But it did more than that: it confirmed other reports that the media had been featuring. It was the biggest news of all and it had broken on the Saturday, just twenty-four hours ago and eleven days after the assassination:

GADAFFI AND PRINCE IBN PLANNED
TO OVERTHROW SAUDI GOVERNMENT

Knight set the papers down. If Ibn's death was a Soviet action, things had gone badly wrong: Gadaffi was in the dock now, not the West. The Saudi Arabia–Britain–US axis would be stronger than ever after this. Either that, or Britain had fabricated the coup, the dead Libyan and God knows what else. Knight shook his head. He was going too far too fast.

He fetched a writing pad from a nearby desk and began to make notes. He stuck to the facts, if that was what they were, as the papers had reported them: only the facts. Thinking would come later. But as for whether any of the events related in any way to Bill Clarke's death or the attempt on his own life, that was a complication about which he still hadn't the faintest idea.

When he'd done he tidied the newspapers away, cut out a few of the key articles and shuffled them together into his pocket.

There was one small cutting, however, that he set apart and left on the table. It wasn't a news story. It was a classified advertisement, from the previous Tuesday's *Times*. It occupied just one column inch and was set inside a single-rule display box.

NASSAU, BAHAMAS
Substantial investor/partner required
for 22–24 apartment development in prime
location. Exceptional profit potential.
Please call our UK offices:
Boyar Properties
01-862-0699

He studied the advertisement for a time before tucking it carefully away in an inside pocket of the mackintosh. Then he checked that the reading room was as he'd found it, turned out the light and made his way back through the darkened corridors of the convent block.

The building was silent, the girls by now being in one of their study sessions. He saw no one as he followed the lane over the fields and up to the retreat house.

He went straight upstairs to the small dormitory and the metal locker where he'd folded away his suit and the clothes in which he'd arrived. The cash that he'd had on him that day was on the top shelf, a neat

232

stack of coins and a few folded notes. He scraped it together and went out to the wooden garage adjoining the house, where he'd left his car. He kept coins for meters in the ashtray; now he cleared them out and added them to his haul from the locker.

Half an hour later, his cap pulled well down and the mackintosh collar up, he had walked the two miles to the railway station. The roads were quiet and no one paid him any heed.

The station was deserted and the telephone box outside the small ticket hall was empty. He lifted the phone to hear that it was in working order, took the advertisement from his pocket and dialled the London number which it gave.

It didn't answer. It didn't even connect. He heard the unobtainable tone, tried twice more and got the same result.

He closed his eyes and laid his head against the thick glass of the side panel.

'Damn,' he whispered. 'Why now?'

When he opened his eyes again he was surprised to find a face watching him, only inches from his own. Serious brown eyes in a large full-moon face peered through the glass at him; the face tilted to one side as he straightened up, then back again the other way, like an inquisitive animal's.

Billy Bowman was a child of six in a grown man's body; he harmed no one and, thanks to the village, no one had ever harmed him.

Knight smiled at him and returned the phone to its cradle. The coins came clanging out. Billy nodded energetically and stuck up a broad thumb. He grinned and wandered off, pausing to wave before he rounded the corner.

The advertisement was still lying on the shelf by the phone. Knight returned it carefully to his pocket. He had another number to dial. He fed in the coins again.

This number was also in London; an efficient-sounding switchboard operator answered after two or three rings. A moment later the man he wanted to speak to came on the line.

'Don't say my name,' Knight told him, and launched into the set of instructions that he'd worked out on the walk to the station.

34

He saw the distrust in the stationmaster's gaze as he fumbled inside the mackintosh for his cash. It was clear that the man didn't really expect him to be able to pay, considering his appearance.

Knight spread some coins onto the revolving tray set in the window, scooped up his ticket, and arrived on the platform just in time to board the London train before it pulled off.

From Waterloo he went to Embankment station and waited on the eastbound Circle line platform until he saw Doug Riley appear. The journalist was carrying a McDonald's takeaway bag. There was no automatic smile on his florid face as there had been in the pub on Shoe Lane.

'It's true then,' he said, staring at Knight's clothes.

'What?'

'I heard they were looking for you. I thought it was just talk.'

'Stop staring.'

Riley turned away and began munching his burger. From the pocket of his city overcoat he took a handkerchief, with which he wiped his lips and fingers from time to time. Knight huddled into the mackintosh. Both of them remained silent as a man drew near and strolled past.

'Something else I heard,' Riley resumed. 'Joss Franklyn. You were there the night he was shot. Oh yes, I know he was shot. You didn't do it, did you? That's not why you've gone to ground?'

Knight glared at him from beneath the tattered peak of his cap.

'Just asking.' Riley gazed along the platform. 'Bill Clarke, Joss Franklyn, now you like this. Am I going to get a story out of this in the end?'

'Maybe. Maybe not.'

'Looks like it's all you can offer. You're hardly in a position to come on heavy this time.'

A train drew in; it was thinly populated and Knight led the way into what he judged to be the emptiest carriage. They settled themselves in a corner, a seat away from each other. A black girl at the far end of the compartment watched them. Knight met her gaze and her eyes shied away.

Meanwhile Riley was staring at Knight's feet.

'The shoes,' he said. 'They're wrong.'

Knight looked down. Unlike everything else he was wearing, the shoes were his own: black Oxfords. He saw what Riley meant. They weren't new but they were hardly in keeping with the rest of his garb.

'You fail the fieldcraft test,' Riley said, and got back to the hamburger. Knight tucked his feet under the seat as the train gathered speed, and drew one of the newspaper clippings from his pocket. Riley was the man to give him the background on them: the real background. As much of it as could be known.

'Saleem Ibn Abdul Aziz Al-Saud,' Knight read out, keeping his voice to what was only just audible over the train's rattle. 'Know much about him?'

Riley nodded while he finished swallowing. 'A fortnight ago I didn't. Half brother of King Fahd of Saudi Arabia. Prince of the royal blood. Held minor office in the Saudi Council of Ministers until his assassination while under what you people call twenty-four-hour protection. Your lot knew it was on the cards, didn't you? That's what all the search and interrogate activity was for the weekend before it happened. You really blew it this time.'

'We didn't know who the target was. Only that a hit might be imminent.'

'Who tipped you off?'

'No one I can tell you about.'

Riley sighed. Mansion House passed.

'All right,' he said at last. 'Get on with whatever you wanted to ask.'

'This Prince Ibn. The press described him as an Islamic fundamentalist. That's unusual in a member of the Saudi hierarchy. Even his name was a giveaway. Ibn – it's what the world called his and Fahd's father: Ibn Saud. He founded the country and called it after himself. So this prince was harking back to his country's origins in choosing Ibn as his short name. A nationalistic gesture.'

Riley grunted his agreement. 'When he was younger he sympathised openly with nationalist and fundamentalist groups. In recent years he stopped being open about it. I guess he had to, given his position. Now it looks like the old sympathies were still there under the surface.'

'Do you believe they were enough to explain these links between him and Gadaffi?'

'Anything's possible with the Arabs.'

Liverpool Street. The black girl stood up to get out. A Chinese couple got on. Knight waited until they settled themselves at the other end of the carriage.

'So tell me about Ibn and Gadaffi.'

Riley shoved a handful of french fries into his mouth. 'After Ibn's death there was confusion. We knew nothing then about the Gadaffi connection. The Saudis were screaming blue murder because one of their VIPs had been knocked off. The other Arab nations were kicking up a fuss too, Libya most of all. As for the conference – well, that was the end of that, before it had even properly begun.'

'The Saudis were talking about breaking off diplomatic relations.'

'Of course. And Gadaffi and some others were urging exactly that, saying that Ibn's death was proof the West couldn't be trusted. Special Branch and your people were hanging their heads in shame.'

The compartment filled up a little more at Euston Square. Most people who saw Knight sat well away from them, but a teenager came within a few seats. As the train moved off, Knight noticed the light-weight earphones that he was wearing and heard the thin scratch of music coursing through them.

'What did Gadaffi mean about the West not being trusted?'

'His first claims were only about Ibn being privately critical of Fahd and Yamani for failing to get the oil price up. It angered Ibn that doubling output was playing into the West's hands.'

'How did we know Gadaffi wasn't lying?'

'From the number of red Saudi faces. The crunch came when he announced outright that the West had eliminated Ibn with the specific purpose of shutting him up. That's what he'd meant about not trusting the West.'

'"The West",' echoed Knight, '– or Britain?'

'Don't know. He never got beyond the usual Gadaffi-speak about rabid imperialist dogs. He alleged Fahd was in on the assassination. He himself – Gadaffi – might be next, he said. He called all the foreign correspondents into that tent of his for a pow-pow and ranted on about Ibn's death proving beyond doubt that Fahd and Yamani were work-ing with the West to keep the oil price down. Proof at last that they were the Western puppets he'd been accusing them of being for years.'

'Did he offer any proof that the West killed Ibn?'

'Of course not. But he was putting Fahd in a tight spot: on the one hand he was furious with us for a catastrophic security failure. He wanted to slate us – not just because we deserved it, but also to show that he wasn't the Western lap-dog that Gadaffi said. But at the same time he didn't want to be seen siding too tightly with Gadaffi. Fahd was torn between Arab solidarity and his wish to stay friends with us for the sake of the fighter planes or arms or whatever it is that he's always after.'

They had come as far as Notting Hill Gate. The Chinese couple got off. A bag lady got on.

'Then,' Knight said as the train pulled away again, 'Lo and behold – one dead Libyan assassin surfaced. Right?'

Riley nodded. 'Ibraham Abukhder. In fact, he surfaced the day after Ibn's death but it took a while to tie him in for sure – while Gadaffi was laying the blame on the West.'

Knight fished out another clipping.

'Thanks to Abukhder,' he said, 'the tables were turned. Abukhder was the evidence that Gadaffi himself was behind Ibn's killing. And then there was this information that Gadaffi had been backing some lunatic plot of Ibn's to get rid of Fahd. Right?'

Riley nodded. 'The coup. If it had succeeded, Gadaffi would be running Saudi Arabia.'

'And the largest oil reserves in the free world.' Somewhere here, Knight knew, was the heart of the matter.

'The disclosure of the coup,' he said. 'As far as I could see, it wasn't attributed, beyond the usual "reliable sources inform us". Where did it come from?'

Riley cast him a cynical glance. 'Where do you think?'

'It was a leak?'

'Not all of it, of course. To begin with, there was Abukhder. No secret that he was the man who killed Ibn. Plenty of people saw him either actually plant the bomb or flee the scene. No secret either that he was Libyan. It went from there. Whoever heard of a Libyan working alone – one isolated maniac with no line to the chief maniac? But at that stage we could only speculate. I reckon your people thought if they announced openly that they had firm evidence that Abukhder was Gadaffi's man, it might look like they were trying to deflect attention from their own cock-up. The same would apply to information about the coup. So they leaked both instead. Television and radio had it by last Tuesday lunchtime, the press ran it that evening or the next morning. When the media had given it a good airing, the government could legitimately say that it had no choice but to admit the story was soundly-based. Which it did late on Friday – in time for yesterday's editions and the morning news bulletins.'

'And it ends up sounding a lot more convincing than if the Foreign Office had announced it from the start. Nice work.'

'So now it's Gadaffi who's the villain, not the West. There's still the question of why he bumped off his fellow conspirator. Maybe they had some kind of falling-out. Or maybe it was simply mistaken identity – Abukhder blowing up Ibn's car when he meant to get Fahd. They were both attending a meeting at Yamani's Surrey estate. Ibn was first to arrive. Fahd was following about half an hour behind him.'

'Who knew about that meeting? It was unscheduled.'

'Was it?' Riley turned to look at him. 'The implication so far has been that it was in the schedule.'

Knight shook his head. 'As late as the day before the assassination, which was the last time I saw a schedule, the meeting didn't exist.'

Riley scribbled a note on a corner of the now-empty takeaway bag and tore it off. 'I'll follow up on that.'

They had gone full circle and the train was pulling into Embankment again. Knight rose and went to the nearest door. Riley scrunched up the empty bag and went out through the other door to catch up with him on the platform.

'Hold on, Edmund. Is that it?'

The teenager and the bag lady passed them.

'Is what it?'

'You've pumped me. All I get is a meeting that wasn't scheduled. Do me a favour, Edmund.'

'Thanks for your help, Doug.'

'You owe me now, Edmund. You owe me plenty.'

Knight pulled an apologetic face. 'That reminds me. The other favour I asked on the phone.'

He thought that Riley was simply going to walk off. Then the big man's hand produced his wallet and peeled off a sheaf of notes. He pushed them into Knight's pocket.

Knight waited until he was out of sight, then made his way through the tunnels of the station to the Bakerloo southbound platform to get back to Waterloo.

On the last train home, except home was the one place it couldn't take him, he turned over in his mind what Riley had told him.

The fragments still refused to fit together. But he was certain that they all originated in a single pattern; ultimately they must reveal it.

The scenario that had been so neatly planted in the world media made no mention of the Spetznaz unit. There were several ways to account for that. If the unit was still being searched for, it couldn't be mentioned. Equally, if it had been apprehended, that was all the more reason to suppress the information; unlike the Americans, the Foreign Office would prefer to use something like that for private diplomatic leverage than for publicly raising the international temperature.

But the scenario remained inadequate and he was no more convinced of its completeness than he sensed was Rily. It was riddled with inconsistencies as glaring as his shoes.

According to the reports, Ibraham Abukhder had a history of only low-grade terrorist connections: he had acted as an occasional courier and message-drop. Why would the Libyans choose such an inexperienced person for a major action? Linking him with the Spetznaz unit didn't fit either; what Spetznaz commander would allow one of his crack units to be endangered by association with such a man?

Next, there was something over-convenient about his corpse turning up the way it had: the perfect thing to swing Arab opinion against Gadaffi. Would the Libyan leader have made his allegations against the West before knowing for certain that his man was home safe? Gadaffi was a maniac but he was no fool. And if he had been conspiring with the Saudi prince to overthrow Fahd, why kill him? Mistaken identity, maybe, since Abukhder was a novice. But that was as over-convenient as Abukhder's corpse. What about the suggestion that they had fallen out? Thieves fell out, so could conspirators. But it was difficult to see what Gadaffi stood to gain from Ibn's death.

The meeting in Surrey that wasn't scheduled: someone had kept Abukhder and/or the Spetznaz unit very well informed. Someone in the Saudi delegation? Or one of the other groups? The problem was that he, Knight, was now in no position to find out how widespread had been the knowledge of the meeting.

The most vexing question, however, concerned the information about the coup itself. Riley's assertion that a deliberate plant had occurred made sense. Obviously the information had come from the intelligence services. That wasn't the puzzle. It was how the information had reached them in the first place that was the real mystery. When and to whom had it come? There'd been no inkling of it at the start of the previous week, when it would surely have been brought to Knight's attention. It was impossible that intelligence of such a crucial nature could come in and be cross-checked beyond reasonable doubt between then and last Thursday or Friday, when it was leaked. Libya was almost impenetrable to the Western intelligence services; even Mossad had virtually given it up. Obtaining such intelligence was one chance in a million; verifying it would have taken weeks of painstaking work.

Knight ran a hand across his forehead and shook his head. He had hoped that Riley could help clarify some things; instead the opposite had happened. He turned to the question of Bill Clarke's death and his own near-miss. Further dead-ends. Why should anyone want him, Knight, out of the way? Gaunt wanted his head on a trophy board with full details writ large underneath, not silent on a platter; he'd want him wrung through the PsyOps mangle of interminable cross-examination until he was dry and flat, not buried with full honours.

He slumped further into the corner of the seat as the train rushed through the darkness and past the lights of empty country stations. He considered his fragments of fact but they were like the drifting spots of colour behind his closed eyelids: they floated away when he tried to look at them directly and he ended up with only the darkness.

35

From the outside Knight's house had changed in only one respect: net curtains had now been fitted to the front windows on the ground floor.

Inside, the reason for the curtains became clear; the place had been gutted. Half of the furniture and other contents had been taken away for examination. The remainder had been torn apart on the spot, picked through with a degree of care that missed not so much as a tack or a button, and piled up afterwards in corners; or it was to be found in the mobile laboratories and offices that were parked in the back garden. Every carpet had been rolled back. The ground floor was found to be concrete and had been scrutinised for false sections, then left alone; but upstairs the floorboards had been stripped to the joists. The attic, garages and garden workshop had been emptied. Men had pored over every inch of the lawns and shrub-beds with metal detectors. Carelessly-filled holes indicated where their readings had told them to dig; the occasional fence-nail or tangle of wire beside the holes suggested that their labours had been less rewarding than they might have hoped.

Gaunt surveyed the mess without satisfaction as he stood on the steps of one of the mobile laboratories. It had rained all morning and the place was becoming a quagmire. The diggings were filled with water and the most heavily trodden routes between the house and the mobile laboratories were turning into muddy tracks.

'Get some walkways laid,' he told Sumner, who was standing behind him. 'Those aluminium or rubber things you see at outdoor events.'

He drew his gloves on over his long hands and tucked his scarf inside his topcoat, then dashed up to the house, zig-zagging around the puddles and the worst of the mud. Sumner followed. In the kitchen they found a still-warm pot of tea. Sumner poured a cup for each of them while Gaunt peeled his gloves off and scraped his shoes on the kitchen floor.

'Nothing,' he said to the window as he straightened up. 'All this and not a damn thing. Two weeks now since he went to ground. And nothing.'

Sumner remained silent.

'Where the hell is he?' Gaunt sipped the tea, pulled a face and tipped the brew into the sink. He watched its brown swirls for a moment before turning back to the kitchen.

'Are those his?' He nodded towards an untidy stack of newspapers piled on the work-surface by the fridge.

'He has them delivered daily,' Sumner said. 'We haven't cancelled them, for obvious reasons.'

'What did he take?' Gaunt picked the top one off the pile. '*The Times*. Not what it used to be.'

He spread the newspaper open on the table, pushing aside the various pieces of electronic gadgetry that one of the search technicians had left there.

'How did he pay his bill?'

'Monthly. We found some invoices. He paid the last one a fortnight before he vanished. So he's about due again. We'll have to say something to the newsagent soon.'

Gaunt turned the pages slowly.

'He had a ladyfriend,' he said pensively.

Sumner shrugged. 'I didn't know.'

'He slept at her place often. That meant he wasn't home every day.'

Sumner listened, not yet understanding.

'He wasn't always home, but he let his newspaper order stand. Yet there must have been occasions when he didn't catch up with the paper for days at a time. Now why would he do that?'

'I suppose he liked to keep up to date.'

'There's TV and radio. He was reading out-of-date papers. Why did he bother?'

Sumner looked baffled.

Gaunt sighed, just as puzzled, and returned the newspaper to the pile, then turned to sifting through the stack of opened mail beside it. After a time he pulled on his gloves again and looked out at the weather. The rain had eased; the surface of the puddles had become smooth.

'Let me know at once if anything turns up.'

In the hallway they encountered a clutter of upended chairs and picked their way gingerly past them. That brought them to the open door of the study, where Gaunt paused to look inside. A technician was moving a cone-shaped gadget over the bare walls. He wore headphones and was watching the needle of a device like a Geiger counter that he held in his other hand. Gaunt stood there for a minute, watching. The room had been cleared of its desk and other furniture. Knight's combined telephone and answering machine had been left on the window-sill.

Gaunt turned to Sumner. 'I want to know if you come across any tapes for that thing.'

'Yes, Sir Horace.'

The respite from the rain had been only temporary. It was starting again, and heavily, as Gaunt stood alone on the doorstep and waved impatiently for his driver to bring the car closer.

'Bloody fool,' he muttered, as the man manoeuvred away from some shrubs against which he'd parked too tightly. 'They're all bloody fools.' Then he added, 'Except you, Edmund. You've been bloody clever.'

Eva recognised the memo's wording as the standard formula provided in the Personnel manual.

'It is policy for all staff to have the benefit of regular medical examinations . . . records indicate that it is just over a year since your last examination . . . appointment has therefore been made on your behalf with the consultant named below at the Middlesex Hospital . . . advise the clinic direct if you cannot attend on the date given and arrange an alternative . . .'

She glanced at her diary, saw that the date in question suited her, and made a note of the appointment.

A tramp, Knight reflected, could hardly march into a newsagent's and buy a copy of *The Times*. In any event there was also the chance that the newsagent, the only one in the village, might recognise him. Besides, Gaunt's people would be crawling all over by now. They'd have prepared a Retrospective on his movements, his habits, people with whom he associated. They'd be talking to locals and tradespeople. Any of them might spot him on the roads or at the shops; or any of the people they interviewed. His venture out on Sunday night under cover of darkness was one thing; but moving about in broad daylight was asking for trouble.

It was a week since the classified advertisement had appeared. If it was genuine, rather than some unnerving coincidence, then today was when it would be repeated. He'd failed to respond to it the first time and the rule was that there had to be a fallback.

He didn't want it to reappear. And if it did, he didn't want to act on it. He was finished; now more than ever. He remembered the morning he had said so to Eva. Maybe by now she had some idea of how much it was that he had finished with.

Eva. Thinking about her had become an occupational hazard of his solitariness in the retreat house. But there was nothing he could do. God alone knew what her view of him was now.

The newspaper; that was the immediate issue. He couldn't risk leaving the retreat house in daylight. He had no choice but to wait until evening, when the girls were at dinner, and go back to the reading room.

So he sat, and walked from room to room, and pretended to read, and put food on his plate which he didn't eat, and listened to the noises that ticked away the hours, and watched from the library window as the light faded on the fields. And he tried not to think about Eva or Moscow or Gaunt or any of it. And when at last it was time, he sighed with relief that at last it was, put on the mackintosh again and hurried through the night to the convent block.

A small corner of his mind, hidden but insistent, had been convinced that the advertisement wouldn't be there. It was wrong. There the thing was.

Waiting for him as he had waited for it since Sunday. No; since twenty years ago. Cold and simple on the page, its words as hollow as an obituary. And just as final and unarguable.

NASSAU, BAHAMAS
Substantial investor/partner required
for 22–24 apartment development in prime
location. Exceptional profit potential.
Please call our UK offices:
Boyar Properties
01-862-1399

Strangely, now that he had it before him and the worst had happened, he felt nothing. It was as if his heart, like the one in the pious pictures of Jesus, had drained itself empty.

His hands were steady as he scored a line with his thumbnail, tore the small rectangle out and folded it away in his pocket along with its earlier version.

He had two days in which to make up his mind; two days to reach his decision.

He had closed the newspaper and was returning it to the rack when a small headline in the news summary column on the front page caught his eye.

MEMORIAL SERVICE TO BE HELD FOR
RT. HON. WILLIAM CLARKE

He glanced through the paragraph underneath; it gave the date when the service would be held but not its location, saying only that it would be in Clarke's parish church. Knight knew where that was. For a moment he pictured it: the same church where he had seen Clarke and Marion married.

243

Then his thoughts returned to the message contained in the classified advertisement.

As he trudged back over the fields, the same question still nagged him as before. Why were they sending for him now?

It was eight fifteen by the time Eva left the office and almost nine when she arrived at Turnham Green. It wasn't so much that her workload that day had been particularly demanding; more the fact that she tended to take refuge in work these days. The alternative was long evenings filled with remorse and waiting for a call from Knight that she knew could never come.

She was exhausted. It was the best way to be; she might sleep tonight. She was also hungry. As she set off from the station on the quarter of a mile walk home, she tried to decide what should come first when she got there: supper or a hot bath. She passed a restaurant and a rich aroma filled her nostrils; the balance tipped in favour of supper.

There weren't many people on the streets; it was the dead hour when most people had long since arrived home from work, the pubs and restaurants hadn't yet discharged their patrons back onto the streets, and the theatregoers were still enjoying the West End shows.

The two men were waiting at the end of her street. She first looked up and saw them when she was about thirty yards away. Somewhere inside her the voice stirred that spoke to everyone who saw strangers ahead in an empty road at night. She herself had heard it many times before; and as before, she told it to be quiet and pressed on.

As she drew closer she saw that they were youths rather than men, in their late teens or early twenties. One was black, one white. They wore jeans and, despite the cold night air, lightweight jackets and open shirts.

The white boy was sitting on the broken bit of low wall at the end of the alleyway between the launderette and the Mini-Market. His hands dangled between his spread knees and he was clapping them gently together from time to time. The other boy was at the edge of the pavement, facing him. He was doing some sort of shuffling dance step. When she came within earshot she realised that they were singing a tune together, very quietly. It was in time to this that the white boy was clapping his hands and the black boy was jiving.

'Cold night,
Moonlight,
See how the stars are all
Shining bright –'

When she was about ten yards away both of them became completely silent. That she didn't like. Their performance, however, continued in mime: the soft claps, the scrape of the black boy's shoes on the paving slabs. It created an unnatural effect that added to her sense of threat.

They didn't look at her, just kept their eyes on each other. She noticed that they were still smiling. She glanced quickly ahead but there wasn't another soul in sight, only passing cars. It was the same when she looked behind her.

'Hallo there, luscious!'

She looked ahead of her again and saw that the black boy had suddenly spun around and planted himself in front of her, feet well apart as if the leap that had brought him there was all part of the dance. In fact, his hips were still swaying to the silent music. He clicked his fingers as his arms made small circles by his sides.

She halted.

'Lusc-ious!' he repeated. He looked her up and down.

'Please move out of my way.'

She was surprised at how calm she sounded, for she felt light-headed with terror. She had been pestered before but something in the boy's demeanour told her that he didn't intend to let her pass. She tried to remember what it was that a woman was supposed to do when she was attacked: kick her assailant in the groin? scream? give in? They all seemed fraught with risks. Meanwhile she became dimly aware that the white boy was rising to his feet, and that alarmed her further.

Frightened of escalating what might still only be horseplay into something more dangerous, she settled for restating her request. Politely.

'Let me past, please.'

'Don't be like that, girl – I just want to be friends. Let's be friends. Friends, huh?'

He stretched out his right hand as if seeking a handshake. When she drew back he smacked its fingers with the other hand, thrust it forward again and grinned.

'Lusc-ious! Lusc-ious!' he chanted softly.

Still watching her, he resumed his jiving motion and circled back to the edge of the pavement. His hand stretched towards her again; this time lower than before, at the level of her crotch. The fingers crooked upwards in a lewd little movement. He grinned even more broadly than before. She recoiled again.

'Awww,' he moaned, 'that's not very friendly.' His eyes were full of hurt. 'Come to daddy. Come and see what big black daddy's got for you. You'll like it. Oh my – you'll love it.'

As he moved towards her she fell back a step. She opened her mouth to call out but at that moment the white boy's hand closed over it. That was when she knew that it was something more serious than horseplay.

She saw jubilation on the black boy's face.

'Yeah, baby! Yeah!'

Barely conscious, she felt herself half dragged, half carried into the alley.

But they didn't rape her. Afterwards, as she sat there, it took a while for that realisation to sink in.

She picked herself up from the filthy ground and began re-buttoning and straightening her dishevelled clothing.

Hands had undone her coat and blouse and lifted her skirt. Her pants and tights had come down, her bra was unclasped; she could remember the cold air stinging her exposed flesh. The hands had fondled and squeezed her. Fingers had invaded her. Only fingers. She replayed the scene in her mind, forcing herself to go back over the details. But there was no mistake: she hadn't been raped.

They hadn't injured her either. She flexed her body as she re-dressed in the dank alleyway but nothing felt broken or sprained. It seemed that she had nothing worse than a few aches from being held down firmly. She probably wouldn't even be bruised, for she'd been too dazed to put up much of a struggle.

They had opened her handbag and stolen some cash from her purse. There hadn't been much but in the darkness she could feel that the banknotes were gone. Not more than twenty pounds, she estimated. They hadn't bothered with the loose change. She was thankful that they hadn't taken the handbag itself or, as far as she could make out, any other of its contents; and mercifully they'd ignored her briefcase.

She made herself decent and struggled out of the alley to cover the remaining couple of hundred yards home. The road was still empty of other pedestrians.

As she entered her own street, thankful at last to be doing so, she weighed the extent of her good fortune. She was shaken and disgusted, but that was all. Things could have been much worse. She yearned for the security and warmth of her own home. It occurred to her that the hot bath, not supper, had become her first priority. That and a stiff drink.

When she reached the little gate in the hedge that fronted her house, she began searching in her handbag for her doorkeys. She always reached for them when she got to the gate. Tonight, however, she couldn't seem to find them. She kept searching as she went up the path, thinking that in the upset they'd probably got buried under everything else.

She was still rummaging when she got to the doorstep. She quickly went through the pockets of her coat, although that was somewhere she just never put keys.

Still no sign of them.

She groaned as she realised that they must have fallen out in the alley. The thought of going back to that place to look for them was unbearable. Although she'd remained dry-eyed throughout her ordeal, tears now began to well in her eyes. In frustration she made a fist and thumped it against the door.

The jangle that followed sent her gaze to the doorlock. There hung the missing keys.

'Oh no,' she whispered. A shiver ran over her whole body and she felt the fine hairs on her arms and neck prickle.

She unlocked the door and stepped into the hallway.

They had left her intact but they – or someone else while they abused her – had vandalised her home instead. It was as if a tornado had struck. She stumbled from room to room, crying out at each fresh scene of desecration. Furniture was upended, drawers and shelves had been emptied on the floor, record albums and books were strewn everywhere. The kitchen was a mess of spilt flour and foodstuffs. Her bedroom was the same, the bedding stripped into a heap, the air thick with talcum powder and the odours of her perfumes.

But it was the bathroom that was worst. In their choice of a final obscenity it was as if they had read her mind. She would have no bath that night.

The policeman and policewoman had been with her about half an hour before she came to her senses sufficiently to work out what it was about them that was making her uneasy.

'Why don't you let us take you down to the rape centre?'

The WPC was a fresh-faced girl with short, practical fingernails. She leant forward sympathetically across the settee and handed Eva a mug of tea. She had recommended against alcohol, instead ploughing through the mess in the kitchen to make tea for all of them.

'I haven't been raped.'

The policeman, who seemed to be the note-taker, stared down at his pad where he'd written down her report of the incident.

'Strange that,' he mumbled.

'What?'

'Not being raped after all that,' he explained, then dried up.

The WPC took his point on. 'You say you don't think they were disturbed by a passer-by?'

'I wish to God they had been. I never saw a soul.'

'And you don't think you fought them off?'

'You're joking. I turned to jelly.'

'Wonder why they didn't go through with it then?'

'God knows.'

'Are you sure you weren't unconscious at some point?'

'Positive. I was dazed but I didn't black out.'

Now it was the policeman again.

'After they left you, how long did it take you to get back here?'

'I don't know for sure. Ten minutes maybe. Not more than fifteen. I wasn't counting, but I wasn't hanging about either. I told you where it happened – it wasn't far.'

The policeman looked around the devastated room. When he and the WPC had first arrived, he'd had to right the chairs they were sitting on.

'They did an awful lot of damage in ten minutes. And there's upstairs.'

'I think they had help.'

'Don't follow.'

'I think someone else did this while they . . . kept me in the alley. They'd have had half an hour altogether.'

'But nothing's stolen.'

'No.'

The policeman chewed his pencil. 'Wonder how they found out where you lived. Maybe one of them read your address in your purse or something in the alleyway. But then, it'd be pitch black in there.'

'Obviously they must have already known where I lived.'

'You mean they'd been watching you.'

'I don't know. Isn't that your job?'

'You don't think you ever saw them before tonight?'

'No.'

'You'd think you'd recognise them, wouldn't you? If they'd been watching you beforehand, I mean. You'd think you'd've seen them. Would you recognise them if you saw them again?'

'I'm not sure. Maybe. I don't know.'

The WPC took over. 'Look, I think you might be in shock. It really would be a good idea to come down to the rape centre and let a doctor look you over. You might feel steady enough now, but sometimes these things catch up with you later.'

'I'm not in shock. I'll be fine. Really, I'd rather you went out and caught them instead of going on at me about the rape centre. I'm sorry, I don't mean to be rude, but we just seem to be losing time –'

'It's just that if you came down to the centre, the doctor could check to see if maybe you were raped after all. Whatever you say, you might have lost consciousness, you know.'

'I told you – I didn't black out, I haven't been raped. I'd know if I had been, whether I remembered it or not. And frankly I've been poked at enough for one night.'

'It'd be a lady doctor,' the policeman said.

'Oh, for Christ's sake. Go out and catch them.'

'That's not going to be easy, miss.'

'Why?'

'You've not been able to give us much of a description. And it all seems a bit – well – a bit uncertain what's happened exactly.'

'Jesus. Get out of here.'

'Miss –'

'Out. Clear off. Since you think I'm wasting your time, clear off. You've had a good look. I made the whole thing up.' She gestured around at the mess. 'I did all this myself. Don't forget the bathroom. I did that too. Support your local police. Good night.'

She hustled them to the door and all but pushed them onto the doorstep. Now she slammed the door in their faces and stood behind it until she heard their footsteps retreat down the path. They were talking quietly but she couldn't make any of it out. Then car doors slammed, an engine turned and after a moment she heard the sound of their car pulling away.

She groaned loudly, thankful at last just to be left in peace, then went to the kitchen and began digging out her cleaning things.

36

By morning Knight admitted that there was no decision to be made, and that he'd known as much all along. The decision had been made twenty years ago. Any residual doubt in the matter was eliminated by his need to find out why they were sending for him now. The time had had to come, of course; he'd always accepted that. But they never did these things at random, they always had a reason. Why not a year ago, five years ago, when he would have complied without complaint? Or a year from now, when it would have been too late and he would have dropped completely out of sight? If they were calling in the debt now, then somehow it had to be part of everything else that was going on. That was what made him fearful: because he didn't understand. If he didn't understand it, he couldn't control it.

After breakfast he fetched the hardcover Master Atlas from his car and made his way upstairs to the library. In a foul temper by now, he slammed the door shut and flung the atlas down on the nearest table. It skidded into a stack of books and sent two or three of them to the floor. Somewhere in the eaves the mice scurried off in alarm.

He calmed himself and sat down. He cleared a space among the books, bringing the atlas back within reach; then he fished the first advertisement from his pocket and unfolded it on the table.

NASSAU, BAHAMAS
Substantial investor/partner required
for 22–24 apartment development in prime
location. Exceptional profit potential.
Please call our UK offices:
Boyar Properties
01-862-0699

Codes were tools of the trade, just something to get the job done. You saved the complex ones for when you needed them; the rest of the time, when the job was simple, you kept the tools simple too. Especially if you were going to have to carry them in your head for two decades.

He unfolded the second advertisment and pressed it flat alongside the first.

NASSAU, BAHAMAS
Substantial investor/partner required
for 22–24 apartment development in prime
location. Exceptional profit potential.
Please call our UK offices:
Boyar Properties
01-862-1399

Nothing he wanted to know, and everything he needed to know, whether he liked it or not. All in less than two lines of newsprint, repeated until he responded to its command.

The Master Atlas was of Greater London; the standard Geographers' A–Z edition. He opened it and began looking to see where the rendezvous was to be.

It grew dark about five o'clock. He waited until six before venturing out, counting himself a fool for not leaving it till later; but he had to make one final check, and the sooner the better.

The station was busy and quiet in waves as each train arrived from London. When he got to the small cobbled square, he stood out of sight in the doorway of the florist's, now locked for the night, to watch the scene.

A train had just been. A queue had formed for the phone box: men with umbrellas and briefcases waiting to call their wives to come and fetch them. Knight waited until they had all been collected before crossing to the box.

He drew the advertisements from his pocket and dialled 100.

'Operator, I've been trying to reach a London number. It seems to be unobtainable. Could you try it for me please?'

'What happens when you dial?'

'I get a high-pitched tone.'

'What is the number?'

He glanced down at the two pieces of paper. It didn't matter which one he selected; he read off the digits from the top one.

'862 1399.' It was the second advertisement.

'Hold the line, caller.'

251

He heard a tumbling series of clicks as she dialled, then the same unobtainable tone that he'd got from the first advertisement.

She tried again.

'I can check for you if the number's been reported out of order.'

'Well, I've got another one here. Perhaps you could try it for me first.'

She sounded weary. 'What is it?'

'862 0699.'

'Hold the line, please.'

Again the tumbling clicks, again the tone.

'Just one moment, please.' She put him on hold. He looked around the square, wondering how long he had before the next train was due. The operator's voice returned.

'I'm afraid neither of those numbers exists, caller.'

'Oh? How do you know?'

She was definitely fed up with him now. 'I checked the list of London exchanges. There isn't an 862 exchange.'

The advertisements were genuine. He hurried out of the booth just as another train was arriving. Head down, he set off back to the convent and the retreat house.

Back at the library, he re-seated himself at the table and looked at the advertisements again.

There were three pieces of information, all that was needed for any rendezvous: the date, the time, and the place.

The year and the month were in the non-existent exchange, though a real one would have done just as well. The date and the location were in the remaining four digits, which could also have been genuine. He had failed to respond to the first signal, so it had been repeated with an adjustment for the date. The time, using the 24-hour clock to avoid ambiguity, was in the reference to the 22–24 apartment development. The rendezvous was good between ten o'clock and midnight.

As for the place, he took the atlas and opened it at page 99. A page that was half white, showing streets and roads, and half green, parks and open spaces. In red were printed the borough names of Wandsworth and Merton; blue print announced postal regions SW15, SW18, SW19, SW20. Bus routes criss-crossed the page in yellow.

Like every page in the atlas, 99 was sectioned by fine blue grid lines into twenty-four squares, each half a mile wide. Four across the page and six lengthwise. His gaze fell to the exact middle, where the central grid lines intersected. Putney Heath.

He took the advertisements from his pocket, dropped them into the atlas and shut it softly, this time causing no disturbance to the mice.

The room in Cricklewood's Mulgrave Road was in darkness. The woman with the black hair and the crew-cut fumbled for the lightswitch and flicked it on. One corner of the bedsitter became bathed in a ruby-red glow. The light was coming from a bulb on an extension cord that ran from the ceiling light in the centre of the room to dangle from a hook in the corner.

Directly underneath the bulb was a deep sink, and on the draining-surface nearby several trays; they contained developing and fixing solutions.

Over the sink an extendable clothes line, the kind that reeled away into a neat tubular mounting, had been opened and stretched across to the other wall. Some items of underwear were tossed over the line at either end, but in the vicinity of the sink a dozen rolls of developed film had been clipped up to dry. They hung in long strips, weighted with bulldog clips to keep them straight.

Over on the table stood a printing frame and a lamp on a stand, and beside them a box of photographic paper.

The black-haired woman crossed to the sink and examined the strips of negatives with the help of a jeweller's eyeglass. She sought out the tiny line of digits in the bottom of each frame that recorded its date and time of exposure. As she found them she shifted the strips of film about on the clothes line until they were all in sequential order.

Then she unclipped the first strip, took it across to the printing frame and set to work.

37

As Knight left Southfields station that night he paused by a rubbish bin and fished out the empty wine bottle that had caught his eye in the glare of the streetlamp. A policeman standing nearby shot him a warning glance and took a leisurely step towards him. It was more ritual than any serious attempt to apprehend him. Knight slipped the bottle quickly into the mackintosh pocket, gave the bobby a wide berth, and made off along Augustus Road.

He came onto Wimbledon Parkside from the northern end of Inner Park Road and turned south, counting his paces under his breath as he shuffled along the wide pavement. He kept the paces as equal in length as he could, folding his fingers into the palm of his hand to mark off the hundreds.

The southern end of the Inner Park Road horseshoe turned out to be 614 paces away. It took him the best part of ten minutes to cover the distance; walking normally, he'd have done it in half the time. He rounded the corner and sat down on the wall that edged the grounds of a mansion block. Parkside was a busy road and traffic whizzed past in a continuous stream, some of it turning off where he sat.

According to page 99, torn from the atlas and folded safely away in his pocket, the horizontal grid line cut across Parkside roughly halfway between the two ends of Inner Park Road. His next task was therefore to double back the way he'd just come, counting again.

As he set off he felt the first spits of rain and pulled his cap down tighter.

At 300 paces he found himself opposite a bus shelter on the other side of the road. He straightened his fingers and stopped counting.

The time was ten thirty. He took the wine bottle from his pocket and staggered into the road, seemingly oblivious to the vehicles that shot past him.

When he reached the opposite pavement he lurched onto one of the folding seats in the shelter and took stock again. Behind him, immediately after the pavement, lay the heath. It was woodland where he had to penetrate it. Looking out from the glare of the streetlamps, all he could see was blackness and the thick trunks of what looked like oaks.

As discreetly as he could, he brought the folded map out and peered at it in the sickly light. To arrive at the point where the grid lines intersected, he would have to go roughly the same distance into the heath as he'd just walked from Inner Park Road: 300 paces.

He allowed 20 paces for the road and took his count from there as he set off through the damp carpet of leafmould behind the shelter. He kept the wine bottle well in view for the benefit of anyone who might be watching.

The woodland was difficult going, made all the harder by the darkness. He'd brought no torch because he'd known that he wouldn't risk using it. So it was a question of feeling the lie of the ground beneath his feet, step by tentative step.

There was no shortage of obstacles: tree-roots to stumble on, brambles that snagged at the legs of his corduroys, a stream that he almost slid into, and bushes and low boughs that whipped his face. He discovered to his relief that there were flattened paths through the undergrowth if he was patient and felt for them. But they zig-zagged back and forth, running off at a different angle or dog-legging each time they crossed a riding-track or stream; to make use of them he was obliged to abandon all attempts to stick to a straight line, instead making the best adjustments he could to his count. And the rain felt like it might be setting in for the night.

As far as he could gauge with any accuracy, he'd come about 250 paces from Parkside, although he'd probably covered half that again, when the woodland began to open out and then ended entirely. The mature trees that had shut out the sky gave way to saplings and smaller shrubs. The ground felt spongier than before and he realised that he was probably walking on low gorse or heather. He had never lost the subdued hum of traffic but now, across the far side of the heath, he saw the glow of headlamps and carriageway lights on the A3. To his right the sky was orange with the lights of the busy Tibbets Corner roundabout.

As if it had been waiting for him to leave cover, the rain got going in earnest. The drizzle became a shower, then a relentless downpour. He swore aloud and looked around for cover; there was none.

A flash lit the sky; he was able to count to nine before the thunderclap followed. He retreated to the edge of the woodland and crouched under a deformed oak. But it was bare of foliage and the rain hammered down on him anyway; after a few minutes he realised that he was also catching the steady trickle from the branches themselves.

Partly because of the lightning and partly because of the drips, he gave the oak up as a bad job and returned to the open heathland.

Already the gorse was awash; the grubby trainers that he'd exchanged for his Oxfords might as well have been tissue paper for all the success they were having in keeping his feet dry. The rest of him was faring no better. Rain poured down his neck, into his eyes, through his matted beard.

Another flash; this time the thunder came after a count of six. His apprehension grew. Surely by now he wasn't more than a few yards from his destination. Ten o'clock to midnight, both advertisements had said. It must be eleven by now. It was good form for the control to be in position from the opening of the rendezvous window. After all, it was he who set the rules; the least he could do was stick to them himself. Surely the man could see or hear him by this time. They'd probably sent some desk colonel from Yasyenevo who hadn't done this kind of thing in years if at all or who was too petrified –

Knight froze as the gun barrel nuzzled the nape of his neck. He closed his eyes. An image appeared there at once, apparently irrelevant but compelling. It was one of the persistent details from the retreat house crucifixes: a punctured side. Another followed it: blood pouring over a forehead from its crown of thorns.

'Welcome, comrade.' The voice behind him was quiet and assured. It wasn't the voice of an incompetent or nervous man.

Knight drew a sharp breath and held it. The tang of the freshly-soaked earth filled his lungs. Even over the rush and roar of the rain, that voice seemed to echo in his eardrums. He knew it. He knew that voice. But so long ago; he was sure it was from so long ago . . . He pushed the crucifixion images aside and searched frantically through others that he summoned up: faces, gestures, events, conversations, anything that could give the voice its context.

The muzzle shifted up towards his skull an inch; he tipped his head back in protest and the gun's forward sight dug into the soft fold of scalp at the base of the bone.

'Please forgive this unfriendly precaution,' the voice went on, in perfect English. 'Unorthodox, I admit. I wasn't sure if it really was you, Boyar. I'm still not. You don't look quite as I expected.'

Now he had the face to fit the voice. No stiff-necked colonel. Perfect English? Yes, and why shouldn't it be? He'd taught it to him himself. That summer, twenty years ago. He opened his eyes and stared at the night.

'You?' he said. His mouth was dry.

From behind him, a soft laugh. 'Yes, I. It's been a long time, yes?'

Uninvited, Knight slowly began to turn around. Streams of rain poured over the tattered peak of his cap as he brought his head level again. The gun remained pointing at him, grazing the layer of beard on his cheek now, but the man made no move to stop him.

The lightning flashed again. Knight's eyes strained to see through the curtain of rain. And there for an instant as the lightning flashed, floating like a pale ghost against the dark trees, was the face he'd conjured up.

One, two, three, he counted; then the thunder rolled. The storm was almost overhead now.

Nikolai Vasiliyevich Serov brought the Makarov pistol down, wiped the rain off its barrel and returned it to its holster inside the black leather greatcoat.

'Shall we find somewhere drier than this to talk, Boyar?' he suggested. 'I underestimated your English weather. It's every bit as bad as you always said it was.'

It was two thirty in the morning when he slouched up the long tunnel that led to Waterloo station. A bitter wind whipped around his legs and through the mackintosh, still stiff from its soaking.

'Yes, sir! Can I help you?'

The sarcasm was as heavy as the hand that suddenly pressed against his chest. He raised his eyes from the pavement to look at the policeman who blocked his path. He remembered the bobby at Southfields station. This man wasn't going to be so easy to shake off.

'I'm going for my train.'

'No trains at this hour.'

'I know. I'm going to wait for the first one.'

'Not here you won't. Anyway – how're you going to pay for a train? Cash in your empties?' The constable yanked the empty wine bottle from Knight's pocket.

'I've got a ticket.'

'Let's have a look.'

Knight fumbled in the other pocket and handed the ticket over. The constable pushed the bottle back at him and pulled out a torch to examine the ticket.

'Nice try.' He tore it in half. 'Yesterday's. Where'd you pick it up? Go on – get out of here. Or you'll come down Kennington Road with me.' He dropped the pieces of torn card into the gutter and began to shoo Knight out of his way.

Knight didn't argue. He couldn't. Somewhere in an inside pocket were his wallet and everything they needed to identify him: driving licence, credit cards, all brought along for the benefit of the man he'd gone to meet on Putney Heath. The man who hadn't needed to see them.

Still clutching the bottle, he turned to go back the way he'd come, and noticed the other policeman for the first time. He'd been standing by the constable's elbow and slightly behind him. He was younger, early twenties. Knight thought he saw a flicker of something in his face; perhaps sympathy.

'Try Cardboard City,' the young bobby said quietly. The older constable glared at him.

'Where?' Knight asked dubiously.

'Cardboard City. You're new. Thought I hadn't seen you before. Come on, I'll show you how to get there.'

Wondering what he was getting into, Knight followed him obediently back down the tunnel. When they got on to the road the rain was starting again. He was in for another soaking. But that wasn't what was running through his mind.

Three hours before. Almost supine in the stitched leather seats of the Ferrari. Serov's Ferrari. A black Testarossa; Knight couldn't even guess how much a car like that might have cost. Warm inside, Knight getting drier, the heater roaring. Rain on the roof like a tattoo. On the car's parcel shelf, a London A–Z like his own. Naturally. Used by Serov or by someone acting on his behalf to compose the adverts.

Passing through streets at random as they talked. Clapham, Dulwich, Lewisham, Deptford, Knight lost track where else. Telling Serov about Kunaev, and the book.

'Inconvenient,' said Serov. 'But now we have bigger things to turn our minds to, you and I.'

'Not me. I'm through.'

Serov smiling in the eerie glow of the dashboard, like a devil in black leather. 'I don't think so, Boyar. Not when you hear what I have to say.'

Then more endless streets. Knight losing track this time because of what Serov was saying. Sometimes in English, sometimes in Russian. Knight not believing what he was hearing; then having to believe it. Glad to believe it in the end because it offered hope, one last chance. Glad too of the bourbon when Serov produced it. Wondering where Serov's pistol was, could he grab it. Lose everything if he were to kill Serov. Serov knew it too, that was why he was relaxed. Knight not even thinking about it any more.

'Those are my terms, Boyar. Take them or leave them.'

'What?' Knight was startled. An end had been reached. It was time to decide. As if there was a choice. As if there ever had been.

'I would take your terms.' He had to say it twice because his voice had cracked. The tension in him, not his soaking, was doing that. 'But I don't see how I can arrange what you want. I want to but I can't see how. I'm through, I said. I have no ways in any more.'

'You'll think of something. You're a resourceful man. We picked you well. And now you're highly motivated.'

One thought, from nowhere.

'William Clarke.'

Serov nodded. 'Your Home Secretary. What about him?'

'His death was part of it somehow, wasn't it?'

'His death was no part of it as far as my planning was concerned. But perhaps he became a casualty. Who can tell how these things come about? Perhaps he made himself unpopular, perhaps he opposed the British–US action.'

The British–US action. Perhaps. Perhaps indeed.

'Did you get all that?' the young bobby asked.

'What?' Startled again.

'The directions.'

'Oh. Yes, I think so. Thanks for your help.'

When he got there, after wrong turnings because he'd hardly heard a word of the directions, the Royal Festival Hall was shuttered and quiet, its legitimate business long since over. But in the walkways underneath it, although they were empty of paying customers, a whole other world had come into existence. A world that now lay sleeping, for that was its only purpose in that place. Huge cardboard boxes, formerly the wrappings of washing machines or freezers, rolls of corrugated packing, newspapers, piles of ratty blankets and coats: these were the bedding of the night-time citizens of Cardboard City.

It was a purgatory where there was no such thing as silence. Snores, mumblings and random cries as pitiful as in any madhouse, subdued laughter or sudden anger over the dregs of a bottle; these sounds greeted Knight as he picked his way through the huddled bodies and along the concrete passageways, looking for a space. He found one, sat down and pulled the mackintosh close about him. He had no other bedding and there were no surplus materials that he could see anywhere; it was a place where you brought your own and took it away again in the morning. No matter; he wouldn't sleep: he was too wet and uncomfortable for that. Not to mention the things that he had to think about.

And there was one other thing that he had, even in this hell-hole; that he hadn't had three hours earlier.

Hope.

38

Moscow

Gramin plodded up the steps of the Serbskiy and paused at the top to catch his breath before pushing the heavy door open. God, how he hated this place. Any self-respecting KGB man did. It might be on his side today; but tomorrow?

Ogarkin was waiting for him in the lobby, talking to one of the armed doormen. He broke off as soon as he saw Gramin enter.

'It's all right,' the professor called to the other doorman, who'd planted himself in front of Gramin to ask his business. 'He's come to see me. Let him through.'

Gramin cast the man a venomous glance as he moved out of the way, and crossed the lobby to Ogarkin.

'Well, comrade Professor. Do you live or die?'

Ogarkin's eyes closed at this greeting. When he opened them Gramin had his finger on the lift button.

'Well?' he repeated.

Ogarkin pulled a tissue from his pocket and wiped his streaming nose.

'We think she'll be all right,' he mumbled. He gave a heavy sigh of relief. 'She came out of the coma late last night.'

Gramin showed no reaction, which made Ogarkin frown.

'That's a major step forward, you know,' he pointed out.

'Is it?'

'Of course!'

Gramin still looked unimpressed. 'So much for her physical condition.'

Ogarkin became agitated, rolling the tissue up into a tiny ball. He knew what the man was driving at; he just wasn't sure how to frame his answer.

'She seems to be as whole mentally as when she came in,' he said at last.

It won him a sneer. 'That's not saying much.'

'It is, comrade, it is! We feared irreversible damage. Not a vegetable, thank God – the EEG and other tests told us she was safe from that – but we feared a much reduced state.' The words came spilling out more hurriedly the more sceptical Gramin looked. 'Physiological damage we wouldn't be able to do anything about, but now it looks like we're no worse off than when we started – just her psychiatric condition.'

'*Just* her psychiatric condition!'

'Please –' Ogarkin lifted his hands and looked around nervously.

'Can she travel?'

The question took the professor by surprise. 'Travel?'

'Some distance. Say overnight by road.'

'I suppose so, but it's not an idea I'd encourage. She still needs rest and close watching. Her psychotherapy needs to resume as soon as she's physically strong enough. Where is she going?'

Gramin looked at him. 'You'll find out. What's keeping this lift?' He pummelled the button with his knuckle. 'Is everything in this place useless? Is that what you specialise in, comrade Professor – uselessness?'

But Ogarkin's thoughts were elsewhere.

'Travelling. Has he sent for her?' There were the beginnings of terror in his watery eyes.

'Not yet.'

'Does he know what happened to her – what she did?' He seemed somehow to underline the 'she'.

'Not yet.'

'Yet?'

'Well, he'll find out sooner or later, won't he? When he sees her for himself. No telling how he'll take it either. He doesn't have a very forgiving nature. Maybe you know that.'

At last the lift arrived. As they stepped inside, Ogarkin moved closer. He wiped his nose again.

'Did you bring me anything?' It was a desperate whisper. 'The general said he'd look after me . . . it was part of our arrangement. For her being here. Didn't he tell you to bring me something?'

Gramin was expressionless for a moment, then he nodded. As the lift doors closed, he took a handful of transparent polythene sachets from his pocket. They were half-filled with a fine white powder. The professor's eyes widened hungrily. Gramin held them up before him for a moment, then dropped them on the floor. Ogarkin fell to his knees and began scooping them up, snuffling all the while. Before he'd collected them all, however, the lift reached its destination, the infirmary floor, and the doors flew open. Ogarkin looked wildly around. The corridor outside was empty but for a stretcher trolley and a corral of rubbish sacks; he returned to gathering up the sachets.

But as he reached out for the last one, Gramin's heel descended on the back of his hand. The professor yelped in pain.

'I've got a job for you,' Gramin said. 'To earn these.' He kept his foot in position.

Tears began to roll down Ogarkin's cheeks, partly from pain, partly from anxiety that someone might appear, but most of all for fear Gramin might take the sachets away again. His fingers were turning a dark red, as if they were filling with blood and might burst. Their throbbing was almost visible.

'What job?' he gasped.

'Accompany her on her journey. Look after her. That should set your mind at rest for her immediate welfare. And you can explain personally to the general what happened to her. Take my advice – it's your only chance.'

Despite his terror at the prospect of having to face Serov, Ogarkin was nodding vigorously; he was ready to agree to anything.

'We leave this afternoon, then. I'll drive us. It's a long way but we'll have a comfortable car – the general's.' He thought for a moment and added, 'It's not an ambulance, though. Does she need an ambulance?'

Ogarkin shook his head.

'Good. You can sit in the back with her. That'd be the best idea.'

He lifted his foot and the professor fell forward and clasped his injured hand to his chest. As Gramin seized the shoulder of his white jacket and hauled him to his feet, however, he remembered to snatch up the last sachet.

'Plenty of that stuff waiting for you when we get there, by the way,' Gramin remarked. 'Mountains of it.'

Some measure of calm was returning to Ogarkin's eyes. He seemed to find Gramin's last comment of particular interest.

'Where are we going?' he asked, still nursing his hand.

Gramin shoved him out of the lift. 'Ever heard of a place called Molodechno?'

Galina dozed for most of the way, curled up under Gramin's greatcoat on the back seat. Ogarkin dropped off as well sometime after Borodino. Gramin switched on the rear reading light and adjusted the rearview mirror to keep a check on both of them.

The roads were bad, once they got outside Moscow. Where wheels had churned the snow to slush, it had frozen into ice, so they made slow progress. Gramin took it just as easy as he had to. In the marshlands beyond Vitebsk they met some pockets of thick, greasy fog, and that slowed them down further.

It took until the small hours of the following morning before they reached the estate. Ogarkin awoke as they slowed for the guardpost, revived by the chill air when Gramin wound down the window to identify himself. The professor rubbed the sleep from his eyes, then gulped at the sight of the machine-pistol barrel that was poking in at him. It withdrew and he blinked stupidly around at the dark forest beyond the floodlights, struggling to get his bearings.

'You don't need to know where we are,' Gramin said before he could ask anything. 'Just somewhere in the hills. Somewhere the general keeps to escape to.'

'Is this where he is now?' There was an unmistakable quiver in Ogarkin's voice.

'No. Relax.'

Some minutes later the fox compound sent up its usual hullabaloo as they passed. Again the professor started in alarm.

'Werewolves,' Gramin told him. 'Nothing to worry about. No worse than you're used to.'

The servant Sinsky, warned by the guardpost that they were on their way, was waiting for them at the door of the great stone house. He and Gramin half-carried Galina to the bedroom that had been made ready for her. Ogarkin followed, lugging his gladstone bag full of medicines and equipment. He gawped at the high ceilings and ran his hand like a child over the carved banisters. But his nose started its tricks again, and as they reached the upper floor he vanished into a nearby bathroom for a few minutes, mumbling apologies. Gramin smiled to himself but said nothing. Sinsky stared coldly at the bathroom door.

Half an hour later they'd eaten a snack of black bread and beetroot soup and were sitting in front of the roaring fire in the dining hall. Gramin poured them a couple of vodkas.

'Absent friends,' he toasted, and watched as Ogarkin swallowed the measure before knocking back his own. 'How was your hit?' He nodded in the general direction of upstairs. 'In the bathroom.'

The professor kept his gaze on the floor. 'I just fall to bits without it, like a puppet with the strings gone.'

Gramin poured two more vodkas. They emptied the glasses again. Two more. Empty again.

'Back to Moscow tomorrow?' asked Ogarkin. 'Today, I mean.'

Gramin noted with disdain that his speech was slurring already. 'No.'

'Oh. I told the Institute I'd only be gone for a day or so. Still, I suppose a bit longer won't matter. I expect you want to recharge your batteries before you tackle that drive again.'

'We're not going back the next day either.'

Ogarkin's small red eyes grew concerned. 'When?'

Gramin refilled the glasses. 'A few days, a few weeks – who knows? The general will decide.'

Ogarkin tried to bluster.

'Shhh, comrade,' Gramin said reassuringly. 'You can phone them. Tell them you're ill. Listen to me – you said the girl needs plenty of watching. Who better than you? You said she needs to start back into her psychotherapy. Well, you know her better than anyone after all these weeks.'

'You weren't so flattering yesterday.'

'I was a little worked-up. I was anxious, that's all. Maybe I was also worrying about how to explain things to the general. He'll be calling me, you see. Here. It might be tonight, it might be another night. But as we agreed, now you're here, you can do the explaining.'

Ogarkin looked scared to death.

'Remember what I promised you?' Gramin said.

Ogarkin shook his head.

'Mountains of the stuff?' Gramin reminded him.

A light came to the professor's eyes.

'It's here,' Gramin whispered. 'Pure. Ninety-nine point nine per cent. It hasn't been cut yet. Clouds of paradise. Now do you still want to leave?'

Ogarkin just stared. His fat tongue came out and licked his lips. He swallowed a quick mouthful of vodka.

'Want to try some?'

Ogarkin nodded.

Gramin smiled and knocked back his vodka. For the good professor, time had just taken a back seat.

39

Sumner felt himself wilting under Gaunt's stare. He had hurried in to
see him as soon as he had finished checking the police information that
had come to him that morning.

'Are you telling me we've got Knight's description at every port and
airport and with every police force in the country, and he's still
somewhere around his home?'

'I think so, Sir Horace.'

Gaunt banged the office door shut with his toe; Sumner braced
himself for the worst. Gaunt crossed to the desk and planted himself on
Sumner's side of it.

'This mental defective – what's his name? Bowman – how did we
come across him?'

'He lives with his father and sister. It was when one of the local
coppers was checking with them that Billy spoke up.'

'What makes you think we can believe him?'

'His father and sister say he's reliable on something like this. We
talked to his GP as well. He says Billy's like a six- or seven-year-old. A
bit vague on things like time but otherwise dependable enough. Billy
knows the whole village and they all know him. He has no other world
and he doesn't make mistakes about it. According to both the GP and
the sister, if Billy says he saw someone, then he saw someone.'

'What did you tell them to account for our interest?'

'Standard story. That we're Special Branch, that we want to interview Knight in connection with passport offences.'

'If this half-wit's vague on time, how do we know he hasn't got the
day of the sighting wrong?'

'It checks out. Billy spent the weekend with his married sister. He
comes and goes on the train and someone meets him either end. This
was the only occasion his sister can recall being late and he set off up the
road on his own to meet her. That's when he says he saw Knight.'

'I want the area knee-deep in police. Get the local men to list
everywhere and anywhere he could possibly be staying – houses, hotels.
Empty properties. Any squats in that area? Garden sheds, if necessary.
If there's a scout hut, turn it inside-out.'

'There's just one thing, Sir Horace.'

'What?'

'Billy said he looked a bit different from usual.'

'What does that mean? "A bit different" – get him to be specific.'

'It's difficult. He's only like a seven-year-old.'

Gaunt leant closer and dropped his voice. 'Then take him into a nice, dark room, lock the door and get it out of him. He can hardly report you, can he?'

Sumner left the office as meekly as if they had been discussing his career prospects; in a way, he realised, they had.

When he was gone, Gaunt turned again to the document that he had been reading. It had been delivered just one hour before.

Preliminary Diagnosis

I saw the subject this morning as part of her clinical examination and have had access to her file notes and certain other material.

She shows a degree of affective disorder in which agitated depression is present, along with some paranoia. It is difficult to say at this stage whether this is severe enough to be classifiable as paranoid schizophrenia.

Supporting Evidence

1. The results of my own observation and those of the subject's recent clinical examination (for which see Annex II). She shows the physiological symptoms of acute stress (blood pressure, agitation, sleeplessness, loss of concentration, forgetfulness, disorientation, etc.). I find that she also voices suspicions and distrust of those around her in her work, particularly her superiors. She is either unwilling or unable to give specific form to these feelings so that they can be evaluated, but is evidently convinced of their legitimacy. This is typical of paranoia.

2. Written and oral reports from her superiors.

3. The Metropolitan Police Incident Report appended as Annex III. This merits further comment.

First the alleged assault. If this did occur it is difficult not to conclude that it must have been far less grave than the subject described: for example, horseplay with no real sexual threat. Had there been a more determined sexual content, it is odd that the event did not proceed to its natural conclusion. This raises the question of why the subject felt impelled to embroider the incident. If this was done unconsciously, then paranoid schizophrenia is a possibility. If it was a deliberate act on her part, some other explanation must be sought.

Following on this, there is the apparent raid on the subject's home. The Police Report raises doubts as to whether or not this was really the work of vandals or thieves. Nothing was stolen; interestingly, the subject is even reported to have claimed that she did it herself anyway. If she was indeed the conscious or unconscious protagonist, paranoid schizophrenia again becomes a possibility.

Conclusion and Recommendations

An intensive programme of psychoanalysis is recommended. Its objective would be to identify the nature and origins of the subject's disorder.

There is every likelihood that the disorder will prove responsive to psychotherapy; this is therefore my second recommendation.

This favourable prognosis might not hold unless treatment is begun as soon as possible.

It has to be my further recommendation that the subject be relieved of her duties with immediate effect.

Gaunt closed the manila folder, laid it on the desk and placed his elbows on either side. He straightened it neatly, steepled his fingers, rested his chin on his thumbs and tapped his forefingers gently against his lips.

He would bend over backwards to handle the whole thing in a humane way, of course: sick leave on full pay, no loss of pension rights. No reasonable person would have any grounds to criticise him.

40

The morning was dry and sunny, the storm of the previous night forgotten. A brisk breeze was helping to dry off the remaining puddles.

Knight's train, the first of the day after his night in Cardboard City, brought him out to the chalk hills of Buckinghamshire shortly after first light. He walked the three miles from the station to the boulder-strewn field overlooking the graveyard where Bill Clarke lay buried and the little Norman church where his memorial service was to be held. The press announcement hadn't given a time, so Knight was resigned to waiting all morning. He still had no very clear idea of what he might be able to do, but he could think of no other way than this.

It was ten fifteen when the congregation began to arrive. They were clearly all family or close friends. The absence of government ministers or top civil servants meant that security was light: when Marion and the two children arrived in the Rover, there was just one female detective in the car with them.

The service was brief. Afterwards Marion embraced or shook hands with the other mourners and walked with some of them through the churchyard to the graveside. They stood together in silence for a few minutes, then began returning to their cars. But as they were passing under the lychgate, she halted and spoke briefly to the others. They nodded and she returned alone to the grave while they climbed into their cars and left. The detective watched her from the edge of the churchyard. The children waited in the car.

Marion stood with her back to both Knight and the detective as she faced the grave, her hands clasped before her. After a moment she knelt in the damp grass and began making some small adjustments to one or two of the wreaths.

Knight found that he was feeling ashamed to be watching this private moment. The detective seemed to be feeling the same way; she turned away and moved across the parking area to stand by the car. Knight saw what she was doing and took his chance, the only one he might have, and made his way quickly down the far side of the hill from the detective, circling around at the bottom to arrive at the side door of the church.

Marion came past a minute later. He simply stepped out into her path and looked at her. She glanced at him in alarm, then quickly away, then her eyes came back and this time stayed on him.

'Edmund? I don't believe it. Christ, you're a mess.'

'Please don't walk any further, Marion – if I go beyond this wall your detective will see me.'

'The whole world's looking for you.'

'I wasn't sure if I'd get a chance to see you if I came. You surprised me.'

She lifted her veil and drew it over her hat. 'How?'

'By going back to the grave.'

'To check who had sent wreaths? What's surprising about that?'

Knight shut his eyes and shook his head. 'Can we talk?'

'Where?'

'In the church. Tell your chaperone you want a minute or two alone.'

'Think she'd believe that? Of me?'

'Look contrite. Pull your veil down.'

'What do you want to talk about?'

He wondered if he really could rely on her. 'I want to talk about Bill.'

'Oh Christ, Edmund. I've had a morning of that.'

'And I need your help.'

'What help can I give you?'

'You're the Home Secretary's widow. That doesn't change, however you and Bill were. I need your contacts. Your ways in.'

'You're losing me.'

'See me in the church and I'll explain.'

She shrugged and went off to talk to the detective. Knight walked across to Clarke's grave. Explain? Yes. Some of it. As much as he had to.

He stared at the dark earth beneath the multicoloured wreaths. After a few moments he picked up a handful of drying soil, crumbled it in his hand, and let it run slowly through his fingers onto the grave.

Serov kept the A–Z on his lap as he took the big Ferrari slowly along West Cromwell Road. He stuck to the inside lane, taking bearings from the roads on his left and keeping one eye on the atlas. He thought how useful such a book would be for Moscow, where the only people who seemed to own reliable maps were the KGB and the CIA, and even the local taxi drivers got lost when they went beyond the city centre.

He took a left turn at the lights and went down North End Road for a couple of hundred yards. Then he swung right and picked his way through the sidestreets.

They fascinated him, these streets. Row after row of tall, terraced houses with columns by their front doors and parapets along their roof lines. Some were private hotels but the rest, judging from the ranks of doorbells, seemed to be split into apartments. It was the variability of the houses, and the mixture of lifestyles they implied, that intrigued him. Seediness next door to affluence. Skips, clouds of dust and workmen identified the properties that were going up in the world. Moth-eaten curtains, peeling doors and cracked columns indicated the ones that were not. In no other city in Western Europe could he recall seeing such contrasts side by side. It was an arrangement that appealed to him. No doubt about it: he was going to like London.

He consulted the A–Z again, then parked. Nearby was a dusty Volvo station-wagon. From the Ferrari's glove compartment he took a yellow plastic lunchbox, quite empty, and finished his journey on foot. It was only seventy or eighty yards and the sun was shining.

He entered Normand Park near the swings, where he saw some mothers with their children, and strolled across to stand by the pavilion and park-keeper's annex. From there he had a perfect view of the bowling green and the rest of the park beyond it. It was a fine day, with spring in the air, but the turf still looked soggy from the recent rain; there were no bowls players today. One or two people strolled around the perimeter of the green, otherwise he couldn't see a soul this side of Lillie Road. In the pavilion itself there were only a teenage boy and his girlfriend, both in school uniform. They puffed defiantly on their cigarettes as he passed. The girl was giggling; the smoke caught her throat and she was seized by a fit of coughing.

He doubled back and turned into the northern corner of the park. Here it became like a secret garden, about half an acre in size and tucked away behind the pavilion. A path encircled a lawned area dotted with trees; behind the path, high hedges shielded the whole area from the street and the pavement outside. There were benches at intervals along the path, set into recesses in the hedges.

Three of the benches were occupied. On one, two old men were engaged in high-volume conversation. On another sat a young mother rocking a pram.

Two women were seated on the third bench. They were in their twenties, attractively made-up and neatly dressed. Nicely turned-out but in an everyday way. They could have been typists, bank clerks, shop assistants, or any of half a dozen similar occupations. One of them was eating an apple, the other a sandwich. On the bench beside them were their lunchboxes: one was orange and the other, exactly like his own, was yellow.

Serov gave the women a friendly smile as he drew near. He saw now that one of them was strikingly pretty, her fine features emphasised by black hair cropped so short that it was almost a crew-cut.

They had been chatting quietly but fell silent as he came within earshot; they ignored his smile.

'Do you mind if I sit here?' he asked politely, indicating the other end of the bench.

The one with the crew-cut glanced in his direction but without actually meeting his gaze. She shrugged indifferently and said nothing. Her companion stared straight ahead, stony-faced.

He sat down and set his lunchbox on his lap, but made no move to open it. Instead, he looked around the enclosed area. No one else had entered it since himself.

'I enjoy eating in the open air,' he announced. Now he set his empty lunchbox down on the bench, next to theirs. Both of them were eating from the orange box, the yellow one remaining tight-lidded.

'It makes me think of that painting,' he went on. '*Déjeuner à l'herbe*. Do you know the one I mean?'

At first they showed no sign of having heard him. Then the woman with the crew-cut said, 'You mean, *Déjeuner sur l'herbe*.'

'Ah yes,' he replied at once. '*Déjeuner sur l'herbe* – silly of me.'

She swallowed another bite. 'We all make mistakes. I sometimes confuse that one with Seurat's *Sunday Afternoon at the Grande Jatte*.'

'Seurat? Don't you mean Manet?'

'No, Seurat.'

Now they turned and looked at each other. A greeting of sorts showed in the woman's face.

'We'll keep speaking in English,' Serov told her. 'It's safer. And you should smile occasionally, now that we've broken the ice. Which of you is the senior officer?'

'I am.'

'What rank?'

'Captain.'

'Make your report then, Captain.'

She dropped the last piece of her sandwich in the wire rubbish bin beside the bench, and wiped her fingers on a paper tissue.

'CIA Langley sent two operatives over. At least one of them, the bald man in these photographs –' she tapped a finger on her yellow lunchbox '– is already known to us. I saw his file in Registry before we left. He was on the list of agents we predicted they might use. The file said he'd operated before in Nicaragua and Seoul.'

'Your memory is impressive,' he said. He smiled and draped an arm across the back of the bench, looking as cheerful and relaxed as any man might who'd just made the acquaintance of two pretty girls. A little way along the path, the young mother vacated her bench and began pushing her pram towards the exit. The old men were still shouting at each other.

Serov helped himself to one of the sandwiches and settled back to listen to what else the Spetznaz captain had to say.

271

At the end of the meeting, he watched from the bench as they strolled off. As far as he could see, no one showed any interest in them.

He stayed on to enjoy a cigar before picking up the yellow lunchbox that the captain had left in exchange for his own, and made his way back to the Ferrari. As he walked, he hefted the box in his hand and noted its substantial weight. The Spetznaz women had amassed plenty of photographic material; he was looking forward to going through it. Looking forward even more to putting it to use.

He decided to find himself a decent restaurant. He was still ravenous. One small sandwich wasn't much to keep going on. After all, the photographs would keep.

Knight's return to the safety of the retreat house was short-lived. It was midnight when Marie-Thérèse came to see him. As soon as he opened the kitchen door to her she hurried past him and inside. She shook her head at his offer of a chair and stood facing him.

'They came looking for you tonight,' she said. 'They've just gone.'

Knight felt a sudden emptiness where his stomach had been. 'Who, Sister?'

'The police. It's all right – we've said nothing. Well, the Mother Superior doesn't know who's over here anyway. They named you and said someone had seen you getting off a bus in the village this afternoon.'

He had no one but himself to blame; he'd broken his own rule against daytime travelling.

'Thanks for getting rid of them.'

'It's our duty. Right of sanctuary.'

'Be careful. That's an old law and it doesn't apply any more.'

Her glasses flashed up at him. 'They can meddle with the laws of the land, but not the laws of God. What are you doing?'

He'd taken the mackintosh off its hook and was putting it on. 'They'll be back. One way or another. I can't stay.'

'If you go out tonight you'll walk slap into them. They've left someone in a car outside the gates.'

'I have to get past sooner or later. I'd rather try my chances in darkness.'

'I have an idea. If you'd be willing to give it a try.'

The winos arrived at ten o'clock sharp the next morning, although not one of them had a watch. There were seven or eight of them and they came up the lane in ones and twos, hands in pockets, watching the ground two paces ahead as if their eyes might burn out if they met another human gaze. It was the saddest little parade that Knight had ever seen.

Their place was by the side door of the dining hall, out of sight of the school block and the classrooms, and they lined up there in mournful silence.

There was no life to them, that was the thing that struck him. They were the cored shells of human beings. Some of them could hardly put a whole sentence together, just strings of unrelated phrases.

Some of the faces were ones that he'd vaguely noticed around the village from time to time; but they'd had no more relevance to him as individuals than stray dogs.

They were given bowls of soup, cups of tea and foil packages of meat and bread to take away with them. Some of them received articles of clothing; the sisters seemed to know which man would fit this sweater or which needed that pair of trousers.

At ten thirty Knight crossed the cattle grid with them and walked out of the main gate. Like them, he had his foil package under his arm, his head down and his eyes on the heels of the man in front.

Twenty yards up the road, the clean, well-fed officers in their white Panda car paid them as little heed as, two weeks ago, he himself would have done.

41

The young man in the Estates Office in Berkeley Square had all the obsequiousness of an experienced courtier.

'Good morning, sir. How may I help you?'

Serov took the chair at which he waved a white hand. The estate agent's bottom remained in mid-air until his own was safely grounded.

'I want to buy a good London property. A home but also a good investment.'

The agent smiled. 'Certainly, sir. Have you had a look at any of the properties we have on display?'

'No.'

The smile was unshakable. 'Did you wish to do so first, sir?'

'No. I will tell you the kind of property I seek. You will recommend some that may suit. I know what I want.'

'Of course, sir.' A pad of forms had appeared beneath the white hand.

Serov adopted a look of concentration. 'I do not mind which area, provided only that it is good. I understand from my English friends that places like St John's Wood or Hampstead would be ideal. You have properties in those areas? Price is not a constraining factor – investment potential is at least as important. It is important that the property is secluded, with good grounds – a country house in town. It must be good for entertaining, it must have adequate guest and staff quarters and be capable of being equipped with excellent security systems. I am not interested in whatever systems any particular property may already have – I prefer to have one fitted to my own requirements . . .'

They spent five or six minutes on the specification; the white hand fairly flew across the pad. Serov gave his name as Lüeck, described himself as a West German 'in electronics', and assured the estate agent that sterling finance wasn't a problem.

'It may be worth mentioning,' he concluded, 'that my business is internationally based. I have financial arrangements in many foreign places – '

The young man was poker-faced. 'It would be against the law to make any payments overseas, sir, in respect of UK property sales. But I expect you know that. You were merely thinking that if the vendor were himself making an overseas move, as you have done to come here, your international contacts might be able to assist him.'

'Precisely. I know how awkward foreign moves can be.'

They understood each other. Serov watched as the soft hands began to leaf through a stack of colourful property brochures, extracting some into a separate, smaller pile.

He lit a cigar and waited to look through them. The estate agent couldn't have been more than twenty-three years old. Serov watched the scrubbed fingers as they flicked over the pages. When they picked up a pen to jot a note, they held it with a poise that told him they'd practised until the most graceful writing attitude had been found. When the agent took a phone call, the way he cradled the phone and his intonation had the same air of studied rehearsal. These were the instruments and routines of his work, and everything about him said that they were important; which meant that he was important too.

Serov thought about another young man of twenty-three. With no studied airs. And no importance. Not then, anyway. And he heard the voice of a dry old man in a dusty room talking down to him.

'It's just that the young people who attend this academy are . . . rather special, intellectually. I'd like my Captain-Adjutant to be able to relate directly to them.'

'I understand, comrade Major. I'll make special efforts.'

'You will. Good. Be seated.'

Kunaev peeled off the pebble glasses, one wire loop at a time, and peered across the desk at him.

'Izmaylovo is one of only three top secret training facilities of its kind administered by the First Chief Directorate. You're very honoured to be posted here, young man. You'll understand that better if I tell you that we were set up by none other than comrade General Secretary Khrushchev himself. And our purpose, Captain? Our purpose is to train a very special type of sleeper agent. You're familiar with the term "sleeper"?'

'Yes, comrade Major. An agent who spends time under cover before he begins operating.'

'Correct. His first priority is to build the credibility of his cover identity – his "legend". When he finally becomes active, perhaps not until several months later, the legend is strong and believable.'

Kunaev rose from the desk and stood by the window to look out into the summer garden.

'The sleepers we train here, however, are unique in certain ways – ways which are of overwhelming importance and on which we never compromise. First, our sleepers are always citizens by birth of the country in which they will operate. Thus, when they're in position there's never any question of them having to adopt a false identity, because after their training they go back to being who they were, where they were. This minimises the risk of detection. Second, their only motivation is ideological; we reject the use of bribery or entrapment as techniques of recruitment because experience has shown that those methods are unreliable in the long term. And, as you'll see, our whole purpose is long term. Third, our agents are drawn without exception from the ranks of the brightest and most promising of their generation. Hence my anxiety about your own limited educational attainments. Fourth –' He broke off abruptly and turned from the window. 'Let me ask you something, Captain. If a few months can build a credible legend for a sleeper, what do you suppose fifteen or twenty years would achieve?'

The question took Serov by surprise. 'I don't know. The best cover possible, I should think.'

'The very best! A virtually impenetrable legend. Think about it – half a man's working life spent building his persona. Friendships, a career, putting down roots, becoming a member of his local community. That agent would be almost unassailable, wouldn't he?'

'That's what you train people for here?'

Kunaev looked pleased with the effect his words were having. 'We prepare such men. And some women too. There'll be more women in years to come, as Western society catches up with ours. Where was I? Yes – time. The fourth fundamental principle of our work is that Izmaylovo-trained agents will not be activated for fifteen or perhaps even twenty years. I see you're still having difficulty with this concept, Captain. You'll grow used to it. As for the reason behind such a strategy – that brings us to the fifth feature that makes us unique.'

He returned to the desk, resumed his seat and replaced the pebble glasses.

'We will activate our agents only when they have ascended to the highest levels of whatever governmental, scientific, military, political or academic establishments they are targeted to penetrate. Then and only then will they begin active work for us. Depending on where we have seeded them and our requirements at the time, this might range from accessing specific intelligence that is available only at that level, to merely acting as agents of influence to foster pro-Soviet opinion.'

Now he beamed with satisfaction. 'That is their ultimate purpose, Captain. It explains why we are prepared to wait so long before activating them. We mustn't use them prematurely to deliver information that we can get by other means – such as the use of less élite agents. You see, there's a rule with sleepers: the earlier they're activated and the more active they become, the higher the risk of them being exposed. All sleeper agents are valuable. They're difficult to insert, difficult to maintain, difficult to replace. Think how infinitely more irreplaceable the Izmaylovo agents would be – the very best, planned to rise to the highest echelons. So we must wait until they get there, Captain. If you look upon them as an investment for our future, then being prepared to wait patiently is how we protect that investment.'

'How many agents does Izmaylovo train at any one time, Major?'

He'd thought it an innocent enough query. But Kunaev stared at him through the thick, round lenses as if he'd just asked the colour of the red flag.

'One, of course, Captain. It's not Red Army squaddies we're training, you know.'

'No, Major. Of course.'

Kunaev continued watching him with suspicion as he picked up his telephone and pushed a button on its base to summon his secretary.

'I'll take you to meet our current trainee,' he said to Serov. 'He's a young Englishman about your own age. Incidentally, our trainees always have codenames. Use them at all times – never their real names. This Englishman's code is Boyar. Can you remember that?'

'I'll make special efforts, comrade Major.'

'I think you'll find that these meet your specification nicely, sir.'

'What's that?'

Serov stared blankly at the earnest young eyes for a moment, then jerked his thoughts back to the present.

'Oh yes,' he said crisply. 'Very good.' He looked down at the sheaf of brochures on the desk.

'I've tried to select a cross-section from a range of districts, sir – all of them first-class, of course. But I thought you might find it helpful to compare the ambiance of each. We like to say that London is really made up of a whole jumble of villages, each with its own atmosphere and character. Do you know London well, sir?'

'Not very well.'

'In that case, would you like to take advantage of our escorted viewing service? One of our senior associates would be delighted to oblige. At no cost – and with no commitment, of course.'

'No, that will not be necessary.'

But the young man had been well-trained in pampering the rich; he found it confusing to be fended off. All kinds of helpful things continued to tumble forth: maps, insurance advice, details of their removals service, warnings not to delay before making an appointment to view. It took Serov fifteen minutes to escape to a coffee shop for peace to go through the brochures by himself.

From Berkeley Square he went to Kensington and turned down Young Street. At its far end was the NCP; he drove up to the uncovered top floor and parked. The block had a lift and two stairways to ground level, but he ignored them and walked instead down the narrow kerb along the side of the vehicle ramp.

He was carrying the yellow lunchbox.

On Level 2 he walked back and forth between the ranks of parked cars, jingling his keys and looking at the cars as if he'd forgotten where he'd parked. He was checking to see that all the cars were empty.

Half a floor down from him was Level 1, partially visible from where he was walking, and vice versa. He went down the ramp and checked it with the same thoroughness.

It was Saturday. There were no vacant spaces on Levels 1 or 2, and the cars that arrived as he was making his checks continued on up to the higher levels, leaving him undisturbed.

Two or three minutes later he returned to the top floor. He was now empty-handed. He unlocked the Ferrari but didn't get inside. Instead he turned the ignition key and wound down both front windows. Before closing the door he switched the telephone over from standby to receive.

He'd parked at the side of the floor that overlooked Young Street. Now he lit a cigar and rested his forearms comfortably on the rampart while he surveyed the view.

Knight made his call from a public call box in Exhibition Road that stank of urine.

Serov did most of the talking. His instructions were crisp and unambiguous, suggesting that he'd prepared them carefully and re-hearsed them to himself in the proper way. He stated them just once. Knight tried to repeat them back to him but found that the line had gone dead.

Glad to be out in the air again after the stench of the phone box, Knight set off at a brisk pace west along Kensington Gore. By the time a bus appeared he'd got as far as the Royal Garden Hotel and the bus wasn't worth boarding.

He found the car park without difficulty and took the stairs at the side of the block, as Serov had advised. The NCP employees at the paybox in the vehicle entrance wouldn't welcome a tramp.

When he pushed through the door onto Level 2 he saw the rubbish bin a few yards away on his right and sauntered over to see if it was the correct one. It was: a cross had been marked on its lid in yellow chalk.

The fried chicken carton was near the top. Inside it, slightly slicked with grease, was a yellow plastic lunchbox. His fingers closed on it and lifted it out.

There was by now a small mound of cigar butts by Serov's toe, in the gutter behind the parapet. He let another one fall from his fingertips onto the pile and stepped on it just at the moment that Knight reappeared on the street below. The mackintosh flapped open as he hurried off towards Kensington High Street, and obscured the article that he was carrying under one arm. But not before Serov had caught a glimpse of yellow and knew that the drop had been made.

He returned to the Ferrari and, with the help of the A–Z, began making his journey-plan for the rest of the afternoon; he had some desirable properties to go and see.

42

Twenty years before, there had been another journey. One that Boyar and he had made together.

They came in from Izmaylovo on Motor Route 17, under a sky tinted pink by the slow dusk at the end of a Moscow high summer day. Boyar had said little on the half-hour journey but Serov had sensed the excitement that lay beneath his deliberate calm. For a month now, the same suppressed excitement had been there; Serov was certain that it was more than the tension of simple lust.

When they reached Inner Ring Road B, Serov turned north and entered the grimy tangle of streets at whose hub lay the Leningrad, Kazan and Yaroslavl stations. The heart of the city now lay to their left, the domes of the Kremlin palaces almost hidden by the ragged silhouette of office and apartment blocks that were starting to spring up all over the city.

What other traffic there was in those days comprised mostly buses and black taxicabs. Up to half the passenger cars would belong to the security forces, the military, or other branches of the government. The majority of the rest would be carrying senior party personel, either owned personally by them or apportioned with their posts.

As if he'd been pondering this himself, Boyar uttered his first remark since they'd set off from the academy.

'This is good of you, Captain,' he said slowly. In those days his Russian was still uncertain. He patted the dashboard and added, 'Your car.'

Serov decided to fish a little.

'It's my job,' he said, then paused. 'There is one thing though, Boyar. Remember the rules. The FCD is an understanding mistress but an unforgiving one.'

'What do you mean?'

'The academy sees to the physical needs of trainees like you because it knows that a three month programme is a long time to be in a foreign country and without a woman. But don't get confused.'

'In what way?'

'Just because no money changes hands, don't forget what these girls are. They're whores. You don't pay them, but they get paid nonetheless. It's only a business transaction.'

'I still don't understand.' But Serov heard the anxiety in his voice.

'It's simple. You've seen a lot of this girl over the last few weeks. Maybe too much. Maybe you're getting confused about her feelings towards you. Or letting yours about her run away with you. But you're just roubles and kopeks to her, comrade. Get that straight. Remember the rules about non-involvement with Soviet citizens. They're FCD rules, don't break them.'

Boyar stared straight ahead; and that was the end of the conversation.

Serov took them through the sooty and now-familiar backstreets abutting the railway line. They came to rest outside a smut-stained tenement block seven or eight storeys tall.

'Be out by midnight, Boyar.'

He watched as the Englishman hurried into the block. The stairwell ran up the street wall, with windows at each landing. He saw him pass the first two, then the angle was too steep to see any more. He shifted his gaze to the right, counted up six storeys, and began studying the window immediately beside the stairs. This he knew to be the whore's sitting-room. Although it was difficult to be sure, he thought he saw the curtain twitching, as if someone were watching the street. Then, just around the time Boyar would have arrived on the floor, the light behind the curtain went on. A moment later a softer light came on in the adjacent window: the bedroom. After a few minutes it was extinguished. But the sitting-room light had remained on throughout; and still did.

It wasn't proof of anything, of course. Electricity was free; plenty of people were careless about switching lights off.

Serov got out his transistor radio, a rare import, and propped it on the dashboard. A female voice was reciting the increases that were being achieved in domestic sewing-machine production.

He slid down a little in his seat and prepared for a long wait.

It was a lively street. As the night wore on, the various brothels caused a steady flow of foot-traffic, all men, to and from the buildings. Hookers prowled up and down the pavements. Occasionally they knocked on his window. He either shook his head or pretended to be asleep. Now and then taxis disgorged men in twos and threes, never singly because of the cost. The clatter of heels, the laughter and cat-calls were drowned from time to time by the rumble of trains passing in the cutting behind the tenements.

There was nothing out of the ordinary about the man who came rolling along the street at eleven o'clock, a little the worse for wear. He was thickly built, his black hair gleamed with cheap oil, and his nose, over a heavy moustache in those days, was flattened like a boxer's. Gramin sang cheerfully, in grating tones but not so loud as to draw himself more than a passing glance, and halted every few steps to top up from a bottle, swaying when he did so. As he progressed he peered at the house numbers. He paid no heed to Serov or his car but grinned with satisfaction when he read the number of the tenement next to it. Then he threw the building's doors open and stumbled inside.

At the sixth floor he thumped clumsily on the door to the right of the stairs.

'Sweetheart!' he bawled when the door opened. He lunged at the woman who stood there, forcing her to sidestep, and more or less fell past her into the room.

'Who the hell are you?' she demanded.

'A friend told me all about you. Said you're the best.' He seized her wrist and pulled her up against his groin. 'Show me what you've got, my angel. I'll show you what I've got.'

As good as his word, he began unbuttoning his flies, still clutching her arm with his other hand.

The whore recovered her voice at last. 'Clear off,' she ordered. 'I'm busy. I'll be busy all night as far as you're concerned.'

She tried to free herself from his grasp but he hung on with drunken tenacity. Suddenly he tumbled towards the bedroom and burst through, pulling her after him.

He stopped short to coo at the sight that met his eyes.

'Oh, you're busy all right. But does he really need both of you?'

The young man in the bed stared fiercely back at him but said nothing. The girl beside him dived under the covers and stayed there.

The whore's fist, landing on Gramin's ear, recaptured his attention.

'Out,' she hissed, pulling him back towards the door. 'Now. Right now.'

The punch seemed to cool him off a bit. He rubbed at the glowing ear, pouting, but let her pull him in the right direction.

'Can I come around another time?'

'No. I'm by special arrangement only. Whoever told you about me shouldn't have.'

'How do I make one of those arrangements?'

'If you don't know, then they're not available to you.'

She pushed him out of the door and slammed it quickly, slipping the security chain in place.

He pleaded with her for a while from the other side, then he belched decisively, rebuttoned his flies and descended the stairs again.

He swayed in the doorway as if unsure what to do next or where to go, before lurching off towards the far corner of the street.

No one paid him the slightest bit of attention, least of all Serov. The voice on the radio was now talking about pig-breeding, reeling off the kinds of statistics that bore no relation to the pathetic supplies of meat that reached the shops. He listened for fifteen more minutes before he turned off and got out of the car, peering up to check that everything was still and quiet on the sixth floor. He locked up carefully, walking around the car to check all the doors, and set off in the direction that Gramin had taken, keeping close in against the buildings.

When he turned the corner he walked on until he came to a red-brick tenement with a fallen porch. In the doorway stood Gramin, now looking not at all drunk. Serov joined him.

'Success?' he asked.

Gramin nodded. 'The whore was as you described her. But she was taking her ease in the sitting-room. The radio was on and there was a book and a glass of tea by the sofa. She was fully dressed. Wearing slippers. Not what you'd call ready for action. She hasn't been near her bed tonight.'

'Did you get into the bedroom?'

'Certainly. There was a man and a girl in the bed. I only got a quick look in the light from the sitting-room, which wasn't much. He was skinny, dark-haired.'

'He doesn't matter. What about the girl?'

'Young. Long blonde hair, very straight. Pretty face. No idea about build. She went under the sheets as soon as I arrived and stayed there.'

'Did the man speak?'

'Not a word. He didn't look pleased, though.'

Serov took out his wallet and handed over some cash. 'You remember I said I might want you to do something else for me tonight?'

'You'd like me to follow the blonde girl.'

'The man will be out by midnight. I want to know who she is, where she lives – everything you can find out about her. Did you see enough to recognise her?'

'I think so. What if she stays the night?'

'Give it as long as you can. If you lose her we'll try again next time.'

'How do you know there'll be a next time?'

'There'll be a next time.' Serov melted into the shadows and hurried back to the pork production figures.

Twenty years ago. There had been plenty of next times.

Serov slipped the last property brochure into its relevant A–Z page and turned the Ferrari's ignition key; five litres of power growled into life beneath him. He took the car slowly down the car park ramps and into the street. As in Moscow, children and men stared as he passed.

But this was better than Moscow.

Much, much better.

Knight sat with his eyes closed and the yellow lunchbox on his lap. Around him the hospital out-patients' area was full and too busy for the staff to keep track of everyone. He would be safe for as long as it took one of the nurse-receptionists to realise that he had no right to be there, that he was waiting for no appointment. Then he would have to move to another waiting area or another hospital. Or somewhere else entirely. He'd never realised before how hard it was to find a warm place to sit in a city without paying for it.

He had gone through the contents of the yellow lunchbox and studied the photographs in it. Most were night-shots. The bald man and his companion. The house where they had stayed, with an NW2 address printed neatly on the back of one of the shots. A white van. The young Libyan, the one whose photograph he had already seen in the news-papers. The van and a black Jaguar outside a small house that he knew would turn out to be Brook Cottage. Just as he knew whose car the Jaguar would turn out to be, its numberplate perfectly visible.

And finally, the bald man leaving the Opera House.

Such an unspeakable trail of death. Clarke, his driver, the Pangton girl and her minder. The Saudi prince and his entourage. The Special Branch men with them. The ordinary people who happened to be on the wrong stretch of a Surrey road at the wrong time. Ibraham Abukhder, no innocent himself. Joss Franklyn. Who should have been him, Knight.

And the ones who were dead in spirit. The ones who had yet to pay. Was he one of them? Perhaps. Hadn't part of him died twenty years ago, when he had chosen this path?

A choice that dated back to Izmaylovo that summer. In Major Kunaev's academy. Long days when the work seemed never-ending; humid evenings when the geese flew overhead and he went to lie in the arms of a forbidden girl.

'I've been told to stop seeing you.'

She pouted at this, then shifted in the bed to lie on top of him. Her hair fell over his face like a curtain. He was looking up at her inside a golden tent that filtered the lamplight and made a soft, dim world that felt safer than any he'd ever known. Her skin shone, her lips and teeth gleamed with moisture that he wanted to taste.

'Who told you that?' she said.

'Just someone.'

'Will you obey this someone?'

He blew a gap in the curtain and watched it fill again.

'You've left your home,' he said. 'Will you ever go back?'

The curtain trembled as she shook her head. 'Home is a man who lives for war and a woman who hates him because of it but won't leave him. So what is there at home for me? No, I won't go home.'

'Then I won't stop seeing you.'

Then afternoon in one of the high-ceilinged rooms in the academy. Bright sunshine out in the garden but so dark inside that he had the ceiling light on. Before him on the table a manual on subversion propaganda.

Suddenly Kunaev was there, entering so quietly that he didn't hear him until he spoke. In English for once.

'You're a member of the Church of Rome, Boyar. I find that intriguing.'

Startled, Knight glanced up to see the major watching him with a bemused smile.

'I don't practise it any more. Not since my father's death. Why should it intrigue you?'

Kunaev looked mischievous, a sign that he was in the mood for intellectual debate. Knight's heart sank.

'The two great opposites,' Kunaev ruminated. 'Rome and Moscow. The two greatest empires the world has ever seen. But diametrically opposed.'

'They have a certain amount in common. Both have been called totalitarian. Both honour the dignity of individual labour but more so when geared to a common goal – in the one societal, in the other spiritual. Both admit of free will but find a higher purpose in subjugating it to the will of the corporate body.'

Kunaev smiled bleakly. 'And both have had great wrongs committed in their name – your Torquemada, our Stalin. Don't look so surprised at my plain speaking, Boyar – Stalin was a mass-murderer and I thank comrade General Secretary Khrushchev for having the guts to say so.'

Knight sat back and closed the manual. 'Your country's purges, Rome's Inquisition. Yet to believers, neither negates the doctrines of their faith.'

Kunaev's eyes were gleaming behind the thick lenses. He was enjoying himself. 'Perhaps you are a philosopher, Boyar. Perhaps we should seed you in a university, where you can tutor the young and bring them to Marxism through Romanism or Anglicanism or Buddhism or Judaism – any ism, we won't mind.'

So saying, he returned Knight's smile and moved away from the doorjamb, producing the book that he'd been holding out of sight behind his back while they talked.

'I always enjoy our debates, Boyar. I think you do too – yes? That is why I thought you might like to borrow this. It is in English, so do not worry – you will be able to read it.'

He handed the blue-bound volume over. Knight took it and read the title and name on the dustcover:

History of Russian Philosophy.
The first comprehensive and complete survey in English.
By N O Lossky.

'Thank you,' he said with as much enthusiasm as he could muster, wondering when on earth he'd find time to look at it.

'No thanks are necessary for broadening the mind of a student of the Izmaylovo academy. I must have the book back, sadly – it is a rare copy. But you may keep it all summer if you like. We will discuss it as you read through it. You will find it fascinating. No one can truly understand Dostoevsky or Tolstoy unless he has met their mentor, Fedorov. And for an examination of so-called religious truths, you will enjoy Karsavin.'

With that he hurried off, leaving Knight to leaf the pages of the book and feel even more intimidated. Perhaps if he managed one chapter a week . . .

'And I did,' Knight muttered. 'And left my fingerprints all over it. Just as you wanted me to, Genrikh Kunaev.'

He opened his eyes to see the hospital receptionist staring down at him. It was time to move on.

43

Moscow

Viktor Chebrikov, Chairman of the KGB, left his offices in Dzerzhinskiy Square at one fifty precisely, was driven through the gateway beneath the Kremlin's Spasskiy Tower five minutes later, and entered the meeting room on the top floor of the Arsenal block at one minute to two.

Marshal Georgi Zavarov left General Staff headquarters on Gogol Boulevard at exactly the same time, fortified himself with a quick swig of brandy in the back seat of his Zil limousine, and saw Chebrikov's car u-turning and parking in the Arsenal courtyard just as his was pulling into it. The KGB man had already been dropped off; four minutes later Zavarov was with him in the meeting room.

Yegor Ligachev only had to walk across the courtyard from the yellow Senate building to the Arsenal block, to join them.

In the meeting room, at the head of the table, Mikhail Sergeyevich Gorbachev was already waiting as each of them arrived. His head was bent over a folder of correspondence that he was speed-reading. He didn't look up or greet any of them; he just kept on reading.

Valets were on hand to take their outer coats, scarves and gloves. The men handed them over in silence and the white-gloved servants padded softly away.

There was no smalltalk as they seated themselves. Ligachev took the number two's customary position on the General Secretary's right, while Chebrikov and Zavarov sat opposite him. On the table between them were bottles of mineral water, drinking glasses and a centrepiece of flowers. Pencils and pads of paper completed the arrangement. But no alcohol, no boxes of Cuban cigars and English and American cigarettes as in the old days. Not even an ashtray, Zavarov noted dolefully.

Eventually Gorbachev raised his head, leant back in his chair and gestured with an open hand at Viktor Chebrikov for him to begin. No preliminaries; there never were these days.

The KGB Chairman acknowledged the invitation with a crisp nod. 'Each of us has seen and heard the Western news reports of the last few weeks. I passed recordings and extracts to you from the West European and American television and press.'

Gorbachev didn't stir but the others nodded. As well as the source material provided by Chebrikov, each of them had kept an attentive ear to the BBC's World Service, Voice of America or *Deutsche Welle*, depending on their linguistic capabilities. Unlike the rest of the country, the areas of inner Moscow and the resort locations where Politburo members had their homes and dachas were kept clear of radio jammers.

'These indicate that the operation is running exactly as planned. To be specific – first, the Anglo-American action has been a complete success.'

'From whose point of view?' Ligachev asked, for the sake of appearances. 'Theirs or ours?'

'Both, Yegor Kuzmich. The assassination went without a hitch. We couldn't have done a better job ourselves. Next, Gadaffi of Libya reacted to it as our strategists said he would, trying to capitalise on it by laying the blame at the West's feet. Naturally, and as we also projected, spokesmen for the British and American governments gave immediate and categorical off-the-record assurances to their press and broadcasting communities that there was no such involvement.'

'Off-the-record?' Ligachev queried. 'Why off-the-record?'

'There's nothing sinister in that. Official statements might have lent some credibility to Gadaffi's allegations or suggested that the British and Americans were worried by them. By handling them in a low-key way, they would have been hoping to reduce them to the level of Gadaffi's usual pronouncements. In my opinion they succeeded. And that's good. Remember – the more successful they've been in refuting Gadaffi's allegations, the better it is for us in the end.'

'And the British and American follow-up?'

'They've laid a convincing false trail. Their strategy has been more or less what our scenarios had led us to expect. Their chosen stooge was a Libyan trainee airman. He was a good choice and has been accepted without question as the assassin. The world is now convinced – more importantly, so are the other Arab nations – that it was Gadaffi himself who ordered the Saudi prince's liquidation. In parallel, word of the intended Saudi coup that Gadaffi was sponsoring was fed by British intelligence to their media mouthpieces. From the British press and television reports the story has spread to the rest of the world. Consequently the tide of Arab opinion is now running strongly in Britain's and America's favour. Their fall from grace will therefore be all the more dramatic, and the Arabs' reaction against them all the more extreme, when we implement the final phase.'

'The final phase,' Ligachev repeated. He turned to Zavarov. 'In connection with which, comrade Marshal, tell us about the Special

Detachment unit, the Spetznaz team. Did it cover everything it was meant to?'

Zavarov nodded confidently. He took particular pride in his Spetznaz brigades. Had he been a few years younger, he would have been tempted to dole out more than verbal encouragement to the two young women who had been detailed to the London assignment.

'Set a pickpocket to catch a pickpocket,' he said, turning to address his remarks to Gorbachev. 'And set an assassin to cover an assassin. He – or she – knows better than anyone else how the other will think, how he'll approach an operation. That was the principle behind our strategy, and – just like the stages of the operation that comrade Chebrikov has described – it has been brilliantly borne out. Our Spetznaz unit has done an outstanding job. Its reports indicate that it was onto the killing unit that the CIA lent to the British from almost their first day of operation. Furthermore, the covers adopted by the Americans, the way in which they had obviously been briefed and prepared for the assignment, their acquisition of the Libyan stooge, their materials and ordnance supply – all these things point to full collusion by the British. So we have everything we need, and more, to prove conclusively that the Saudi was the target of an Anglo-American action.' He paused, looking pleased, before adding, 'And I understand that comrade Chebrikov's agent has now been able to make contact in London with the Spetznaz unit.'

Chebrikov sat forward again. 'Correct. He waited until he'd established good cover in London and was confident that he wasn't under surveillance. Now he's not only made contact, he also says that he's taken delivery of the evidence – photographic and documentary – that the Spetznaz unit has amassed.'

At the end of the table Gorbachev still sat listening, though not looking at any of them. He sat sideways to the table, gazing instead at the bleak sky outside. One hand was laid flat on the papers that he'd been reading earlier; now his fingertips rose one inch into the air and came gently down again. It was the smallest of gestures but every one of the other three saw it.

'This agent of yours,' he said, turning to Chebrikov. 'Aren't you being rather modest on his behalf? I believe he's quite a senior man.'

Chebrikov frowned, momentarily disconcerted. 'That's correct, comrade General Secretary.'

'A top man. Director of the First Chief Directorate, in fact.'

'Yes, comrade.'

'General Nikolai Serov.'

'Yes, comrade.'

'Isn't it unusual to risk a man like that in the field?'

Chebrikov had regained his composure. 'It is unusual. But so is this operation, comrade General Secretary. I specifically asked the director to handle it personally. In the service of the Soviet peoples, naturally he didn't hesitate.' He looked thoughtful for a moment, sucking in through pursed lips. 'Even though great personal sacrifice will be involved.'

Gorbachev looked at him in silence for a moment.

'I commend your decision,' he said at last. 'And the General's dedication. This operation is crucial to the country's future.'

Chebrikov allowed no outward sign of his relief to show. 'Thank you, comrade General Secretary,' he said stiffly.

Ligachev stirred and glanced from Chebrikov to Zavarov.

'We have mentioned the final phase,' he said. 'Will you both be ready for it?'

Chebrikov was confident. 'In the next few weeks my people will be sent to Tripoli with the next batch of the comrade Marshal's military advisers. There they will await my signal.'

Ligachev turned to Zavarov. 'And the fleet?'

Zavarov also was ready. 'On manoeuvres in the Mediterranean. Within a couple of days of the Gulf of Sidra, perhaps less. We have a few stragglers from the American Sixth Fleet watching us, but nothing could happen quickly enough to block us.'

Now, their account complete, Chebrikov turned back to Gorbachev.

'In brief, comrade General Secretary,' he summarised, 'all aspects of the operation to date have been satisfactorily executed, and all future aspects have been prepared for. We're in fine operational status.'

'I don't think it's premature or complacent,' added Zavarov, 'to mention that it's demonstrated how effectively our military and intelligence services can work hand in hand.'

The Marshal and the KGB chief fell silent. Ligachev settled back in his chair, through this change in position tactfully yielding control of the meeting back to Gorbachev.

If any of them had been hoping for grand words or some other measure of congratulation from their leader, they were disappointed.

'Then I await developments,' he said. 'You'll keep me informed.'

That was all. Without another word, he picked up his file of papers and rose abruptly to his feet. The others hurriedly followed suit.

'Good day, comrades.'

He'd left the room before they'd even finished returning his farewell.

'We're not on dry land yet, Viktor Mikhailovich,' Zavarov said to Chebrikov. Now that there was no one to stop him, he was fumbling for a cigarette. He found one and lit it. 'Better pray he doesn't get to hear about your little difficulty in the London *rezidentura*.'

'The young cipher clerk?' Chebrikov batted the cloud of cigarette smoke away; he seemed to be dismissing Zavarov's anxieties at the same time. 'I've already told him about that. It's nothing more than a minor inconvenience. I'm not worried – why should Mikhail Sergeyevich be?'

'A minor inconvenience? Then obviously you haven't told him what Serov is reporting – that your cipher clerk may have wrecked everything by his exposure of Serov's sleeper. I'll wager you didn't spell that out to him. And while we're on the subject of Serov, I didn't like all that fishing Mikhail Sergeyevich was doing about him.'

Ligachev was frowning across at them.

'Enough!' he whispered. 'Find a deaf office if you want to talk. Not here. And you, Georgi Fedorovich – put that cigarette out. Nowadays walls don't just have ears – they have noses too.'

Chuckling quietly, the three men stood up as the valets, magically appearing at that moment, stationed themselves behind their chairs and shook their outer coats open for them.

Zavarov dropped the cigarette into his water glass as he left, and thought happy thoughts about the Zil's well-stocked liquor cabinet.

44

Knight's priority was the Spetznaz photographs: to get them in a safe place. And to get them copied.

A chemist shop in Victoria provided the solution to both. The manager was wary at first: he wasn't used to down-and-outs bringing him business. But Knight produced the remains of the money that Riley the journalist had lent him and agreed to pay in advance. Many of the prints in the yellow lunchbox depicted nothing that was in itself alarming: faces, locations, and vehicles that were all quite innocuous unless their context was known. Even the close-ups of the Libyan, Abukhder, were scarcely recognisable from the mugshots that had appeared in the newspapers. The exceptions were the photographs of the Windlesham bombing, worthy of any sensationalist tabloid. They constituted a risk that Knight had already decided he had to take; he could see no way out of it.

The chemist confirmed that he could copy the prints without having the negatives, and that he had no problem if Knight took a week or two to collect them; they would wait safely and anonymously until then in his photographic drawer. So Knight handed the prints over, paid a small fortune, and loitered as inconspicuously as he could outside the shop for half an hour or so, watching to see if the chemist examined the prints. He didn't; he went to lunch and his female assistant took over.

For a week thereafter Knight followed the same routine. He slept in Cardboard City, he ate Salvation Army meals to eke out what was left of the money, he thought about using some of what he saved to pay for showers at public baths, but never did. As for the days, he passed them not in hospital waiting areas but in a variety of public libraries, any that would let him sit in peace at a table in their reference sections. Here he wrote in a lined A4 pad, making many false starts and copying to start again. He referred to the notes he'd made at the retreat house, now giving them their true meaning through what he'd learnt from Serov. What he wrote he kept on him at all times, wrapped in a plastic food bag, and each evening he burnt the rejected material in a brazier down by Charing Cross Pier.

Each evening he also phoned Marion Clarke. She was waiting for his call and he never had to give his name. The calls were always brief because she had no news for him.

But on the sixth evening she said: 'There's a chance it might be tonight. A good chance. If he does make it, it won't be till sometime after midnight.'

Dear God, he thought; she'd done it.

Midnight came and went, cold and windy in the concrete labyrinths of Cardboard City. The place was packed with its usual clientele, the usual noises echoed back and forth. Knight sat in a corner by himself, his mackintosh buttoned tight about him, a few layers of cardboard between him and the numbing floor.

At one o'clock there was a flurry of movement along the tunnel. Knight sat abruptly forward, staring and listening hard. A low murmur of voices reached him, completely different voices from those which usually punctuated the night.

He rose to a crouch and strained to see what was going on. The dim security lights set into the tunnel's ceiling were next to useless. All that was clear was that people, he had no idea yet how many, had congregated at the far end. Their silhouettes blocked out the glow that was usually visible from the river and embankment.

The movement and murmur of conversation drew nearer. It was a stop-go kind of progress as the group, four-strong as he could now see, halted occasionally to chat among themselves; there was the occasional gruff interjection as they brought one of the tunnel's awake or more sober residents into their conversation.

The four men were walking two in front, two behind as they approached. Knight reckoned that the man for whom he was waiting would be one of the pair in front. The two behind would be his personal detectives.

They stepped into clear view at last and there was no longer any doubt. Knight rose to his feet and stepped quickly over to the man in the Barbour jacket.

The royal visitor showed no alarm, but his detectives sent cardboard bedding flying left and right as they leapt forward to seize Knight.

'Mr Knight?' the man said. 'Mrs Clarke has told me about you. You have a remarkable story that you would like to tell me, I believe?'

'Thank you, sir,' Knight said.

First to be called the following morning was the Conservative party chairman. After him were the leaders of the three main parliamentary opposition parties. The Lord High Chancellor made the phone calls personally. The Liberal leader, at his home in the Borders, was flown south by RAF jet, the others, all based in London or the Home Counties, were fetched by police cars to Westminster.

The constitutional crisis that brought them together had thrust a critical role on the Lord Chancellor. His was the oldest office in the kingdom, older than the Norman Conquest. As President of the Supreme Court of Judicature, the nine judges in the House of Lords who made up the final court of appeal in the land, he was also the lord of the Law Lords themselves: there was no higher legal authority. In the matter of calming the constitutional waters that the government's senior ministers had stirred up, there was no one else on whom the task could fall.

On that Saturday the four politicians came to his office behind Chancellor's Court in the Palace of Westminster and listened with growing repugnance and dismay as the truth behind Ibn's assassination unfolded.

'Why?' asked the Conservative chairman, his shoulders sagging. 'Why on earth did they do it?'

The Lord Chancellor peered at him over the top of his gold-rimmed glasses. 'They couldn't risk letting the Saudi Arabian coup go ahead.'

'But they only knew about it because the Soviets fed it to them as part of the set-up. Our intelligence people and the Americans' have been played for idiots.'

The Lord Chancellor nodded. 'I cannot deny that. They felt that they had two choices: tell the Saudis or sort it out themselves. They judged that the first was no good – King Fahd would merely have executed his renegade prince, the Ibn fellow, or flung him in prison. Ibn was already a focus for fundamentalist forces – he would have become a martyr for his cause. They concluded that the only safe thing was to remove him permanently and arrange to put the blame on Gadaffi. So they kidnapped the young Libyan, Abukhder, and constructed what they hoped would be enough circumstantial evidence to make his guilt obvious.'

'Killing him in the process,' the Liberal said.

'Sadly, yes. One more death among many. The intention was that the other Arab nations would despise Gadaffi for assassinating one of their own. That would negate his plan to be some sort of chieftain of them all. Also, with Ibn out of the way, there could be no question of the Saudi Arabian coup going ahead.'

'And all the time they were doing everything the bloody Soviets wanted. The cretins.'

'Nothing to add to that,' the Lord Chancellor said mildly.

'The government must resign.' It was the Labour leader this time. The others turned to stare at him.

'If it won't do so voluntarily, it must be dissolved.'

The Conservative made to reply but the Lord Chancellor held up his hand to stop him. 'Dissolved? How?'

'Crown prerogative.'

The Lord Chancellor let out a long sigh and shook his head. He had said nothing about how the facts behind Ibn's killing had reached him: nothing about Edmund Knight nor the man who had met with him and then dragged the Lord Chancellor from his bed, demanding this meeting and the decisions that had to be made at it. They were matters that no politician needed to know; politicians had done enough already.

'Involving the Crown would be a legal quagmire,' the Lord Chancellor said. 'The Crown wouldn't want to be brought into something like that. It could be accused of unwarranted interference with the democratic process. Leave the Crown out of it.'

'A straight vote of censure, then. One of us will move a censure debate, the others will back him. The Whips will be powerless in the face of national opinion and pressure from the media. We'll carry the vote easily.'

Content to have won his point, the Lord Chancellor sat back as they debated this suggestion. It was the Social Democrat who brought it to a conclusion.

'No.' Quiet though it was, the single word silenced the others. 'No, we won't have a vote of censure. National opinion? Media pressure?' The Democrat shook his head. 'No. What this government has done is beyond all excuse; but if we expose it we'll undermine not just it but the country's standing in the eyes of the civilised world. The standing of our allies as well. The Soviets have duped us – we'd be a laughing stock if what happened wasn't so obscene. The same goes for the intelligence services, America's and our own. If we disclose anything, we'll make it impossible for them to function with any effectiveness ever again. There'll be an outcry here for greater controls, for making the intelligence services more accountable – demands for Select Committees and God knows what.' He shook his head sombrely again. 'That's a high price to pay for vengeance on a rogue Prime Minister and a few madmen. Neither Washington nor ourselves must ever let this get out.'

The Lord Chancellor nodded, letting them know that he found that a satisfactory conclusion. Now there was just one more point to cover, one more safeguard to arrange.

'One last thing,' he began. 'Best you should know everything. The fact is, we're in an odd legal position ourselves. Concerning this meeting.'

They looked at him, waiting.

'The government of the day hasn't been dissolved or suspended. Nor, as we've discussed, is it likely to be. Yet we must take certain actions – executive actions – on its behalf. But it has not given us the authority to do so.' He sat back in his big wooden chair and stuffed his hands in the pockets of his baggy trousers, where they drummed up and down on his thighs for a moment while he chose his words. 'Technically, it is conceivable that we are all committing treason.'

The silence that followed lasted for the best part of a minute. Then the Labour leader began to laugh.

'I don't believe you.'

The Chancellor shrugged. The laughter petered out.

'You've boxed us in,' the Liberal said bitterly.

'Have I?'

'We're damned if we reveal what you've told us or what action we agree on, and damned if we don't.'

'Congratulations, Lord Chancellor.' This now from the Labour man, whose face was crimson with rage. 'You must be proud. You've served your nation well this day.'

'There's something I want to ask,' the Social Democrat said slowly. 'We've heard some insane things today. I hope you'll understand this question in the light of them.' He paused. 'Bill Clarke's death. That was about the same time as all of this was going on. I – all of us, probably – heard some outlandish stories that were circulating in the Bar and the Tea Room –'

'Oh, for goodness' sake!' The Conservative was shaking his head despairingly. 'You don't give any credence to those slanders, do you?'

'What I give credence to is neither here nor there – particularly after today. Could I just ask – Clarke's death wasn't anything to do with this, was it?'

The Lord Chancellor took his glasses off slowly and slipped them back in his pocket. Then he folded his hands and stared hard at all of them.

'That would be a foul suggestion for anyone to make,' he said coldly. 'We have had enough unpalatable fare on our plates this morning without looking for more. William Clarke died in a road accident – I have no evidence whatever to the contrary.'

The Conservative settled comfortably back in his chair. The Democrat shrugged indifferently. 'Just wanted to hear it from the horse's mouth.'

'Gentlemen,' the Lord Chancellor said. 'We come now to the matter of the further action on which we must agree. It concerns our Libyan friend, Gadaffi. According to my information, the worst is yet to come. We must decide on what we are going to do to prevent it and what assistance we require from our American colleagues. Now that we're clear where we all stand, shall we turn to that?'

No one dared raise any objections.

Gaunt was called that weekend as well; not, however, by the Lord Chancellor.

What he heard seemed at first to please him.

'Given himself up?' he repeated with relish. 'That's excell—'

His features froze.

'Who did you say? Who did he give himself up to?'

As the answer was repeated, he sat slowly down in the chair by his telephone table.

'What kind of complications?'

He listened very hard for several minutes. His long head fell gradually forward until his chin touched his chest and he was staring at the rosewood surface of the telephone table.

When at last he spoke again, his voice, despite having said so little, was hoarse.

'I'll leave at once, Prime Minister.'

His hand trembled as he replaced the phone. When he raised his face from the table, it was pale. He could smell his own sour sweat. The entire room seemed suddenly full of the odour.

He didn't leave at once, as he'd promised. He sat on for five or ten minutes, pale and sweating, staring across the room at nothing.

In the comfort of his hotel suite in central London, Serov welcomed the call that came through to him.

'I have found my way in,' the voice on the line said. 'I am progressing matters exactly as we discussed. I expect you to honour your terms in the same way.'

There was no more. Serov hung up.

'I knew you were resourceful, Boyar,' he said.

Events were drawing to their conclusion. Precisely as he had planned them. It was a time for congratulation.

But he felt no pleasure; only the impending sense of loss. He poured a stiff bourbon and unlocked one of his suitcases. Within was the steel-lined briefcase that he'd packed before leaving his Moscow apartment. He sprung the combination locks and opened it flat.

The photograph album lay beneath a clutch of telexes and bank statements that spilled across the table as he drew the album out and spread it open.

The bourbon stung his throat; he knocked back another large mouthful and began to flick through the pages. Katarina, Galina, Katarina, then only Galina. Blonde hair, green eyes. Devastating.

He took a cab from outside his own hotel to another one that was conveniently near. Its foyer had the benefit of enclosed payphones for privacy, and provided greater security against his next call being eavesdropped on or traced. He took with him a pocketful of coins.

He placed the call to Molodechno via the international operator, reciting the digits slowly and carefully so that there would be no mistake.

When the number finally rang, Gramin's voice came on the line so rapidly that he must have had the phone at his elbow.

'I want an update,' Serov told him without preamble. 'It is time.'

'Very good. And good also to hear from you, comrade.'

Behind the ingratiation there was something else in Gramin's voice: a guardedness that went beyond what was necessary. Something was wrong.

'Is everything all right?'

Serov tried to tell himself that the question was purely professional, for the sake of the operation.

'There have been certain difficulties, comrade. And a new development.'

He knew now what he was hearing in Gramin's voice: fear. He felt the roots of his hair prickle.

'What difficulties? What development?'

'The professor is here. He'll explain.'

Before Serov could argue, Ogarkin came on, stammering and sniffing. Serov fumbled nervously for a cigar and heard him out in silence.

Afterwards, when the change ran out, he put the phone back on the hook and stood there trying to absorb what he had just been told.

Then, silently, his back pressed against the payphone door, he wept.

45

Byelorussia

'Back to Moscow tomorrow, comrade Professor.'

As he spoke, Gramin pushed a log back into the fire with the toe of his boot, and returned to his warm seat. Two days had passed since Serov's call.

Relief and disappointment battled for control of Ogarkin's face, like conflicting weather zones.

'The general sent for her when he spoke to you?' he asked.

'He's sent for her.'

'What about her psychotherapy, without me?'

'She'll have plenty of witchdoctors.'

They were at the vodka again. There wasn't much else to do of an evening out there. The cocaine kept Ogarkin fit to work, but Gramin had been rationing it day by day. When evening rolled around, it was vodka-only time.

'You'll be sad to leave here, comrade Professor.'

'The Institute won't complain.'

Gramin laughed darkly. 'I was thinking of the clouds of paradise.'

Ogarkin sighed and looked bereft.

'Wait here,' Gramin said, and left the room.

He returned a few minutes later with what looked like a small silver jewel case. He set it in Ogarkin's hand and eased the lid carefully open. It was full of the white powder.

'God of mercy!' Ogarkin gasped.

Gramin moistened the tip of his finger, dipped it into the powder and ran it around his gums, smacking his lips and sucking in air as if he'd eaten something hot and spicy.

'A little thank-you present,' he said. 'Not just the contents – the box. I liberated it from a Georgian who let me down on a deal. Would you like it?' He squeezed the professor's shoulder. 'I know we've said a few rough things to one another in our time. But that's all in the past. Yes?'

Ogarkin stared in awe at the gift in his hand, his nose running again at the very prospect of its almost infinite portions of heaven.

A tiny measuring spoon and a razor blade were set into the lid of the box, along with a small tube a couple of inches long and not much greater in diameter than a drinking straw. The spoon, the tube, and the razor's sleeve were all made of silver, engraved in a pattern to match the box.

'Take a snort now if you like,' Gramin continued. 'Why not? You're off duty. I've got a few tasks to do later but I needn't trouble you.'

Ogarkin didn't need telling twice. He closed the silver lid with reverence and set off for his room.

When he'd gone, Gramin uncurled his fist. The finger that he'd dipped into the powder was still white with it, except where its damp neighbour, the one that he'd run along his gums, had rubbed some of it off.

Carefully, he stretched his hand over a corner of the fire and poured vodka over it straight from the bottle, washing the fingers and palm thoroughly. The high-proof alcohol splashed into the flames, damping them down at first, but flaring up a beautiful yellow as it evaporated and caught.

Then he put the bottle to his lips for another mouthful, and settled back to enjoy the interlude of peace.

He heard the jet come in over the house at nine thirty, on schedule. He rose unsteadily, kicking over the empty vodka bottle as he did so, and lumbered up the stairs to the circular window that looked down towards the airfield. Through the top fronds of the aspens and firs he could make out the parallel lines of lanterns flashing along the runway; after a moment the lights of the aircraft became visible as it turned to taxi towards the apron.

Sinsky was already standing ready when he turned from the window. He led the way along the corridor, pausing outside Ogarkin's room to look back enquiringly at Gramin. Gramin shook his head. For an instant the faintest flicker of a smile twitched at Sinsky's rocky features; then he stood back from the door.

Gramin entered the room and, ignoring the splayed figure on the bed, collected the gladstone bag.

They walked on to Galina's room.

She stirred as they entered and sat up, shaking the golden hair from her face and blinking against the light from the corridor.

She screamed when Sinsky held her down for Gramin to administer the injection. His thick fingers were surprisingly nimble and he wielded the syringe like an expert, finding the vein quickly and easily; he'd watched Ogarkin often enough.

Her screams were futile; there was no one to pay her any heed. Within a minute, as the sedative took effect, they subsided to a sob, then a low moan, and then she was unconscious. They wrapped the bed-clothes about her like a cocoon and carried her down the stairs and out to the Chaika.

Armed men had taken up position at the entrance to the airfield. The runway lanterns had been extinguished temporarily and the only lights burning were the floodlights that had been set up around the aircraft, an Antonov An-72 military transport. Half a dozen workers from the estate swarmed around it, standing on stepladders and hastily erected scaffolding. The pilot fussed among them like a mother hen, scrutinising their every movement. They were masking the transport's insignia markings with quick-drying acrylic paint. It wouldn't take them long. Unlike conventional military aircraft, the An-72's markings consisted only of red stars on the tailfin and wings, plus a small code number on the fin; the large identifying digits that it would have borne on its fuselage in normal service were absent.

Gramin took the Chaika to within a few yards of the aircraft and waited until the work was done and the workers had withdrawn. Then he and Sinsky carried Galina up the steps and into the passenger cabin.

Here the comfort of the fittings was a further indication that this An-72 was no regular troop or equipment transport. Gramin's gaze took in hide upholstered seats, more like armchair recliners, tables, soft lighting and a large video screen.

A nurse was waiting for them.

'There are sleeping facilities,' she explained. 'Bring her and I'll show you.'

She led the way through a door set into a bulkhead midway along the fuselage; beyond it were two private compartments. She unlocked one and they laid Galina gently down on the bed, blankets and all. On Gramin's nod, Sinsky returned to the car.

The nurse crouched down beside Galina and began lifting her eyelids and taking her pulse.

The co-pilot appeared and watched them in silence. As with the nurse, Gramin offered him no introductions.

The nurse finished her checks and Gramin began to strap the bed's safety harnesses securely about Galina. Now he glanced over his shoulder at the co-pilot.

'Opened your flight instructions yet?' he asked him.

The airman nodded.

Gramin looked more closely at him in the dim standby lights of the compartment. The tension on the man's face made him laugh.

'Afraid we might be shot down?'

The nurse started at this; clearly, Gramin noted, she knew nothing yet.

The airman remained sombre. 'It's not a destination I would've expected.'

Gramin chuckled. 'For an aircraft of the personal flight of the Chief of Staff of our glorious armed forces, you mean?'

'For any Soviet military aircraft.'

'Marshal Zavarov has many friends in high places, comrade. Don't you expect that? Who says they all have to be in our country?'

He looked down at the nurse and winked, then finished drawing Galina's harnesses tight.

'Sometimes, my friend,' he continued to the airman, 'matters of state require the conventions that you and I take for granted to be set aside. What are borders for if not to be crossed?'

'She's a matter of state?' the pilot queried. He gazed at the huddle of blankets.

'Oh yes, comrade. Believe that.' Gramin paused. 'You won't be shot down. And by the saints, you'd better not crash either.'

The airman stared at him, then at the unconscious girl for a moment longer, before giving a resigned shrug and heading back to the flight deck.

'We'll be safe enough,' Gramin said to the anxious-looking nurse when he'd gone. They returned to the narrow corridor outside Galina's compartment.

'Where are we going?'

'You won't even know when you get there.'

'What was all that about being shot down?'

'A joke. Nobody's going to shoot us down.'

'Why did you say it?'

'Because after we refuel in East Germany, we'll be flying beyond Warsaw Pact territory. But our pilot's got everything he needs to get by without problems. A path's been cleared right through to our destination for us. People in high places – remember?'

If she was feeling reassured, she didn't show it. Gramin grinned at her. She was a good-looking woman. A nurse too. There was a lot to be said for nurses. And he'd been stuck in this Byelorussian wilderness for a mighty long time.

'It'll be a lengthy flight,' he said. 'Gives us plenty of time.'

'What for?'

'To get to know each other a little better. We'll be old friends. Not to mention the trip back.'

'We do come back then?' she said with irony. 'When?'

'Right away. That's why we're refuelling in East Germany: so we can turn around and come straight back. We just stay long enough to drop off this cargo –' He nodded towards Galina's compartment. 'And pick up some more.'

'Similar?'

'Wait and see.'

A low whine that swelled quickly to a growl indicated that the pilot had fired the An-72's twin turbofans.

'Time we strapped in for takeoff,' she said.

Gramin didn't move.

302

'I thought I might give the other compartment a try,' he told her. 'The one with the other bed.'

She stared at him for a long moment.

'Why not?' she said at last. The engines were revving at almost full throttle. It was a short-takeoff plane; any second now they'd shoot up the runway and be airborne.

'See you when we get there.'

She tossed him the key and returned to the main cabin.

By the light of a cold moon, Sinsky dragged Ogarkin's body across the cobblestones of the courtyard. The heels of the professor's steel-tipped shoes kicked sparks from the flint where the yard had been brushed clear of snow, throwing out brief orange arcs and leaving two fine trails of scratches.

Sinsky left the yard and took the stepped path down the wooded hillside, shortcutting the road. Ogarkin's feet and legs now cut two parallel tracks through the deep snow.

When he got to the foxes' compound, Sinsky hauled a bunch of keys from his pocket and unlocked the trapdoor in the roof of one of the cages. The clamour of the foxes became deafening; they slavered and tore at each other as the trap creaked open.

Just before he dropped the body in, Sinsky thought about the shoes; a few cotton garments were one thing, but even these creatures couldn't eat leather and steel. He whipped the shoes off and let the body go; it didn't even get as far as the floor of the cage, riding instead on top of the snapping jaws.

Sinsky held one of the steel-tipped shoes against his own sole for size, and grinned when he saw how closely the two corresponded. He relocked the trapdoor, not even bothering to glance inside, and returned up the hill. He was content; it had been a good night's work. As he plodded through the snow, his ponderous brain considered the production process of which Ogarkin was now part, and the Western women who'd end up dabbing essence of the professor over their sleek bodies. It was a thought that pleased him even more than Ogarkin's shoes, and he stood roaring with laughter until his stomach muscles cramped and his sides ached.

Then, still chuckling and winking at the cold moon, he went inside to see what liquor Gramin had left.

London

The Lord Chancellor hadn't had much of a weekend, Knight reflected; thanks to him.

Evidently the Lord Chancellor agreed.

'My fervent hope is that you and I never set eyes on each other again, Mr Knight. I daren't think how many years you've taken off my life.'

Knight smiled wryly at him. He was bathed and scrubbed, in fresh clothes, but for the present retaining the beard that had grown over the last three or four weeks.

'I'll assume that your comment is solely a professional one, meaning that everything's been arranged as I said it should be.'

'Requested,' the Lord Chancellor corrected him. 'It's not up to you to dictate. As it happens, I have been asked to relay some agreements to you.'

He glanced down at the papers on the desk; they were several copies of a two-page memorandum. From where Knight sat, he could see that, after a few opening paragraphs, it consisted of a list of points, each briefly stated, and some summary paragraphs at the end.

'No legal proceedings will be initiated against you,' the Lord Chancellor read. 'Your resignation will be accepted. You will be awarded a commuted lump sum instead of a pension. Attached to this letter is the calculation pertaining to this. Your house will be restored to good order. You will be compensated for damage to its contents. You will be provided with the documentation necessary for a fresh identity.'

He stopped and looked questioningly at Knight over his glasses. Knight nodded to signify that, as far as he was concerned, that part of the list was as it should be.

'In return,' the gravelly voice resumed, 'you will honour certain reciprocal obligations that have already been discussed with you. You will participate willingly in any further debriefings that may be called for by senior officers of Counter-Espionage Branch or any other intelligence personnel that may need to be involved. You will sell your home and move to a different part of the country. You will not, however, move abroad to live permanently or travel abroad other than for holidays or in connection with any business with which you may subsequently be earning your living. You will inform Curzon Street before you go on any such trip, and give full details of your travel arrangements. You will not seek to make contact with any members of the security or intelligence services, present, future or former. You will avoid any such contact if other parties seek it. The sole exceptions to this arrangement will be to communicate your new location and to comply with any follow-up interviews that you may be required to attend. There is no time limit on this. You will not speak, write or in any other way communicate with journalists or anyone else about the matters in which we have been engaged and which have occasioned this agreement, or about your intelligence career or any operations in which you have been involved or of which you have any knowledge, however acquired.' He looked up again. 'And finally, you will hand over the document and other items that you have admitted to preparing.'

'At the right time,' Knight said.

'This is the right time.'

'Nice try, Lord Chancellor. Did they ask you to try? The articles are safe where they are. They're staying there until the right time.'

'You said you would hand them over when your requests had been met.'

'Fulfilled, actually.' It was Knight's turn to do the correcting. 'I said I'd hand them over or destroy them when my requests had been fulfilled. At this stage they've been agreed to, that's all. Just words. When my house and compensation are sorted out and I've got my lump sum, I'll hand the materials over. Till then –' He shook his head. 'And my arrangement for their disposal remains unchanged – namely, if the person or organisation I've lodged them with doesn't hear from me regularly, they'll make sure the materials get into hands that would make embarrassing use of them. I think that's clear enough, Lord Chancellor. Don't you?'

The law lord looked at him without answering for a long moment. Then he returned his attention to the letter, scrawled his surname on each copy, and slid them across the desk for Knight to do the same.

Knight obliged. It was just words, after all.

46

When the letter arrived at breakfast time, Viktor had known that it had to be from the university because it was addressed to him in his new name. As he picked it up his hands were trembling. The crest on the flap confirmed its origin.

Anna glanced up from settling Andrei in his chair and watched him anxiously as he opened the envelope. He slid his knife under the flap and sliced the paper slowly; to find out that they had rejected him would be worse than knowing nothing at all.

His eyes scoured the single page, up and down, side to side, not taking in its content but trying to pick out the simple yes or no from the midst of the courtesies and formal prose. In English it was so much harder than in Russian.

Anna waited.

His eyes stopped roaming the page and read and re-read a single phrase; then he read the bit before and the bit after, to make sure that there was no mistake.

When at last he looked up, he was beaming.

'Anna! They've said yes!'

Her broad smile reflected his delight back at him. Andrei began to laugh as well, catching their mood, and she reached across to cuddle him.

'Papa is going to be a teacher, Andrei. Imagine! In a big university. As big as Moscow State! Perhaps one day he'll teach you. Viktor, how wonderful!'

She stood up to lean across the table and kiss him. He passed the letter over to her, and she kissed it too. Andrei giggled.

'Oh, Viktor!'

It was the best breakfast they'd ever had in Stratfield Saye; or anywhere else, he decided. No: the best breakfast since the day Andrei was born!

'I'll thank Mr Sumner,' he said later in their room, as he wrote his acceptance.

'Thank him, yes,' she said. She came across and stroked his hair, laid her hand on his shoulder. 'But remember – you did this, Viktor Genrikhovich. You earned it.'

'I know, but Mr Sumner helped. He took me to them. He introduced me to the right people. It's his old university. They're his friends.'

'He didn't pull strings. He told you he wouldn't do that. They're taking you because they know you'll be a brilliant teacher of philosophy – like your father could have been.'

'I hope so, Anna. I'll make you both proud of me.'

It was settled. The gruelling weeks with Sumner and the others were over: the weeks of remembering and talking, describing and repeating. Their future was settled. They were new people, with new identities, and now he had a new job to look forward to. A little money had been provided, enough to start them in a modest home, and they could borrow the rest: a mortgage, it was called. Soon they would make new friends; they'd have to gloss their past a little, of course. That was an uncomfortable way to start friendships, but they'd get used to it. At least they wouldn't have to disguise where they'd come from. A population almost the size of London's had left the Soviet Union in the last forty years. Thousands were allowed to emigrate each year, despite the emigration authorities' mixture of inefficiency and obstructiveness; it gave a measure of the many thousands more who were waiting in line behind the lucky ones. He and Anna and Andrei would be virtually untraceable.

Later they went walking in the quiet country lanes around the house; they were allowed to do that now, although someone always stayed with them, trailing a few yards behind.

'Suddenly there's a lot to do,' she said, awed at the prospect of their new future. She was more animated than she'd been for weeks, almost dancing along by his side, catching his arm, laughing and swinging Andrei. 'You'll have lectures to prepare, we'll have to start looking for an apartment or a little house –'

'Two,' he corrected her.

It was a mistake; she glanced over her shoulder at the security man.

'Our guardians,' she muttered. 'I forgot.'

Suddenly the spark was gone. Her head drooped. He put his arm about her and squeezed her close.

'It's not for forever, Anna. Look at me. Just a few months, probably. Maybe a year. Until they know we're not being searched for.'

'You said it could sometimes be as much as three or four years. Sometimes even for the rest of a person's life.'

'Oh, that's so unlikely, Anna. Even three or four years. That was just something I said to show you how careful these people are prepared to be if it's necessary. I said it to make you feel safe. To reassure you. But they only keep someone with you if they think there's a continuing risk. If I'd been a high-ranking person, for example. But we're not that important. After a few months, who in Moscow will remember Viktor and Anna Kunaev?'

307

'The FCD has the longest memory in the world.'

'Yes, but times change, people move on, get promoted, get fired. New problems come along and the old ones – old names too – are forgotten. Why would these people want to keep guardians with us any longer than necessary? It all costs money, Anna.'

'Pah! Money!'

'Of course, Anna. Be practical. Our guardians have to be a couple, for them to be inconspicuous, they have to be housed and paid, one of them has to be found some kind of job to stay close to me. That's why Mr Sumner had to help me – so that one of them can have a university post. But they refund the university. It's all money, Anna, and they don't want to pay it for any longer than they have to. Do they?'

'Just as I said to you – everything comes back to money.'

'Let's think about the nice things.' He squeezed her again, and reached down to snatch up Andrei. 'Here's a young man who needs a school! With luck, we'll be settled just in time for him to start. Won't that be fun, Andrei! We'll buy a little car. We will! Oh – and English lessons for Andrei. We'll have to work on that.'

So they strolled on through the moist Hampshire lanes, and eventually he brought her around and was rewarded as the laughter returned to her eyes.

And when he closed his own eyes, the picture of a small boy growing up in a free country didn't seem as elusive anymore as for a time it had been.

But that had been in the morning. At lunchtime the message came from Sumner. One line, dictated over the telephone and jotted down by the female security officer. Be packed and ready to leave, it said; from anytime after ten tonight. No explanation, no reasons given; only those few dreadful words.

The day, that had started as fresh as spring itself, became agony. Sumner never called back and the guards said he couldn't be reached.

It was ten thirty that night before he came. They were ready and waiting, had been for an hour; there was precious little to pack anyway. They'd put Andrei to bed as normal. He could be lifted and wrapped in his dressing-gown for the journey. Whatever and wherever it was.

Viktor hurried out to the hallway as soon as he saw headlights in the drive. He was taken aback by what met his gaze when the security man opened the front door. Sumner was climbing out of a large van with black side-windows, like the kind Viktor had seen carrying policemen about in London. There were four police motorcycle outriders with him.

'What's going on, Mr Sumner? Why all this?'

Sumner looked at him without saying anything. He led the way into the living-room, where Anna and their two suitcases were waiting. There he planted himself in the middle of the floor and looked from one to the other. Viktor saw that he was as jumpy as a flea.

'I apologise for the suddenness of this,' he said. 'But we think it's wise to move you from here. Without delay.'

'Why?' Viktor felt a knot harden up in his stomach.

'We don't think there's any real danger – let me make that absolutely clear – but we don't want to take any chances.'

'Danger?' Anna's eyes were large with fright. 'What danger?'

Sumner seemed to gather his thoughts for a moment. Then he looked back at her. 'The Spetznaz unit that your husband warned us about. We have good reason to believe they're still in this country.'

Anna made a small noise in the back of her throat. Viktor sat down beside her and put his arm about her.

'Dear God,' he said quietly.

'We don't know for certain that they're interested in you. But it's a possibility. That's all we can say at this stage. And obviously we don't want to take the risk. The man you helped us identify as a Soviet sleeper, he's confessed. He's given –'

'Who is he?'

'He's given us further information – I can't be more specific – and we're acting on that. What I will tell you is that it suggests that, after the murder of the Saudi prince, the unit may have been set a further objective of some kind.'

Anna turned her pale face to Viktor. 'So much for us not being important enough,' she whispered.

Viktor thought of Andrei sleeping peacefully upstairs and suddenly felt an overpowering urge to go and grab him at once. He was thankful when Anna, clearly seized by the same need, rose and hurried out of the room; he heard her clattering up the stairs.

'You think they might know where you're keeping us, Mr Sumner?'

'Possibly. The man you uncovered insists that he hasn't passed any details over, but we're playing safe.'

'Thank God. So where are you taking us?'

'To another house a couple of hundred miles from here. Partly to get you into a new place but also because it's in a spot that's even quieter than here, where anyone or anything out of the ordinary will be very obvious.'

'And we drive there tonight?'

Sumner shook his head. 'We wouldn't feel happy about going all that distance by road. You know how mobile these units can be. If they do know this location, they may be watching the area. They might not try a hit or a snatch tonight, but we don't want them following us.'

'How do we get there?'

'We fly you. We drive you from here to a military airfield and put you on an aircraft that'll take you the rest of the way.'

'Won't we be in danger between here and the airfield?' Viktor's thoughts were racing. 'Shouldn't we go there by helicopter?'

'Couldn't land one in this area – too many trees. I've brought an armoured van instead. And you saw the escort we've got.'

Viktor felt a measure of relief. Sumner seemed to have covered all the angles.

'Thank you, Mr Sumner. You're looking after us well. I'll go and fetch my wife and child.'

He left the room and Sumner stood alone, looking at the two pathetic suitcases and the little mound of toys on the floor. He felt sick with guilt.

At 23.30 hours mid-European time, 22.30 hours Greenwich Mean Time, the An-72 crossed into West German airspace in the vicinity of Brunswick and held its course along the civil air corridor towards Hanover. Hanover logged it as far as the Netherlands, where Amsterdam picked it up. It continued to the coast, veering out over the North Sea and towards Britain. By the time it crossed the English coast at Clacton-on-Sea, Amsterdam had handed it on to the London air traffic control centre at West Drayton.

At each leg, as it blipped across the radar screens of north-western Europe, the jet identified itself to the air traffic centres with the call-sign of a privately-owned civilian aircraft. This aircraft was one that belonged to a billionaire entrepreneur whose dealings over more than half a century in both Eastern and Western Europe had made his plane, with or without him on board, a familiar user of the international airlanes. No one saw the jet that was laying claim to his reporting signal that night, so no one had any reason to challenge it; and, as Gramin had said, the aircraft's route had been pre-notified in the normal way.

Consequently, its passage through the skies that night was unexceptional and immediately forgettable.

Knight got to RAF Northolt at eleven thirty. It was a crisp, dry night, no fog, and with only wisps of cloud veiling the stars here and there. His first stop was at the Meteorological room in the Operations block, where he learnt that the perfect conditions were much the same over the North Sea and across most of north-western Europe, and were forecast to stay that way for the next thirty-six hours.

When he got to the section of the aerodrome that had been reserved for them, he found a barrier across the approach road and three RAF service policemen manning it. They made him step out of the car and open the bonnet, tailgate and all of the doors. Two of them checked the car visually, including passing a pole-mounted mirror and light underneath the chassis, while the other verified his identity against some details on a clipboard. Knight noticed that they were armed with sidearms. He deliberately inched his way to their glass-fronted hut as he chatted with the third officer; three machine-pistols were tucked handily under the counter beneath the window.

Further on, at the spot to which the tower would direct the aircraft to taxi, there was a scattering of bored-looking RAF ground staff, two more Land Rovers of service police and a couple of cars. As Knight parked and stepped out onto the tarmac, he realised that one of the cars was Gaunt's. A shadowy figure sat motionless in the back seat.

He turned in the opposite direction and strolled across to the other car. Four men were inside it. He introduced himself, giving his name and describing himself as 'Military Intelligence', and waited pointedly to hear what was their business there. Grudgingly they owned up to being customs and immigration control officers who'd been dispatched from nearby Heathrow. Knight wondered privately what genius had found time to think about inviting them. They explained that they would take no part in the immediate proceedings; papers could be sorted out later. They'd been sent along only to ensure that no one and nothing disembarked other than what was specified on their Home Office advice notices. One of them waved a copy under his nose. Female; Caucasian; one. Nobody wanted any nasty surprises later. Did they? Sir.

Thinking about nasty surprises of many different kinds, Knight returned to his car to sit and wait.

47

When the men on the ground in Northolt saw the lights in the eastern sky at midnight, they had no way at first of telling whether or not it was the craft for which they were waiting. Only when it was down and was undeniably taxiing towards them were they sure.

Knight's hands, clenched about his steering wheel, were suddenly slippery with sweat. They left glistening marks on the padded rim when he removed them and wiped them on the car seat.

He got out and began walking the hundred or so yards to where the aircraft had been guided and flagged to a halt by one of the ground staff. Its engines remained at idling speed. He forced himself not to hurry. The service policemen had now also emerged from their Land Rovers and were standing in a rough semicircle twenty or thirty yards from the plane. As an extra reminder of their presence, they'd turned on the flashing lights on the roofs of their vehicles. The flood-lights that had been set up on the tarmac behind them came on, bathing the aircraft and the area around it in light. The policemen supplemented the glare with the headlamps and spotlights of the Land Rovers.

Gaunt stepped out of the Jaguar; he glanced across at Knight from twenty yards away and their eyes met. For a moment only. Then Gaunt turned away.

More lights, moving fast, appeared on Knight's left. He turned his head and saw that a tight formation of vehicles was accelerating away from the security barrier and towards them. After a second he made out the shape of a large van behind one pair of the bright lamps; the others were motorcycles. It would be Sumner and the Kunaevs.

As he resumed his steady progress towards the plane, he realised that his heart was pounding like a jackhammer.

He passed beyond the floodlights, halting when he drew level with the line of policemen. The passenger door on the port side of the aircraft began to swing open.

What Viktor could see through the black windows was far from clear at first. An aircraft, yes, but many more people than he'd been expecting.

Most of them were policemen, judging from the flashing roof-lights. And the place was lit like a film set. Clearly, Mr Sumner was taking no chances whatsoever.

It was only when the van swung around to face the aircraft directly, and he was able to see it through the clear windscreen and between the shoulders of Sumner and the driver, that something began to trouble him. Something he couldn't put his finger on.

Andrei had been jolted awake by the stop-start process of negotiating the aerodrome; now, excited by the blazing lights and the racket outside, he leant across from where he sat on Anna's lap and tugged his father's arm.

'Yes, yes,' Viktor muttered absently, still trying to pin down what was troubling him.

Then they were parked and Sumner was out of the van and pulling open its door. Andrei tumbled out at once, breathless to see all that was going on, his blue dressing-gown billowing behind him; Anna leapt out laughing in pursuit, her earlier fears forgotten in the boy's exuberance. They ran on ahead between two of the security officers who'd travelled with them from the safe house.

On the tarmac, Sumner was urging Viktor to hurry. But Viktor paid no heed. Across the growing distance between Anna and himself, he heard her laugh as she caught up with Andrei.

'Yes, Andrei!' she called, 'It's for us, this big plane! We're going to fly up into the sky in it! Yes – it's just like your toy one – but real!'

While Knight watched, figures appeared in the doorway, averting their eyes from the harsh lights, and waited for the ground staff to wheel a set of steps into position.

Two figures.

No, three. One of them, a man, was supporting someone close by his side.

Just like the toy plane?

But the toy one had markings. Red stars on its tail and wings, call letters as tall as the pilot on its fuselage. This plane had nothing. Nothing at all. Not even so much as a dancing lady by the cockpit, like Andrei's had. This plane apparently belonged to no nation, had come from nowhere. This plane wanted no one to know of its existence.

Viktor froze on the door sill of the van and tried to make sense of the scene.

Quickly! his mind screamed.

As Anna and Andrei drew further and further away from him. Closer to an aircraft whose snub-nosed silhouette, with its drooping wings and huge engines mounted forward of them, was starting to seem disturbingly familiar.

The figures were coming across the tarmac towards where Knight and Gaunt and the policemen waited. Surely, Knight decided as they drew closer, that third figure following the others was a nurse.

The man supporting the other figure, now visible as a slim, long-haired girl, halted ten yards away. He shielded his eyes from the battery of lights to peer at the row of men facing him.

'Boyar!' he roared above the shriek of the engines. It was a demand, not a question.

Some intuition made Knight look over at Gaunt again.

'Where are you, Boyar?' In Russian.

Gaunt returned Knight's stare, unblinking.

'Boyar!'

Knight took a step forward.

'Come get your daughter, Boyar!'

Not in the air now. Not flying. Being walked across a great open space of some kind. Cold; she was cold. Where had her warm cocoon of blankets gone? Glaring lights that hurt her eyes when she tried to open them. Flashing lights too. On and off, on and off.

People everywhere. If she squinted through her lashes she could see them better against the lights. Men in uniforms, with caps. But some who weren't.

Who was that bearded man? Beneath the beard a face from some-where. A face that she remembered trying to remember many times before but always it had melted into Nikolai's before she could fit it where it belonged. Dear Nikolai. But he wasn't dear Nikolai any more and anyway his face was broken now. Just chickenwire and torn clay. Whoosh! Split with the cleaver.

One blow.

It wasn't just the aircraft that bothered Viktor. It was the people too. That man Knight was there. Why? What had this to do with him? They were only being moved, Anna and Andrei and he. Weren't they? Why had Sumner ignored him when he'd asked who the sleeper was? And over there, a few yards away from Knight, was another man that Viktor didn't even recognise. He was no policeman and, judging from his bearing, was no security officer either.

Quickly! his mind screamed again.

'Come on, Viktor,' Sumner said. 'We don't want to lose any time.' There was far more anxiety in his tone than a few minutes' delay should have occasioned.

Something else. If the aircraft was for them, who were the people that were getting out of it? And didn't the policemen and the others look more like a reception committee for them than a guard for Viktor and Anna and Andrei? Look at how they were facing. They were watching the aircraft; they should have been standing over here, by the van, if their purpose really was to watch out for him and his little family.

And what was it that was going on out there anyway, between the people who'd got out of the plane and the others?

The demand was repeated. 'Come get your daughter, Boyar!'

Knight closed the distance between them and looked down at her. The face he hadn't seen for so long. He looked at her with eagerness. But with foreboding as well. Why was she slumped like that? Why did there have to be a nurse?

He stared. It was her and yet not her. A broken face. Whole, unmarked; but broken. Broken inside. Like a doll whose vacant eyes would rattle in her hollow head if you shook her.

Christ, what had the bastards done?

He raised his gaze to the other face, that of the man who'd brought her. A squat lump of a face with a flat nose. Under it, a sardonic smile. Magpie-bright eyes that watched him with detached interest. Somewhere he'd seen it before. Moscow?

'Fuck your mother,' Knight told the Soviet, very quietly and deliberately, in the man's own language.

The eyes widened and the smile became a low, rasping chuckle.

'*My* mother, comrade?' he echoed. 'No – not *my* mother!'

He looked down at Galina and laughed some more.

Knight stretched out his arms to take her from him, but the man drew back sharply.

'You owe first,' he growled. The chuckling had stopped.

Suddenly a hoarse cry behind Knight made him swing around; a man's demented scream fought against the roar of the jet engines.

'Anna! Anna! Stop! Come back! Andrei!'

Then everything happened at once. Galina's limp body thudded into Knight from behind. He spun around to catch her and was in time to see the Soviet, who'd flung her at him, lunging instead at a small boy who had dashed within reach. It was the Kunaev child. A gun had appeared in the Soviet's fist; he pulled the boy to him and rammed the end of the barrel against his skull. Knight heard the crack as it connected; the boy cried out in pain and fear.

Somewhere close by, Anna Kunaev launched into a piercing, primordial scream of pure terror. Further in the distance, her husband's cry had become a howl of agony. A babble of voices had broken out; a clatter of confused footsteps. And one distinctive sound that made the hairs rise on the back of Knight's neck and arms: the slap of a dozen palms on a dozen leather holsters.

'Stop!' the Soviet bellowed, in English.

Instantly, astonishingly, everyone complied. Viktor. Even Anna. There was a dreadful stillness, as if they were all frozen in time.

'No guns!'

Knight glanced around and saw the policemen's hands drop by their sides.

'Up!' The Soviet gestured briefly with his free hand, then locked it back in place on the boy's throat.

The policemen raised their hands clear from their sides as they'd been told, away from the holsters. Knight noted that the man closest to him, like several others, had got as far as undoing the flap of his; now it sat wide open, the butt of his pistol protruding.

'Kunaevs – in airplane!' The Soviet looked directly at Anna and repeated the order in Russian.

'Yes, yes,' she gasped, and hurried forward, turning to search for her husband. Then she bent towards her child and said something reassuring to him. He was beside himself with fear and stretched his arms out to her; the Soviet smacked them down and the boy burst into more tears, wailing with despair and incomprehension.

Knight stared at him, that small boy with a gun pointed at his head, who wanted his mother.

For a lifetime he stared at him.

Ah, how she hurt! Why had she been thrown like a piece of garbage so that she ached like this?

The lights were behind her now. She was looking up at that strange-familiar bearded face. And over there, look: a little boy. Footprints through the snow? Look down, look down. No snow, no snow, just black tarmac. But a little boy. He was real. And he was crying. Perhaps he couldn't keep up.

> *There are shadows on the snow, mama.*
> *Two shadows side by side, papa; two shadows waiting.*
> *I fell behind.*
> *I stumbled.*
> *The wolves have stopped their howling.*

They had, too; they had stopped. There had been howling, but now there was only the lost boy.

'Mama!' he cried.

Two shadows side by side; they melted into one, parted again. Two faces. Nikolai's and this man's. That signature on Mama's letters. Shadows on the snow.

Snow? No snow. Spring, then.

Spring.

A picture in a gallery. A woman before a log cabin, a woman naked in defiance of the snowflakes, welcoming her little girl with warm love, asking her where she'd been. A living woman, not wet rags beneath the iron wheels on the metal tracks and then a rotting thing beneath the snow in a cemetery where the crosses marched all the way to the horizon.

'Mama!'

Once, she had cried like that. Yes, reverberating in a long gallery.

Oh! The man hit him. That man with a gun hit the boy. The man who'd brought her here. The man who'd taken her to that house; who'd injected her.

'Mama!'

'*Nyet!*'

The scream was hers. It came unbidden and it shocked her with its force, it tore from her like an exorcised demon and it left her throat raw and throbbing. But she'd stop the man hitting the lost boy. She would. She'd stop him.

The scream set Knight's ears ringing. Before he knew what had happened, Galina had torn herself from his arms and was rushing at the Soviet.

Knight's response was pure reflex. He saw the man's mouth drop open. The gun shifted from the boy's head and wavered in Galina's direction for an instant. But he wouldn't pull the trigger; in that millionth of a second Knight knew he just wouldn't pull the trigger.

The policeman's 9mm Browning was already in his own hand and the safety catch was off, his feet were planted apart and his knees flexed, his left hand rose to steady his aim, wait, wait, for God's sake wait till Galina was out of his line of fire; and then the kick along his arms told him that the bullet had gone.

Half the Soviet's head vaporised into the night, like a burst melon. His bulging eyes still stared. But not at Knight; at empty space where Galina had been. Until he crumpled like a felled ox. One leg flapped uselessly against the tarmac for a moment, then was still.

He hadn't even seen where death had come from.

Had Katarina? For she was dead, wasn't she? Knight had to face that now. Whatever Serov said.

He lowered the gun, its smoke stinging his eyes, then stepped forward, over the Soviet's body, and lifted Galina to her feet.

All over.

Anna Kunaev folded her small boy in her arms and, sobbing, carried him back to safety.

48

Serov heard the single shot. At that still hour of the night he couldn't fail. He stepped out of the Ferrari and stood in the sleeping suburban road with its neat semi-detached homes, and listened.

There were no more shots.

When he drove back to the gates of the aerodrome, all was as quiet as it had been earlier. Then, while he sat there, an ambulance came speeding along the road, its flasher going but its siren silenced. The gates opened to admit it and closed again.

Serov sat on.

After another few minutes the gates reopened and two police motorcycles emerged. This time the gates stayed open. The motorcyclists stationed themselves on either side of the gates and on opposite sides of the road, setting their bikes to block each traffic lane. Each man turned off his engine as he propped the motorcycle up on its stand, dismounted, and held up a hand to halt what little traffic there was. Then they remounted the bikes; one of them spoke briefly into his radio mike.

A Jaguar emerged, with Gaunt in the back seat. It rushed past Serov's Ferrari and towards London.

Seconds behind it the other two motorcycles sped through the gates, followed closely by the van with the black windows. Neither the van nor its outriders stopped as they hit the road, roaring off the way they'd come on their arrival.

The first two motorcyclists restarted their machines and raced off after them, leaving the handful of stopped cars to sort themselves out.

Again Serov sat on. Again the gates remained open.

Then Knight's car appeared. Unlike the van, it had to stop for the road. Not for long, for the small jam had cleared easily enough.

Long enough, however, for Serov to see Knight's passenger.

He waited until Knight's car had disappeared, then set off back to London. Behind him, the aerodrome gates remained open; for the ambulance. A medium-sized jet aircraft lifted into the night sky and climbed towards the stars. It was all a matter of indifference to Serov. He'd seen what he'd come to see. What he'd never wanted to see.

'Bourbon.'

'On the rocks, sir?'

'Plain bourbon. A large one.'

He pushed the room card towards the barman and signed the chit, writing in a generous tip to keep the man interested.

When he swung around on his stool the woman was still watching him. He lifted the glass to his lips and calmly returned her stare.

She was about thirty-five, well dressed or they wouldn't have let her into the casino, tall, with a broad, full mouth and her hair flicked back off her face to accentuate it. That mouth was her best feature and she knew it.

'You know what the lady in the corner's drinking?' he asked the barman.

'I do, sir.' The barman was drying glasses. He looked up to meet Serov's gaze. He seemed to consider for a moment whether or not to say any more.

'But it's not necessary,' he finally added and held a glass to the light.

'What's not necessary?'

'Buying her a drink, sir. If what you're looking for is an introduction. She's not that kind of lady.'

'So what kind of lady is she?'

'You know, sir.'

Serov knocked back the bourbon and slid the glass over the counter; the barman caught it just as it tipped over the edge.

'Another,' Serov told him. 'Large. No ice. And one for the lady.'

When he took the drinks over and sat down beside her she told him her fee. It was high but he'd stopped being shocked at London prices for anything.

'All right,' he said.

She picked up her handbag and began to rise. He laid his hand on her arm.

'I'm not in a hurry.' He pushed the drink towards her.

She looked earnestly at him. 'We stay here and the meter's still ticking.'

'So it ticks.'

'You want to talk?'

'No. Drink your drink.'

She made it last but he had two more, nodding at the barman to bring him scurrying over each time. Then he took her into the main part of the casino and they strolled around a few tables, not playing any but just watching the cards, the wheel, the hands, the eyes. Some of the men were bold enough to wink a discreet greeting to her. One or two of them nodded at him as well, marking his admittance to their private society.

Later, in his suite, she earned her money well. He paid her more than she asked.

'Anytime,' she said, pleased by his generosity. 'You know where to find me.'

Another cold dawn was stretching across the sky as he stood by the wide window and dropped another cigar butt into a full ashtray that spilt ash over its table. He saw his eyes in the glass top and they were dark. Darker than bourbon and sleeplessness could cause.

So he lit another cigar from the burning butt and let the years roll back, like jagged skin from a wound.

The summer went and so did Boyar. The leaves fell, scurrying where the wind blew them and lining the pavements of Moscow with gold and amber.

Then came the dark eternity of winter: steel skies that pressed down on the city like a lid.

Until at last the snow retreated and the first flowers reappeared. The parks grew green again and the birds sang from dawn to dusk.

The year's cycle was complete.

She was twenty now, the girl with the long blonde hair, from the tenement street where the whores lived and the trains thundered past below. And when Nikolai Serov walked up to her in Sokolniki Park that summer, her green eyes made his breath catch in his throat.

'I see you every day,' he said.

The eyes were quizzical. Amused. Perhaps even sceptical. But not nervous.

'And every night,' he added softly.

That made her laugh.

'How every night?' She rocked the pram gently back and forth; the baby slept on peacefully. 'I come here every afternoon. For Galya. But never at night. Galya keeps me safe at home at night. How can you see me every night?'

'I dream,' he told her.

It was a courtship. The only one he had in his whole life. Every day he met her. Sometimes in Sokolniki, sometimes in Gorky Park, sometimes on the embankment under the Kremlin's two Nameless Towers, or by the Moskva Swimming Pool, or sometimes in the Alexandrovskiy Gardens. It was a week before he touched her hand, two weeks before they kissed.

'Eduard was a poet,' she said when she was ready to talk about the fictitious father she'd conjured up for her child. 'He used to go to the demonstrations in Mayakovskiy Square. Things got rough. The lucky ones got arrested. The militia kicked Eduard to death. By then I was carrying Galya. I didn't want an abortion. I wanted him or a part of him. That part is my little Galina.'

These were her lies. But she told them the same way she did everything else: beautifully.

'You've been very brave,' he said.

'Are you a poet, Nikolai?'

'I don't think so.'

'You might be. With my help.'

He waited two months before he took her to bed. Never had he waited so long for any woman. He never looked at another while he was waiting for her, not even a whore.

She was shy to start with, then she fell upon him.

Izmaylovo no longer existed by then. When Khrushchev went, it went too: an experiment that was too subtle for the new Neanderthals. Old Genrikh Kunaev was sent off to moulder in a harmless teaching post somewhere and the rest of the staff were scattered.

Katarina stuck to her story of her Eduard; Serov never challenged her.

But twice every year Boyar returned to Moscow to watch his child grow. Always around the time of her birthday, in June, and again in the winter. Like Druids marking the solstices, he and Katarina kept faith. Even when Galina was a teenager, Katya would still be taking her out to Sokolniki. And by then it had grown into its own mother-and-daughter tradition that couldn't be broken: an established ritual that cloaked one that was even older.

For the first few years Boyar and she would talk for an hour or so. But as Galina grew, that became impossible; a toddler could talk and ask questions, report and remember. From then on, the Englishman kept his distance, just watching them and listening.

He was breaking every rule in the book, of course; starting with Galina's existence in the first place. As far as Yasyenevo was concerned, had they known, they'd have given him a simple choice: the first plane back to England, never to return, or a bullet in the back of the head. The experiment at Izmaylovo and its two sister academies might be over, but that was no excuse for jeopardising the investment. Serov knew that it lay in his power to put an end to Boyar's visits. But he never did.

And all the while Galina was growing. Galina. Blonde hair, green eyes, milky skin; like her mother. Devastating. And untouched. But, by the blood of Christ, so tempting.

49

The last Tuesday in February dawned cold and clear.

In the heart of the city, gangs of workers, KGB staffers to a man, arrived to put the finishing touches to the flags and staging of the Kremlin's Palace of Congresses. Later that morning, under the severe gaze of a colossal portrait of Lenin, the Palace would receive five thousand delegates from every corner of the country. They would be assembling for the 27th Congress of the Communist Party of the Union of Soviet Socialist Republics.

As the yawning workers set about their task, two men were meeting in an old-fashioned dacha deep in the woods in the Kuntsevo region, ten miles west of the city.

The dacha belonged to Mikhail Sergeyevich Gorbachev. His visitor was Abel Aganbegyan, the economist who had brought him the report of the secret committee known as Oligarchy.

'I'm just an economist,' said Aganbegyan.

'The best in the Soviet Union.'

'The best engineer on the railway doesn't know how to drive the train. I can't understand the things you're telling me.'

Gorbachev smiled tolerantly. His eye fell on the mantel shelf where, among a range of other ornaments, there stood a hand-painted wooden Matrushchka doll, about four inches tall. He rose to his feet and lifted it down. The doll, whose name meant 'little mother', had the rosy cheeks, curls and traditional peasant garments, all painted on, that had made the puzzle toy a folk-symbol of Russia the world over.

'Let me explain,' Gorbachev said. 'How better than with the help of this lady? Nothing could be more fitting.'

He placed the doll in front of Aganbegyan.

'For a few moments, Abel,' he began, 'role-play a little with me. You are the British. Or the Americans – it makes no difference. This lady –' he tapped the Matrushchka '– is the situation as you perceive it.'

'Namely?'

'You learn that Gadaffi is plotting with Prince Ibn to overthrow King Fahd. The intelligence seems to come from *bona fide* sources. You investigate further and discover that Gadaffi's motive is simple enough. He wants to sell Opec oil to the Soviets. Naturally, you are horrified.'

'This much I understand,' put in Aganbegyan, 'The price of oil is at an all-time low. It has brought Gadaffi near to bankruptcy. He doesn't like Fahd's policies, especially since they help the West. He knows that we in the Soviet Union need more oil to support industrial expansion – more than we can force out of our own reserves, large though they are. Our nuclear power programme is badly behind target and can't make up the difference – not to mention the dangerous condition and poor design of most of the reactors. One of these days the RBMKs will explode in our faces. This energy crisis – this is what Oligarchy was about. Gadaffi has second-guessed our predicament. Am I right so far?'

Gorbachev nodded.

'But in this scenario how does Gadaffi think we'll pay? Like the other oil producers, he wants paying in US dollars. But these days you'll find a Jew in the Politburo easier than a dollar bill in the Central Trade Bank. Our main source of dollars used to be our oil exports – when we had a surplus to export. Now we've barely enough for our own needs. What little there is has been reduced in value by the falling oil price – just like Gadaffi's own revenues. So – this Libyan colonel, is he going to take roubles from us?'

'Hardly, my friend. To him that doesn't matter. What's driving him to bankruptcy is his spending on arms and militarisation, his crazy wars with neighbours like Chad, and his egotistical civil construction schemes – roads, buildings and dams. Although times are hard, he refuses to cut back on anything. He'd be happy to trade his oil for Soviet armaments, where he's one of our largest debtors anyway. Or for our help – material and expertise – in his construction schemes. Besides, he knows that as soon as the West hears he's trading with us, they'll pay any price he wants for his oil – and in dollars – to stop him. Either way, he thinks he can't lose.'

Aganbegyan gazed down at the Matrushchka doll. 'Meanwhile, the British and Americans decide they can't let it come to that. They have to block his plot. And they do.' He cocked a forefinger and thumb at the doll, like a pistol. 'They kill the Saudi prince whose coup Gadaffi is backing. Yes?'

Again Gorbachev nodded.

'What now, Misha?'

Gorbachev picked up the doll, unscrewed it at the waist into its two halves and set it aside. His fist remained closed.

'Behind the situation that the Western powers see, just as you have seen the first doll, is this.' He opened his fist; an identical but smaller Matrushchka now stared round-eyed up at Aganbegyan. Gorbachev set it before him. 'This is what they don't see – my plan to entrap them.'

'Through their killing of the Saudi prince?'

'By putting that killing on record with evidence that would be irrefutable in the eyes of the world. The Arab world in particular.'

'This is where I become confused,' Aganbegyan admitted. 'Please take the train slowly along this stretch of track.'

Gorbachev obliged. 'Gadaffi accuses the West of being behind Ibn's death. The West denies it. Just as we have seen. They produce the corpse of a young Libyan terrorist, with apparent evidence that he killed Ibn. But this is a lie and we have proof that it is. Irrefutable proof. For the present, we keep it to ourselves. Now, comrade –' He rose to his feet, swept along by his own thoughts, and gestured at the economist. 'I want you to imagine something else. Imagine that in a few weeks' time, after Gadaffi's allegations, the West's denials and then the discovery that Gadaffi was to blame for the Saudi's death have echoed around the world, Gadaffi himself is assassinated. Who do you think would be blamed for his murder?'

'It depends who the accuser is,' Aganbegyan said slowly. 'There would be those in Libya who would accuse the West, of course. Again.'

'There would. Especially if we encourage them to do so. Now think on. What would the West do in response?'

'Refute the allegation, of course.'

'In the same way as they refuted the allegation about Prince Ibn's assassination?'

'Undoubtedly.'

Gorbachev's eyes glinted. 'So what would happen if our irrefutable proof of Britain's and America's guilt of Ibn's assassination were then released to the world's media?'

A smile of understanding spread across Aganbegyan's features. 'Not only would they be known to be guilty of Ibn's killing, but their denials of responsibility for Gadaffi's death would also ring hollow.'

'How would the rest of the Arab world respond to that, including the Opec nations?'

'Deep revulsion and anger against the West.'

'More than that, comrade. There is in Libya a man called Major Abdul Salem Jalloud. He is Gadaffi's right-hand man. But he's also an ambitious man. Ambitious enough to have been involved in some of the attempts on Gadaffi's life. Jalloud would be one of the contenders for power after Gadaffi's death. There would be chaos then, with all the competing cliques trying to seize power. We would give Jalloud all the help he needed – we have our military infrastructure in the country already, we could airdrop many more troops, and our fleet is now within a few hours of Tripoli. With our support, Jalloud would quell resistance within days and stand as the unchallenged leader of Libya. He would become our mouthpiece. Through him, Fahd and the Saudi ruling cabal would be accused of complicity in the assassinations of Ibn and Gadaffi, to serve the Western interests that many Arabs suspect them of being enslaved to already. The Arab world, my friend, would be in uproar. Fahd would fall or at least lose all credibility, and Jalloud would emerge as the natural leader of the Middle East oil nations and of Opec.'

'And he'd be our creature,' breathed Aganbegyan.

'Indeed. Opec would be ours. All the oil we could ever need, and the ability to make the economies of the West rise and fall at our whim. Suddenly, they'd be paying sky-high prices for Arab oil – and not just in dollars, Abel. They'd have to share their technological advances with us, and anything else we stipulated. Even Japan would be at our feet – mighty Japan, potentially the world's greatest economic power, but with no oil reserves of its own.'

'It'd be a master stroke,' Aganbegyan whispered.

But Gorbachev's smile had vanished. His face darkened as he screwed the second doll apart. 'Yes, Abel. Except for one thing. This isn't reality at all, it's just a little wooden doll – a façade masquerading as truth. Flim-flam tricked out to be the most daring international gambit in our history.'

Looking as if he were tempted to crush it in his hands, he set the hollow second doll aside. A third was revealed inside it, smaller again. Again he set this Matrushchka before Aganbegyan.

'Here we have the next layer of truth,' he said softly. He returned to his chair and pointed at the little wooden ornament. 'Comrades Zavarov, Ligachev and Chebrikov. The men who constructed the façade. A clever façade. Clever men. Well, some of them anyway. Men who planned to fool me.'

'Don't go too fast for me, Mikhail Sergeyevich,' the economist cautioned.

But the doll-puzzle had all of Gorbachev's attention.

'Their plan,' he went on, 'which they have now implemented, is that Gadaffi's death will never occur. Because the Western powers will prevent it happening. Exactly how doesn't matter – they'll find a way.'

'Comrade? How can this be?'

Gorbachev frowned and sat forward, his hands clasped between his knees. 'The operation has been exposed. The West has been alerted to it.'

Aganbegyan was thin-lipped. 'By the three who conceived it – Zavarov, Ligachev and Chebrikov?'

Gorbachev shook his head. 'Those three did not conceive the operation. I didn't say that. I said they constructed its façade. Someone else conceived it. But yes – all along their intention has been that it would be exposed.'

'The old guard,' Aganbegyan said quietly. 'The soldier, the party man and the KGB chief.'

Gorbachev said nothing.

'How have they done this, Misha?'

Gorbachev stared across the room. 'That needn't concern us now.'

'You mean it needn't concern me.'

Gorbachev shrugged. 'I tell you much, Abel. I trust you. But I needn't tell you everything. The important thing is that these three want to neutralise me. That's their motive for this. They want to lead me into a foreign policy blunder of such magnitude that it undermines my position as leader. Our good comrades are implementing a coup of their very own.' He stared blackly at the little doll.

'This would never be enough to topple you,' Aganbegyan said. 'Even if you were accused of error, leaders have erred before.'

'Toppling me isn't necessary. My judgement would be shown as unreliable – that's all they need. I'd forfeit support right across the senior and middle ranks of the party hierarchy. How would I build caucuses to back me under those circumstances? My whole reform programme – the programme that was making them and others like them so uncomfortable – would have to be tempered to what this country's old guard finds acceptable. You know as well as I do, that would get us nowhere.'

Aganbegyan leant forward, to peer into Gorbachev's face. He saw plenty of anger in it. But his instincts told him something else: it wasn't the face of defeat. Not by a long way.

'Misha,' he said slowly, 'Are you telling me they've succeeded? Are you telling me the old guard has won?'

Gorbachev took a long time before he looked up from the doll and met the economist's gaze. Then he picked the toy up and yet again unscrewed it into two halves. A fourth Matrushchka, tiny but solid this time, the kernel of the puzzle at last, fell into his hand. As with its predecessors, he set it before Aganbegyan. It rocked gently back and forth.

'No, Abel,' Gorbachev said simply, and smiled bleakly. 'The old guard has not won.'

They rode downtown together in Gorbachev's limousine.

'What will you do with them?' the economist asked. 'Brezhnev or Andropov would have stood them against the nearest wall and had them shot.'

Gorbachev seemed to find the thought amusing. 'Not good for the image, comrade, as the Western public relations men would say. This is the age of enlightenment in the Soviet Union.'

'Disgrace and imprisonment, in that case. Pack them off to a camp.'

'No.'

'What, then?'

Gorbachev stared out at the Kuntsevo parkland as it glided past.

'Nothing,' he said.

Aganbegyan swung around in his seat and stared at him in disbelief. 'Are you serious?'

Gorbachev nodded.

'You're demoting them at least?'

Gorbachev shook his head.

Aganbegyan was aghast. 'But they're traitors, they plotted against you. They tried to bring you down.'

'Their punishment will be subtler than any you mention. And of more benefit to me.'

Aganbegyan became intrigued again. 'Go on.'

'Take Zavarov. If I demote him or lock him up, I need to replace him. Who with? A younger man you'd say, one with new ideas. Fine, comrade, if I knew one I could trust. But in the whole of the Soviet military, I don't know of such a man. Do you?'

'Appoint a civilian.'

'Ho! There speaks a civilian!' Gorbachev relished the idea for a moment. 'The Red Army wouldn't take kindly to that, Abel. Maybe one day it's a possibility. In a year or two. But maybe by then I'll have found a soldier I can trust anyway. What I need now is time. Time to watch, time to decide. No –' He shook his head again. 'I don't need to send Zavarov to prison. I have him there already. This plot was to get him out. All I have to do is keep him there. That's his punishment.'

'And Chebrikov?'

'The same thing applies. He's younger than Zavarov – he can give me even more time. And if it's difficult to know whom you can trust in the military, imagine what the KGB is like. Chebrikov also stays where he is. I knew him well enough before this started – now I know him even better. What more can any leader hope for than to know his enemies – and keep them close?'

'Ligachev,' Aganbegyan said. 'He doesn't have age on his side. He ought to go for that reason alone.'

But again Gorbachev was shaking his head. 'Who knows the party caucuses better than that old fox? Ask yourself, Abel – what must I have over the next few years? I told you earlier – a network of caucuses across the country to support my policies and watch my back. I've drawn what little fire Ligachev had left. He's a spent force. But he's still an encyclopaedia of information on the party's operations and people. I'll keep him by me till I've drawn out everything he has to teach me.'

Aganbegyan remained doubtful. 'They've made a fool of you, Misha.'

'In whose eyes? Not the Western powers. They've seen that I can bite as well as smile. It's good that they know I was prepared to go through with the whole operation. So what if I was led into it? What leader isn't the object of such intrigues at one time or another? Maybe next time the scenario will be of my own making, and then they'd better watch out. In

327

politics, it's final survival that counts, not the skirmishes along the way. The Western leaders understand that just as well as us. Now they have to wait and see what I'm going to do. If the conspirators remain untouched, that leaves the West all the more baffled. "What's Gorbachev's game? Does he know about the conspiracy or not? Has he been weakened or not? Was there more to this than we've been told?"'

He broke off, thought for a moment, then added quietly, 'The conspirators can't weaken me, Abel. I've turned their own gun on them.'

'How?'

'They'll find out,' was all Gorbachev would say.

London

In Curzon Street, the sharp-faced woman from Personnel arrived as Eva was loading the personal contents of her desk into a stout carrier bag.

'Mind if I come in?' she asked, and did so without waiting for an answer. She stood for a moment watching what Eva was doing.

'Hope you'll let Security vet that lot before it leaves the building,' she said. 'Hope you don't mind me saying so. You know the rules, I daresay.'

'I don't mind you saying so. I know the rules.'

'Good.' The woman patted the folder she was holding against her flat chest.

'I've got a few forms here. Just one or two really.'

'Yes?'

'We like people to fill them in when they're leaving. Standard debrief procedure. What job are you going to next, has it been security-cleared in relation to the position you held with us, why have you decided to leave – that sort of thing.'

'I know the sort of thing.'

'You don't mind, do you? Most people don't.'

'I don't mind. Give them here.'

The woman set the folder down on the cleared desk and picked out several forms: more than the one or two that she'd promised. She handed them over.

'Thank you,' she said, clutching the folder to her chest again, like a shield. 'Pop them in on your way out. Well – I won't trouble you any more.'

'No trouble,' Eva said. With great care, she tore the forms in half, shuffled the halves together, tore them again, and pushed them back inside the folder.

'No trouble at all.'

328

A mile away, in Westminster, the Lord Chancellor was not a happy man. He liked things fair and square. He'd kept his side of the bargain, after all. The cheques for the commuted pension and the housing compensation had cleared, and he'd burnt Knight's document personally.

The letter was just two paragraphs long.

> *Dear Lord Chancellor,*
>
> *You will recognise the enclosed photocopy as a single page from my account of recent events. Needless to say, I have copies of the rest of it. Also of the photos showing the CIA hit team, establishing their involvement in the killings of Prince Ibn and Bill Clarke, and the recording of Bill's message to me, when he was clearly about to blow the operation open. All of these things are safe somewhere. Just like me. Let's hope we both stay that way. I'd be grateful if you'd pass this on.*
>
> *Of course I'm not where the postmark suggests. Doubtless someone will track me down eventually. Hope you make sure they read this first.*
>
> *Yours, etc.*

'Damn you, Knight,' the Lord Chancellor said. He picked up the telephone. He'd better do as the man said: pass it on.

A mile and a half north, in Fleet Street, journalist Doug Riley found his letter more entertaining.

> *Dear Doug,*
>
> *Herewith is a cheque that won't bounce. Thanks for your help.*
> *The story will have to wait. Sorry to let you down. One of these days you might get it. If you do, send me some flowers. If you can find out where to send them.*
> *Best regards,*

For a man who suspected that he'd just missed the story of the decade, Riley took it surprisingly well. So well, in fact, that he adjourned to the pub. He had someone's health to drink.

A mile to the east, Bolton's Restaurant, between Fenchurch Street and Lime Street, was the ideal watering-hole for the money men of the City of London.

The hubbub was at its merriest that lunchtime as two bankers followed the maître d' across the floor. They were a contrasting pair. One was pot-bellied and middle-aged, the other was younger and taller, with long ears.

Both men were drinking large gins, which they carried with them to their table. As they seated themselves they looked around automatically to see who else was there.

'Well, I've had a useful morning, old boy,' said the younger man, tugging on an earlobe.

'Really?'

'Chap walked in off the street. Had a couple of letters of introduction with him from West German banks. He's West German, you see. Something in electronics. Turns out he's come here to do a little company shopping.'

'Hmm. Never sure about Germans.'

The younger man grinned and polished off his gin. 'This chap's cash-rich. Looking for ways to soak it up. I saw his balances. He authorised me to check them directly, bank-to-bank. He's got accounts all over the place. Took me half the morning.'

'What's he want from you?'

'A front. He wants to be able to wheel us in when he decides who he's going after and makes his offer for them. Wants to do it through us. He'll stay out of sight.'

'Sounds straightforward enough.'

'A licence to print money. We take a management fee for expediting the purchase, then we pick up the business's account afterwards.' The young banker dropped his voice to a whisper. 'Might even be some side action for chaps like you and me. Want me to keep you abreast?'

The pot-bellied banker didn't look very interested. 'Depends on the return.'

'Can't fail to be outstanding. Know who he's planning to go for?'

'How would I?'

The young banker rattled off a list of eight or ten company names, none of which meant anything whatsoever to his companion, whose face said as much.

'Sunrise industries,' the younger man explained. His fingers worried vigorously at his right lobe.

The pot-bellied one shook his head. 'What?'

The young banker launched into a further explanation, full of phrases like 'ultra hi-tech' and 'leading edge technology'. The pot-bellied one just continued staring blankly at him.

'Military application, some of it,' the younger man concluded in some despair. 'Defence contracts. From the Americans. Guidance systems – Star Wars stuff. Could be worth a packet, old boy.'

'Ahh!' At the mention of Americans, the fat banker understood. He saw dollars, military men who didn't know a budget overrun from a tomcat, and whole days spent entertaining them at Ascot and Henley.

'He'll need security vetting,' he said. 'This German of yours. The government won't let just anyone start buying up possible defence contractors.'

'No problem. Got friends in high places, this chap.'

'That's all right, then. Looks like you're made. Lunch on you, by the way? Old boy?'

Berkshire

Marie-Thérèse took the phone call as usual in her neat little office with its Sacred Heart picture and its crucifix over the door. On her wall she also had a portrait of Pope John Paul that had been painted from a photograph by her nephew in Ireland. As was her habit when she was on the phone, she gazed at the portrait as she spoke.

'Good morning, Mr Knight. Are you well? Are you having nice weather? Oh yes, we're all perfectly well. Yes, all the girls too.'

She listened for a moment, then smiled.

'Yes,' she said, 'It's safe. Don't worry. No, no untoward visitors. Good, yes, I'll hear from you in a month then.'

She hung up.

'Excuse me, Holy Father,' she said as she moved John Paul to the side and unlocked the wallsafe behind him.

Yes, the yellow lunchbox was safe and sound.

50

Moscow

It was the last day of the Congress.

For a fortnight a tidal wave of speeches and lectures had washed over the delegates. But in the millions of words that had echoed around the vast conference hall, there was one that had rung out again and again. That word was reconstruction. Reconstruction of the country's threadbare economy, of its industries, even of society itself. As for Gorbachev, he could hardly have spoken more plainly. There was nowhere to run to, he'd said, nowhere to hide; the Soviet Union had to reform and match the West's economic power or be prepared simply to wither away. After this Congress, he warned the delegates, they had to go home ready to tackle the task with every ounce of energy they possessed; if they weren't committed to that, there could be no place for them in tomorrow's Soviet Union.

So by the time the delegates were gathering for the closing speeches on that final morning, they'd learnt beyond a shadow of doubt which way the wind was blowing the top of the tree.

That left but one question to be answered, a question that swept through the side lobbies and toilets where they whispered together. In their political system, it was the make-or-break question.

So much for the top of the tree, they said to each other; but would the branches beneath it be blowing the same way?

In the Arsenal block, Gorbachev's office door opened and Zavarov, Ligachev and Chebrikov were shown in. Gorbachev turned from the window to watch them, noting with grim satisfaction that all of them looked rather ill at ease. They were meant to be. His summons for them to come to him, issued only ten minutes earlier, had been calculated to achieve precisely that, catching them when they least expected it, on this of all mornings.

He offered them no greeting. He went to his own seat behind his desk and waved them into the chairs arranged in front of it. No meeting of equals around a table, this.

One detail caught the eye of each of his visitors as he sat down:

although there were only the three of them, a fourth chair had been set out in that neat line before the General Secretary's desk. It sat empty. Gorbachev made no attempt to explain it and it was as if a ghost were sitting there watching them.

'So, comrades,' Gorbachev announced heartily, 'We come to the end of Congress for another five years. It's been an exciting one – don't you agree? – new ideas, a new path for our great country. What stimulating times we live in!'

They watched him uneasily.

'And today, of course, as is our tradition, the closing speeches will affirm the commitment of the Politburo and the Central Committee to that new path and the changes it will entail.'

He paused to look slowly from one to the other of them, his gaze settling first on Ligachev.

'Changes such as the overhaul of the party's structure and organisation.'

Then to Zavarov.

'The fact that military spending will continue to be held in check and absorb less of our national wealth.'

Finally, his gaze went to Chebrikov.

'Then there is our commitment to gutting the State Security apparatus clean of corruption and laziness.'

The three men exchanged discreet glances but still said nothing.

'As for those closing speeches, their words will be scrutinised, messages will be read between their lines. Here is why I called you together this morning. Comrades, make no mistake – every word, every coded signal in those speeches, will declare unequivocal support for the policies to which I have committed myself, and to the path of change on which I have set the Soviet peoples.'

That did it; Zavarov finally spoke up.

'Comrade General Secretary, perhaps this is the time for us to raise a small matter with you. It concerns the Middle East project on which we've all been engaged.'

But Gorbachev raised a hand to stop him.

'I want to talk about the same matter,' he announced. The faces before him looked warier than ever. 'I believe that in it we will find the grounds for my confidence regarding your support. Sadly, however –' He gestured at the empty chair. 'One important person cannot be here today. But he asked me to pass on to you his fraternal good wishes and his assurance that he will be with you in spirit, though he cannot in person, when you declare your complete and unstinting support for me. Complete and unstinting, comrades. Nothing less will do.'

'Who is this mysterious absentee?' Zavarov growled.

'I didn't say? Forgive me.' Gorbachev took his time. 'A good friend of yours. General Nikolai Vasiliyevich Serov.'

In the apartment on Kutuzovskiy Prospekt the letter arrived unopened: the Soviet Chief of Staff and his wife were spared the indignity of having their mail tampered with; visibly, at any rate. This one certainly hadn't been touched: all the edges and corners were sealed with transparent tape. An old trick. For all their clevernesses, that was one simple precaution the KGB hadn't found a way around.

Olga Zavarova held the unexpected envelope gingerly, at arm's length, as she studied it. Letters were usually bad news. Hadn't it been a letter that sent Georgi Fedorovich off to Afghanistan? On the other hand, it got him out of her way for a while; something to be said for unexpected letters after all.

She brought her glasses down from where she'd propped them on the crown of her head and peered more closely at the envelope. This letter wasn't for Georgi and it wasn't from the Kremlin. It was for her and it had apparently come from Great Britain, of all places. Unless her English was letting her down completely, that was what she could read on the poorly-inked postmark. She walked over to the light from the window. The postmark yielded no further clues: the town or city of posting hadn't printed.

She turned the envelope over; no sender's address on the reverse, a normal precaution with mail from the West. She looked at the front again. Her name and address were in proper Cyrillic script, not the Latinised form that she might have expected on a letter from England.

Whom did she know in England? More to the point, who in England knew her?

Olga shrugged. Only one way to find out.

She had always told Georgi he had hands like a peasant and fingers to match. But now, as she wrenched at the envelope, it seemed that she was just as bad. She swore nervously at her incompetence.

Suddenly the tape and paper parted, her hands sprang apart, and something fluttered to the floor. No, two somethings. Pieces of card. Olga grunted and bent over to retrieve them.

Even before her fingers touched the nearest rectangle, she saw what it was. It lay face up and she stared at it, not believing what she was seeing.

Her fingers trembled as they picked up the photograph. Faded monochrome. Grainy. Torn at one corner and cracked across its surface. And so familiar.

The trembling spread to her whole body as she crossed the room to the Steinway and held the photograph next to the print in the silver frame.

Two identical prints from a single negative. A soldier of the Red Army with captain's boards on his shoulders. Taller in those days. Slimmer too. Broad shouldered even if he did have peasant's hands. A proud, good-looking wife by his side.

And there, gazing out from the picture with those serene eyes, their beautiful daughter.

Suddenly Olga's head was swimming.

'Katarina,' she whispered. The name set her lips tingling; she hadn't said it aloud for years, not even to Georgi. Hah! Above all, not to Georgi.

She let herself flop down onto the nearest couch and continued staring at the black and white photograph. Then she remembered the other piece of card that had come in the envelope.

She went back and fumbled to pick it up off the floor. It seemed to be a photograph too, but it had fallen face down.

Finally she had it in her hand and turned it over.

'Dear God in heaven.'

She sat down heavily. This photograph was modern and in colour. She stared at it for many minutes. She had no need to compare it with the first one, the older one. Nor did it matter that the older one was monochrome. She was a mother: she could remember the blonde hair and the green eyes, like jade. They were the same hair and eyes as in this colour photograph. A generation apart, but the same.

'To the life,' she whispered. 'Katarina to the life.'

There was no letter of any kind in the envelope. Nothing but the photographs.

It was dark when Georgi Zavarov got home from his fateful Congress. He was exhausted, empty and about as low as he could be. And, damn it, on this of all days there was no one at the door to take his coat and put a friendly drink in his hand. Infuriating. Ratushny no longer worked for them, of course. And Olga being Olga, she'd found something wrong with every replacement that they'd offered her, and had sent them all away. Under the circumstances, was it unreasonable of him to expect that the least she could do was see to his needs herself?

Suddenly he stopped his mental grumbling and listened. His heavy coat hung from his hand. He let it fall.

'Tchaikovsky,' he whispered.

It was true. The unmistakable strains of a melancholy Nocturne drifted along the hallway.

Slowly, soundlessly, he pushed the drawing-room door open. The only light was what fell into the room from the kitchen. And there, at the Steinway, sat Olga. She was playing without benefit of any score or the light to read it by. Playing like her husband hadn't heard for years.

Zavarov ignored the torn scraps of envelope on the floor and crept quietly to an armchair. She hadn't noticed his arrival. He wouldn't make a sound to disturb her. He only wanted to hear her play.

335

It was a nice little town. Not very large, just a harbour and a beach really. Dead quiet at this time of year. The shops hadn't even got around to stocking up on beach balls and flip-flops yet. They'd do that for Easter. Which would be early this year, only two or three weeks away.

'Stuff your psychiatrists,' was what Knight had told Welfare. 'I know all about your psychiatrists. She'll be fine with me.'

And here they were. He wouldn't be telling Curzon Street where either. He'd used some of the cash to buy a new car, just to make things harder for them. Not in his own name, of course. Nor the new one they'd given him. Just like the house wasn't rented in either of those names. His solicitor had power of attorney to sell the place in Berkshire. The money would get to him in the end. He still had a trick or two.

The days slid by in a lazy stream. Swanning about like schoolkids in the long holiday. They walked in the forest above the harbour. He talked to Galina a lot, mostly in her own language, sometimes in his, which he was beginning to teach her. He cooked them plain food and made sure she ate all he put before her. She painted a little but showed no inclination to sculpt. He took her swimming in the nearest big town. They explored all the coffee-shops and tea-houses for miles around. They went boating on a lake, wrapped up against the March wind. They drove to look at the countryside. They listened to all kinds of music, from classics to rock. He rented movie videos from one of the shops; in fact, it amused him that she seemed to be becoming a television addict. Not that he ever said anything about that: there were worse things.

According to the local doctor, the baby that she was carrying was just fine. But after his first examination of her he'd asked Knight about the scars on her wrists.

'I guess she lost a lot of blood,' Knight admitted.

'I was wondering how she got the scars, actually.'

'It's because of the blood loss I was worried about the baby.'

'The baby's perfectly healthy. The scars look a few months old. The pregnancy can't have been very advanced at the time. Care to tell me what happened?'

'I'll bring her again in a month's time, doctor. Thanks.'

She'd be all right. They all would. All three of them. Spring was in the air. Buds, new life.

The dying was over.

He left it a while before arranging to see Sir Marcus Cunningham. They had brought him out of retirement for a while to keep an eye on Gaunt.

It was all very discreet. Gaunt still held the position and title of Director General; Sir Marcus was merely there 'in an advisory capacity'.

Knight and he met by the boating lake and Galina waited in the car while they strolled along the marina.

'Pity about that bloke and his book,' said Sir Marcus. 'The fingerprints.'

'Viktor Kunaev? Yes, sorry about that. All those years and I never knew.'

'You were young.'

'I was soft.'

Sir Marcus smiled. 'Weren't we all once?'

'Once.'

They stopped to watch a windsurfer. Sir Marcus had brought his binoculars. When the surfer finally fell over, they walked on.

'Trouble is,' Sir Marcus resumed, 'we've lost you just when you were going to be some use to us. Activated, you might have stood a chance. Now I don't know how we track down the others – whoever they are.'

He stopped walking and had another squint through the binoculars. The surfer was upright again.

'How is Gaunt anyway?' Knight asked.

'He doesn't like me being his shadow. I'll have to call a halt soon. The politicians won't like it but that's too bad.'

'Keen to get back to your retirement?'

Sir Marcus brought the binoculars down and shook his head. 'With me around we'll never get anywhere with him. He won't make a move. They wouldn't even activate him. If he is theirs.'

'I suppose so. What will happen to him in the end?'

'He knows he's got to go. They'll let him claim personal grounds or something similar. Spend more time with his family – that sort of line. In a year or so. That's why I'm concerned. It doesn't give us long. He'll have to do something soon or not at all. I suspect it'll be not at all.' Sir Marcus sighed and lifted the binoculars to his eyes again. 'How's the girl, by the way?'

'She'll be all right.' Knight had said nothing about the baby and didn't intend to.

'You were silly, weren't you? All those years ago.'

Knight shrugged. 'I was young.'

'You were soft.'

'Weren't we all?'

Sir Marcus brought the binoculars down; his grey eyes scanned Knight's face.

'Not as soft as that,' he said.

The office was deserted, the Minister who occupied it attending a Cabinet meeting.

It was an office that offered few clues to the personality or private life of that Minister. It was clearly meant to be a work-station, nothing else. A stack of three red boxes occupied the top of the bureau by the desk. On the desk itself a full in-tray and even fuller out-tray took up one corner. A file of letters and memoranda for signature waited on the plain blotting-pad in the middle. And in the other corner was an untidy pile of three or four of that day's newspapers. It was untidy because each paper had been read or at least skimmed, in the process losing its morning crispness.

The topmost paper was the *Financial Times*. Unlike the others, it hadn't been closed before being consigned to the pile. It lay folded open at a page of classified business-to-business advertisements. Halfway down that page a faint pencil mark had been made along the side of one of the advertisements.

FINANCE FOR EXPORT/IMPORT
Substantial funds available for
export-import-UK trade.
Also back-to-back letters of credit.
Strong core of 18–20 blue-chip investors.
Please call our UK offices:
Terem Investments
01-863-1261

Apparently, here was a politician whose interest in commerce amounted to rather more than a cursory speech at Budget time and the occasional business lunch.

Serov had just stepped out of the shower when the phone rang. He left wet footprints across the luxurious pile of the bedroom carpet as he hurried to pick it up. Water dripped from his hair and body to form a damp circle around his feet.

'Yes?'

'They're still convinced it's Gaunt,' the voice at the other end said.

Serov frowned. 'This is an open line. Be careful. Where are you?'

'Go to hell. The deal's complete now. I said I was through.'

The line went dead. Serov dried the handset with the towel and padded back to the bathroom.

'Gaunt,' he repeated, towelling his chest. He chuckled softly. 'Thank you, Boyar.'

He reviewed the situation as he dressed.

The money was the key, of course, the money that had passed so fleetingly through Director Smolny's hands in the Foreign Trade Bank in Moscow and had been all around the world since then. Zavarov had been the only one authorised to trigger the military procurement account, Chebrikov the KGB one, and Ligachev the Central Committee funds. Not even the General Secretary could override their personal authority over their own budgets. It was an operational safeguard that had been instituted after Stalin.

Now that the accounts had been penetrated, however, and the laundering network established, it would be simple enough to step up the flow of funds. That could start just as soon as Gorbachev had spelt out his terms to Zavarov and the others. Which would be any day now; if it hadn't happened already. Then they'd find that rather more cash would be siphoned off than any of them had planned. That was business. The high-technology companies that Serov would purchase would be an important factor in bringing the Soviet Union up to technological parity with the West; buying them was something that the West itself had made necessary by its restrictions against exporting high technology to the Eastern Bloc. If some of the companies thus acquired happened to be engaged, now or later, in defence contracts, well then, so much the better . . .

There was a knock on the outer door of the suite. Serov glanced at his watch.

'Punctual,' he remarked approvingly.

Dressed now but for his tie and jacket, he strolled unhurriedly through to the hallway and had a look through the spyglass in the door. One man stood waiting outside. Serov unlocked the door and opened it wide.

'Mr Stephens?' he asked.

'Correct.' The man handed him a business card. It carried his own name and, above it, that of a leading international detective agency.

'Come in, Mr Stephens.'

He poured himself a glass of bourbon but Stephens took only a soft drink. They settled themselves in the armchairs in the suite's sitting-room.

'Shall we get right down to business, Mr Stephens?'

'That suits me.'

'There are two parties I want you to find for me. One is a young family – a husband, a wife, and a little boy.' He took a draught of bourbon. 'The other is a man about my own age and a younger woman. Much younger. She's pregnant.' He broke off, remembering his feelings that night in the payphone booth when Ogarkin had told him. Bad enough that he'd traded her; but the child as well? Would he have traded his child if he'd known? Could he have done that?

339

Stephens was staring at him. He finished the bourbon and stood up to avoid the man's perceptive look.

'I will give you their names and last known locations, but all will have changed.'

'Mind if I make a few notes as we talk?'

'Not in the slightest.'

Serov poured himself another bourbon and they talked for an hour.

When Stephens had gone, he finished dressing. He should choose somewhere special to dine tonight, he decided. The best that this city had to offer. But not one of those dull places that the British seemed to favour. Somewhere lively, with music and women. He needed cheering. Perhaps reception would advise him.

Before leaving the room, he checked his appearance in the mirror. He was satisfied with what he saw.

Grey suit, white shirt, dark tie. The very picture of a prosperous Western businessman.

Apart from the heavy Makarov pistol in his hand.

AFTERWORD

In the small hours of Tuesday morning, 15 April, American bombers from USAF bases in Britain bombarded the Libyan capital, Tripoli. In the course of the attack, Gadaffi's base, the Bab Al-Aziziya barracks, was hit.

It appeared that the raid's objective was to assassinate Gadaffi. This was what most commentators in the Western media decided. With some pride, many US citizens reached a similar conclusion.

However, certain facts contradict their belief.

To begin with, there was the formidable technological sophistication of the American assault aircraft. They had the ability to target with pinpoint accuracy yet they failed to hit a single one of the places in the well-lit Aziziya compound where Gadaffi was known to work or sleep. One bomb did land close enough to his two-storey house to kill his fifteen-month adopted daughter and injure two of his other children; but nothing short of a direct nuclear hit could have harmed them if the family had been in the nearby bunker that had been built for them and where they should have been sleeping.

As for Gadaffi, he wasn't even in Aziziya that night. He was probably at his main command centre two hundred kilometres south, in the oasis town of Jufrah. If the US military planners didn't know this for sure, logic would have suggested it to them. Jufrah was where he always went in times of emergency. That period was one of emergency and had been ever since the skirmishes three weeks earlier in the Gulf of Sirte between the US Sixth Fleet and Libyan forces.

Finally, prior to the Tripoli raid the US president's military and intelligence advisers had offered him several alternative methods of assassinating Gadaffi, any one of which would have been more certain to have achieved its aim and some of which could have been completely clandestine. The president rejected them all.

Far from being eliminated by the raid, therefore, the Libyan leader became a virtual recluse because of it. In so doing, he placed himself beyond the reach of any assassin, Soviet or otherwise.

In other words, the West had found a way to keep Gadaffi alive.

As Gorbachev had told Aganbegyan it would.

In Saudi Arabia, King Fahd made a concession or two to his critics. Sheikh Yamani was the fall guy; Fahd sacked him from his position as oil minister. His passport was confiscated and he was forbidden to leave the country.

Eventually, some measure of accord was achieved in Opec over output and pricing. But although prices stabilised to an extent, they never returned to anything like their peak levels.

Nor did the power of the Opec cartel.

In Moscow, Gorbachev was saluted by four standing ovations at the close of the 27th Communist Party Congress. His final message to the five thousand delegates was typical of the new leadership style that he was setting. Rejecting the cheer-leading approach of his predecessors, he simply wished the delegates good health and told them: 'Now go back home and work hard.'

Politically, he had good reason to feel that the Congress had been a personal success. Over half of the three hundred-plus Central Committee were new men of his caucus. For any leader to bring in so many new people so quickly without a bloody purge was unprecedented.

Yegor Ligachev's speech at Congress was strongly supportive of his leader. He commented favourably on the personnel changes, contrasting them with the Brezhnev-type policies of keeping people in jobs for years, which had produced only 'self-isolation and stagnation'. It was a further warning shot across the bows of the remaining members of the audience whose appointments dated back to the Brezhnev years.

The Congress pursued two broad strands of thought. There was the need for change at home: again and again Gorbachev hammered home the need to get the economy moving, reduce central control, offer more worker incentives, achieve cost-effectiveness and high quality of production, and introduce flexible pricing of goods that would reflect basic laws of supply and demand.

On foreign policy his prescription for change was no less startling. World communism, although still desirable, was relegated to a distant goal instead of an immediate priority that would be allowed to dominate everything. In other words, military adventurism abroad was to be scaled down. He told the amazed delegates that Western imperialism was no longer a mortal enemy to be quashed at all costs, but merely 'the society with which we have to co-exist and seek paths of accommodation.'

But in the months that followed, despite Gorbachev's political success, progress was slow on other fronts. A solution to Afghanistan remained out of reach for over two years. Success in arms control proved hard, despite some bright public-relations highspots. At home, the more that corruption was rooted out, the deeper it seemed to be

344

ingrained. Economic growth continued to lag; workers and management were reluctant to give up the old, comfortable ways of working.

As for the energy crisis, oil production stayed behind target and the foreign earnings shortfall continued.

There was something worse.

On Saturday 26 April, at one twenty-three in the morning, a fearsome explosion tore apart one of the RBMK nuclear reactors that had worried Aganbegyan and the Oligarchy committee.

The accident at Chernobyl crippled the Soviet nuclear energy programme and was the worst nuclear accident the world had ever known.

In Britain the government continued on a stable course with a strong majority in Parliament. After a general election the following year, it went on to a third term. There were no high-level sackings in the intelligence organisations.

However, a series of deaths began to occur among workers at some of the companies involved in high-technology defence research. These took the form of bizarre and not entirely convincing suicides. The news media were interested for a time, but the stories grew stale.

The deaths remain unexplained.